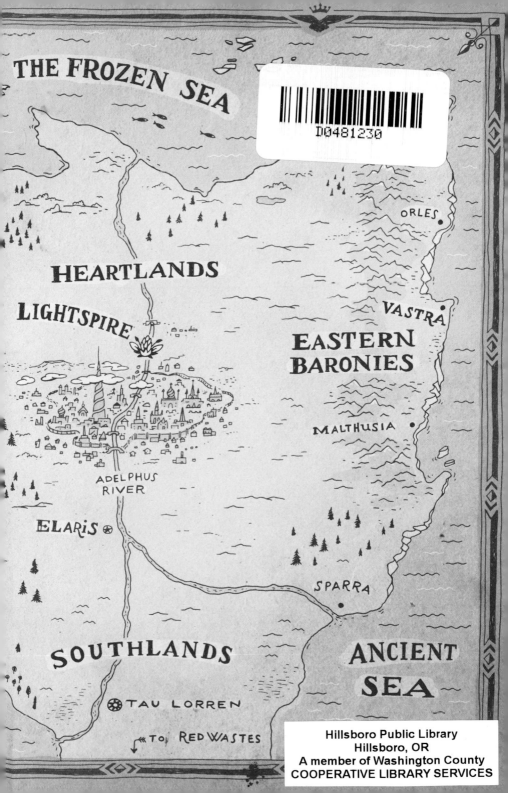

THE FROZEN SEA

ORLES

HEARTLANDS

LIGHTSPIRE

VASTRA

EASTERN
BARONIES

MALTHUSIA

ADELPHUS
RIVER

ELARIS

SPARRA

SOUTHLANDS

ANCIENT
SEA

TAU LORREN

TO RED WASTES

WAR OF THE BASTARDS

WAR OF THE BASTARDS

ANDREW SHVARTS

HYPERION
Los Angeles   New York

First Edition, June 2019
10 9 8 7 6 5 4 3 2 1
FAC-020093-19109
Printed in the United States of America

This book is set in 12-point Minion Pro, Avenir/Monotype; Amulet/G-Type Fonts
Designed by Tyler Nevins

Library of Congress Cataloging-in-Publication Data
Names: Shvarts, Andrew, author.
Title: War of the bastards / by Andrew Shvarts.
Description: First edition. • Los Angeles ; New York : Hyperion, 2019. •
    Series: [Royal bastards ; 3] • Summary: A year after the Inquisitor Miles
    Hampstedt usurped the throne of Noveris, Tilla and her fellow bastards
    continue to fight tyranny as they contemplate a pact with the people of
    the Red Wastes.
Identifiers: LCCN 2018053813 • ISBN 9781484767641 (hardcover)
Subjects: • CYAC: Fantasy. • Adventure and adventurers—Fiction. •
    Insurgency—Fiction. • Illegitimacy—Fiction. • Fathers and
    daughters—Fiction. • Magic—Fiction.
Classification: LCC PZ7.1.S5185 War 2019 • DDC [Fic]—dc23
LC record available at https://lccn.loc.gov/2018053813

Reinforced binding
Visit www.hyperionteens.com

33614081654310

For all the bastards out there

one

We hit the caravan just after sunrise.

This was down the southeast border of the Heartlands, where the flowing wheatfields gave way to grassy foothills and sprawling forests. It was a beautiful morning: the air had that earthy smell of fresh dew, the first rays of morning crested the horizon, painting the sky an ethereal ghostly purple . . .

And here we were, armed to the teeth, planning to kill a man.

The caravan was a modest thing, three wagons long, escorted by a dozen marching soldiers in heavy armor. They wore my father's colors, red and gold, but that didn't mean they were Westerners; their faces were hidden behind bulky helms, and you never knew who you'd find fighting for him. In the early days of my father's reign, when he'd first demanded all the able men of the Kingdom take up arms in his name, we'd held out hope that the people of Noveris would rise up in defiance, that they'd sooner choose death than serve a usurper king. Then Miles took up the mantle of Inquisitor and the culls began, as his bloodmages tore through the Province, leaving a trail of burning villages and mutilated corpses in their wake.

Turns out? Pretty much no one *ever* chooses death.

"There," Lord Galen Reza said as the last wagon rolled into sight. We were up on a hilltop, six of us, huddled in the shadows of a birch grove. We wore the de facto uniform of the Unbroken: leather armor, hoods up over our heads, black bandanas pulled up over our faces like masks. Galen had his fork-tipped daggers, Zell his curved nightglass blades, and I had Muriel, my short sword, the one weapon I was pretty damn good with.

The wagons rolled closer, turning the bend to cross a narrow little valley between a pair of hills. I squinted at the driver of the middle one, a pale old Westerner with a shaggy beard. It was definitely a royal caravan, but that didn't make it worth ambushing; the last thing we wanted was to kill a dozen men over a few wagons of grain. "You sure Vladimyr is in there?" I whispered to Galen.

"Oh, he's in there." Galen's curly black hair was pulled back in a warrior's bun, and a long white scar cleaved his cheek in half. He looked about a decade older than he had when I'd first met him, back when he'd been the young Heartlander lord of a minor House, before he'd hardened into the brutal rebel leader he was today. "The Raven said Vladimyr would be here. And the Raven's never wrong."

I nodded. The Raven was our best contact in Lightspire, a high-ranking nobleman who seemed to know every detail of my father's regime. It bothered me sometimes that we were attacking people on the word of someone whose real name we didn't even know. But I wasn't the leader of the Unbroken. Galen was. Which meant he called the shots.

The last wagon fully rounded the corner, putting the whole caravan between the two hills. My stomach fluttered, and my hands tingled with pins and needles. It had been a year since the fall of Lightspire, a year since my father had taken the throne and become King Kent, a year since our tiny band of refugees had coalesced into a Kingdom-spanning rebellion. It had been a year of resistance and warfare and midnight raids, a year of blood and pain, a year of killing and running and killing some more.

And even after all that, after a year of pure frozen hell, I still got nervous before every battle.

I glanced to Zell for reassurance and found his eyes above his mask, soft and brown, the eyes I stared into every night, the eyes that often felt like the only calm, reliable thing in the world. He nodded, the tiniest bit. I took a deep breath. I could do this. I could *do this.*

"All right, kids," a gruff voice said from my left. A massive slab of a man stood there, a grizzled old warrior with biceps the size of my head and the deepest wrinkles I'd ever seen etched into his dark features. This was Manos Vore, a Heartlander general who'd lost his entire company to my father's men, which gave him a, shall we say, unique outlook on the conflict. "Let's kill us some traitors." He grinned and tightened his grip on his massive iron warhammer.

Galen pulled down his mask enough to put two fingers in his mouth and let out a loud whooping whistle. The guards by the caravan froze, spinning our way, which was perfect because it meant they weren't looking at the *other* hill, the one across from us, where all our archers were rising up from their hidden position, longbows nocked. The wagon driver, the old man with the beard, let out a yelp of surprise, but it was too late now. The early morning air sang with the whistle of a half-dozen longbows shooting at once, and a hail of arrows streaked down into the company below. Two guards dropped right away, one with an arrow in the throat and another with one through his skull, and a third caught one in the side and lurched over, still alive but bleeding out fast. The other guards scrambled into a defensive formation, shouting to one another, pressing themselves against the wagon, drawing their blades as they braced for the second volley. . . .

Which meant it was go time. Galen moved first, unsheathing his daggers and sliding out of cover, and the rest of us followed. We raced silently down the hill, a swooping shadow, a clenching fist, our weapons glistening like shooting stars. There was one second, one lingering second, where the poor sons of bitches guarding the caravan realized what was about to happen.

Then we hit them, hard, and there was just the screaming of men and the clanging of steel. Zell struck first, as always, leaping forward to plunge a blade down into a man's chest. Galen was next to him, daggers a blur as he cut through the ranks. And Manos came charging up behind with a bellowing roar, swinging his hammer in a broad arc to cave in a terrified guard's skull.

I hadn't chosen a target, not really, but I didn't have to. One of the guards charged right at me, a broadsword raised high over his head. I could see just a little of his face through the slits in his helmet: pale skin, furious green eyes, a few wisps of curly blond hair. A Westerner. A boy.

He swung his sword in a downward chop, and I dodged it, weaving to the side in a little bound. His blade hit the dirt uselessly, a total amateur move, and I almost felt bad for him.

But my feelings didn't matter now. My body was in control, the khel zhan my guide, and it knew what to do. As he looked my way, eyes wide with horror, I whipped Muriel up and drove her through the gap in his armor just below his armpit.

Twenty-seven.

The Westerner dropped like a stone as I jerked my short sword out, her blade slick with crimson, and not a moment too soon. Another guard was on me, and I didn't get a good look at him because I was too distracted by the sword he was swinging at my damn head. I jerked Muriel up in a fumble, just barely blocking him, our blades hitting with a resonating clang. He was stronger than me, no question. The force of his hit spun me around, and I nearly lost my grip on my sword. But the khel zhan was all about beating stronger opponents, about using kinetic energy and movement to your advantage. I kept the spin going, whirling in a circle, dodging his next thrust . . . and driving the edge of Muriel into the back of his head, right where the skull met the base of the neck. He let out a gurgle, and collapsed into the dewy grass.

Twenty-eight.

I fell back, taking stock. Most of the guards were dead, along with one of our men. Someone in the wagons was screaming. Galen was crouched low, his knee pinning a struggling man down as he pushed his daggers into him. Manos had driven his hammer into the side of the carriage and was trying to pull it out. Zell had a nightglass sword in each hand and was fighting two men at once, blocking the attacks of the first while finishing off the second.

And beyond him, at the front of the caravan, was the wagon driver, the old Westerner with the shaggy beard. He hopped off his perch and glowered at us, raising his hands, and the veins in his eyes flared a throbbing sickly green.

Oh shit.

"Bloodmage!" I screamed, as the air around pulsed with a sticky moist squelch, as my ears buzzed with the rustle of leaves and my nose flooded with the smell of freshly cut grass. Vines emerged from the palms of his hands, dense rope-like vines covered in thick thorns, and they streaked toward us like pouncing eels. They tore open the side of Manos's arm and shot past him, hurtling blood-tipped toward the rest of us. But they were too slow—too slow for us, anyway. Galen dove aside, neatly rolling under them, and Zell shoved the guard he'd been fighting forward, right into their path. The man shrieked as the vines hit, their ends splitting open as they entangled him. The bloodmage let out a gasp, struggling to pull his vines back . . .

Which meant he was vulnerable. I let out a battle cry of my own and raced toward him, my feet padding over the ground, my body a blur. I leaped over a guard's fallen corpse, streaked past Zell, an arrow on a collision course with no turning back. The bloodmage jerked back, raising one hand, and I weaved below it, under the new vine bursting forth, and drove Muriel's point straight into the underside of his chin.

Blood bubbled from his lips. A wet wheeze escaped his throat. The green glow faded from his eyes as he slumped down and lay still.

Twenty-nine.

And then it was quiet, that sudden, restless, panting quiet that only comes at the end of a battle. All twelve guards lay dead at our feet. I lurched away, heart thundering, suddenly aware of how weak my knees felt. Galen's nostrils flared as he rose up, and Manos just stood there, warhammer at his side, casually pulling twisted thorns out of his bloodied bicep like they were berries on a bush. "Vines, huh? That's a new one."

Zell rushed toward me, pulling down his mask. "Tilla! Are you hurt?"

"No," I said, even as I stared down at the body in front of me, the bloodmage with my sword through his head, the man I'd just killed. "I'm fine. Really." I mean, my hands were shaking, but that was normal. That happened all the time.

"Clear!" Galen shouted up to our archers, which was helpful because I'd forgotten all about them. He walked over to the first wagon and threw it open, revealing bags heavy with gold, and the second, filled with metal chests. Galen leaned in to open one, and there, inside, were rows of syringes, neat little vials filled with lightly glowing crimson. Miles's serum. The secret to my father's army. Capable of turning anyone into a powerful mage.

Made from the blood of our captured allies.

I exhaled sharply. There was no turning back now.

Galen threw open the third wagon, the one where the screaming was coming from, and exposed a man hiding inside, a trembling chubby Easterner with thick jowls and bushy purple eyebrows.

And even while I was relieved that it was our man, that this hadn't all been for nothing, a tiny part of me was upset. Because that part knew what came next.

"Vladimyr Cel De Naro the Fourth," Galen said, arms folded across his chest. "End of the line."

We pulled him out of the carriage, crying and flailing, and dragged him up the hill, where we forced him to his knees. There, we gathered around him in a semicircle as our archers joined us, as the sky's purple just barely started to fade into pink. Galen nodded at Zell, who strode over to Vladimyr and drew his swords.

"Please," Vladimyr begged. "You have to listen to me. This is all a misunderstanding. I've done nothing wrong!"

I clenched my teeth, forced myself to look away. Because I knew that if I kept looking, I'd start to believe him, start to listen, start to feel the natural empathy that's unavoidable when a man is crying and begging for his life. No matter how many times I did this, I always *wanted* to believe them.

Galen, for better or worse, didn't have that problem. He reached into his bag and took out a rumpled handwritten parchment. "Vladimyr Cel De Naro the Fourth," he read. "You have trafficked in blood stolen from loyal mages, and partaken in the creation of abominations. You have betrayed your countrymen to the hounds of the Inquisitor. You have collaborated with the Usurper King. Do you deny the charges?"

"I . . . I . . ." Vladimyr stammered, his eyes flitting wildly from side to side as he struggled to come up with an excuse. I hoped he wouldn't try to lie, because it was always so pathetic when they lied; he had to know that with a caravan full of mage blood, we had him dead to rights. "It's . . . it's not what it looks like. I had to do it! I had to help them! They would have killed me if I hadn't!"

"I'll take that as an admission," Galen said, and resumed reading. "You are guilty of treason against the crown. By the order of the one true Queen and the lawful ruler of Noveris, Lyriana Ellaria Volaris, you are sentenced to death." Without a word, Zell crossed his arms, laying one blade flat on each of Vladimyr's trembling shoulders. "Do you have any last words?"

I glanced back and there were Vladimyr's eyes, wide, terrified, glistening with tears. "This is so pointless," he cried. "They won. You lost. It's over."

"Do it," Galen said, and Zell swung his arms out in a lightning-fast scissor chop. Vladimyr's head tumbled off his shoulders and rolled down the hill. His body sat there for a moment, then crumpled down into the grass, blood pooling around the stump. "May the True Queen reign," Galen said.

"May the True Queen reign," we repeated, and Manos spat on the corpse.

I didn't add Vladimyr to my count. I mean, I know I probably should have. But I had to draw that line at only counting people I killed with my own two hands. If I had to keep track of everyone who died as a result of my actions, everyone whose death I was indirectly responsible for—well, that was a road I couldn't go down.

Twenty-nine. My number was twenty-nine.

Zell reached out, gently squeezing my arm. I leaned into him, pressing against his side, resting my head on his shoulder. Everything in the world was broken. But this still felt right.

"Come on," he said softly. "Let's go home."

TWO

HOME WAS A HALF DAY'S RIDE AWAY, IN A FOREST BY THE edge of a murky green lake. The Unbroken couldn't stay in any one place for too long, not without drawing the attention of the Inquisitor, so we lived out of tents and wagons, a makeshift camp ready to run at a moment's notice. Right now, we were holed up deep in Vanshire, a border region at the foot of the Evergreen Mountains, made up mostly of dark oak forests, lily-covered ponds, and tiny rustic villages, the kind with the wooden huts and the muddy roads and the villagers who scowled at you as you rode by. It was a sprawling, sparsely populated region, easy to get lost in, notable only as the region you had to ride through if you were going from Lightspire to the Eastern Baronies. Which made it the perfect place for us to lie low and strike.

In the early days of the rebellion, we were the most-wanted fugitives in the Kingdom and had to move constantly to escape my father's men, running from the vineyards of Ashelos to the narrow alleyways of Trellbein. Then the

Southlands had declared secession and my father's priorities had shifted, the war down there taking up most of his resources, buying our homegrown rebellion a little breathing room. When I was feeling exceptionally petty, I pictured my father on his throne, King Elric Kent, swamped with reports of rebellion, frantically putting out one fire after another, overwhelmed with the nightmare of ruling a Kingdom that loathed him. He had all the power, the throne he'd coveted his whole life, and I prayed to the Old Kings that it made him so, *so* miserable.

We rode in a line through those spindly trees, our horses trotting over mossy stones, the canopy of leaves filtering the hot afternoon sun to just a few golden rays. We'd been here for a month now and I still had absolutely no idea where to go, but Zell led the way and we followed. Riding through forests had been pretty much the high point of my childhood, but those had been the fog-shrouded redwoods of the West, not these creepy Eastern trees with their gnarled branches and whispering briarbirds.

We crossed a small gurgling brook, one I recognized, and then I heard the familiar tooting of horns from nearby. The watchmen had spotted us and were blowing the call of safety, which was great, because it ensured we wouldn't get peppered with arrows as we approached. I spurred my horse to get closer to Zell, and our eyes met again. He nodded. I smiled. These days we didn't even have to talk; he just *knew*, and I did too, and that was enough.

The camp loomed up ahead, fifty tents in a lakeside clearing, surrounded by a makeshift fence made of sharpened logs. Sentries kept watch from platforms built into the tallest trees. I could hear the sounds of the camp as we got closer:

the chatter of voices, the neighing of horses, the thump of wooden swords against training dummies. The guard at the gate saluted Galen, fist pressed to his heart, and then he did the same to me and Zell. On the long list of things I wasn't used to, getting saluted was near the top; I'd somehow managed to accept myself as Tilla, Citizen of Lightspire, but Tilla, Respected Rebel Warrior, still didn't make any damn sense.

We stabled our horses and took off on foot through the crowded tents. Chickens flapped by underfoot, and I could smell stew cooking from the canteen. There were members of the Unbroken all over the Kingdom, from lowly blacksmiths in backwater towns to spies in the castles of traitorous Lords, but we were the single largest group, a traveling band of seventy-five or so people. Most of that number were warriors, the most-seasoned rebel fighters, but we also had the leaders, the tacticians, the last few surviving mages. Also . . . we had the Queen.

Galen broke off toward the round central tent that was our command center, and Zell headed toward the armory to put our swords away. I needed a hot bath, and a good meal, and a strong drink, but right now, more than anything else, I needed a friend. So I made a beeline toward a tent at the far back of the camp, the only tent with a dedicated guard out front.

Lyriana was inside, seated cross-legged on her bed with a heavy tome in front of her. She glanced up as I entered and smiled. "Tilla! You're back!"

Looking at her now, it was almost impossible to recognize that naive, sheltered girl who'd sat at the Bastard Table in Castle Waverly just two years ago. Her luminous raven hair was cut short, shorn nearly to the scalp. Tattoos covered her arms, decorating the black skin: the Crest of the Titans on her left forearm, the elderbloom sigil of her family on her right, and the names of her murdered mother and father circling her biceps in the runic script of the Titans. When I'd first met Lyriana, she'd never worn anything but a dress, but now she looked natural in a loose cloth shirt and riding pants, brown leather boots halfway up her calves and an iron bracelet around her wrist. Only her eyes were the same, a glowing gold that seemed to give off a light of its own. She wasn't a Princess anymore, not by a long shot, but she made for one hell of a rebel Queen.

"That I am," I replied, and took a seat next to her. Lyriana's tent was unquestionably the nicest in the camp, with its own table, chairs, and stacks upon stacks of books. Most of us slept on mats or rugs, but Lyriana got an actual bed. A small, crappy bed with scratchy sheets and a fur blanket, but hey, a bed nonetheless.

"How did the mission go?"

"Successful. Only lost one man. Chalk? Chalko?"

"Chelkon," Lyriana sighed. "Father of two. A farmer, before the war. We'll have to hold a funeral." She glanced away uneasily. "Did you get Vladimyr?"

"We got him. He pled guilty. Zell . . . well, you know."

Lyriana nodded to herself, taking it in. I knew it weighed heavily on her, having to sign off on warrants of execution, the knowledge that we were out there killing people in her name. "I met Vladimyr, you know. At the Ascendance Day Masquerade a few years ago. He'd come along as a member of Baroness Celeste's retinue, and he was just so happy to be in the city. He gave me a little stuffed horse." She shook her head, her voice tight. "He seemed nice."

"He had a wagon full of mage blood, Lyriana," I said. "Vials and vials of it."

"Oh," Lyriana replied, and her face hardened. After the Ascendance Day Massacre, the common people of Noveris had been given the choice to bend the knee to my father and accept his rule. The mages, though, hadn't been so lucky. They'd all been rounded up, hunted, arrested, executed. Thousands died in those first few terrible months, a slaughter that put even the worst of the Volaris oppression to shame. Only a hundred or so mages survived that, but their fate wasn't much better; they were carted off to Miles's camps, kept alive so their blood could be harvested for his serum, tortured and experimented on whenever he needed new subjects. The era of Lightspire mages was over, the orders of Knights and Sisters and Shadows culled; now, there were only Miles's bloodmages, and the people terrified of them.

"The serum?" she asked.

"We burned it." There were some in the Unbroken who believed we should use the serum, make bloodmages of our own. But Lyriana had drawn a hard line at that. If we went down that road, we were no better than my father.

"Good," she said, then cocked her head to the side, scrutinizing me. "Tilla . . . are you all right?"

"Me? Yeah. I'm fine. Why?"

Lyriana shrugged. "You seem off. Not quite yourself. The whole terse words, haunted eyes, cold demeanor. You sound like Zell."

I blinked. It was true, I guess, that I felt like I *got* Zell much more now, that a year of bloodshed and turmoil had brought us closer together than ever. But it was still weird to think that I was becoming more like him. "I'm just a little messed up from the battle. My knees are still shaking, and I keep thinking about . . . I don't know." I sighed. "I thought it would get easier. But it hasn't. It's still just as awful as the first time."

Lyriana wrapped an arm around me and pulled me into a hug. "I should be out there with you, fighting by your side. It's not right that you're risking your life, putting yourself through hell, and I get to sit here, safe and warm in my tent. I'm the Queen, for the Titans' sake. . . ."

"Which is exactly why you can't fight with us and you know it," I replied. There weren't a whole lot of Volaris left in the world, after all. Lyriana's little sister, Aurelia, had made it out of Lightspire with us, but a rebel army was no place for a little girl. We'd sent her, disguised as a servant, to some loyalists in the Eastern Barony of Saile, where she'd be safe from my father's reach. That meant the entire legitimacy of the Unbroken hinged on the fact that we had Lyriana with us; with her, we were the champions of the true Queen, but without her, we were just a band of outlaws. The last thing I wanted to do was rehash this argument yet again, but I didn't have to because right then the earth started shaking.

Lyriana let out a little gasp and I clenched my teeth, resting my hand uselessly against her bed frame. This was just a thing that happened now: every few weeks or so, the earth would shake and tremble underfoot, rattling walls and knocking over shelves. It had started about eight months ago, and the tremors had been getting more and more frequent. Most weren't bad, just a little rattling that went for about a minute. The worst one had been four months ago, when we'd been back in Trellbein, a solid five minutes of quaking that had toppled buildings and torn deep rifts in the dirt. In that chaos, I'd genuinely wondered if the world was ending. Some days, I still wasn't sure.

This wasn't a bad one. The tent rumbled for a minute, candles swaying, and then went still. Outside, I heard a few men shout, and the horses neigh.

"Titans grant mercy," Lyriana said softly, instinctively. There were a whole lot of folks who believed the quakes were a sign of the Titans' displeasure, the Ascended gods angry at what my father had done. Much as I wanted to believe that, I couldn't, not after what I'd seen down in the catacombs below Lightspire; I still didn't know what the rotting ghoulish husks we'd encountered were, but they sure as hell weren't gods.

But I wasn't about to get into that, so I nudged the book lying on the bed, a heavy leather-bound tome with a picture of a severe-looking woman on the cover. "What're you reading?"

"A History of Queen Corellia II," Lyriana replied, because of course it was boring ancient history. I missed Markiska and her filthy romance novels. Really, I just missed Markiska. "Corellia came to power during one of the greatest periods of unrest in the history of Noveris and managed to restore peace and order, putting down the Bandits' Revolt and ushering in the Golden Age."

"I see the book's appeal."

Lyriana gave a sad little smile. "As a little girl, she was always one of my favorites. I thought it was just so amazing what she did, how much she accomplished. And now? All I can think about it is how easy she had it. I mean, she had Lightspire. She had hundreds of mages. She had her family advising her and her brother leading her armies and so much else. If she had all that and still struggled, how am I not completely doomed?"

Honestly, it was a pretty good question, but I wasn't about to tell her that. "She might've had a lot . . . but did she have a kickass best friend? One who always had her back *and* taught her all the best drinking songs?"

Lyriana grinned. "*Now* you sound like yourself."

"Yeah, well, you bring it out in me," I said, and it was mostly true. "I don't know how and I don't know when. But we'll win this thing, Lyriana. We'll get you back your Kingdom, and make my father and Miles pay for everything they've done. I know it."

"I wish I had your optimism," Lyriana said, and I kept up my smile. The thing is, it wasn't optimism. It wasn't certainty. It was desperation. I believed it because I *had* to believe it, because if I doubted it, if I questioned it, then I would just lie on the floor every morning and never get up. It was a load-bearing conviction, and the house of Tilla the Rebel depended on it.

"Enough talk," I said. "Want to grab a drink at the canteen?"

"I should stay here and finish this," Lyriana said, as if we were still at the University and she still had homework. "But you ought to stop by the canteen anyway. Ellarion's been there since morning and . . . he could probably use a friendly word. I'd go, but you know how he gets with me. Like I'm still some little girl he has to protect."

"Oh." My smile faded. I felt bad because Ellarion was my friend and deserved my support, but at the same time, I was looking to get comforted, not console the inconsolable. Not that I had any right to complain, of course. As bad as I had it, he had it so much worse. "Okay. Yeah. I'll stop by." I hugged her again, then glanced down at the portrait on the cover of the book. "By the way, you're, like, a hundred times prettier than her."

"She was in her fifties, you jerk." Lyriana laughed and shoved me off the bed. "Thanks for coming by, Tilla. Really."

Well, I felt better, if only a little bit. I would've given anything for a long soak in a hot bath, but had to settle for a dip in the lake instead, in a private spot a small walk away from camp. I stripped down and washed off the sweat and the mud, and as I ran my hands through my hair they came back bloody, which was just great. I'd loved reading about war as a kid, but none of the books had driven home how messy it is, how loud, how gross and squalid and wet. You never realize how fragile humans are, how brittle and breakable, until you've killed twenty-nine of them.

With a shudder, I washed my hands in the river a dozen times, then got dressed and headed back to camp. Ellarion or not, I needed that drink.

We called the common area "the canteen," but that was being generous; it was just a few long tables at the edge of the camp, next to a tent that served food and drinks. As soon as I got close, the smell hit me, savory roasting meat and freshly baked bread, almost as good out here as it had been in Lightspire. I grinned and waved, and from the canteen tent, a pair of friendly faces smiled back: Marlo and Garrus, ex–Ragged Disciples, devoted rebels, and the cutest couple I'd ever seen. Marlo ran provisions for us, hustling every caravan and small-town merchant, and Garrus had turned down the opportunity to fight to be a full-time cook, bringing all his baking skills to our meager little camp. Things could be tough out here in the woods, sleeping on mats, pissing in bushes, and constantly swatting away flies, but no one would ever say we didn't eat well.

"Tilla!" Marlo beamed, his smile big and infectious. "Tell

me you're hungry. Garrus has whipped up, and I'm not exaggerating here, the best mudrabbit stew you've ever had. . . ."

"That's a low bar," Garrus grumbled, stirring a pot with a wooden ladle. "But I'll admit, this is pretty damn good."

"Give me a bowl," I said. "And a glass of ale. The good stuff."

"Coming right up." Marlo grinned and turned to his apprentice, a scrawny young recruit we'd just picked up a few weeks ago. "Ein! You heard what the lady said!"

"On it, sir!" Ein replied, in that overeager way you had in your first month on a job. He scrambled forward to pour the stew, and only dropped the ladle once.

"Never too early for a drink," a voice called from one of the tables. Ellarion. He sat hunched over, bleary-eyed, with what I'm sure wasn't his first glass of ale in front of him.

"Can I join you?" I asked.

He glanced up at me, eyebrow arched. If Lyriana didn't look like the Princess she'd once been, then Ellarion was damn near unrecognizable. Back in Lightspire, he'd taken meticulous care in his appearance, always the sharpest-looking guy in the room, but now his aesthetic could best be described as "frightening hermit." His black hair was messy and wild, hanging in wide curls down his back. A thick beard covered the lower half of his face, stretching down to his collarbone, and his red eyes looked dulled, bloodshot, framed by heavy bags.

And then there were his hands. I tried not to look, to be polite, but my eyes instinctively glanced there anyway, to the clicking mechanical prosthetics at the ends of his wrists. Ellarion had lost both of his hands protecting us from the explosion at the Ascendance Day Masquerade. We'd scored him the prosthetics during a visit to the black market of Trellbein, and they were the nicest money could buy, elaborate

Artificed bronze hands with inlaid gemstones and flexible gold bands for the knuckles. Inside were thousands of tiny clockwork gears that gave life to fully functioning joints and bending fingers, linked magically to his mind. They could grasp things and make gestures and do pretty much everything non-prosthetic hands could do.

Except magic. For some complicated reason I couldn't begin to understand, mages needed their hands to channel magic, to funnel the energy running through their blood out into the universe. And whatever that conduit of energy was, it didn't work with Ellarion's mechanical hands, no matter how hard he tried. Ellarion Volaris, the former Archmagus, once the most powerful mage in the Kingdom, had lost his magic.

Which brought us to where he was now. Slumped on a canteen table in a rebel camp.

"Did my cousin send you?" he asked. "Because I don't need a pity check-in."

"Relax, tough guy. I'm just here to get a drink." I took a seat at the opposite side of the table, and even from there, I could smell the booze on his breath. "Started early, huh?"

"That, or I'm just still going really late. Hard to tell sometimes." He shrugged. "How'd the raid go?"

"Good. We got Vladimyr." I cleared my throat. "Your tactics worked out perfectly. The archers on one hill, the rest of us on the other . . ."

"I'm not so drunk I don't remember my own plan," Ellarion said, though I would argue he very much looked that drunk. "You don't have to praise me. Seriously. It was a basic high-ground rout, nothing to write ballads about."

"It just worked, is all," I said softly. Figuring out Ellarion's role in the Unbroken had been one of the more painful challenges of the past year. He'd spent fruitless awful months trying to regain his magic, sweating and grimacing in our training grounds, his metal hands trembling uselessly in front of him, the anguish in his eyes too terrible to look at. After that, he'd wanted to be trained in the khel zhan, to fight alongside us, but Galen had forbidden it; even without his magic, he was still one of the few remaining Volaris, and we couldn't risk losing him on the front line. Galen had wanted to send him east with Aurelia, but Ellarion had put his foot down, insisting he stay with the Unbroken.

So he became our tactician. And honestly, it was a good fit. Ellarion was smart as hell, and he'd read pretty much every book there was on military strategy. He worked alongside Galen in the command tent, poring over maps and scrolls, fielding letters from spies, plotting the course of our tough little rebellion. He was good at it, damn good.

And I knew he hated every second.

"Your soup and ale, miss," Ein said, placing a ceramic goblet and a wooden bowl in front of me. The goblet was full of cheap stolen beer, but my eyes were on the bowl right now, and the steaming, savory stew inside: diced rabbit, potatoes and carrots, a little dash of some peppery spice.

"I'll have another beer, too," Ellarion said, knocking over his empty goblet with a stray gesture. Ein shot me a glance, the kind that said *For the love of the Titans, deal with this guy*, and hurried off.

I ate a spoonful of stew and slumped back in my chair, savoring it. I knew objectively it probably wasn't that good and my standards had just plunged since we'd become a rebel band, but I also knew that it tasted amazing. Ellarion watched my face, and his cracked lips twisted into a little smile. "Know what I miss most about Lightspire?"

I arched an eyebrow. "Everything."

"Yeah. But especially the fruit. What I'd give right now for a thick juicy pear or handful of sweet cocoaberries . . ." He shook his head, his shaggy beard swaying with it. "Every morning of my life, I woke up to a bowl of amazing, ripe, perfect fruit, cut and peeled and ready for me. And I never appreciated that until now. Do you know what I mean?"

"No. I don't. I'm a bastard from the West, remember? I appreciated the hell out of every single bite of Lightspire fruit I had."

"Fair point. Fair point." Ellarion rubbed at his eyes with the back of a metal hand, which always made me wince a little. "Ein's not bringing me that beer, is he?"

"Nope. And with good reason. You are pretty damn drunk." I worried he might argue, but he just nodded and slumped forward, resting his head in his hands. "Can I ask what happened?"

"I just hate days like today," he grumbled. "Sitting back here all cooped up, no idea what's happening with you all out there, no way to know if my plan worked, just wondering if today'll be the day, the day it all comes down . . ." He let out a sigh and sat up. "Shit. I'm sorry. You . . . you shouldn't see me like this."

"It's okay. Really. The way the world is, I can't blame anyone for getting drunk."

"It's not just the world. It's . . . I . . . this . . ." He breathed in deeply, eyes shut, and then let it out. "I'm sorry, Tilla. I should go. Before I say anything else."

"Ellarion, it's fine. You can talk to me," I tried, but he was already up on his feet, lurching toward the tents. "Guard my food!" I yelled to Marlo and then rushed over to catch Ellarion, pulling one arm under his to keep him from falling over, and together we made our way across the camp toward his tent. I could see a lot of the other rebels eyeing us with annoyance. If anyone else had acted like this, they'd be disciplined within minutes. But Ellarion was a Volaris, and that carried special weight, even here.

I got him into his tent and flopped him down on his mat, where he sprawled, eyes shut, legs splayed. "I'm sorry, Tilla," he slurred, already half-asleep. "This is embarrassing."

"I once held your cousin's hair while she puked into a potted plant. Taking care of drunken Volaris is pretty much my thing."

Ellarion made a sound that was half chuckle and half snore. And as badly as I wanted to leave, there was one last thing I had to deal with. "Ellarion," I said quietly. "Your hands."

He let out another sound, this one an angry sigh, and then clasped his hands together, so the clockworks fingers of one came together at the wrists of the other, where polished metal met blistered, burn-scarred skin. He pressed down lightly on a smooth button at the base of the hands, and with a slight rush of condensed energy, a faint tinkling whistle, they tumbled down, falling flat onto the tent's floor. Even the best Artificed prosthetics had their limitations. They couldn't feel. They couldn't do magic. And they had to be taken off every six hours, to prevent overexposure.

The hands lay on the ground, fingers twitching as the magic left them. Ellarion kicked them away lazily and rolled onto one side. This wasn't the first time I'd seen him this drunk, or the dozenth. I knew how this would play out. Tomorrow, he'd walk out of his tent sobered up, act like nothing had happened, swagger his way to the command tent and shoot me a knowing glance, like *Heh, wasn't that funny?* Then we'd go a few weeks doing fine, and then it would happen again. I didn't judge him for it. It's just how life was.

I turned to leave, but as I did he spoke again. "Tilla. Can I tell you something? Something I haven't told anyone?"

"Okay..."

When Ellarion spoke, his voice was distant, a thousand miles away. "When I was a kid, I was scared of the dark. Like, really scared. Terrified. I'd lie awake in my dark room, holding the blankets, afraid of closing my eyes. And then my father showed me how to make these little lights, Candleflies, blue and yellow and pink, that could flutter in the dark and keep me safe." He closed his eyes, lost in the memory. "And they did. I made the Candleflies come every night, and I stopped being afraid." His voice choked up. "I can't make the Candleflies come anymore, Tilla. They're gone. Forever. And now all I have is the dark."

I didn't know what to say to that, what I could *possibly* say to that. So I just stood there in the tent's entryway, frozen, until I heard his breathing go shallow, and turn into a light snore. Then I left and stepped back into the camp, the sun hidden behind a gray cloud overhead, the whole forest a dusky gray.

It wasn't just the world that was broken. It was us.

I ate my stew and drank my beer, taking way less joy in them than I would have liked, and made my way back to my tent. Zell was waiting there, wearing just a drying cloth around his waist, his taut muscular torso still glistening from his own trip to the lake. His slick brown skin was decorated with scars, some old, some new: a jagged line across his chest from a Westerner's sword, a small white triangle from an arrow he'd taken in the shoulder. I crossed over to him wordlessly and kissed him, running my hands through his neatly-cut black hair, gazing into his eyes, tasting his lips, breathing in that smell of first winter frost.

"Tilla?" he asked, even as his broad hands worked their way down my side, easing open the clasps of my shirt.

"Just kiss me," I said, and we sank together onto the bed.

Later, we lay together, my head nestled in the crook of his shoulder, his fingertips running gently running along my bare back. This year had changed me too, given me a body I couldn't always recognize: firm and hardened, my stomach taut, my thighs strong, my biceps actual biceps. A warrior's body, as hard as that was to believe, decorated with a litany of scars of my own.

Night had fallen outside, so our tent was dark, the only illumination a few rays of moonlight ghosting in through the slit. It was quiet out there, the only sounds the occasional murmurs of a conversation, the crackling of a dying fire, the hooting of a distant owl. There was something soothing about the forest at night, almost magical, that made you feel like you were alone in the world. It was here, in the still forest night, safe in Zell's arms, the heat of his skin against mine, that I felt like I could be really honest, that I could give words to the fears and truths that raged within me.

"Zell," I whispered. "What if this all isn't worth it?"

"What isn't?" he asked, his voice husky and low.

"What we're doing out here. This rebellion. This whole life. What if it isn't worth it?"

I felt him shift, turning his head so he could look at me. "The man today. Vladimyr. His words affected you."

He could read me like a book. "Yeah. A little, I guess. I

just keep thinking about it. What if he's right? What if they *have* won? What if we're wasting what little time, what little freedom, we have with this pointless fight?"

Zell exhaled, his chest rising and falling beneath me. "And what would we do instead?"

"Run away," I said, my voice so quiet it could barely count as a whisper. "Somewhere far, where they'd never find us. Take up new names. Build a little house. Raise animals and grow plants, go into town once a month to sell them. Maybe . . . I don't know . . . make a family." This was heavy shit, even for us, but once I'd broken the dam the words just kept spilling out. "What if this is our one life, Zell? What if this is our only chance at happiness? Are we making a huge mistake in giving that up?"

We lay in silence for a long time, and I listened to the steady beating of his heart. "And what of the people who can't run away?" he asked at last. "What of the people who are locked away in your father's prisons, the people trapped in his cities, the people he's already killed? We just abandon them?"

"I don't know," I said, even though I did know.

"This is my fault, Tilla," Zell said. "If I hadn't helped the Ragged Disciples, if I hadn't let them take over Lightspire, none of this would have happened. This world, this nightmare, is my fault. And I can't rest or settle or even dream of a peaceful life until I've atoned for my mistakes. When I die and stand before the Crone, I need to show her that I did everything I could." He pulled me in tight with his arm. "I dream of that life too, Tilla. Of that little house. Of . . . a family. But I can't be that man. Not yet."

"I know," I said. And of course he was right. More than right. Because this wasn't just his fault. It was also mine. Sure, he'd helped the Disciples, and that led, in some small way, to Lightspire falling. But it was my actions all the way back in Castle Waverly that led to Miles discovering the secret of magic, my actions that brought my father to Lightspire, my actions that broke the world. And if Zell was guilty, then I was guilty too, guilty of so much more.

I didn't believe in his Gods, didn't believe in the Titans, didn't really believe in any judgment after death. But I knew just as well as he did that I wouldn't be able to live with myself if I ran, no matter how doomed or pointless this fight was. I was in this till it killed me.

"You're right," I said, then turned onto my side. "It was just a dream."

He wrapped his arms around me and pressed his chest to my back, entangled his bare legs with mine, kissed my neck. "A beautiful dream," he whispered, and sleep took us both.

THREE

Two weeks went by without any more raids. I settled into the dull routine of camp life: days practicing in the training grounds, nights lounging by the fire with Lyriana or learning military history from Ellarion or wandering the forests with Zell. I swam in the lake. I broke my knuckles on practice dummies. Garrus tried, and failed, to teach me how to bake. It was nice, boring even, but that was okay. I welcomed boring.

Then the messenger came, one humid summer morning. Galen communicated with the rest of the Unbroken through some elaborate coded network of Whispers and human messengers. It was always a big deal when they came in, the few outsiders who knew our location, our most trusted contacts, bearing news from the rest of the Kingdom. Some days it was massive, like when we'd received the missive that the Southlands had declared secession; that night, the whole camp had celebrated, even as Galen had urgently penned letters trying to form an alliance with their upstart Dyn.

Other times, the news was smaller, more disheartening, like when the messenger came to tell us that Miles had created another hundred new bloodmages, that they marched openly in the streets of Lightspire, that three dozen citizens had been executed for treason without so much as a trial. I'd seen all kinds of news pass into camp, but I'd never seen anything like this.

The messenger came at us galloping through the forest, so quickly that the scouts blared their horns and the guards at the gate drew their swords in alarm. He tumbled off his horse as he drew near, his ruddy face streaked with sweat, holding out a crumbled scroll in his hand. "An urgent dispatch from the Raven!" he bellowed, even as the guards tackled him to the dirt. "Please! You have to read it *now!*"

I watched as Galen took the note out of the man's hand, watched his expression darken as he read it. Then he crumpled up the paper and spun around. "Command tent. Now."

The command tent was big enough to fit a dozen, with a heavy table in the middle covered by an intricate map of the Kingdom. We gathered in a circle, the leadership of the Unbroken: Galen, Lyriana, Ellarion, Zell, and I, plus Manos Vore and the young scholar Kelvin Del Te Rayne. Galen laid the letter flat on the table in front of all of us, and we all stared at its blocky script.

"The Raven," Galen said, "has been captured."

An uneasy murmur passed through the room. The Raven was our absolute best contact, our most valuable spy. He'd first reached out to us six months ago through a series of intermediaries, gifting us the location of one of Miles's blood-harvesting prisons. The prison was incredibly secret, its location known only to maybe a dozen people; it was also absolutely fucking horrifying, which we discovered when we attacked it and freed the few prisoners who were still alive. There were still people out there who refused to join the fight, who lamented that both sides of the conflict were the same. Bullshit. After what I saw in that prison, I knew there was a right side and a wrong side. And I knew which I'd fight for.

After the dispatch about the prison, the Raven stayed in touch, sending us a tip every few weeks. Some were big, like a list of which Provinces the Inquisitor was searching, and others were smaller, like the travel route of an Eastern merchant collaborator. Speculating on the Raven's identity was a common pastime in the camp, and we always came up blank. None of us had any idea who he was, just that he was someone very high up in my father's court, someone with access to all kinds of secret information . . . and someone who really, really hated the bloodmages.

"What do you mean he's been captured?" Ellarion asked, his eyes flaring red at the thought. He might not have been able to use magic, but it was still in him, running through his veins.

"According to the letter, Inquisitor Hampstedt was able to identify him as a rebel contact," Galen said. His voice was flat, emotionless, but that didn't mean he wasn't angry. "The Raven has been arrested and thrown into prison. He was able to bribe a guard into relaying this message to us. He doesn't think he'll be able to do it again."

"Titans be damned," growled Manos. His frizzy gray hair hung down his back in four tightly wound braids, and salt-and-pepper stubble dotted his slab of a jaw. "We need the Raven. Without him, we're up shit creek."

"That's not all," Galen said, and oh, were we *just* getting to the bad news? "The letter says that Inquisitor Hampstedt has called a meeting of Lords a week from now at the castle of Lord Delaux in Fallowfields. He's bringing the Raven with him, to make an example out of. The Raven will be publicly tortured and killed." Galen glowered. "He's a dead man."

The tent was silent for a moment as we all took the weight of that in—a silence Lyriana vehemently broke. "We have to rescue him!" she implored. "After everything he's done for us, everything he's risked for us, we can't just let him die."

My instinct was to agree with Lyriana. I'd grown attached to the Raven, thought of him as one of us. Leaving him to die just didn't seem right. "Plus, there's probably a lot more he knows, right?" I said, not sure if I was convincing the others or justifying it to myself. "If we saved him, he'd probably still be really useful."

"Maybe," Galen said, and I could practically see the thoughts whirring through his head, the gears of possibility spinning away. "Or maybe this whole letter is just a trap to lure us in."

"We have to take that chance," Lyriana said.

"And how would we do that?" Ellarion replied. "We're not talking about raiding a caravan or hitting some remote prison. We're talking about riding straight into the lands of Lord Alayne Delaux, one of King Kent's most loyal allies. And not just that, but doing it while the Inquisitor is there himself. You know how Hampstedt travels. There'll be a whole company of soldiers with him, and dozens of bloodmages." He drummed his fingers on the table as he talked, with the heavy thuds of metal on wood. "What you're talking about is a suicide mission."

"It's probably a real letter, then," Kelvin said quietly. "The ratio of cheese to mousetrap is all wrong." He was a handsome young Easterner in his mid-twenties, with curly blond locks and sparkling blue eyes. He was one of the Kingdom's brightest minds, and before the war, he'd been on track to become a professor at the University; when my father had burned it to the ground, he'd come running to us instead. He was useful, sure, but something about his haughty manner always set me on edge.

"So what?" I asked. "We just let the Raven die?"

"Better that than dying ourselves," Galen replied. "There's just no way."

"No way to do a direct attack, sure," Lyriana said. "But we don't need that just to rescue one prisoner. We could send a small group in. We sneak in disguised, grab the Raven, and get out before anyone even knows we were there."

Galen arched a skeptical eyebrow. "I notice you're saying 'we.' I can't imagine you think for a minute I'd let you be a part of this."

Lyriana glared at him, then sighed. She raised a slender hand, and the Rings on her fingers pulsed a dazzling color, a swirl of turquoise and emerald. The air around us crackled with the electric hum of magic. I tasted lavender, I think, and felt an odd heat on my skin, like a ray of sunshine on a cold day. Lyriana scrunched up her face in concentration and spun her hand in a delicate circle before pointing her fingers directly at Manos. The room around him seemed to throb and pulse, a contraction of light, and the air around him shimmered like an oil spill. I blinked, or the room blinked, and suddenly Manos wasn't there at all anymore. He was gone, the only sign that he'd ever been there a faint shimmer over his chair.

We all gaped. Kelvin's jaw fell open in shock. Even Ellarion sat up, dazzled.

"What?" Manos demanded, and okay, his voice coming out of thin air was pretty damn funny. "What is it? What are you all staring at?" Kelvin lifted up a mirror so Manos could see, and then his chair toppled over as he fell back in surprise. The illusion vanished as soon as he hit the ground, the shimmer disappearing to reveal Manos's sprawled form. With a rush of air and the tingle of a cold breeze, the magic left the room, and Lyriana slumped back down in her seat.

"How in the frozen hell did you do that?" Galen demanded.

"It's a new Art. One I invented. I call it Glimmering," Lyriana said, beaming. "I can do it for all of us, and keep it up for twenty minutes at a time."

"That's incredibly powerful magic," Kelvin said, staring at the Queen with the world's most obvious schoolboy crush.

"It's something, all right," Ellarion said, and I could hear it in his voice, a pained mix of pride and jealousy.

Lyriana either didn't see it or decided not to acknowledge it. "Here's my proposal. A small group of our best rides out to Fallowfields. We keep our distance and take stock of the situation. If there's an opportunity to rescue the Raven—and I'll fully admit that's an enormous *if*—I'll use my magic to hide us, and we'll sneak in and rescue him. What do you say?"

Manos nodded. "I'm in. Without the Raven, we've got nothing but piss and dirt."

"I'm in, too," Zell said, and I nodded. The Raven deserved this much. And I'd be lying if I said there wasn't a part of me excited at the prospect of being in the same room as Miles, of finally getting revenge on the boy who'd cost me so much.

"Well, I'm not." Ellarion folded his arms across his chest. "There are so many unknowns, so many things that could go wrong! We're talking about sending the Queen . . . *the Queen* . . . out into the field on the most dangerous mission we've ever done, with barely any intel or planning, using untried magic, and . . . and . . ." He threw up his hands. "Come on! This is madness!"

"It is." Galen nodded. "But everything we do here is madness. If we back down from this, from saving a loyal ally who risked his life to help our cause, then we're admitting defeat. And if we're doing that, then we might as well just surrender right now." He picked up the letter and crumpled it in his fist. "I'm in, too."

"Are you serious?" Ellarion yelled. "This isn't like you, Galen. What game are you playing?"

"The game where I'm the leader of the Unbroken, and you're just a tactician," Galen replied, and I actually winced. "The mission stands. We ride tomorrow."

FOUR

I didn't get to talk to Ellarion again before we left, because he stormed out of the tent in a huff, but he was there when we rode out, waiting by the camp's gate the next morning. There were five of us going on the rescue mission: me, Zell, Galen, Lyriana, and Manos. Ellarion watched us all go, one by one, and he gave a little wave at Lyriana as she passed him, and a sad little smile at me. With us gone, he was in charge of the Unbroken. He took it seriously, but I knew he'd give anything, *anything*, to be going with us.

The Fallowfields were a dusty windswept region on the Heartlands' eastern border, right at the base of the green hilly mountains that separated the Province from the Eastern Baronies. The name, it turned out, was right on point. The fields and forests gave way to vast plains of brittle gray dirt, interrupted only by scraggly black trees, towering rock formations, and looming canyons so jagged they looked like they'd been cut into the earth with a massive blade. This was a mining region, Lyriana explained, famed for its rich quarries and deep caves. The people who lived out here were hard folk, prospectors and pilgrims and outlaws, and they were ruled over by Lord Alayne Delaux, a hawk-faced old man legendary for his cruelty and pettiness.

"Delaux was one of the few Lords who survived your father's coup, and he eagerly bent the knee," Galen said with disgust, as our horses tromped over a craggy outcropping. "He'd always felt snubbed by the Volaris, like they treated him and his people as if they weren't important. He took the first chance he could to get revenge."

"How'd he survive the bombing of the Masquerade?" I asked. "I thought all the Lords of the Heartlands were in that ballroom."

"*Most* of the Lords," Lyriana admitted. "Lord Delaux and a few other lesser ones weren't invited."

Zell and I shared a look. "So . . . you *did* snub him and treat him like he wasn't important?" I asked.

"I . . . We . . . I mean . . ." Lyriana stammered, and Galen just shrugged. "It's complicated."

We wore our cloaks with the hoods up and traveled by backroads, avoiding settlements and trade routes. I didn't think anyone was looking for us, not out here, but we were better safe than sorry. After four days, riding through the day and sleeping under the stars, the spires of Delaux's castle loomed on the horizon.

They called it the Dragonsmaw, which was both needlessly dramatic and totally accurate. A sprawling castle made of sturdy gray stone, it sat in a stretch of gravelly emptiness, like a massive skull bleached in the sun. Dozens of pointed towers reached up into the sky like teeth, framing a round central dome. The banners of House Delaux hung off the tall gray walls:

black and red, with a skeletal serpent wound around a spear.

But it wasn't the banners that caught my eye as we lay on our bellies on a flat outcropping about a mile away, staring at the castle through Artificed telescopes. Stretching out from the castle's drawn gates was a long dirt road, and lining the road on both sides were dozens of tall wooden posts, standing out like nails driven into the earth. At first I thought they were signposts or monuments or something, but then I saw the shapes on them, slumped figures, some scorched black, some still writhing. "By the Old Kings . . . are those people?"

"That they are," Manos growled next to me.

My stomach roiled. There were at least thirty posts out there, and each had a person hanging from it, bound up high with a thick rope, their arms folded behind their backs. Looking at them through the telescope, I could make out men and women, burned and tortured, hung out to die in the hot sun. Each had a sign around their neck, and I could read a few of them: TRAITOR. REBEL. SPY.

"Gifts for the Inquisitor," Galen explained. "He likes to know that Lords are doing their part in purging disloyal citizens. So they've taken to putting up this kind of display."

"Are they actually rebels?" Zell asked, and I could hear the coiled fury in his voice.

"Some might be. Most aren't. It's the gesture that matters." Galen let out a terse breath. "Welcome to life under King Kent."

We didn't talk much after that, just lay there waiting for Miles and his company to arrive. I knew I should have been more worried, but for now, we felt safe; the plan was just to scout and not go in unless we were absolutely sure we could pull it off, and I had enough faith in everyone's sense of self-preservation that we wouldn't do something *too* stupid. Besides, the outcropping we'd picked gave us a good view of the castle and the surrounding fields, while keeping us hidden from view no matter which road they came from.

Too bad they didn't come on a road.

We heard it before we saw it, a low hum from somewhere past the horizon, a vibrating pulse like you felt in the walls of the Godsblade. Lyriana perked up, eyes darting around, and I could tell she felt it in her bones, the surge of looming magic. "Something's coming," she said. "Something big."

And oh yeah, was she ever right. Galen was the first to spot it, a dark looming shape in the sky, approaching through the clouds like the world's fastest thunderhead. I whipped up my scope to get a better look, and nearly fell off the outcropping in shock. Because this thing wasn't a cloud, not at all. It was a ship, an enormous rectangular metal block of a ship, hurtling through the sky in a way that defied all sense or reason. It was massive, as big as a galleon, but it had no mast, no riggings. The front came together in a jagged point lined with shimmersteel windows. Heavy iron cannons jutted out of slats on the side, and six wings hung above them, three on each side, gently swaying and turning. The whole thing practically *oozed* magic. The air around it wavered and trembled, and the ground below it quivered as it passed, the light bending and arching in impossible ways.

"The Skywhale," Galen said, and I don't think I'd ever heard awe in his voice before. "I heard rumors that Hampstedt built this . . . but I never thought I'd see it with my own eyes."

"Titans grant us mercy," Lyriana whispered.

"Forget mercy," Manos grumbled. "Titans grant me a damn catapult."

I turned to Zell to see what he thought, but he just muttered something in Zitochi, a prayer maybe. Never a good sign.

The Skywhale drew closer, that low hum growing louder and louder until I could practically feel my bones grinding together. I wondered if we ought to move, if we'd be exposed from above. But it stopped by the side of the castle, a good ways off. The wings rotated, turning sideways, and as they did the whole ship slowly descended, like a leaf fluttering off a tree, before coming to a rest on the brittle earth and sending a cloud of gray dust billowing up around it. It was impossible, unfathomable, one of those things you see in a dream that doesn't make sense but still chills you to the bone. It reminded me of how I'd first felt when I'd gotten to Lightspire, the sheer staggering awe, the sense that nothing could ever triumph over something so vast and powerful.

But Lightspire had fallen. And so would my father.

We watched through our telescopes as the ship's front slid open like a gaping maw, revealing a long ramp that descended down into the dirt like a tongue. First came the soldiers, at least three dozen men in red-and-gold armor, wielding jagged spears and heavy broadswords. The bloodmages came after them, ten or so, Western men and women. They wore plain leather armor and brown hoods, and most were unarmed, but you could tell they were bloodmages by the quiver of the air around them, the steam billowing off their shoulders, the crackle as they walked.

The soldiers and the bloodmages marched through the curved gate of the Dragonsmaw, and then a man emerged after them. He was a Westerner, tall and thin, wearing a tight gray robe and walking with his hands folded behind his back. His silver hair was tied back in a ponytail, and a perfect pointed goatee framed his lean jaw. The air around him shimmered weirdly, and as I squinted I could make out shapes moving behind him, just barely there, like a trick of the light: tendrils of spectral darkness, emerging from his back like the legs of a spider.

A pang of stress curdled in my stomach. I'd never seen the man before, but I knew him by reputation. Archmagus Jacobi. My father's enforcer. The most dangerous bloodmage in the Kingdom.

Jacobi had been a House Hampstedt scholar, a mentor to Miles long before the war had broken out. He'd been one of the first to volunteer for the bloodmage injection, and the most successful at harnessing its powers. Most bloodmages came away with one Art, maybe two, but Jacobi had been able to master dozens, including the dark tendrils of the Shadows of Fel. There were all kinds of rumors about him: that he'd single-handedly wiped out a company of mages, that he never slept or ate, that he personally tortured prisoners for the thrill of it. Looking at him now, his lips a hard line, his gray eyes smoldering with black veins, I believed all of it.

Jacobi marched forward, after the soldiers, and once he was at the gates he turned around, gesturing, just barely, toward the ship. Then another man walked out, and at the sight of him my heart lunged up into my throat.

Miles Hampstedt, the Bloodhawk, Inquisitor of Noveris, descended down the ramp out of the Skywhale. The last time I'd seen him had been in my room in the Undercity, where he'd grabbed my face and slammed me against a wall. The sight of him still made me feel sick. He wore his Western General's uniform, a long black coat that trailed after him as he walked, and he'd taken on the sigil of the Inquisitor, an iron eye hanging over his chest by a chain. His curly blond hair hung long around his shoulders, and a golden beard framed his jaw. Despite being the guy who'd invented the bloodmage serum, Miles refused to use it, determined to keep himself clean. Not that he needed the extra power. He walked with the confidence of a man who had nothing to fear, a man who had the world laid out in front of him like a buffet, a man going through his life with a perpetual self-amused smirk.

I had never wanted to punch someone so bad.

Then he strode on, toward the gates of the castle, and one more man walked out after him, and now I actually gasped out loud. Because I'd steeled myself to see Miles, prepared myself for the surge of fear and anger and hatred I knew I'd feel.

But I was totally unprepared to see my father.

He hadn't changed much since that day in the throne room a year ago. He had the same brown hair, neatly cut at his shoulders, the same pointy beard, the same contemplative scowl. He'd traded his plain Western robes for a more ostentatious look, with a trailing red cape and a sparkling golden breastplate and a delicate shimmersteel circlet, thin and subtle on his forehead. He looked like a King right out of the history books, regal and commanding and maybe even wise, the kind of King I always imagined when I heard the stories of the Old Kings of the West. The kind of King he must have always dreamed of being.

My gut lurched, and I had to fight back a sudden rush of vomit. My eyes burned. How did he still make me feel this way? How could I feel so many different things at once, and every one of them so overwhelming?

"Fuck me in both eyes," Manos growled, and that kind

of grounded me, because it was pretty clear he only felt one thing. "The Usurper himself."

"The Raven didn't say anything about him being here," Lyriana murmured.

"The Raven's locked up and bribing jailers. He must not have known," Galen replied. His voice was flat, his brow furrowed in deep concentration. I could tell he was plotting something, and I was a little afraid to ask what.

My father entered the castle's gates. Four more soldiers emerged out of the maw of the Skywhale after him, and took up posts just past the ramp. Sentries, then, to guard it. Probably from the likes of us.

"They didn't have a prisoner with them," Lyriana said. "The Raven must still be in the ship."

"Forget the Raven," Galen said. "We've got a bigger target." We all turned to him, confused, and he looked back at us like the answer was self-evident. "We're taking the Skywhale."

"Wait, what?" I said, a pit of dread tightening in my stomach.

"We can get in with Lyriana's Glimmer Art, just like we planned. Then we find whatever they use to fly that thing, take control of it, and steal it for ourselves." Galen grinned, and I'm pretty sure it was the first time I'd seen him smile since the coup. "And then we unload every cannon it has right into that castle."

Manos laughed, a low booming thunder. "Oh, Lord Reza. I love the way you think."

"Well, I don't!" Lyriana replied. "I appreciate your enthusiasm, but we have no idea how that thing works! We don't know what kind of magic powers it might have or how to fly it or anything! How do you expect to steal a vessel you don't even understand?"

"It's a ship." Galen shrugged. "It'll have some kind of deck and some instruments to control it and a navigator who knows how it works. I say we put a sword to his throat and make him do the rest. It's no different than taking a boat in the harbor."

"A boat in the harbor doesn't fly," I said quietly.

"We came out here to rescue the Raven," Lyriana insisted. "That's what this is about. Saving a loyal and faithful ally!"

"Your Majesty, with all due respect," Galen said, in a voice that most certainly did not have all due respect, "we're talking about a chance to kill King Kent and Inquisitor Hampstedt in one fell swoop. We'll never get an opportunity like this again."

I had a thought, a sudden thought so loud I couldn't keep it from tumbling out. "Did you know this was going to happen?" I asked Galen. "Is that why you agreed to come out here?"

Galen's gaze flitted away. "I'd suspected it *might* happen. But that's not why I agreed."

"You *agreed* to rescue the Raven," Lyriana insisted. "That's what we all agreed to."

"Your Majesty—" Galen started, but Lyriana cut him off.

"I *am* Your Majesty," she said, harder and more forceful than I'd ever heard her talk to Galen. A part of me had always suspected a confrontation between the two of them was coming, but I couldn't think of a worse time or place. "And I'm giving you a direct order. We're here to rescue the Raven. And that's what we're going to do."

"Why don't we do both?" Zell said, before Galen could reply. "We sneak in there and find the Raven. Odds are good he'll know how the ship works. If he thinks it's feasible, we steal it with his help. If not, we run."

We all turned and stared at him for a long, silent minute. "Damn it," Galen said at last. "That *is* a good plan."

"It is," Lyriana said, though she still eyed Galen with a measure of suspicion. "Which is why we're going to follow it."

So we made our way off the outcropping, as close as we could without being seen, and in the dusty basin below we armed ourselves for battle. I put on Western armor I'd stolen during a raid, chain mail sleeves and a leather helm and a metal breastplate adorned with an eagle. Zell crossed his blades across his back in an X; Manos held his hammer at his side; and I strapped on Muriel, snug in a sheath at my hip.

Then came the Glimmering. We'd realized pretty early in our planning that the one downside to a magic that made us impossible for our enemies to see was that we couldn't see one another, either. So we stood together in a tight pod and tethered ourselves with thin ropes hooked at our hips. It felt unnatural, restrictive, but it would keep us together, and safely within the five-foot radius Lyriana insisted her Art was good for.

"All right." Galen cleared his throat. "Let's do this."

Lyriana closed her eyes in deep concentration, her lips moving just barely in some inaudible chant. She wove her hands in precise delicate motions, bending and releasing her fingers like she was playing a giant invisible mandolin. The world around us was already pulsing with the hum of magic, but I felt something else, a warmth in my skin, a tingle deep in my bones. Motes of dirt lifted up from below our feet and spiraled around us. The air shimmered with that oil-slick multicolored glow.

Galen vanished first. Then Manos, then Lyriana, then Zell. I was about to ask when it was my turn, and then I looked down and realized my body was gone.

It didn't matter how prepared my brain was. Looking

down and seeing nothing made my gut churn. "Whoa," Manos said from somewhere, his voice queasy, and I heard Zell sharply draw in his breath. It was weird—profoundly, disorientingly weird. There was always an innate wrongness to magic, to seeing the rules of the world bent and broken, but I'd never experienced it firsthand like this.

Then I felt something else, a pressure on my hand, warm and tight. Zell's grip. And I closed my eyes and took a deep breath and in that darkness I was just a girl holding hands with her boy. That was all. So long as I had that, his hand in mine, I'd be okay.

It took us about ten minutes to get to the Skywhale. It was even more impressive up close, a colossus of metal and shimmersteel, at least twice the size of the largest galleon I'd ever seen. Squinting through the big window in the front, I could make out what looked like a deck, but my eyes were mostly drawn to the dozens and dozens of cannons along the side. I hated to admit it, but I was impressed, blown away by the ingenuity of my father or Miles or both. That they were capable of building something like this was amazing. If only they'd put their talents toward something good.

I'd worried a little that the sound of our footsteps would give us away, Glimmered or not, but it turns out I had nothing to fear; even at rest, the Skywhale was noisy, that hum of magic we'd heard from afar a deafening roar, like waves crashing into cliffs. The ground underfoot rumbled constantly, which had the nice added benefit of throwing up a small cloud of perpetual dust that obscured our footprints. The whole area around the ship surged with energy, loud and unstable.

That just left the four guards stationed outside the Skywhale, standing ramrod straight, spears in hand, grim expressions etched on their faces. My brain knew they couldn't see us, but that did jack shit for my heart, which was thundering with the absolute certainty we were about to get caught. I sucked in my breath and followed the gentle pull of the invisible rope, even as it led me closer and closer to the guards, to the ramp that led right into the ship itself. Every step we took felt more doomed than the last, and then we were on the ramp itself, walking up, right between the guards, who had absolutely no idea. I wish I could have seen Zell's face, just so that I could have shared the total absurdity of what was happening with someone else. But there was just the roar of the ship and the feel of the metal underfoot and the blank expressions of the guards, feet away, looking at me, *through* me, with no idea that I was actually there.

I let out that breath once we were in the ship and not a second earlier. The ramp led to a long metal hallway, stretching all the way to the back of the Skywhale itself. It was cold inside, the walls stark and bare, the only light coming from white Luminae bulbs mounted in the ceiling. I don't know what I expected, a nicely furnished cabin maybe, but this was all business, harsh and functional. The cannons outside weren't an embellishment, they were the whole point. The Skywhale wasn't some fancy galleon; it was a battleship, a weapon of war.

None of us had any idea where to go or what to do once inside, so we just quietly shuffled forward, invisible, following the tug of Galen's rope at the lead. We passed long benches, clearly made to fit dozens, and a handful of side rooms: a picked-over armory, a tiny canteen, narrow shafts that led to cannon platforms. All of them were empty, though. This was a troop transport, after all, and all the troops had gotten off to march into the castle, which meant the ship was pretty much ours. The only people we saw at all were in the shafts that led to the wings. There, behind iron-barred prison doors, were bulky men in brown robes, standing over wide round grates that trembled with magical energy.

"It's the same principle as the floating platforms in the Godsblade," Lyriana whispered, and holy shit was it weird to suddenly hear her voice. "The manipulation of air currents to achieve flight, just on a larger scale."

I didn't realize it was safe to talk, but I guess that's what we were doing now. "Those are prisoners, aren't they?" Zell asked. "Not bloodmages."

"Correct. Those are captured Hands of Servo," Lyriana replied. "Perhaps the bloodmages haven't mastered that Art."

"All the more reason to take the ship," Galen whispered. "Come on. Let's find our Raven."

That long hallway led to a door at the end, which opened up to a spiral stairway, leading both up and down. I was starting to get a feel for the ship's layout: the middle floor we were on was the main galley, where the soldiers rode. Above us, the stairs led to an ornate wooden door that I guessed went to the captain's quarters or the deck. So instead we went down, pushing together on that narrow staircase, which brought us to a thick metal door. The rope pulling me along stopped, and even though I couldn't actually see Galen, I could picture him perfectly, crouched against the door, one hand on his dagger, prepared to strike.

"Ready?" he whispered.

I sucked in my breath and wrapped my fist around Muriel's leather pommel. I was as ready as I could be, I guess. Which never felt like enough.

The handle twisted, turned by Galen's invisible hand, and

the door flew open. Through it, we could make out what was very definitely a prison, a small unfurnished metal room with three heavy doors, the kind with the little barred windows at the top. A single yellow Luminae burned in the ceiling, revealing a table covered in torture tools: curved daggers, jagged hooks, iron manacles, and glass syringes.

And standing in the middle of the room, head cocked toward us with mild confusion, was my father, Lord Kent himself, in a plain gray shirt and trousers, his hair loose around his shoulders.

No. That was impossible. I'd seen him just a half hour ago, walking out of the Skywhale after Miles. This didn't make sense. Something was wrong, very wrong.

But I didn't have time to question it, because I felt the rope on my waist tug tight and then rip off. The air in front of me shimmered and rippled like the surface of a lake, and Galen burst through it, lunging out of the radius of Lyriana's magic, appearing out of nowhere with a dagger in each hand. My father let out a yelp of surprise, his green eyes widening, but that was all he got out, because Galen crossed the distance between them in two strides and drove a dagger up to the hilt into his chest.

Holy shit.

Holy holy holy shit.

My heart thundered so hard I was sure it would burst out. My eyes stung. My breath was like a swig of whiskey, burning in my chest. I couldn't breathe. I couldn't stand. After all this time . . . after everything . . . my father was . . .

There was a sharp contraction of air, like the world gasping, and the Glimmer around us vanished, probably because Lyriana was too shocked to keep it up. She appeared next to me, alongside Zell and Manos, and, you know, the rest of my body. And we all just stood there, stunned, staring at Galen with his dagger in my father's chest.

"May the True Queen reign," Galen hissed and jerked his dagger out. Blood blossomed like a rose in my father's shirt, and he slumped down, wheezing, grasping toward Galen with trembling hands. As his body hit the ground, as he gasped his last breath, he shimmered as well, a sickly purple ripple like the air around him was curdling, tendrils of smoky light bending off his features as they twisted and changed.

The man lying on the floor, the man Galen had killed, *wasn't* my father. Not anymore. He was a middle-aged Westerner, a ruddy man with messy blond hair and a thin beard. He lay there, staring up at Galen with dead eyes, eyes that were a bleary, veiny blue, eyes that were very distinctly not my father's.

It wasn't him. It was an impostor, a bloodmage.

How was it possible that I still felt relief?

Manos was the first to break the silence. "Someone want to explain what's happening here?"

"I don't know. I don't understand." Lyriana hunkered down by the man, turning over his bare arms to see the purple bruises on his skin. "He's a bloodmage, certainly. He was performing a Mesmer Art to mimic Lord Kent's appearance."

"But why?" I asked. "Why would a bloodmage be impersonating my father?"

"A double," Zell said, fists tightening around his swords' hilts. "To draw out assassins. This is a trap."

"No. Not a trap. Just bad timing," a voice called from behind one of the barred doors. It was a man's voice, ragged, hoarse, the kind of voice you get when you're either sick as a dog or you've been screaming for hours. "You're my rescue party, I assume?"

"And you are?" Manos demanded.

I swear I heard the voice sigh. "The Raven, of course."

We all looked at each other uneasily, none of us quite sure what to do from here. We needed more time, to think, to discuss, to try to make sense out of all this, but time was the one thing we very much didn't have. So Galen stepped forward, sheathing one dagger, and with his free hand turned the door's metal handle and pulled it open.

Behind it was a tiny unlit cell, barely bigger than an outhouse, its floor and walls bare. A man sat on the floor in the middle, hands bound with manacles. He was tall and gaunt, clad only in his underclothes. Stringy hair, mostly gray, hung long and messy down to his shoulders. A thick beard framed his jaw. A big purple bruise blossomed on his cheek, the kind you got when someone punched you really hard, and his nails were cracked and bloody.

Still. Even in this state, his eyes were the same. Sparkling green. Defiant and proud. My own eyes, staring right back at me.

"Tillandra," my father said.

"You have got to be shitting me," Manos grumbled. "Another one?"

"It's him," I whispered. "For real this time." And I just knew, knew for sure, knew in a way I hadn't with the impostor we'd just killed. His eyes met mine, and for one second, I swear I saw something else in them, a hint of relief, of joy, of pride. A look I hadn't seen in years.

Galen stormed over, jerked my father up by his collar and slammed him against the cell wall. "You've got ten seconds to explain what's happening here," he said. "What do you mean, *you're* the Raven?"

"Exactly what I said," my father replied, totally unfazed by the impact. "For the last six months, I've been feeding information to the Unbroken through a network of couriers. The prison camp in the fields of Amalore? The weapons depot in Trellbein? The travel plans of the Eastern blood-mongers? All of that was me."

It checked out. I mean, the names and places were right. But that didn't mean it made sense.

"You're saying you've been helping us," Lyriana said, and her eyes were glowing hot, the air around her tense and crackling. She looked ready to *kill*. "You. The man who murdered my parents. The man who stole my Kingdom. You really expect us to believe you're on our side?"

My father's nostrils flared, his hands tense with barely contained rage. "I made a terrible mistake appointing Lord Hampstedt to the role of Inquisitor," he said, and I don't think I'd ever heard him admit a mistake, *ever*. "I led my revolution to bring freedom to this Kingdom. But Miles and his blood-mages have turned it into a charnel house, carving a bloody trail from coast to coast, a pall of tyranny more terrible than the darkest days of the Volaris." Which yeah, true, but holy shit, hearing it from the person we'd thought was responsible. "All Miles knows is fear and blood, power and control. I ordered him to cease the production of the serum, to rein in his bloodmages. But he defied me, first behind my back, then to my face."

"You're the *King*," Zell insisted. "Forget the rat Miles. Surely his men answer to you."

"No. Miles makes the serum. He gives them power.

Without him, they'd be nothing," my father said. "If it came to a war, they'd choose him over me, and the chaos of that battle would scorch what's left of the Kingdom to the ground. I couldn't challenge him directly. So I sought to undermine him instead."

"All the messages you sent us," Galen said with dawning comprehension. "They were undermining the bloodmage operation."

My father nodded. "I'd hoped that between your attacks from within and the war with the Southlands, Miles would become vulnerable enough that I could remove him from power. But one of my messengers betrayed me, and Miles discovered what I'd been doing. His men came for me at night, slaughtered my guards, and threw me in a cell."

"Why not kill you?" Manos asked. "I mean, I would've. Still might."

"As far as everyone in the Kingdom is concerned, I'm still the King. The Lords of the land, especially in the West, still respect that. Without me on the throne, they'd begin scheming and conspiring, plotting a way to take the crown for themselves. Killing me would make Miles's life much harder. So instead he keeps me in this cage and has his puppets take my face, parading from Lord to Lord, giving whatever orders he tells them to."

"Mesmering another person's face requires looking right at them . . ." Lyriana said. "That's why he keeps you alive."

"It was the perfect coup." My father nodded. "Miles stole the Kingdom right out from under me, and no one even noticed."

The sheer enormity of what he was saying dawned on me, and I felt the world lurch underfoot. Because as horrible as things were out there, as terrible as the past year had been, I'd still assumed we were fighting a rational, logical enemy. My father could be ruthless and terrifying, but he was still a man driven by principle, by ideals, a man who could be reasoned with and beaten. But Miles? Emotional, impulsive Miles? The Miles who'd betrayed all his friends because I'd broken his heart, the Miles who never gave a shit about anyone but himself?

I remembered his face back in that room in the Undercity. I remembered his anger, his resentment, his seething, childish fury. *That* Miles couldn't be reasoned with. He'd burn the whole world down just to take it with him.

After all the horrors I'd seen in the past year, few things could still frighten me. Miles in charge of the Kingdom? That did the trick.

"Madness. Utter madness." Manos spat to the side. "Whole world's gone mad."

Zell shook his head. "World's always been mad. It's just catching up to you."

Galen had no time for their philosophizing. He actually laughed, that kind of half-crazed laugh someone does when they're about to completely lose their shit. "If what you're saying is true . . . if that weaselly coward Hampstedt really is in charge of everything, if you're nothing but a husk for his bloodmages to copy . . . then there's no reason I shouldn't kill you right now." He jerked a dagger up, pressing its point to my father's throat. "After all, like you said, you dying would make his life a whole lot harder."

My father didn't even flinch. "I always knew there was a good chance it would end like this. If you're going to do it, do it quick."

"Wait," I blurted out, even as Galen drew back his blade. "Don't!"

Galen turned back to me, slowly, hesitantly. "Why the hell not?"

"Because . . ." I stammered, even as my brain struggled to find an answer. "Because . . ."

"Because we can use him," Lyriana said coldly, her eyes blazing daggers.

Manos cocked a skeptical eyebrow. "For what?"

When Lyriana spoke, each word was forced out, and I could tell it was taking every ounce of her willpower to be rational and measured, to not let Galen do what she so badly wanted. "We could send him out there to tell the people that Miles is a traitor. We could have him publicly denounce the bloodmages. We could use him to rally the Western Lords."

"I could do all of that," my father said quietly. "And I could also help you take control of this ship."

Now even Galen was silent. He just stood there, breathing deep, and then lowered his dagger. "Keep talking."

My father's lips twitched with the tiniest hint of a smile. "The mechanism's simple. Bronze tubes run from the deck down to the mages in the wings. The captain gives orders into those tubes, and they comply. All we have to do is take the deck, and they'll follow any order we give them. You just have to know the jargon. And I do."

"How many guards on deck?" Zell asked.

"Ten to fifteen. No more. Mostly soldiers."

Manos grinned, hefting his warhammer. "Now we're talking my language."

"The door at the top of the stairs goes directly to the deck.

With the roaming sentry dead, there shouldn't be anyone else in the ship, so we can make our way straight there and—"

"Hold on a second," I cut in. "What was that about a roaming sentry?"

"You know. The soldier that patrols the whole ship, walking up and down all three floors to look for intruders." My father blinked. "You *did* kill the roaming sentry, right?"

Something creaked from the stairwell. We all spun around, and there he was, standing just outside our door with a stunned expression, a young Western soldier with a whistle clenched in his teeth.

Zell moved first, hurling one of his swords. It streaked through the air like a spear and plunged right into the soldier's chest, but it was too late; even as he fell back, he blew into the whistle, a piercing deafening shriek that rattled all through the walls of this metal monstrosity.

"Block the door!" Galen yelled, but Lyriana was already on it. Her hands flew up, fingers clawed, Rings glowing, and she jerked them in a series of harsh chops and pulls. The door slammed shut, the handle ripped clean off, and tendrils of metal snaked around the cracks like grasping vines, sealing it shut like a rope around a chest.

More whistles sounded from above, and then something else, a low braying horn, the kind you'd hear on a frigate, so loud it made the walls vibrate around us.

"That's the alarm of distress," my father said with a weary resignation. "It'll summon Miles and his men back to the ship. They'll be here in minutes."

I looked at the sealed door, bound shut with those metal bands. "That'll hold, right?"

"Against soldiers? Sure. Against bloodmages? Not for

long." Lyriana's eyes darted around the room, wide and worried. There was no other way out, no escape, no doors save the ones for the other cells. We were trapped.

"Is there anything you can do?" I pleaded with her. "Some Art that can get us out of here or keep us safe or . . . or . . ."

But in her eyes there was only defeat. There was a second of silence, a heavy silence as we all realized just how doomed we were. Galen breathed deep. Manos hefted his hammer. My father closed his eyes and slumped back against his cell wall. I looked to Zell, and he reached out and took my hand, squeezing it tight. I was going to die here. But at least I wasn't going to die alone.

Then a voice spoke, a new voice, from one of the other cell doors. "I can get us out," it said. "But you must set me free."

Every head turned. It was a woman's voice, low and husky, with an accent I couldn't place: rolled "r"s, hard consonants, and a measured way of speaking that suggested every word was being chosen carefully. "And who's this now?" Manos demanded.

"No idea," my father replied. "I didn't even know there were other prisoners."

Footsteps clanked above us, the frantic pounding of men running back and forth. I could hear more on the stairs outside, the clanking of armor and metal, and the pounding of gauntlets on the sealed door. "I have magic," the voice said. "Powerful magic. But I cannot help you from here."

I could see Galen gearing up to ask a question, but honestly, we didn't have time for that. I reached over, grabbed the handle, and threw open the cell door. Inside, sitting on the floor with her legs crossed, was a young woman. She was small and thin, bony even, and I could see olive skin through the holes in her ragged nightgown. Strange tattoos covered her arms, circular knotted bands and curved runic hooks that crept from her wrists to her shoulders. Her head was hidden under a rumpled black cloth, and her hands were bound to the walls with iron chains. Which was a lot of extra restraint for a girl already shoved into a cell in the bottom of an armored ship. Whoever she was, Miles wanted her locked up *tight*.

Lyriana flicked her hand through the air, and the chains binding the girl's wrists burst apart. She stood up, pulled the hood off her head, and tossed it to the side. The first thing I noticed was her hair: long and straight, cut jagged above her shoulders, and a color that didn't make any sense, the darkest lushest black interrupted by streaks of vibrant radiant blue, like a sapphire flame. She looked young, my age, and her face was lean and angular, high cheekbones and a sharp chin, a spattering of brown freckles across her nose. And then there were her eyes: sharp and bold, with heavy black lashes and irises that burned a vivid orange.

"A Red Waster," Lyriana said softly. That explained the girl's accent, and why I couldn't place it. The Red Wasters were some of the most reclusive people in Noveris, a culture who lived, against all odds, in the impassable deserts south of the Southlands. I'd seen only a few in my whole time at Lightspire, travelers clad in ochre robes, their faces hidden behind featureless white masks. I'd never been so close to one, much less heard one speak.

"Who are you?" Galen demanded, but she didn't even acknowledge him, which, okay, was pretty cool. She just walked out of the cell, bare feet padding silently over the cold metal floor. I could see now that she was tall, a good head taller than me or Lyriana, and she walked with a measured pace that seemed totally wrong for our desperate situation. She went straight to the torture tools table, where she threw aside the daggers and hooks and left the only things I couldn't identify: a pair of stone orbs, maybe the size of oranges, their midpoint lined with what looked like a ribbon of razor-sharp metal.

"Um . . ." I said.

The girl didn't move. She didn't raise her hands or arch her fingers or anything else that I associated with magic. But all the same, the orbs moved, rising up from the table to hover at her shoulders, spinning slowly beside her like levitating tops, their sharp edges sparkling in the light.

Lyriana let out a gasp, and even Galen looked rattled. The only people who could naturally do magic were natives of Lightspire, those born close enough to the Heartstone that they'd been steeped in its raw energy. That meant she had to be a bloodmage. But that didn't seem right either. For one thing, her slender arms were bruise-free, no marks of injection any-where on them. And there was something else, something fundamentally different about what she was doing, about the energy around her . . .

"How . . . how are you doing that?" Lyriana asked, mouth agape with wonder, and I realized what it was. There was no hum in the air, no pulse, no shimmering lights or rush of smells and tastes. The weird thing about the energy around her was that there *was* no energy, no trace of magic, none of the telltale sensations or feelings that came from being near someone working an Art. She just . . . *was*.

Horns sounded from above us, and I could hear more and more footsteps now. Definitely more than fifteen men, which meant that Miles's soldiers and bloodmages had returned. Time was running out.

The girl's dark eyebrows furrowed in concentration. The orbs whistled forward, spinning so fast they were just a blur, carving a rectangle the size of a brick into the room's wall. That shape, that section of the wall, glowed for a minute and then . . .

It didn't fall out or turn into smoke or anything. It just vanished in a blink, like it had never been there. Sunlight streaked in through the little slit, and I could see the dusty fields stretching out beyond the Skywhale, the faint blue shadows of the mountains in the distance.

"So now we have a window?" Galen asked. The pounding on the door had stopped, and the footsteps had grown oddly silent. That couldn't be a good sign.

"I need to see where we're going to take us there," the girl replied, which helpfully explained nothing. She stared out that little window intently, arms stiff at her sides, and her orbs whirled around her now, spinning around her body in diagonal orbits that seemed like they ought to collide. "I must concentrate. Please."

The pounding outside the door stopped abruptly, and the soldiers' shouting went silent. There was a chill in the air, not like a breeze, but more like the warmth itself had been swallowed, sucked away by something cold and terrible.

"Archmagus Jacobi," my father said. "He's here."

Manos made a face that was somehow a grin and a grimace at the same time. "Always wanted to kill him." He stepped in front of our group, meaty hands wrapped tight around his warhammer's shaft. "You lot want to take your chances with mystery magic girl? Be my guest. I'm going down fighting."

I glanced back at, uh, mystery magic girl. Her expression was more intense than ever, teeth gritted, breath quick, sweat streaking down her brow. The orbs were spinning faster and faster now, weaving around her in increasingly complicated spirals. I tried to steady my breath, to channel the khel zhan, to steel my nerves. At my side, Zell closed his eyes and whispered in Zitochi, a prayer that I knew was the Grayfather's Oath: *I fear not pain, that I may serve you. I fear not death, that I may sit by your side.*

Something was happening to the sealed door. It stiffened and shook, almost like it was freezing. Inky black tendrils hissed around, prying through the cracks like eels, wrapping around the metal frame. It buckled and trembled, and the bolts binding it popped and creaked.

"Almost there," the Red Waster girl choked out. The orbs around her were whistling so fast I couldn't even see them anymore, just streaks of sparkling light. "Just . . . a little more . . ."

The door shuddered again, and this time the whole thing bent inward, away from us, the metal itself crumpling. Lyriana raised her hands, and I could feel flames crackling around her. "May the True Queen reign," Galen growled.

Then the tendrils tightened all the way and the door flew off its hinges, pulled back into the hallway, and there he was, Archmagus Jacobi, glaring at us with those sick pulsing eyes and a look of dry bemusement, like a cat about to pounce.

Manos let out the loudest, angriest war cry I'd ever heard and rushed toward him. He swung his hammer in a broad arc, his huge muscles clenched tight, and the big metal head swung right down towards Jacobi's skull.

But before it could hit, Jacobi flicked one hand in its direction, and the hammerhead dissolved in midair, the thick metal sloshing down in a torrent of water that hit the floor with a wet splash. Manos stumbled forward, uselessly, and Jacobi shoved his hands forward, and jagged black tendrils, sharp as blades, shot out of them, tearing clean through Manos and out his back like he was made of paper. Lyriana screamed. My stomach turned. And Manos Vore, general of the Kingdom, strongest warrior I'd ever known, howled as Jacobi lifted him up into the air and tore him clean in half.

"No!" Galen roared, but before he could rush forward, something happened behind us. There was a rush of air and a wrenching feeling, like an invisible hand had reached out and grabbed me and jerked me back. The Red Waster's orbs streaked out in front of us and then they cut through not just the air but through *reality itself*, two jagged lines that formed an X in the skin of the world. Time seemed to slow down, to stretch for an unbearable eternity. That pulling feeling, that wrenching, grew deeper, harder, like my bones were being ripped out of my skin, like my every molecule was being sucked into that impossible X. I couldn't even scream, couldn't even gasp, couldn't even breathe.

There was darkness.

There was pain.

And then suddenly there was dirt rushing at my face.

I had just enough time to realize I was falling before I hit the ground. Dusty earth flooded my mouth and stung at my eyes, but that barely mattered because what in the frozen hell had just happened?

I scrambled up to my hands and knees, gasping for air like I'd just been drowning. I was outside now, somewhere up high, I think, a clearing by a cliff on the edge of a forest. I could smell fresh air and see the sky overhead. The others lay around me, gasping and writhing, Zell and Lyriana and Galen and my father. My brain felt like it was on fire, and my heart like it had burst. What . . . Where . . . How . . . ?

I lurched toward the edge of the cliff, and then I saw it. The dusty windswept plains of the Fallowfields. The rocky outcropping where we'd lain hidden. And there, just beyond it, the distant towers of the Dragonsmaw and a little gray shape that had to be the Skywhale resting right in front of it.

We were in the mountains. The mountains miles away from the castle, the mountains that had been a faint blue silhouette through the window.

"Impossible . . ." Lyriana choked out, her voice tiny and awestruck. "No one could . . . no one has ever . . . but she . . ."

I followed her gaze and there she was, the Red Waster girl, standing barefoot among the trees just a few feet away from us. Her eyes were bleary, her face slick with sweat, her breath short and ragged. Her orbs jerked around her in twitchy spurts. She looked ready to collapse. Whatever that had been, whatever magic she'd worked, it had taken everything out of her.

Our eyes met, and then her orbs whistled up, forming another rectangle of light around her. "Wait!" I screamed, but it was too late. There was another rush, another hiss of air, and she was gone.

Zell came over and helped me up. Galen slumped against a tree, clenching and unclenching his fists. I looked around instinctively for Manos before remembering what had happened.

"Well," my father said, pushing himself up to one knee. "I have to say, that—" and I never got to find out what he was going to say next because Galen walked over and punched him in the face.

FIVE

ONCE WE'D ALL RECOVERED FROM WHATEVER HAD JUST happened to us, Galen and Zell sneaked off through the forest and came back with four horses. I didn't ask where they got them, but given that they all had Western army saddles, I doubt they were wandering a meadow. Galen and Lyriana took one each. My father got one of his own, but only after Galen bound his hands and gave him a long and involved threat on what would happen if he tried to run. Zell and I shared the last horse. I loved riding like this, my chest pressed to his back, my hands around his waist, his shoulder so conveniently located for me to bury my face in. Even out here, there were seconds where I could lose myself in him. Those seconds were what I lived for.

We rode quietly, in shadow, avoiding all roads and traveling instead along the rocky banks of the rushing Yagmaw River. We slept under the stars and ate roasted rabbit and took turns sitting by the fire, keeping watch. I don't know what happened back in the Skywhale after we disappeared, but I'm pretty sure it involved Miles being extremely *pissed*. Knowing him, he probably had every soldier under his command tearing across the countryside looking for us. Luckily, he had no idea where we'd gone or where we were heading or if we even existed anymore. After a full day on the road, with no sign of him, I was pretty sure we were safe. Still, every time a cloud passed in front of the sun and a heavy shadow fell over us, I found myself panicking, just a little, searching the sky for that massive metal ship.

I woke up early on the morning of our second day to find Lyriana sitting by the embers of our cooking pit, staring at them with a troubled look. Around us, the camp was still; Zell was off hunting, Galen on watch, and my father sat silently against a tree, his wrists still bound with a thick rope. I hadn't spoken to him since the rescue, but he hadn't spoken to anyone; he was a prisoner, plain and simple, and right now we were all just focused on making it back to camp safely. Once we got there, we'd interrogate him. We'd figure out how to use him. And we'd almost certainly execute him, the way we executed everyone else who'd played a part in his regime.

I didn't want to deal with any of that. So I yawned and made my way over to Lyriana's side. "Hey," I said, and she barely nodded, lost in her own musings. "Thinking about that Red Waster girl?"

Lyriana sighed. "Am I that obvious?"

"Only to me." I smiled. "I'm guessing her magic didn't make sense to you, either."

"No. Not at all. Nothing about her did," Lyriana said. "Back in Lightspire, Ellarion showed you the Heartstone, didn't he? He told you how it worked?"

I nodded, remembering that trip to the very top of the Godsblade, that last peaceful day before everything had gone to hell. The Heartstone was an enormous, writhing, iridescent boulder made of pure energy, sealed in a shimmersteel dome on the tower's highest floor. It was also, apparently, the source of all magic in the world. The Titans had left it behind when they Ascended, just like they'd left behind the tower itself, and its leaking power had altered the citizens of Lightspire, turned some of them, over time, into mages. The Rings they wore were just tiny shards of it; their blood, now stolen by Miles's creatures, was just a conduit of its energy. Everything magical always came back to the Heartstone.

Which is why a mage from all the way out in the Red Wastes didn't make any sense. "Could she be a bloodmage?" I asked.

"I doubt it," Lyriana said. "There were no marks on her arms, no scent of corrupted blood. When bloodmages work their Arts, it feels sick, rotten, a perversion of energy, a literal blasphemy. She didn't feel that way. She didn't feel like . . . anything."

"Another of Miles's creations, then. Like the Skywhale."

"Maybe, but . . . that doesn't feel right, either." Lyriana shook her head. "The way she moved, the way she used those orbs, it was so graceful, so precise, so disciplined. It was like something you'd expect from a master, from someone who'd been doing it for years."

"You sound impressed."

"I am," Lyriana said. "What she did, transporting five people to a location miles away, unharmed, all on her own? No one's ever done anything like it. No one's even *attempted* it. It's magic on a scale I've never seen before. And I know there are more important things happening, I know we need to figure out what to do with Lord Kent. But I just can't stop trying to figure her out. I can't figure *any* of this out." She sighed. "I miss when the world made sense. It was flawed and broken and unfair, and it needed a lot of work, but at least it made sense."

"I know what you mean." I hugged her close with one arm. "It feels like every time we get our bearings, the earth shifts under our feet."

Lyriana rested her head on my shoulder. "Everything changes so fast, so often. Every day brings some new horror, some new calamity, some new reality we just have to accept and live with. And I don't know what's worse: feeling perpetually lost . . . or just growing numb to it all."

"Not all change is bad," I tried. "I mean, look, we have King Kent as prisoner. That's a huge win for us. The biggest we've had."

"I know it is in theory," Lyriana said. "And yet I don't feel any more certain, any more sure, of what lies ahead." She let out a deep, shuddering breath. "Let's imagine that this actually works. That we take back the Kingdom, that we defeat Miles, that I sit once more on the throne. What then?"

"I don't follow. Isn't getting the throne back the goal?"

"For you, maybe. For Galen and all those others out there. But for me? It's just the beginning. I still have to rule. To mend this Kingdom. To right all the wrongs and restore justice and rebuild everything that's been broken. And it's not just that, it's also . . . it's also . . ." She hesitated a moment, like this was something she was struggling to admit. "I keep thinking about the Undercity."

I blinked. The Undercity had been the hidden hideout of

the Ragged Disciples, a village of the destitute and desperate built in the Catacombs beneath Lightspire. "What about it?"

"Those people were my citizens, Tilla. We drove them there, beneath our very streets, drove them there with oppression and injustice. They would never have taken up arms against us, would never have become pawns of your father, if it hadn't been for the way my family had ruled."

"You can't blame yourself," I said, partially because I meant it and partially because that was an emotional rabbit hole I had to avoid at all costs. "My father and Miles, all of them, they chose their own path. They chose to kill all those people."

"I'm not making excuses for them. I'll never forgive what they did," Lyriana said, that hard edge back in her voice. "But they would never have been able to pull it off if there hadn't been hundreds, thousands, of people willing to support them. And those people were there because of the choices *my* family made. The oppression, the inequality, the culture of fear and war and conquest . . . I feel like this was the only plausible outcome. It's like every generation of Volaris ruler was raising the temperature on a pot of water, one degree at a time. Sooner or later, it had to boil over." She craned her head up, golden eyes looking right into mine. "We can't just go back to the way things were. But we can't keep living like this either. How are we supposed to do this, Tilla? How do we fix a broken world?"

"I don't know," I answered honestly. "But I feel like all we can do is try."

It was easy enough to say, especially because it made Lyriana smile. But my thoughts were just as preoccupied as hers. Every day as we rode on, I found myself staring at my father, trying to read some meaning into his distant scowl, wanting him to look my way and see just how I felt. Except how I felt was all over the place. Some moments, I felt anger, so much anger, a burning fury that made my hands tremble and my eyes burn. I'd think of Markiska and those people in the Godsblade ballroom and Jax, of every innocent person who'd died because of him, and I'd feel so livid that it took real restraint not to just run over there and start kicking him, punching him, hurting him for all the pain he'd caused me.

But then there were other, rarer moments when I'd feel something else, something closer to pity. For the first sixteen years of my life, I'd looked at my father like a god, a man who never felt fear or worry or regret, a High Lord of the West driven by the noblest of principles, dedicated to his people above all else. I'd never seen him cry or beg, never seen him show a moment of weakness. But here, dragged along by Galen, his hair tousled, his face messy with dirt and bruises, his clothes ragged . . . he just looked so pathetic. He wasn't the King or the High Lord or even My Great Amazing Father. He was just a broken man coming up on what was almost certainly the end of his life. And it was hard not to feel bad for him.

I knew that I should keep my distance, that talking to him would only make things more complicated. I was a rebel, and he was a tyrant, and that was how I needed to think. But after four days on the road, my resolve broke. That night, as we sheltered in an abandoned barn, I took a shift on watch and walked over to him when everyone was asleep. He rested against a mossy wooden beam, eyes shut, and I kicked him gently in the side of the leg. "Hey," I whispered. "Father. Wake up."

With a grunt, he shifted over and opened his eyes. The roof of the barn had mostly collapsed overhead, giving way to a clear night sky full of radiant stars, and in that bright moonlight I could see his face up close. By the Old Kings, the last two years had aged him. Heavy bags hung under his eyes, and deep wrinkles creased his forehead. His beard was more gray than brown, and his gaunt features looked sunken, haunted.

We stared at each other in silence. "Well?" I said at last. "Are you going to say anything?"

"Like what?"

Okay, this was going to be one of the angry moments after all. "Like . . . sorry? Sorry for getting my brother killed? Sorry for murdering my friend? Sorry for starting a war that destroyed the Kingdom? Sorry for ruining my *fucking life?*" The last one, I almost yelled, and nearby Galen shifted in his sleep. I took a breath and lowered my voice. "How about, sorry for being the worst father ever? Let's start with that."

His pinched lips didn't betray even the slightest hint of emotion. "I already told you what I had to say, way back in the Nest." That felt a lifetime ago, all the way back in our journey to escape the West. "I should have trusted you from the beginning. I should have brought you into my plan. It should have been you, not Miles, by my side."

"That's not what I'm talking about!" I said. "I don't care that you didn't loop me into your stupid plan. I care that you did this. All of this. That you started this war. That you killed all those people. There were children in that ballroom, Father. Children." It was taking all my effort not to cry. "And I swear by the Old Kings, if you say anything about all wars having casualties, I'll punch you in the face myself."

My father didn't say that. But his eyebrow arched, just a tiny bit. "'By the Old Kings'?" he repeated. "Not 'by the Titans'?"

"*That's* what you're hung up on?"

"Yes. Because it tells me who you are," he said. "You may have thrown in your lot with the Volaris. You may have betrayed your family and your Province. But in your heart, you're still a Westerner. And you always will be."

"Can you stop? Please? For just one moment?" I pleaded. "I don't want to talk about Westerners or Volaris or hear another big speech about freedom and tyranny and all your bullshit. I just want to talk about *people*. About Markiska and Jax. About me. You've hurt so many people."

"And you haven't?" he asked. "How many men have you killed, Tillandra? How many sons of the West, how many boys just fighting for their land, their King?"

Twenty-nine.

"That's different," I said. "I did that because I had to. And I would've given anything to choose a different way. Every time I close my eyes, I see their faces and feel horrible." The tears were getting harder and harder to hold back, but I gave it my all. "Don't you feel any regret? Any remorse? Don't you feel *anything*?"

He paused for a long time, saying nothing, just breathing deep, and when he spoke at last, his voice was terse, guarded. "When I was seven years old, a group of soldiers woke me from my bed and dragged me down to Castle Waverly's Great Hall. The Archmagus was there, Rolan's father, along with a company of Knights of Lazan, and they made our whole family gather to bear witness. My grandfather, High Lord Tobias Kent, was accused of treason, of spreading seditious talk and conspiring against the crown. I don't know if he was guilty or not. Knowing him, probably. But I was seven at the time. I didn't understand any of it. I just knew that they had my grandfather on his knees, the sweet old man who took me fishing and taught me knots, who called me 'Little El' and told me stories of the Old Kings. And they made me watch. They made me watch as they pronounced the sentence. They made me watch as my father begged, as my mother sobbed. They made me watch as they burned him alive from the inside."

My knees were trembling. "I thought he died of an illness. . . ."

"The Volaris didn't want to turn the High Lord into a martyr, so that's the story they made us tell. His death, his torture, that was a lesson for the Kents alone. For me." His eyes were hard slits, his hands clenched tight. It was like every word of this was a dagger he was forcing out of himself, like every sentence caused him pain. Had he told *anyone* about this? Or had he just kept it inside, all his life, a raw wound still bleeding behind a dozen layers of armor? "Whatever you're looking for, Tillandra, whatever ember of remorse or compassion, you're not going to find it. The Volaris took it from me that day. They made me who I am." He closed his eyes. "Everything I've done, every action I've taken, every person I've hurt, has been in service of our people. I fought and killed for a better world. And I will not apologize for that."

I stepped back, in part because I could see the others stirring but mostly because I just had to get away. "Eighteen years, I've dreamed of getting to know the real you. Of meeting the man behind the facade, of talking to you just as a daughter to a father. But the man doesn't exist, does he? This *is* you. This is all there is."

I turned away and walked across the barn, to fresh air, to anywhere else. But as I reached the threshold, I heard him sit up and say one more thing.

"Not eighteen."

I stopped. "What?"

"You're not eighteen yet," he said. "Your birthday's next month."

I shoved my way outside, into the sprawl of wild wheat just outside the barn. The world throbbed around me, and my lungs felt tight, crushing in, that horrible overwhelming sensation of just feeling too much. I stumbled away from the barn as far as I could, and then I collapsed to the ground and sat there, hands wrapped around my knees, letting it all out, the tears, the sobs, the heaving waves and shudders.

The stalks in front of me rustled and parted, giving way to the one person I'd want to see. Zell. His jet-black hair shone silver in the moonlight, as did the nightglass blades on his knuckles. He was wearing just a cloth shirt, pants, and riding boots, while the rest of us were bundled up under furs and cloaks. That was one thing about Zell. He never got cold.

He took a seat next to me and wrapped an arm around my shoulder, and I leaned into his warmth. "Hey," he said.

I sniffled. "Did you hear all that back there?"

He nodded.

"I don't know what I expected. But it wasn't that." I squeezed Zell close. It was like he always had a little fire burning inside him, just radiating out through his skin. "How does he still have this much power over me? Why can't I just hate him?"

"Hate comes from ignorance," Zell said. "And you know him too well to hate him."

"Everything he's built has fallen down around him. He's a fugitive in his own Kingdom. And he knows it, he knows he created this nightmare, he knows it's all on him . . . and still, he just holds on to these convictions." I sighed deep. "But I guess so do I. Even now, I keep hoping he'll change. I keep hoping he'll listen. Why do I do this to myself?"

"Because he's your father." Zell's calloused palm gently rubbed my arm. "My father tried to kill me with his own hands. He betrayed our Clan, betrayed our people, betrayed our family. When I think about what he did, my heart burns with rage. But if he were to appear before me now? If he were to ask for another chance, to extend his hand?" He shook his head. "I'd take it. I'd have to."

I appreciated him saying that, even if it wasn't really a possibility; we'd left his father under a pile of rubble in the Nest, so a reunion wasn't exactly on the table. "You're objective. Or at least not as biased as me. Do you think my father could ever be redeemed?"

Zell thought this over for a while. "In the lakes near my home, there's this creature. Similar to what you call eels, but bigger, blue, with scales like snowflakes. We call them *rellzars*. They're brutal predators, lean and fast, but more than anything, they're always moving. They can't stop. They swim, they hunt, they eat, and then they immediately swim again. Even when they sleep, they keep moving." A cloud passed in front of the moon, casting us, for just a moment, into darkness. "Your father reminds me of a rellzar, but instead of hunger, he's driven solely by belief, by certainty. He can't rest, can't stop, can't question for even one moment. Because if he does, if he allows himself even a second of doubt, then everything he's done will come to drown him."

"That's a no, then," I started to say, but never got to finish because an earthquake hit. This one was small, just a soft rumbling beneath us, but it made all the wheat stalks sway and rustle. I clutched Zell tight and felt the earth buckle and groan.

When it had settled, Zell spoke. "The shamans teach that earthquakes are a sign that the Gods are displeased. When one happens, it is customary to take the next day to reflect on your actions, to consider ways in which you can improve yourself. We call it *Vask Denaro*. The Calm After the Quake."

"So what does it mean when we have a quake every week?"

He pulled me in tight and held me there, even as the stalks kept swaying. "Perhaps we all have a great deal of changing to do."

SIX

We got back to the Unbroken camp a week later, the horns of the watchmen bellowing with even more excitement than usual as we approached. That should've been the first sign that something was up. As we cleared the tree line, the whole camp seemed to be out to greet us, all the soldiers and followers gathered around at the gates, pushing over each other to get a look. There was something off about their expressions though, something troubling. They looked happy to see us, but also alarmed and confused, maybe even wary. Ellarion was the first to break the line. He rushed out of the gate toward us, meeting us before we could even dismount. "Oh, thank the Titans," he said, clutching Lyriana's hand, tears glistening in his crimson eyes. "When we got that letter, I just thought . . . I mean, I assumed . . . But now you're . . ." His words were a messy stammer, his voice choked. "How did you . . . I mean what . . ." His voice trailed off as he laid eyes on the last horse in our procession, on my father. "Oh. *Oh.*"

"Quite a lot has happened," Lyriana said, and I could tell

even she was a little caught off guard by the display. Other people had spotted our prisoner, and I could hear a sound running through the crowd, somewhere between a murmur and a growl. I tightened my grip on the reins nervously, digging my fingernails into the leather. Every last person in the camp had lost someone to my father's reign; some of them had lost *everyone*. And here we were, bringing him back, like a pig for the slaughter.

Galen, alone, seemed focused. "What letter? What are you talking about?"

Ellarion gulped, collected himself, and wiped his eyes with the back of a wrist. "I think you should probably just see it for yourself."

The crowd pushed forward, clamoring for a look as we tied up our horses and walked through the camp. These were hardened Unbroken, soldiers and refugees, but pressed together now, they looked more like an unruly mob. It reminded me of that night back in Lightspire, the Festival of Tears, where the lovely gathering had turned to a bloody riot in the blink of an eye. I tried to imagine how I'd feel if I was one of them, if I could see him as just the man who'd destroyed the kingdom, and not the father who'd raised me. I guess it'd be sort of how I felt about Miles, which didn't bode well for him.

Kelvin, the scholar, was waiting for us in the command tent, standing behind the sprawling wooden table with a stunned look on his face. We all marched in, and Ellarion pulled the tent's flap shut while Galen shoved my father down on his knees on the floor. "Well?" Galen said. "Is someone going to tell me what's going on here?"

Kelvin stared at us with his jaw hanging open, and Ellarion gently nudged him. "Read them the letter."

"Right. Yes. Of course." Kelvin fumbled on the table for a moment before finding a curled scroll. In the wan candlelight I could see a sigil on the back, an open watchful eye, the sign of the Inquisitor. "Five days ago, there was a flurry of Whispers from the Dragonsmaw, flying to Lords all over the Kingdom. We shot one down and . . ." He cleared his throat and began to read. "'It is with a heavy heart that I inform you of the passing of our King, the Great Liberator Elric Kent. While visiting Lord Delaux to plan a course for victory against the Southland Secession, he was ambushed by a group of cowardly traitors, and was mortally injured. As his children are too young to assume the throne, I, Inquisitor Miles Hampstedt, will act as Regent, and assume all the duties of the King until his heirs come of age. Rest assured, these treasonous assassins will face justice for their heinous act. As Regent, I will not rest until every last member of the Unbroken has been put to the sword.'" Kelvin paused, skimming the scroll. "Then there's a lot of proclamations. A week of mourning . . . renewed conscription of able-bodied men . . . mass executions . . . oh, and this." His eyes flitted down, to my father on his knees. "'We believe the assassins were able to breach the King's security through the cunning use of Mesmers, and they plan to use his likeness to target other loyal Lords. Do not be fooled by this ruse. Anyone bearing the visage of our departed King is a traitor, and should be killed on sight, alongside all of their companions.'" He hesitated for a moment, like he was saving the worst for last. "'Anyone who provides information as to the location of a Mesmer wearing Kent's face shall be rewarded with a manor in Lightspire, fifty thousand in gold, and the title of Lord.'"

The room was as silent as a crypt. "Sneaky little shit," my father growled at last.

"He learned from the best," Lyriana replied, harsher than I'd ever heard. I remembered the letter we'd read all the way back on the Western shore, the one that had blamed us for Rolan's murder and put a bounty on our heads.

"It was a lie, then," Kelvin said, and you know, for a scholar, he seemed a little slow on the uptake. "Misdirection. A ploy."

"That's putting it lightly." Galen let out a low, bitter laugh. "So much for parading Kent in front of the other Lords or using him to denounce Hampstedt. So much for getting any use out of him at all." He knocked my father over with a kick, sending him tumbling to the tent floor. "All that trouble we went through to save you. And Miles just had you killed anyway."

My gut plunged. I hated Miles, hated that devious mind of his, hated his way of always ending up one step ahead. "Will people believe this?" I asked.

"Of course they will. Why wouldn't they?" Galen shook his head. "The second we take Kent out anywhere someone can see him, we'll end up riddled with arrows. And it's only a matter of time before someone in our camp gets tempted by that reward and decides it's a safer bet to turn on us."

"So what do we do?" I asked.

"Only one thing we really can do." Galen drew one of his daggers, its blade gleaming. "We execute him."

"Whoa," I said, before I could think twice about it. "Hang on. Just like that?"

Galen's head swiveled slowly toward me. "We kept him alive because he was useful. He's not useful anymore."

"Galen's right," Ellarion said, eyes burning with hate. Technically, he'd only found out about my father, like, ten minutes ago, so I'm not sure he was in a position to talk. But also, my father was directly responsible for what happened to his hands, so I guess he had the right to be a little emotional. "Every moment he's alive, we risk someone getting tempted by Miles's bounty. We should kill him here and now."

"I . . . I just mean . . ." I tried, but my brain couldn't find the words to justify what my heart was screaming. I knew intellectually that sparing him was indefensible. I knew that there was no world where I could make that case. I knew, deep inside, that what I was feeling was driven by the fact that after everything else, after everything that he'd done, he was still my father, still the man who'd chased me giggling around the castle courtyard, who'd hugged me when I came running with a skinned knee, who'd taken me on those long rides through the Western forests and told me all the great history of our family line. He was still my father, despite it all.

"Tillandra," my father said quietly. His eyes were shut, his teeth gritted, the dagger's point still pressed to his forehead. When he spoke, his voice had no emotion, just the flat distant cadence of resignation. "Walk away. You don't need to see this."

But I couldn't. I wouldn't. Even if it made my eyes burn and my knees tremble, I couldn't just turn away. I had to see it through. "No," I said, and my father just nodded. Galen drew back his blade.

"Wait!" Lyriana said, and the whole room froze. "No. Not like this. We must have a trial."

Galen swiveled his head toward her with weary irritation. "What now?"

"We still live by the laws of the Kingdom. That's impor-tant. Now more than ever." And even though Lyriana was stopping Galen, her voice was cold and hard. This wasn't about saving my father. This was about making sure the justice was *hers*. "If he is to die by the Queen's justice, I must pass a sentence. And I won't do that without a trial."

"Your Majesty," Galen growled, "you know as well as I do that the trials are mostly a formality. . . ."

"Not in this case," Lyriana insisted. "Think of all those people out there, all the Unbroken. Think of how much this means to them. If there was ever a time for a show of justice, it's now. They deserve to see a trial, to see Kent held accountable for every murder, every crime, every drop of blood he's spilled." Her gaze narrowed. "There *will* be a trial. Consider that a royal decree."

Galen glared for a moment, then sheathed his dagger. "As you wish," he said. "First thing tomorrow morning, then. The trial of the Usurper."

I let out a deep breath. I'd been ready, totally ready, to see my father die. And yet I still felt such relief that it wouldn't happen for at least another day. I looked to Lyriana, and mouthed *Thank you*. She shook her head. This wasn't for me.

"What do we do until then?" Ellarion asked.

Galen shrugged. "We pour a drink for Manos. We honor his courage, his sacrifice. And then I'm calling it a night. We've all been through enough. We could use a break." He reached down and took my father by the rope binding his wrists, jerking him back up to his feet. "Not you, though. You've got a lovely little spot waiting for you in the stockade."

We followed Galen toward the edge of the camp, to the building where we kept prisoners. It wasn't much, a crude wooden structure barely bigger than a closet, with stacked logs as walls. A peg was driven into the earth inside, a pair of manacles attached to it. We mostly used the stockade to punish disobedient rebels for things like stealing or brawling, occasionally to hold a captured soldier for interrogation. It had never had a prisoner like this.

The crowd of Unbroken framed our path, and with each step we took, the mood soured. As Galen marched my father along, jeers started to break the silence. Cries went up all around us: *murderer, traitor, usurper.* A woman stepped forward to spit in my father's face. One bold rebel even threw a clod of dirt that exploded against the side of his head, sending him stumbling down. Galen shot a quick glance the dirt-thrower's way, a look that was disapproving, but just barely. *Not yet,* it seemed to say.

Then they were at the door of the stockade and vanishing inside, the shouts of the crowd louder and angrier than ever. As Galen pushed my father in, he turned him around, just for a moment, and our eyes met. I saw no fear. No pain. Just calm, proud defiance.

I turned away, and found Zell standing there, watching it all. I hugged him, buried my face in his chest, felt the comfort of his arms. "I hate this," I whispered.

He held me close, pressed his head low to gently kiss my forehead. "Lyriana gave you another day. A chance to find some peace. After that . . ."

I nodded, closed my eyes, and tried to let everything in the world fade away. "After that, he dies."

seven

I took a bath. I ate Garrus's stew with a crust of bread and drank a beer quietly as I listened to Galen deliver a eulogy for Manos. As night fell, I tossed and turned in my tent, hoping desperately for rest that wouldn't come, and then I finally got up and went over to talk to Lyriana.

She sat on her bed as usual, reading a massive book by candlelight, but she wasn't alone. Ellarion sat in a chair nearby, goblet in hand, legs up on the table. The two of them glanced my way as I came in.

"Can't sleep?" Lyriana asked, and I nodded. "I'm the same way. There's just so much going on in my head, so much to consider . . ."

"After what you went through, I'd be surprised if you ever slept again," Ellarion said, taking a small sip.

I took a seat next to Lyriana. I don't know what book she was reading, but it was open to a giant picture of vibrant dunes the color of a ripe apple, so I'm guessing it had to do with the Red Wastes. "Moved on from impressive Queens of yore, I see?"

"I thought there might be something helpful in here," she sighed. "But there's nothing. Nothing I don't already know."

"That's your fault for already knowing everything," Ellarion said, and Lyriana threw a boot at him. He dodged it with a grin. "I never thought I'd be so happy to have a boot hurled at me. But here I am."

I realized I hadn't talked to him since we'd gotten back to the camp, and felt a pang of guilt. "You holding up okay? That couldn't have been easy. Thinking we were dead."

Ellarion kept smiling, but something flickered in his eyes, something lost and devastated. "No. It wasn't easy. It was the hardest three days of my life."

"I'm sorry."

"Don't be. Truth is, I barely had time to process anything, much less grieve. With Lyriana gone, I was next in line. The..." He paused, as if just saying the words was a struggle. "The True King. Everyone looked to me for guidance, and that was so exhausting and unbearable I couldn't even think straight." He shook his head. "I spent most of my life dreaming of being in charge, of being the Archmagus, giving orders and taking command. What in the frozen hell was I thinking?"

"Ellarion," Lyriana said, and she looked like she was going to say something else, but I never got to learn what it was, because all of a sudden, the Red Waster girl was in the tent with us.

It's not so much that she appeared. There was no rush of air or cloud of smoke. She was just standing at the side of the room, casually, like she'd been there all along.

Lyriana let out a little shriek and jerked back in the

bed, and I clasped a hand over my mouth. Ellarion sprang forward, jerking a knife out of his boot and holding it out in front of him.

The Red Waster didn't immediately say or do anything. She just stood there, staring at us, head cocked slightly to the side. She'd managed to find clothes, the kind of clothes I'd seen her people in before: a burnt-orange robe held tight at the waist with a sash, leather sandals that laced up her calves with thin straps. Her hair was pulled back in a braid, and it looked different now, more muted, like some of that vibrant blue had been drained out of the streaks. Her bladed orbs were back too, hovering at her shoulders with slow, lazy spins.

In the flickering candlelight, I got a better look at her face. She was pretty in an odd way, her features a little too asymmetrical, and her eyes weren't just orange; they were orange with flecks of gold and purple, a sparkling mix of colors, like looking into a geode cut in half.

"It's her." Lyriana pointed with a trembling hand. "The Red Waster girl."

"Yeah, I guessed that," Ellarion replied. "Who in the frozen hell are you? What do you want?"

"My name is Syan Syee of Benn Devalos, Torchbearer, Daughter of the Storm," she said, as if she expected any of that to make sense to us. "And I want to talk."

Ellarion jabbed the knife her way. "Drop the weapons, and I'll think about it."

The Red Waster—Syan—blinked at him. "Weapons?" Then she realized he was talking about her orbs and let out a soft, little laugh. "These are not weapons. They are my zaryas. They are more like . . . like . . ." She paused, searching for the word. "Like the line a man uses to catch a fish."

"They're flying balls covered in sharp-ass blades," Ellarion said. "If that's not a weapon, I don't know what is."

Syan stared at him for a moment, then sighed. "Fine." The zaryas stopped spinning and fell to the ground with metal thuds. "Now will you speak with me?"

Lyriana stepped forward, gently pushing Ellarion aside. "I am Queen Lyriana of Noveris. I speak on behalf of the Kingdom."

The girl nodded. "I know. That is why I have sought you out."

"I have so many questions," Lyriana said, sounding a lot more like an eager schoolgirl than a reigning Queen. "Your magic, what you did back in the Skywhale, your zaryas . . ."

"What is your question?"

"It's . . . I mean . . ." Lyriana struggled for words. "How?"

Syan shrugged. "The Cutting is one of the more difficult skills, but all advanced Torchbearers can do it. There is no 'how.' We simply can."

I expected Ellarion to call bullshit, but he actually slumped down with resignation, easing his knife to his side. I guess seeing really is believing. "Red Waster magic. It's actually real. Titans have mercy."

"So it's not just you?" Lyriana pressed. "There are other mages among your people?"

"Every Izterosi . . . every Red Waster, as you call us . . . is touched by the flame," Syan said, with the cadence of someone struggling to find the words to explain something obvious, the cadence you'd use with an overly inquisitive child. "Without the flame, we could never survive the wilds or brave the storms. It is the lifeblood of our benns, the blood in our veins."

"And you've just managed to keep it secret from us all this time?" Ellarion said, and there was that telltale skepticism. "How is that possible?"

"Our flame is not like your magic. We draw it in, and we release it out. It is a part of Izteros, our land, as we are a part of it." Was anyone following this? Because I wasn't. "When we leave Izteros, the desert, we leave that flame behind. Only a few, the most gifted, can carry it with us, inside us, to the world beyond. I am the first such person to venture into your lands."

"Torchbearers," Lyriana said, repeating what the girl had said earlier with a tone of quiet reverence. "It's amazing. All our scholars and historians, they never knew. Your people managed to hide this from us for centuries."

"An ancient law among all Izterosi. The fire of our people must always be kept secret from the Stillanders." I'm guessing that meant us. "Your kind is greedy, untrustworthy, always grasping, always conquering. If you learned what we have, you would come for us, with war and death."

"Tell us what you *really* think," Ellarion grumbled.

"But there are your kind among us," Lyriana said. "I've seen them in Lightspire, in my father's . . ." She paused. "In the King's court."

Syan nodded reverently. "They are heroes, the most loyal and devout among us. They venture out past our desert, losing all bond with the flame, so that we may see what is happening in the Kingdom of the Stillanders and report back to the benns."

"They're spies," Ellarion snorted.

"Heroes," Syan repeated. Her face was calm, inscrutable, but on that word her eyes narrowed, and I could swear they pulsed orange.

"Can I ask a question?" I said, in part because I wanted to

move on from the increasingly tense vibe in the room. "What were you doing in that cell in the Skywhale?"

Syan inhaled sharply, as if sinking back into a terrible memory. "They began four months ago. The dreams. First the children had them, then the elders, and then all of us, every night. Dreams of fire and pain, of war and ruin. Men flayed alive, bodies tied to posts, a terrible monster with tendrils of darkness." I glanced at Lyriana uneasily. I had no idea where the metaphors stopped with this girl, but I'm pretty sure that one was literal. "And every dream . . . every last one . . . ended with *Zastroya*."

"Zastroya?"

She glanced away, and her voice dropped to a hushed whisper. "The Storm That Will Consume the World."

There was no wind, but the room seemed to get colder all the same. "So you started having these dreams," I said, "and that's how you ended up out here?"

"We received word of your new King, of the abominations he creates, of the devastation he has caused. The elders of Benn Devalos believe that he is responsible for the dreams, that he will cause Zastroya if he is not stopped. So they sent my brother and me to talk to the King and warn him." Her eyes narrowed with anger, and on the floor, her zaryas twitched. "We encountered the Inquisitor's men. They killed my brother. And he kept me, tortured me, tried to discover the truth of my power."

My chest tightened, and I swallowed my breath. Dead brothers had a way of doing that to me.

But Ellarion just shrugged. "So we have a common enemy."

"I would like to inflict on him a great deal of pain," she said, and the streaks in her hair flared bright.

I couldn't help but smile. "Welcome to the club."

"This is great, then," Lyriana said, rising up with excitement. "With your power, your 'Cutting,' we have an advantage Miles won't see coming. You can get us into his—"

"No," Syan said. "What I did back in the Skywhale drained much of my flame. I have enough left for some small skills, but I would not stake a victory on them." There was an overarticulation to the way she talked, a stilted formality, the way nobles talked in the old fairy tales. "I must return to my home to rekindle my flame. And you must come with me."

I blinked. "What now?"

"I refer to Queen Lyriana, though you are welcome to join us."

I turned to Lyriana, who looked equally bewildered. "I'm not sure I understand. Why would I come with you?"

Syan hesitated for a moment, and when she spoke again, her voice was quiet. "There was something else in our dreams," she said. "A symbol, etched in stone, or written in blood, or glowing in the sand. Again and again, the same symbol." She pointed to Lyriana's right arm, to the ornate symbol tattooed there: an elegant rune, like a V wrapped in thorns with a sword jutting through. "*That* symbol."

"The . . . old seal of the Titans?" Lyriana asked. "Why would you have dreamed of that?"

"I don't know," Syan said. "But it can't be a coincidence. We're being sent a message that we must join our flames, to fight this together. You are the rightful Queen of this land. If you come to the elders of my benn and appeal to them, promise them peace and sovereignty, they may elect to join your cause. There are at least fifty more Torchbearers in my benn alone. With their flame, you could take back your Kingdom and defeat the abominations." She closed her eyes, and I noticed for the first time that her eyelids were darker than the rest of her, like they'd been painted or burned. "And we can keep Zastroya away."

Fifty mages doing that Cutting stuff seemed like a pretty good deal, but Lyriana looked torn, struggling for words. "I can't," she finally got out. "As much as I want to. These are my people, my Kingdom. I can't just leave them." She shook her head. "Perhaps an envoy . . ."

"No," Syan insisted. "It must be you. They will not trust an envoy, but they may listen to the Queen herself. Especially if she bears the mark from our dreams."

Ellarion snorted. "That's a hell of a lot to ask for a 'may.'"

Syan shot him a glare. "I cannot promise their help. My people have never taken part in a foreign war. But I do believe if your Queen comes to ask for their aid, they will listen."

"I'm sorry," Lyriana said. "I can't abandon my people."

"What people? This camp? These broken men?" Syan shook her head, and there was something unsettled about her, a hint of desperation beneath her poise. "You must come with me. It is your only hope. My only hope." As she spoke, her orbs lifted up, slowly, steadily, turning in silent, deliberate circles. "The only hope for all of us."

Lyriana's eyes flitted from orb to orb, and I could see her hands tensing, her Rings beginning to glow. "And if I don't?"

"I will give you a day to consider," she said. "Call for me when you have made up your mind." Her orbs zipped forward in front of her, crossing in a perfectly symmetrical X. There was that rush of air, that tugging feeling . . .

And then she was gone.

We sat in stunned silence for what felt like a while. Then

Ellarion slumped down onto the ground, the knife tumbling from his hands. "Titans above," he said. "Real mages existing outside of Lightspire. I never thought I'd feel so exhilarated to be proven wrong."

"Do I get to say 'I told you so'?" I said. "Because I'd love to say 'I told you so.'" Ellarion rolled his eyes at me, and I kicked at his side. "Are we really going to turn her down, though? Fifty mages like her . . . I mean, that feels pretty big."

"A journey to the border of the Red Wastes could take months, and runs straight through the Southlands. And who knows how long it will take to reach her people, her 'benn,' or what dangers I'd face out there." Lyriana shook her head. "Our group here is fragile enough as is. If I were to leave for months, or if something were to happen to me, it would all fall apart. I can't risk that on some long-shot plan."

"No, you can't," Ellarion said. "So we'll just have to convince her to take me instead."

Lyriana and I stared at him and he shrugged. "What? It makes sense. I'm second in line for the throne, which makes me almost King. And if I can bring back even a handful of those Torchbearers, it'll be worth it."

Lyriana wasn't having it. "No. It's too dangerous."

"For you? Sure. For a third-rate tactician who's spent the better part of a year drinking himself into oblivion?" He smiled, and I felt a pang of sadness, a yearning for something I hadn't realized I'd missed. How long had it been since I'd seen him smile? "This is my choice, Lyriana. And I choose to go with her."

I could see Lyriana thinking rapidly, trying to come up with any counterargument, and coming up short. And honestly? Ellarion was right. I didn't like the idea of him heading somewhere dangerous, but . . . how many times had he been in our position? Wasn't it our turn to sit and worry?

"Look," Lyriana replied at last. "Syan said she'd give us a day, right? Let's sleep on it and talk to Galen tomorrow."

A flicker of annoyance danced across Ellarion's face, but he didn't say anything. "Sure," he said. "We'll talk tomorrow. Seems like delaying till then is the go-to solution for all our problems." He stood up, stretching his arms, casually cracking his neck. And there was something off about him, some nuance I was missing, some hidden motivation. "I think we've all got some thinking to do. I prefer to do mine alone in my tent, with a little wine and a comfortable mat."

"I suppose I have some reading to do." Lyriana looked down at the tome on her bed, still open to that page with the bright red dunes. Looking closer at the picture now, I could see that what I'd thought was the night sky was actually a mass of dark clouds, swirling together over the land like an ink blot, lit up in a few places by bursts of vivid purple or sickly yellow. What had Syan called herself? A Daughter of the Storm?

I hugged Lyriana good night and stepped out with Ellarion, the two of us walking to our tents in the brisk night air. There was still that pep in his step, that odd energy. I mean, I sort of got it. Between capturing my father and this whole development with the Red Wasters and their mages . . . it felt like maybe things were turning around. Like after a year on the run, a year of suffering and killing and watching our enemies grow stronger, maybe we had a chance. Like we could actually win this thing.

But that wasn't all of it, and as we reached the entrance to Ellarion's tent, my patience ran out. "What's your deal?" I asked.

He looked at me all innocent. "What do you mean?"

"You're acting weird. Like you're hiding something or thinking about something or— I don't know. But there's something up with you."

He paused for a moment, head cocked and even under that beard and messy hair I could still see him, the boy who'd walked around Lightspire like he'd owned the place, the mage who'd rolled coins of flame across his fingers when he was bored and made roses of light to impress pretty girls. "When that girl did her magic, did you notice her hands?"

"No."

"Exactly." He grinned, and stepped back into his tent.

I turned away, shaking my head, taking it in. The camp was quiet, asleep, save the sentries in their tower and a few soldiers finishing their beers by a fire pit. Marlo was still up, wiping down the tables of the canteen with a wet rag, and I could see the glow of a lantern from Galen's tent. Even though I didn't want to, I glanced toward the stockade, which was as stark and dim as ever. I imagined my father sitting in there on the ground in the darkness, hands bound, just awaiting the end. . . .

I looked away, back at my tent, and smiled. Zell was standing there in the entrance, watching me with the flap pulled back. His lips curled the tiniest bit upward at the sight of me. I took a step his way, and then I heard the horns.

Three sharp blasts, then three more, from the guard platforms.

Alarm.

Instantly, the mood changed. Soldiers burst out of their tents, scrambling to the armory. On the walls, the archers nocked their bows. Voices shouted all around, panicked and urgent. The horns blared again, even more frantically. "They're coming!" a guard screamed from one of our platforms, a rickety structure just behind the camp's wooden wall. "Defensive formations! Now! They're co—"

But he never got to finish because the wall just past him exploded, blowing apart the tower and the guard in one thunderous blast.

A concussive burst of air hit me, knocking me down, sending tents flying like sheets of paper in the wind. Dust filled the air, stinging and thick, as fire roared somewhere beyond. I staggered up to one arm, coughing, scrambling to see what had just happened. There was a hole in the camp's wall, a massive hole of splintered wood and broken, burning logs, and through that haze of flickering flame, I could see at least two dozen men charging our way, men wearing red-and-gold armor, men with their faces hidden behind slitted helmets, men wielding swords and crossbows and axes.

Miles's men.

They'd found us.

EIGHT

I SCRAMBLED UP TO MY FEET, TRYING TO LOOK FOR SOMEONE, anyone, but it was impossible in the darkness and dust. All around me, the camp was chaos, a whirlwind of scrambling soldiers and screaming voices. Injured guards lay in the ground by the hole, faces bloodied, limbs severed, shrieking and gasping. Archers fired from the remaining walls, a volley of arrows that took out a few of the soldiers but left most of them still charging. My hands darted for the sword at my hip, except it wasn't there, because I'd left it back in my tent like an idiot. And Miles's men were charging closer and closer, fifteen feet away, ten, five . . .

The first row of soldiers burst through the hole in the fence, storming into our camp through the darkness. I wanted to run, to hide, to fight, but my stupid legs were paralyzed with shock. That front row of soldiers drew their crossbows, leveled them, and fired, right at us, right at me. I threw up my hands with a scream . . .

Then there was a crackling surge of magic from behind

me, and a deep guttural howl of primal fury. A shimmering purple curtain billowed out before me, hanging in the air like the membrane wall of a giant bubble, and the crossbow bolts hit it and shattered, their shafts collapsing in on themselves in sprays of splintering wood. I spun to see Lyriana standing behind me at the far end of the camp, hair messy, hands outstretched, Rings pulsing. She let out a booming roar like a howling thunderclap, then twisted her hands into claws and jerked them straight up.

The ground beneath the rushing Western soldiers shot up, pillars of stone rising like teeth in a hidden jaw. They screamed as it hurled them up in the air, screamed as it blanketed the camp in an impenetrable cloud of dust, screamed as it sent them crashing back down. Armor shattered, bones broke, men slammed into the ground like sacks of meat.

I turned back to Lyriana with a whoop, even as she geared up for another strike. Ellarion was by her side now, standing askance with blood streaking down from a gash in his left leg. And there were two other figures coming up behind them, Unbroken soldiers, swords drawn. One of them was an old veteran, a bearded bald guy whose name I couldn't remember, and the other was Ein, that ruddy-faced boy who worked the canteen with Marlo.

But then I saw the way they were walking, tense, quiet. I saw the way they glanced at one another as they crouched up to Lyriana, a single charged conspiratorial glance. And I saw them raise their swords, not at our enemy, but at Lyriana's turned back.

"Behind you!" I screamed.

Lyriana jerked aside, surprised, and Ein's blade cut

through the empty air where she'd been standing. The veteran's blade caught her in the right shoulder, sinking deep into her flesh, sending rivulets of blood streaming down her chest. She screamed and crumpled to her knees, her hand twitching uselessly at her side. Ellarion spun on them, his hands flaring out in an instinctive casting form. But no magic came out, not even a flicker, and Ein smashed him in the side of the head with the pommel of his sword. Ellarion crumpled down with a whimper, and the veteran jerked out his blade, pulling it back for a final thrust.

Lyriana's left hand jerked up, a clawed grip that froze the veteran in place. Her golden eyes blazed with fury, two smoldering stars. Her blood flared a dazzling gold as it dripped down her side. She snarled and twisted and jerked back, and the veteran's rib cage ripped clean out of his chest with a wet spray, hovering in the air for a moment before Lyriana threw it across the camp like a dirty rag.

That . . . was a new one.

The veteran flopped down into the dirt, his chest a gaping cavity. Next to him, Ein spun around, trying to flee, only to run straight into the point of a dagger, one that drove clean through his chest like a hammered nail. He toppled down next to his companion, and standing in his place was Galen, face contorted into the angriest grimace I'd ever seen. "Your Majesty!" he yelled.

"Galen!" she said, the fire leaving her eyes, replaced by a stunned grimace that had to be the pain kicking in. She was bleeding hard, her whole body soaked. "I . . . he cut me . . ." she said, her voice distant and soft, her eyes on her ragged wound. "Why . . . why would he . . ."

She slumped back down, but Ellarion was there, catching

her even as he bled from his own gash on his temple. "I've got you, Lyri," he said, holding her close. "I'm sorry. I'm so sorry . . ."

"Be sorry later!" Galen barked. "Right now, you need to get her to safety!"

"But . . . I . . ." Ellarion stammered, struggling to hold Lyriana up. I turned back to the front of the camp, trying to see through the dust and shadow. Lyriana had stopped the first wave, but the next was coming. I could hear men shouting, pulling each other up, drawing their blades.

"Now!" Galen screamed again, his eyes so big they looked ready to burst out of his head. Second to the throne or not, Ellarion listened, pulling Lyriana up and dragging her toward the end of the camp, where it met the placid waters of the lake. She was still breathing, I think. She'd be okay. She had to be.

Galen had other concerns. He whipped out his daggers and strode forward, toward the billowing dust and the enemy within. "What are you all waiting for?" he roared to the stunned camp. "This is our moment! Attack!" He sprinted across the camp, daggers twirling, right into the cloud of dust, and as he did a half-dozen of our soldiers, the few who'd managed to pull themselves together and grab a blade, joined him. I could see Garrus among them, Garrus who'd sworn off fighting, charging into the fray with a burning log of a club. "For the Unbroken!" I heard the rebels yell. "For the True Queen!"

I didn't see the impact, but I heard it, the trampling of bodies, the clanging of swords, the grunts of wounded men. I didn't understand what was happening, didn't understand any of it. How had they found us? How many of them were there? Why were our own people attacking Lyriana? What could I—

"Tilla!" Zell's voice pulled me into the moment, a hard jerk into the present. He stood next to me, unarmored, a sword in each hand, raring to go.

Right. Questions later. Fight now.

His eyes met mine, and I could see the uncertainty in them. He didn't want to leave me.

I was having none of that shit. "Go!" I yelled, because even though I couldn't tell what was happening, I was pretty sure any chance we had at survival hinged on our best warrior getting in the mix. "Now!"

He gritted his teeth in frustration and took off, hurling himself into the billowing cloud with a barely restrained growl. I saw his blade flicker through the dust, saw a streak of red follow a gurgling shriek, then another. My heart beat against my ribs and my stomach clenched tight and I hated that I couldn't see him, hated that this could be it, the last time I saw him. . . .

No. Not if I had anything to do with it.

I couldn't see the armory but I knew where it was, a long rack of weapons along the camp's easternmost wall. I sprinted there now, still barefoot (why hadn't I put on shoes?), eyes stinging, mouth flooded with dust. The sounds of the battle raged around me, louder and louder, and there were other noises there too now, noises I liked a whole lot less: the crackle of flame, the hissing of steam, the sloppy wet rending of flesh.

Bloodmages. Because of course.

The dust cleared in front of me, enough to reveal the rack of weapons. Most had been claimed, but there was a figure standing behind the rack, and even through the cloud I could make out the husky frame and the roped hair. Marlo. "Tilla!" he yelled. "Here!"

He grabbed a short sword off the rack and tossed it my way. I caught it effortlessly (which, okay, not bad) and spun around. Not a moment too soon because there was a Western soldier there, rushing at me with the point of his broadsword. Rookie mistake. Coasting on pure instinct, I slid to the side, letting him streak by right into the weapon stand, and then jammed my own blade into the base of his skull, just below the helmet.

Thirty.

"Titans have mercy!" Marlo gasped as the soldier flopped down to the ground, and I thought he was just horrified at the body before I saw the reflection in his eyes and realized there was another soldier, a silhouette marching toward me. Even through the dust I could make out the flickering white glow of his eyes.

Screw that. I wound up and hurled my sword directly into his face.

Thirty-one.

Except wait, no, not thirty-one, because he whipped a hand up and my blade stopped, frozen in the air just inches in front of him. That wasn't good. I had just enough time to dive to the side as he flicked his wrist my way and the sword came hurtling back, spinning wildly end over end. I was fast, but not fast enough; the tip clipped my bicep, slicing it open, which hurt like hell. I stumbled to the side, wincing, clutching my arm as blood trickled through my fingers. I'd been cut more times than I could've ever imagined, but every time I was still shocked by the pain.

Still, that was the least of my concerns, because the blood-mage was marching toward me, arms outstretched. His eyes were pure white, no irises or pupils, marked only by throbbing black veins. I scrambled for another sword, but before I could grab it, he twisted his hands in circles and my own wrists jerked back hard, like they were being pulled toward him by an invisible force, one that was squeezing tighter and tighter, crushing so hard it hurt. I kicked and flailed, my feet dragging streaks through the dirt, but it was no use. I was like a fish on a line, being pulled into his clutches, toward those awful eyes and wheezy breath. He raised his hands up to the sky, and I went with them, lifted into the air so just my toes scraped the earth, hanging like a horrible flailing marionette. His magic coursed through me and it felt horrible, like beetles crawling through my veins, spiders scratching behind my eyes. He strode toward me, and now I could see all of him, his husky frame and bushy black beard and grief-weed-rotten teeth. He clenched his hands into fists and then there was another crushing feeling, this one around my waist, like I was being flattened in the palm of a giant. I gasped for air as none came. . . .

Then the bloodmage let out a hacking gasp of his own and suddenly all that magic vanished and I fell down onto my knees with a thud. The bloodmage was the one kicking and struggling now, and I couldn't quite see the figure standing behind him, but I could see the thick iron chain it was holding against the bloodmage's neck, jerking him back in a violent choke. The bloodmage's hands flailed uselessly, pawing at the figure's face, but the chain dug in deeper, deeper, deeper, and then there was a wet brittle crack and his head lolled forward like a broken doll's. The figure let go, tossing the bloodmage aside like garbage, and stepped forward into the light.

I didn't need to see his face. I'd known the second I saw the chain. But still, there he was, my father, the traitor, the usurper, the murderer, and he'd just saved my life. He was breathing hard, hands soaked red, a long gash running down his left leg. And he looked relieved.

For a moment, anyway. Then he spun back around, toward the hazy chaos of battle, where the screams were getting louder and closer. "Tillandra!" he shouted. "Sword! Now!"

I stared at him, then at the swords lying next to me, then at him, then at the swords. "Sword!" he yelled again, more urgently, but still I just lay there. Because throwing him a sword felt wrong, monumentally profoundly gut-wrenchingly wrong, even though it also seemed liked the obvious thing to do.

He was my father. But he was also the enemy. He'd saved my life. But this could also all be a trap. If I didn't do it, we'd both probably die. But if I did, maybe I'd be playing right into his hands.

It was all too much, too fast. Every choice felt wrong, every outcome doomed, and every passing second was a moment I wasted. "Tillandra, please!" he yelled again, his voice somewhere between desperate and commanding.

Behind him, the dust was finally settling, and I could actually make out the camp, or what was left of it, what I could see in the light of the dozens of smoldering fires. Most of the walls had collapsed, and the few that remained were blackened husks. Burning tents billowed like flags and flakes of ash danced and spun in the air like falling leaves. Bodies lay everywhere, twisted and charred, limbs splayed, the ground around them stained red. Some survivors huddled to the sides, scrambling to get out, clutching their wounds. The battle, as far as I could tell, had died down to just a few people, maybe eight or nine Western soldiers, a pair of our rebels, and one last bloodmage, this one enveloped in ribbons of flame, throwing gusts out like whips. And my friends . . .

Kelvin and Marlo hid crouched behind the weapons rack. Garrus leaned against a wall, panting, clutching a bloody mess that was all that remained of his right hand. Lyriana and Ellarion were gone, escaped hopefully. Galen hunched over a Western soldier, pressing down on his chest with a knee as he choked the life out of him. And Zell was still there, still fighting, face streaked with sweat and blood, hunkered against a wall in a defensive crouch as two Western soldiers closed in.

"No," I whispered, because there was no way I could get there fast enough, nothing I could do. "Not now."

"Not now," an accented voice said behind me in agreement. I spun around and there she was, Syan Syee the Red Waster, striding into the battle with her hands folded together in front of her chest, and the confident air of someone about to lay some shit *down*. Magic ran through the blue streaks in her hair like surging rivers, and her tattoos glowed a vivid blue. Her zaryas spun over her shoulders, fast and irritated, jerking back and forth like caged dogs straining to break free.

"Do it!" I yelled, barely knowing what *it* was. "Do your thing!"

She glanced back at me out of the corner of her eye, and I could see the tiniest flicker of a smile. "With pleasure."

She didn't move, not an inch. But her zaryas streaked forward, zipping across the camp like a pair of homing hummingbirds. One caught the closest Western soldier in the side of the neck, and he fell to his knees, his life shooting out of him like he'd sprung a leak. His companion spun to gape and the other zarya thing zipped into him, punching a hole clean through his chest and bursting out the back of his armor like an arrow shot through a sheet of paper. My father and I shared a look of astonishment, but the zaryas kept going, zigzagging across the camp, stinging like a pair of hornets, dropping one guy after another. A soldier raised his sword, only to lose his entire arm; the one who'd been coming at Zell tried to run and took the hit in the back of his neck, his head popping off with a surprisingly gusty spray.

The bloodmage was the last Westerner standing, and he let out a furious roar, pulling his hands back as the air around him sizzled and wavered. Jets of flame shot out of his palms, catching one of the zaryas midair, but it didn't burn or fall, just froze there, enveloped, hovering. Syan dug her feet into the dirt and breathed a little harder, forehead beaded with sweat. The zarya spun faster now, in the other direction, and the jets of flame were moving into it, around it, like thread winding around a spool. The bloodmage gaped and clenched his fists shut, but it was too late. The zarya kept spinning, spinning, a cyclone of fire, and then all at once it stopped and shot it all right back, a curtain of flame that swallowed the screaming bloodmage whole. I could actually see the flesh fly off his bones, and yup, that was an image that was going to haunt me for the rest of my life.

Syan crumpled down to her knees, gasping, and her zaryas fell with her, *thunk*ing down into the dirt. That glowing blue had vanished from her hair, leaving only flat black, and, in a few places, new strands of dull gray. I didn't know a whole lot about magic, especially not Super Mysterious Red Waster magic, but I'm pretty sure that meant it was gone.

The camp was still for one second, one second that stretched into eternity, and then everyone still alive moved at once. My father rushed over to Syan's side, catching her with his bound hands as she collapsed. Marlo stumbled toward Garrus, wrapping a thick cloth around his mangled hand. Zell stepped away from the wall, lowering his swords. Our eyes met with wordless gratitude, with breathless relief, with the knowledge that no matter what else happened, we'd at least have another day together.

I staggered toward him, the enormity of what had just happened catching up to me along with the soreness in my legs and the burning pain in my bicep. We'd won the battle, I guess, but the war wasn't looking good. We'd been found. The camp lay in ruins. Moans of the wounded and dying filled the air. Looking around, I could see maybe thirty Unbroken left standing.

Galen broke the silence with a scream, at once triumphant and furious and agonized. He rolled off the body of the Westerner he'd been choking, who I'm pretty sure had died a good five minutes ago, and staggered up to his feet. He kept screaming, his whole body shaking, and he kicked the corpse again and again, smashing the heel of his boot into the head until it collapsed in with a meaty crack.

"Galen, enough," a voice called from behind me. Ellarion. He'd made it, thank the Old Kings, and Lyriana had too, walking alongside him with an arm draped over him. Her shoulder was wrapped up in a bandage, and she ran one hand idly along it, Rings glowing the gentle green of a healing Art.

The sight of her seemed to calm Galen down, or at least

jerk him out of his fury. "Your Majesty," he said, crossing to her side. "Are you all right?"

"I'll live," she replied, staring out at the smoldering camp around us with a look of utter anguish. "By the Titans . . . how could this happen?"

The remaining survivors were huddling closer to us, drifting from the fringes of the camp, limping our way. I could hear their voices above the moans, the urgent questions getting louder and louder, and I could see their eyes, their anger, turning toward the back of the camp, where my father sat by Syan's huddled form.

He had to know where this was going, so he stood up, staring down the crowd pretty much ready to tear him apart. "I don't expect you to believe me, but I had nothing to do with this," he said. His face was caked in dirt, his wrists bleeding from where the chain had dug into them.

"Bullshit," Ellarion said. "You must have tipped Miles off."

My father shook his head with weary indignation. "If Miles himself had known your location, he would have sent a hundred men and Jacobi, and probably flown out here himself in the Skywhale. My guess is that this was a local garrison. And if you're wondering who tipped them off . . ." He jerked his head toward the limp forms of the two Unbroken soldiers who'd attacked Lyriana. "I'd start with those two."

Right. Ein and the veteran. With the chaos of the blood-mages, I'd forgotten about them. Even now, I didn't want to think about it, because the idea of our own people turning on us was too much. All of this, it was too much.

Lyriana crossed to the two of them and hunkered down. The veteran was as dead as anyone could be, his entire chest ripped out, but Ein was still breathing, barely, tiny choking gasps that made blood bubble out of his lips. Lyriana gently lifted his head in her hands, and he stared at her, this boy of no more than sixteen, stared at her as he drowned in his own blood. "Why?" she asked.

But Ein didn't answer, couldn't answer. He didn't need to, not really; that enormous bounty for my father's capture was answer enough. He just lay there, in Lyriana's arms, letting out those sad, gasping wheezes, staring up with those wide terrified eyes. He breathed once, twice, three times, and then went still, and Lyriana gently laid his head back down in the dirt. Her own eyes were shut, but I could see a single golden tear streak down her cheek. Even after what he'd done, Lyriana could still cry for him.

"Titans have mercy . . . they've destroyed us . . ." a trembling voice said. Marlo, still huddled by Garrus's side, cradled tight in one of the big guy's meaty arms. "What do we do now?"

"We keep fighting," Galen replied, his eyes hard narrow slits. "For every man we lost today, we take a dozen of theirs. We make them pay in blood!" He slammed a fist into his chest as he talked, hard, and at least a half-dozen of our survivors let out grunts of agreement. I got the sentiment, in theory, but right now, more blood was the last thing I wanted. "We need to move now. Collect everything we can and head east, into the mountains. We can lay low there for a few weeks, gather our strength, marshal up some new recruits, come up with a new plan of attack. Maybe move into the Eastern Province, take aim at the grain supply. With Queen Lyriana at our side, we can—"

"No," Lyriana said, and every head turned, mine included. She was standing now, hands at her side, and that look of anguish had been replaced by something else, a resolve, a determination.

"What do you mean, no?" Galen asked.

"You can do that. You *should* do that. But I'm not coming with you." She turned to the back of the camp. To Syan. "I'm going with her."

The Red Waster girl was still sitting where she'd fallen, hunched low on the ground on her hands and knees, breathing hard. She looked up at Lyriana when she spoke, and even though her expression was hard, guarded, I could swear I made out a glimmer of relief.

"What are you talking about?" Galen demanded. "Going with her *where*?"

Lyriana walked over to Syan and knelt down next to her, extending a hand. Syan eyed it warily for a moment, then reached out and took it, clasping Lyriana's hand just above the wrist. And maybe I was just imagining it, but it felt like when they touched, something happened, something subtle and indefinable but real nevertheless. It was like the light around them vibrated, glowing just a little brighter, like the air hummed with the undercurrents of simmering magic. Lyriana's Rings flickered, the tiniest hint of pink, and the strands in Syan's hair let off a soft glow. They stared at each other, eyes locked, with something unspoken passing between them. . . . Understanding? Connection?

"Thank you," Syan said.

"No." Lyriana turned to look at the camp, at the dead bloodmages, at the zaryas lying still in the dirt. "Thank *you*."

"I'm sorry, I know a whole lot has happened, but I'm pretty damn sure I'm missing something." Galen paced over to Lyriana and I followed, along with Zell and Ellarion. When he spoke now, his voice was low, not quite a whisper, but low enough so that the rest of the camp couldn't hear. "What's happening here? What are you talking about?"

"I wish to bring the Queen to my home in Benn Devalos," Syan said. "She may be able to convince the other Torchbearers to join your cause. To defeat the Inquisitor and prevent Zastroya."

Galen just stared at her.

"More mages like her," I tried to clarify. "You saw how powerful she was, right? How she pretty much just saved all our asses? Now imagine fifty more of her, fighting at our side, but only if Lyriana can convince them to." I paused for just a moment, because I didn't really have to think about what came next. "I'm going with them, by the way. In case that wasn't obvious."

"As am I," Zell chimed in, and Ellarion nodded and said, "Me too."

"We'll travel light, then. Just the five of us," Lyriana said, and unspoken in that was the sentiment *Only people I can trust*. "And we'll return with an army that can change the tide of this war."

Galen sucked in his breath, choosing his words carefully, like a parent patiently explaining to his son why he can't be a bear when he grows up. "Look. I understand the appeal of that, especially now. But it's just too dangerous, too unknown. We can't send the last two adult Volaris, our only claims to the throne, off into the unknown with some complete stranger, on the promise that there might be more help out there. We just can't do it."

"And *I* can't keep doing this," Lyriana said. "Hiding on the fringes of the kingdom, measuring our victories only in how many men we execute, so worn out from fighting that even our own people are turning on us . . ." Her gaze flitted over to Ein's prone form. "We need something else, Galen. We need hope."

"There's a difference between hope and madness."

"I'm not so sure there is," I chimed in, which earned me Galen's withering glare. I knew intellectually that he was probably right, that this was a bad idea that would end in disaster. But my heart was with Lyriana, and maybe always had been. She'd put into words the despair and hopelessness that had been festering within me for the past six months, the sense of uselessness that cast doubt on every raid, no matter how successful. I wouldn't say it out loud, because Galen would probably blow his lid, but I'd rather die chasing hope than keeping on living the way things were.

Galen's brow furrowed in concentration, and he switched his approach to tactical. "And how exactly do you plan to get to the Red Wastes? The only way there is through the Southlands, which, you might recall, is a war zone crawling with the armies of the Inquisitor. And in case that wasn't enough, just to get there you'll have to somehow cross the biggest river in the continent!"

"If I may speak," my father said, and every head spun to him. "I might be able to help there."

"You're lucky I don't end you right now," Galen growled, but Lyriana silenced him with a raised hand.

"Speak," she said.

"Yours wasn't the only rebel group I was feeding information to," he said. "I have contacts at the border. A group of fighters that smuggled supplies into the Southlands. They should be able to get us into the Province safely." Even on his knees, hands bound, he talked with the confidence of a man in charge. "You'll need to take me along. As a hostage, of course."

"Why don't you just tell us about the rebels, and we'll meet them ourselves?" Lyriana asked.

"Because then you'd have no reason not to kill me." My father shrugged, brutally honest. "If you want to get to the Southlands, you need my help. It's as simple as that."

Lyriana glared at him for a long time, then let out a frustrated sigh. "He's right. We have to take him."

Galen laughed out loud. "You can't trust him. . . ."

"I trust that he wants to take down Miles," I said, hoping I wouldn't make it worse.

"And the second he moves to betray us, I'll cut his throat," Zell said, matter-of-factly, and my father just shrugged.

"Then it's settled," Lyriana said, and I felt a lightening in my chest that might have been relief. "You take care of the Unbroken, Galen. Do what you do best. Rebuild our numbers and hold down the line." She reached out to gently squeeze his shoulder. "And when we return, we'll win this war together."

He glanced down at her hand uneasily. "Is that a promise from a friend? Or an order from my Queen?"

Her eyes flared up to meet his, burning a regal gold. "Both."

"I would like it noted, officially, that I think every part of this is a terrible idea, and you're dooming us all." Galen turned away, exhaling slowly. "But you are my Queen. Your word is my command."

"Thank you. My friend." Lyriana smiled, a sad smile with more pain than joy. We could cling to hope as much as we wanted. But the odds were, we'd all die before seeing each other again. Which was something I'd gotten awfully used to thinking.

Just like that, it was settled. For better or for worse, we were really doing this. We were heading to the most dangerous region of the continent to find a secret society of mages, led by a girl we'd spoken to for, maybe, twenty minutes. That was actually the plan.

And I'd be lying if I said I wasn't excited.

nine

In a better world, we would've packed carefully, and made sure we had everything we needed for a long journey into the south. But we had no idea who else knew the camp's location, or when the next company of royal soldiers would arrive. So after a frantic hour scrambling to throw together what we could, an inspiring speech from Lyriana to the crowd, and a tearful good-bye to Marlo and Garrus, the six of us set out on horseback. Ellarion led the way, with Syan and Lyriana close behind, then me and Zell, and last of all my father, his bound hands hidden under a blanket even as he held his reins.

Galen took the rest of the Unbroken into the hills of the east, which was both safer and more predictable. They'd find allies there, but it's also where Miles would come looking once he got word that a whole company of his soldiers had been wiped out. Heading south meant no one would be looking for us, but it also meant we'd be totally on our own.

Just to be safe, we kept off the main roads and stuck to the forest, trotting together through those spindly trees, slowed only by the occasional bubbling creek or mossy hill. And for some reason I couldn't put my finger on, I actually felt . . . good? Or at least less bad, lighter, like I'd been poisoned by some horrible toxin for months and was finally getting it out of my system. Maybe it was the residual adrenaline from the attack, or maybe the promise of a new way forward, or maybe I'd just finally lost my mind. I couldn't tell you what the reason was. I found myself breathing easier, feeling the warmth of the sun on my skin, breathing in that lush forest smell and listening to the whispering of the briarbirds in the thickets.

And also? I couldn't stop looking at Zell. He was dressed simply, a tight gray shirt, cloth pants with riding boots, a leather sheath over his back with swords crossed. But there was something about how he looked that day, riding through the woods on horseback, gazing forward with a look of solemn determination, black hair sparkling in the sunlight . . .

He caught me glancing one time, and arched an eyebrow. "Sorry. Just the way you look today . . . brings back memories."

"Of our ride through the West," he said with a smile. "I was thinking the same thing."

I guided my horse a little closer to his. "I can't believe that was only a year and a half ago. It feels like it was a lifetime."

"So much has changed since then. We've been through so much." He glanced down at his hands, at the nightglass knuckleblades holding the reins. "Feels like we were different people."

"Is it weird that I kind of miss it?" I asked. "I mean, we were terrified and fleeing for our lives, but . . . I don't know. A part of me would go back there, if I could. Things were simpler, at least." I shot him a playful grin. "Know what I miss? Early morning fight trainings."

"You miss me throwing stones at your head and pinning you to the ground?"

"Let's be totally honest. We both liked the pinning." I grinned, and then there was a soft cough from behind me and I turned around to see, oh, right, my father, his face blank, his gaze averted. My cheeks burned with embarrassment, which, really? The man was a tyrant, a mass murderer, a remorseless killer destined to hang for his crimes. And I still felt mortified at him overhearing me flirt with my boyfriend.

This was going to be one long journey.

We made camp as night fell, tethering our horses to some trees in a mossy grove. We ate dried meat and gathered mushrooms, and, by the flickering light of a campfire, huddled up as Ellarion unrolled an elaborate yellowed map. "Not to put too fine a point on it, but the Southlands is a big, messy Province. Where exactly are we headed?" He glanced over his shoulder to a tree on the grove's edge, where my father sat alone. "That's a question for you, Kent."

My father didn't move. "The rebels I was corresponding with were in a town called Torrus, right on our side of the Adelphus's eastern branch. They should be able to help us cross, far from Miles's army."

"Funny how it's now *Miles's* army, when I'm pretty sure you're the one who declared war." Ellarion clenched and unclenched a fist, knuckles grinding together. "Fine. So these rebels get us into the Southlands. Then we make our way to the Red Wastes?" He pointed at the map's bottom edge. "All the way down there. South of the Province."

"Literally off the map," I said.

"It's quite a wide border," Lyriana mused. "Syan, do you know where we should be heading?"

Syan scooted forward up to Lyriana, wiping some crumbs off her chin as she glanced down at the map. Despite the fact that she was sitting next to the rightful Queen of Noveris (not to mention a bunch of armed strangers), she seemed completely at ease. She took a long look at the map and shrugged. "I don't know how to answer that."

"Why not?" Lyriana asked.

"We don't use maps like this," she said, as if the very idea was beneath her. "It is not our way. But . . . if you're asking me where to enter Izteros, I believe we should start with Tau Lorren."

"Izteros is what she calls the Red Wastes," I whispered to Zell, and he nodded, like, obviously.

"Tau Lorren," Ellarion repeated, tapping a broad circle near the map's base. "The capital of the Southlands, home to the Dyn and most of his army. Why would we possibly go there?"

"One cannot simply ride into Izteros on horseback," Syan replied with an incredulous little scoff. "We will need provisions, gear, terzans." She didn't bother explaining that last word, and no one asked. "There is an Izterosi community in Tau Lorren. They helped my brother and me when we made our way here. I believe they will help us return."

"It might have been nice to tell us that earlier," Ellarion grumbled. "It's one thing to cross the Province by backroads, it's another to head right into their capital city." He looked at Lyriana, then at my father, then down at himself. "Call me skeptical, but I don't think we'll be exactly greeted with open arms."

Zell cleared his throat. "I don't know very much about the Southlands. Would someone mind filling me in?"

Good thing he asked, because then I didn't have to. Everything I knew about Southlanders, I'd picked up from my time around them in Lightspire. I knew they had bronze skin and shaved heads, that they ate spicy food, and kept to themselves and regarded everyone else with a lot of skepticism. I knew they'd had a long history of wars with the Volaris, and that a lot of them were considered heretics by the church. That . . . was about it.

Luckily, Lyriana never passed on an opportunity to play professor. "In the old days, after the Titans Ascended, the Southern Empire was the greatest power on the continent. Their Kings, *Dyns* in their tongue, conquered all the lands south of Lightspire, and a good stretch of the Eastern shore as well. Their armies were unparalleled, their cities glorious. They were truly Noveris's first great civilization."

I knew what came next, because I'd sat through enough history lessons in Lightspire. "Then you guys happened."

Lyriana nodded. "Lightspire was just a city-state at that point, a hub of commerce and scholarship with no real political influence. But that all changed when my ancestors, the ruling family entrusted with studying the Godsblade, discovered the Heartstone. When we discovered magic." She hesitated, real guilt in her voice. "Within a century, Lightspire had conquered nearly all of the Heartlands, and built up a massive army of its own. That was something the Southern Empire could not abide."

"War," Zell said.

"The greatest war," Ellarion replied. "It lasted nearly half a century, and killed a million. By the time it was settled, the

Southlands were a scorched ruin. Those great cities were rubble. Those armies wiped out to a man." He didn't sound proud of it, not exactly, but he was still too matter-of-fact for my comfort. "What was left of their population bent the knee at last. The last living member of their royal family, some ten-year-old kid, became the High Lord. And the Southlands became the first occupied Province of the Kingdom of Noveris."

"Sounds familiar," I said, and fought the urge to glance back at my father. "I'm guessing they weren't exactly thrilled?"

"There's always been some resentment, but by and large, they've accepted our rule," Lyriana said. "There have been flare ups of conflict. A rebellion here and there, a trade dispute, a feud between our priests and theirs. But nothing significant, not even on par with the War of the West. Not until now, that is."

"Things had been getting a little tense the past few years," Ellarion went on. "They didn't like all the new taxes being levied on them, they didn't like how Lyriana's father favored the Eastern Baronies, and they really didn't like how we were demanding their Houses send soldiers to fight alongside us in the West. So when last year's Ascendance Day rolled around, the High Lord of the Southlands, Rulys Van himself, came out to Lightspire to meet with the King. He brought his family along too, just to make a good impression. His wife, his younger sons, even his mother." Ellarion's eyes met mine, their usual red glow a smoldering angry crimson. "You see where this is going, right?"

"They were in the Godsblade," I said, my heart sinking. "When my father blew it up."

"Another lovely consequence of his incredibly well-thought-out plan," Ellarion growled, and my father, thankfully, said nothing. "The only surviving member was the High Lord's oldest son, a real firebrand named Rulys Cal. When he got word of what had happened to his father, to his family, well, he didn't take it lightly. He refused to accept King Kent's rule. Instead, he declared the Southlands a free Kingdom and took up the title of Dyn once again. It's been bloody war ever since."

"I'm guessing he won't be thrilled if he finds my father," I said.

"Or you," Lyriana said. "Or me and Ellarion, for that matter. He holds us just as responsible for failing to keep his family safe. And from what I've heard, he's not exactly the merciful type."

"Which brings us right back to my question." Ellarion tapped the map, the circle labeled Tau Lorren. "Namely if we're *really* going to ride right into the single place he's most likely to find us."

"I do not know the intricacies of your many wars and petty conflicts," Syan said, in a tone that weirdly stung. "I only know the journey we'll have to make through Izteros to reach my benn. Without the proper supplies, we'll be swallowed by the storm."

"Just once, I'd like some unexpected good news. Is that so much to ask? Just once in my life?" Ellarion sighed. "Fine. So we get to Torrus where Kent's rebel contacts get us into the Southlands. We ride all the way through the Province to Tau Lorren. We supply up. And then . . . into the wastes."

The plan was settled, I guess. Ellarion rolled up the map, and Lyriana put out the fire. We all got up and started to head toward our sleeping rolls, and that's when my father spoke.

"I didn't know they'd be there."

A silence lingered over the camp as every head turned his way. "What?" I asked at last.

"Rulys Van and his family. I didn't know they'd be at the Masquerade," my father said. His voice was as emotionless as ever, but there was something different, a hesitancy to his words. Was it actually guilt?

Whatever it was, it just made everyone angrier. "And?" Ellarion demanded. "So what? Is that meant to exonerate you?"

"I'm just explaining myself," my father said. "I never intended war with the Southlands. I'd hoped they'd see me as a liberator. What happened was . . ." He hesitated again. "Unfortunate."

"Unfortunate?" Lyriana repeated. "Unfortunate?" And then she was on the move, striding at my father with her fists clenched. Her eyes burned so bright they gave off their own light. "How dare you? How fucking dare you?"

Full honesty? Even after everything I'd seen, fought, and been chased by, Lyriana swearing was the scariest thing in the world.

"Lyri," Ellarion said, but she cut him off with a withering glare. One way or another, this was happening.

"You killed my mother. You killed my father. You killed my little cousins and my friends and pretty much everyone I've ever known. Innocent people! All of them!" She jerked her hand up, and my father's head slammed back against the tree with a hard thump. "So you don't get to say a single word about 'unfortunate.'"

"I understand," my father choked out, and I could see the creases on the sides of his head, like it was being crushed by an invisible fist. "I was just . . . clarifying . . ."

"You don't get to do that. You don't get to clarify or explain or justify yourself. You help us out for as long as we need you, and that's it." Lyriana clenched tighter, straining beads of sweat out of my father's skull. "Let me be very clear, Lord Kent. This is not your redemption. This is not your path to a pardon. You're here to help us. And as soon as you have, as soon as I sit on my throne, you'll face justice for everything you've done. Understand?"

Even through the pain, my father stared Lyriana down. "I've long accepted that," he said. "Miles betrayed me. He stole my throne and destroyed everything I've worked for. The only thing I care about . . . the *only* thing . . . is making him pay."

Zell's gaze narrowed. "The enemy of my enemy . . ."

"Is still my enemy," Lyriana finished, and jerked her hand to the side, sending my father tumbling into the dirt. Ellarion helped her up, guiding her away, and even Zell left after a moment, shaking his head.

But I stayed, waited until it was quiet, and then I slid over to my father's side. The moon was blocked by a thin veil of cloud, so I had to squint to see him. He was rubbing at the back of his head where Lyriana had slammed him into the tree, and he barely looked up as I approached. "What is it?"

"Would you have done anything different? If you'd known Rulys Van and his family had been in the Masquerade? Would it have stopped you, even for a second?"

He finally looked up at me, his green eyes meeting mine. Then he looked away.

His silence was answer enough.

TEN

I SLEPT RESTLESSLY, MY MIND RACING WITH THOUGHTS OF the journey ahead, and I woke up early, just after sunrise. Zell was still asleep next to me, his chest moving up and down with each measured breath, so I took one long minute soaking up his warmth, then I eased his arm off, gave him a little kiss on the forehead, and stood up. Holy mother of hell, I ached all over. My thighs throbbed from all that riding and my neck hurt like someone had tied a knot in it. Normally, I'd have asked Lyriana to do some of that sweet healing magic on it, but she was sound asleep, sprawled on her side, snoring away with a distinctly un-royal puddle of drool under her mouth.

There was only one other person awake. Syan sat by the edge of the grove on a log, a leather bag by her side. I made my way over to her with a stretch and a yawn, and took a seat next to her. "Hey," I said. "Can't sleep either?"

She turned to me, and I saw heavy bags under her eyes, a distant weary look. "Bad dreams."

"Yup. Believe me, I can relate."

Syan nodded, turning away with the tiniest hint of a smile. This girl was so weird. She was like one of those optical illusions, where it looked like a rabbit from one angle and a mermaid from another. At some moments, like back in the camp when she'd been wiping out those Western soldiers, she looked like a goddess, glowing and powerful, beautiful beyond words. But now, up close, she looked achingly human. Her black hair was tangled, the blue streaks so dull you could barely see them. Her robe hung loose on her frame, and I could see how thin she really was, her collarbone pressing out against her skin. And there was something else about her, a deep exhaustion that made her look so much older than her years.

"Tilla," she said at last, her accent making it sound more like *Teela*. "Your name is Tilla, yes? May I ask you a question?"

"Of course."

"Kent . . . King Kent . . . he is your father." I had a feeling I knew where this was going. "But you are not a Princess? You oppose him?"

I sighed. "By the time he'd become King, I was already kind of on the other side. Also, like, I'm a bastard daughter, so I was never really his heir. Not unless he legitimizes me. Anyway, it's . . . the whole thing is complicated."

Syan nodded. "In Benn Devalos, we say that our world is a straight line, and the world of you stillanders is a tangled knot. I had always heard this, but I had not known how true it was until I came out here." She kicked idly at a clod of dirt. "There is so much I yet do not understand."

"Honestly? I grew up in Noveris, and I feel pretty much the same way," I replied. "You only got sent out here . . . what did you say? Four months ago?"

"Yes. It was my first time leaving Izteros. My first time seeing the rest of the world." She craned her head up at the sky, olive skin glowing in the wan light. "On the way north, my brother and I rode through this forest, or one much like it. I still remember it so vividly. How wonderful it seemed. How truly magical. We have no forests in Izteros, you understand. Nothing like this."

I nodded, but given the way she was talking, that muted-pain tone, I was pretty sure this story wasn't really about the forest. "We rode through it side by side," she went on, "just staring up at how tall these trees were, barely able to believe it. My brother, fool that he was, boasted that he could climb all the way to the top. I told him he couldn't, and the next thing I knew, he was off, scrambling, leaping from branch to branch, until he was at the peak, tossing cones down on my head." She laughed, and a tear ran down her cheek. "Such an idiot."

I hadn't meant to walk into a superheavy conversation, but now that we were here, there was no way back. "What was his name?"

"Kalin," Syan said. "He was born a year after me, but we were as twins, always inseparable. The elders had planned to just send me to meet with your King, but he insisted that he come out on this journey with me. He claimed he'd keep me safe."

I felt that familiar tightening in my chest, that plunging in my abdomen like my heart had become a sinking stone. Jax's laughter rang in my ears. "What happened?"

"On our way up to the Heartlands, we came upon a massacre. A group of royal soldiers and bloodmage abominations, attacking some pilgrims. I still don't know why. I just know they were killing everyone." She breathed deeply, and when she spoke her words were even slower and more measured than usual. "I wanted to keep riding, but Kalin couldn't let it slide. He rushed in, trying to save them, and a battle broke out. We fought well, but we'd never faced something like that before. Kalin was killed. Turned to ash right before me." She swallowed deep. "And then I was alone."

"I'm so sorry," I said. And there was so much more I wanted to say, so many thoughts and feelings that I didn't know how to put into words. Because there was a shared pain between us, the never-ending agony of a lost brother, and a shared rage, a rage at Miles and his regime and everything he'd taken from us. But at the same time, this pain was so personal, so specific, that I couldn't even begin to know what she was really feeling. Her brother had died . . . what? Three months ago, tops? I'd lost Jax almost two years ago, and I could barely remember what it had felt like in the early months, like the memories were lost behind a fog of grief.

If that's where she was now, I couldn't begin to touch that. So I did the only thing I could think of and reached out and gave her a little hug.

She pulled away sharply, so apparently, that was the wrong call. "It's fine," she said. "We come from sand, and we return to the sand. What matters is what we do with the time we have."

I didn't know what to say to that, but luckily, I didn't have to reply, because right around then, Ellarion strolled over, rubbing at his eyes. "This the early-riser club?"

Syan shifted uncomfortably, and I cleared my throat, both of us pulling together like that moment hadn't just happened. "Hey, Ellarion," I said. "We're just, you know. Catching up."

"I see," he said. "Listen, Syan, if you have a moment, I . . . was hoping to ask you a question."

She turned to him. "What is it?"

"Do you think you could . . . I mean, if it's not like a secret . . . see, I . . ." he stammered, and what was up with this awkwardness? The last year had changed Ellarion, sure, made him harder and sadder, but I'd never seen him like this. "I was wondering if you could teach me how you do your magic."

"Teach you *my* magic? You mean, how I control the flame?"

"Sure, whatever you call it," he said. "See, I . . . used to be a mage too. A pretty powerful one."

"I know. I can see the fire within you. So much of it. It's like . . ." She gestured around him. "Like a bottled storm."

"Yeah. That's how it feels," Ellarion said, nodding. "Problem is, I can't unbottle it. Not with these." He raised his arms and turned his metal hands around. "I've been trying for almost a year now. And just . . . nothing. I can't even do the simplest Art. I still see beams. I still feel the energy of the world all around me." I remembered that moment back in Lightspire, when he'd grabbed my hand and I saw the world through his eyes, saw the dazzling pillars of energy all around us. "These hands, though . . ." Ellarion reached out with his right fingers elegantly curled, the way he used to when he'd make flames dance around. Nothing happened. "It's like the beams pass right through them."

"Beams," Syan repeated, head cocked to the side with curiosity. "We call them strands of power."

"Then you see them, too!" Ellarion exclaimed, trying to contain his excitement. "But you control them without using your hands at all! How? Please, I'm begging you. Teach me how."

But Syan was uncertain. "It's not so simple. Torchbearing is not something you can just teach, like the patterns of the stars or which plants are safe to eat. It's something you *feel*." She rose to her feet, and I noticed for the first time she and Ellarion were almost the same height. "Your magic, it comes from here," she said, gently tapping the side of his head. "From study and practice, from learning all of these techniques. But ours is different. Ours comes from here." She tapped her chest with two fingers. "The mastery doesn't come from learning what to do. It comes from learning how to be."

"I'm not going to pretend I understand what that means," Ellarion said. "But I'm willing to learn, no matter what it takes. I have the power. At least let me try."

Syan considered it for a moment, then shrugged. "Stillander magic comes from controlling the strands, the 'beams' as you call them. You reach out and touch them, bend them to your will to reshape the world. But our way is different. We don't touch the strands. We bend the world *around* them, move the energy from one place to another without ever truly coming into contact." She opened her leather bag and turned it over. The two zaryas tumbled out onto the grass. "The zaryas are the key to our power. They are the conduit through which we influence the world, through which we wind the strands."

"Okay. Good. Yes." Ellarion planted his feet in the dirt and clasped his hands together. "So. How do I make them move?"

Syan let out the world's weariest sigh. "You don't make the zaryas move. You *become* the zaryas. Then it's simply a matter of moving yourself."

I could see Ellarion struggling for the most polite words.

"I . . . understand this can be difficult to explain in our language. But I'm just not following."

Syan paced around Ellarion and stood right behind him. "Take off your hands."

"What? Why?"

"The magic flowing into them is a constant distraction," Syan said. "You won't be able to focus so long as it's there."

"I . . . well . . . okay." Ellarion sighed and folded his hands together. With that hiss and crackle, they tumbled down into the ground, leaving his wrists bare.

"Good," Syan said, then reached out with both of her hands, wrapping them around Ellarion to rest on his diaphragm. "Breathe."

"What?"

"Just breathe."

Ellarion inhaled deeply, then let it out. "Good," Syan said, pressing her hand firmly against him, moving it in and out. "Now again. Slower. Deeper. Breathe in and out."

"Okay, but I d—"

"Shh," she cut in. "Now. Look at the zaryas. Focus on them. Let them become the only thing in the world. Let everything else fade away. The ground beneath them. The log behind them. The whole world. Let it dissolve."

Ellarion's tongue poked out beneath his upper lip in concentration, and his gaze narrowed. Syan kept her hand where it was, and he kept taking those breaths, and as she spoke, her voice felt mesmerizing, hypnotic. "Good. Keep breathing. Keep focusing. And as the world melts away, let yourself melt away as well. Let go of that pain. Let go of that anger. Let go of Ellarion Volaris." I wasn't even the one up there, but I could feel my heart starting to race, my skin prickle with goose bumps. "Let go of everything but the zarya."

Ellarion's nostrils flared and his chest heaved up and down. His brow furrowed. A sweat drop streaked down his forehead. The air around him seemed to stiffen and crackle, nearly invisible fissures wavering in the light. I scooted forward on the log, barely realizing I was holding my breath. . . .

But for all of that, the zaryas still didn't move.

After a minute, Syan stepped back, letting go of Ellarion's chest. He let out a harsh sound, somewhere between an exhale and a groan, and wiped the sweat off his brow. "It didn't work."

"I'm sorry."

He shook his head. "No. It's fine. A first try. No one gets anything on their first try." He paused. "Please. Just . . . let me keep trying. I'm sure I can figure it out."

Nothing about Syan's expression gave any indication that she thought that was true, but she nodded nonetheless. "As you wish."

We rode on. There's this haze that comes from days of riding, where the thoughts bouncing around your head blur with the gentle bobbing of your horse, where minutes blur into hours and time loses all meaning, where you blink and suddenly it's nighttime and you're miles from where you thought you were. I hit that headspace maybe three days into our journey, zoning out for huge stretches, snapping out of it only when we made camp or when someone shouted my name at least three times.

There were little things I did notice, though. Gradually, the lanky forests I'd gotten used to faded away, clearing out for wide hills and open sky. There was still vegetation here, scatterings of bushes and short, stubby trees breaking up the stretches of brown dirt. Here and there, tall pillars reached out of the ground like stalagmites, culminating in flat, smooth plateaus. There were few signs of life, though, outside of the occasional bounding hare or grazing sheep or the screeching hawks circling overhead. This was a badlands, Lyriana had explained. Most of the civilization was further west, along the Adelphus, which was also not coincidentally where the war was raging.

I didn't mind. There was something soothing about this place, its stillness, its quiet. At night, curled up against Zell, I'd stare up at that infinite spread of stars, a hundred thousand diamonds glistening in a sea of darkness, and almost feel at peace.

After a week on the trail, we began getting nearer to the Adelphus's eastern branch. I could hear the rushing of the river faintly, like a whistling breeze that just wouldn't stop. Signs of civilization began to crop up again: an abandoned barn here, the faded cobblestone of an old road there. I figured that would be a good sign that we were close to the village of Torrus, where my father's contacts would help us. But his expression was just going from grim to grimmer.

"Something's wrong," he said at last. It was late afternoon, the setting sun painting the sky a dusky orange.

"What are you talking about?" Ellarion asked.

My father squinted toward the horizon, at the incline of a wide hill. "We're a mile from Torrus, two at most. We should've seen someone by now. Scouts, merchants, something." He reached a finger out into the air, then tasted it. His expression somehow got even grimmer. "Ash."

We all looked at each other uneasily, sharing that same sinking dread. I felt the hairs on my arms stand on end, and a cold chill ran down my spine. It wasn't too late to turn back. To look for another way. Maybe even to head back to Galen. But we rode on, cresting that hill, and saw the town of Torrus.

I wish we'd turned back.

Torrus was a quaint little fishing village, home to maybe a hundred, built up alongside the bank of the Adelphus. When I say *was*, I'm emphasizing the past tense, because all that was left of it was a scorched ruin. The entire town had been razed, leaving just a few blackened posts and frames, the skeletal remains of the houses that had once been. Flaky ash coated the ground, fluttering here and there like a snowfall. The broken husks of boats littered the river's bank. The town's gate remained, a wide arch, and a half-dozen bodies hung off it, their faces burned beyond recognition. Above them, on the gate's wooden frame, words were carved in a crude scrawl: DEATH TO TRAITORS.

We rode down in silence. The town had been razed some time ago, but the air was heavy with that suffocating smoky smell. Ash crunched under our horse's hooves. Lyriana clutched a hand over her mouth, looking like she was about to be sick. Ellarion's eyes burned furiously. Zell just had that expression, that hard stare, the look that meant there was a fury raging inside him and he was doing everything he could to keep it down.

Syan reached out, touching a jagged post that might have once been a family's home. Her fingers came back coated in ash. "Zastroya," she whispered.

It took us getting to the center of town, a sprawling courtyard around a blackened ring of stones, before anyone else spoke. Ellarion. He turned around slowly, and forced his words out through gritted teeth. "Kent. What in the frozen hell is the meaning of this?"

"It must have happened after Miles betrayed me," my father said, and even he looked ready to scream. "His men must have learned the rebels were based here. But razing the whole village, killing everyone . . . it's low, even for them."

I tried not to look, but I still saw charred bodies in the rubble, scorched shriveled frames, men, women, children. Some of them so small. I hadn't seen anything like this since the bombing at the Godsblade. "It feels pretty on point to me," I said softly.

"They'll pay for this," Lyriana said. "All of them."

"You lured us here," Ellarion grumbled, and I'm pretty sure if he could use magic, his hands would be aflame. "You knew, you son of a bitch, but you lied to get us to bring you along. . . ."

"I had no idea . . ."

"It doesn't matter," Zell cut in. His voice was flat, emotionless, which always meant he was at his most emotional. "The question is, what do we do now?"

I followed his gaze, out of the town, toward the Adelphus River. It was bigger here than it had been back in Lightspire, so wide that I had to squint to see the bank of the other side. And it was faster too, the current surging past us with a roar. No way in hell could someone swim across. We'd need a boat, a good one. And considering all the shattered frames lining the shore, the royal soldiers who'd destroyed this village had done a damn good job of making sure there weren't any left.

"Do we look for another town?" I asked.

"Too dangerous," my father answered. "If the soldiers

have come this far east, they've likely hit every town along the river searching for rebels. Best-case scenario, the townsfolk capture us on sight and turn us in. Worst-case . . ." He gestured at the ruins around us.

"What about your power, Syan? That thing you did back in the Skywhale, where you made us appear somewhere else?" Zell asked. "Could you do that to get us to the other side?"

Syan shook her head. "No. It's too dangerous. I've spent too much of my flame already. If I tried, we might end up in the middle of the river. Or in the ground beneath it."

"Unbelievable. *Unbelievable*," Ellarion said. "All the way out here, and we're blocked by the oldest barrier in the continent."

I wasn't giving up that easy. "What about your magic, Lyriana? Couldn't you, like, Lift us across?"

Lyriana gazed out at the river's surge. "I don't know. Lifting five people, including myself, and carrying us that distance . . . it'd be extremely difficult. Maybe impossible. There's a reason Mages don't fly, you know."

I hadn't actually put much thought into it, but I guess that made sense.

"I could try," Ellarion said, and it was clear even he didn't really believe it. I'd seen him every morning, practicing with Syan. I'd seen those zaryas lying still.

"But mages do fly," Zell insisted. "Miles and his blood-mages made that whole metal ship fly. And back in the city, they made those platforms go up and down, the aravins. Couldn't you do the same with us on a raft?"

"That's different. They weren't doing a Lift. That was them working together to manipulate air currents and . . ." Lyriana stopped. "Oh. Actually . . . yes. I suppose we could try something like that. But it'll be difficult to raise us *and* move us myself. That's two different Arts."

"I might be able to help with that," Syan said. "Taming the wind is one of the first gifts that Torchbearers master. If you can get us into the air, I could try to guide us. I might have enough flame left for that."

"Might?" I asked. "And if you don't?"

"Then we crash into the river and drown," she replied, way too casually.

"Anyone got a better idea?" Zell asked. We all looked back and forth at each other, hoping someone would say something. But no one did. "All right, then. Let's find ourselves a raft."

There was no raft, not really, but we found a big wooden platform at the fringes of the town, a building's wall that was mostly unburned. We carried it down to the river's edge, laid it flat on the bank, and loaded it with necessities: a few days' food, our waterskins, our weapons. After a moment's debate, we let our horses go, sending them running back into the hills. They deserved better, but we didn't have a choice. Just getting us across the river would be challenge enough.

By the time we were ready, the sun was halfway down to the horizon, the sky almost red. We huddled up together on the platform, which was barely big enough for all of us to stand together. Lyriana took a few metal rods that Zell had found, and placed them upright against the platform. With a wave of her hands and a brownish glow from her Rings, their bases glowed, fusing them into the wood.

"What're they for?" I asked

"To hang on to," Lyriana answered. "It's going to be a bumpy ride."

Syan and Lyriana took up positions at the platform's rear. I reached out and grabbed the nearest rod as tightly as I could. Zell, next to me, did the same, as did Ellarion, grudgingly. My father alone was left at the front, and he hooked the chain binding his wrists around his rod. Seemed a little risky, but it's not like he'd be able to swim with them anyway.

"Are you ready?" Lyriana asked Syan, and she nodded. Her zaryas lifted up, hovering around her shoulders, spinning in slow, measured rotations. "Titans, grant us this crossing," Lyriana whispered, and then, with a deep inhale, raised her hands. Her Rings flared a vibrant white. Below us, the platform wobbled, and then lurched up, lifting a good fifteen feet into the air.

I let out a gasp as the thrust tossed me up, then brought me down. The platform buckled beneath us, the wood straining and splintering. Zell sucked in his breath, and Ellarion whispered a prayer to the Titans, the first I'd heard from him since Lightspire fell. I glanced down, over the edge, and saw the ground below us, and the river's edge.

How had this *ever* seemed like a good idea?!

"Now!" Lyriana said, and Syan focused hard, brow furrowed. Her hair and tattoos glowed again, but it was a duller glow, faded, like a shirt that had been washed too many times. Her zaryas sprang into action, hovering behind the platform, chasing each other in circles like a pair of flirty birds.

And then the wind rushed, an upswell from below, that pushed the platform forward, out, over the river itself. It lurched, sending us sliding and clutching our rods, but then Lyriana corrected it, grunting and straining, raising her left hand higher than her right. The platform leveled out, and then it sailed forward, over the river.

This was working. It was actually working. "Hold on tight!" Zell yelled, and we kept gliding through the air, like a giant leaf, streaking out over the Adelphus's surge. Lyriana's hands clenched tight, her whole body tense as she kept us up, and Syan's breath came in hard gasps as her zaryas spiraled around, pulling up the gusts of wind to keep us going.

I grinned, despite myself, and next to me, Zell let out a little whoop. "I feel like a girl from a fairy tale," I said to him. "Like the Princess of Jakar, who sailed around the world on a flying carpet. . . ."

"That was always my favorite," my father said softly, and I remembered, oh, right, that's where I'd heard it. Sitting on his lap in his study, nestled snug against him, while he read from that huge leather-bound tome, *Tales from the Old Kingdoms* . . .

Nope. Nope nope nope. Way the hell too many feelings there. I shoved all of that down, deep down, and focused instead on the world rushing by.

We were nearly halfway across the river now. I could see the other bank a lot more clearly, the sweeping plains of the Southlands. Peering over the platform's side, I could feel the spray of the water below. If it had looked like it was rushing fast from the shore, it was so much more intense from above, a torrent blasting out to sea. When was the last time I'd gone swimming? Did I even remember how?

And right then, the platform lurched forward, hard, plunging down.

I screamed and grabbed my rod, my body falling forward as the nose of the platform tipped down toward the river. Zell's hand shot out, grabbing my shoulder, but he was barely hanging on himself. I heard Lyriana let out an agonized gasp and the front of the platform pulled up, but now we were banking hard to the side, a lateral swing that sent Ellarion tumbling over. He caught himself halfway down, his metal fingers digging into the platform's wood, his feet dangling clean over the edge.

"What's happening?" I screamed, and now we were just spinning in a circle, the platform groaning beneath us, dipping up and jerking back down.

"I'm sorry!" Syan shouted back. If her magic had been a faint glow when we started, it was almost all gone now, the streaks in her hair a dull gray, sparkling, just barely, with blue shimmers. Her tattoos were faded altogether. "My flame, it's not strong enough. . . ."

"Just get us as far as you can!" I yelled.

"And fast!" Ellarion replied, his feet kicking over a fifteen-foot drop into a raging torrent.

"Just a little more," Lyriana choked out. Her magic was keeping us up, sort of, but without Syan's wind, we were spinning wildly, falling lower and lower.

"I'm trying," Syan pleaded. Even back in the Skywhale, with Jacobi bearing down on us, she'd been cool as ice, so seeing her terrified now meant things were *real* bad. Her zaryas zipped around wildly, uncontrolled, and the left one wobbled, dropping, barely staying in the air. "I'm trying, I'm trying, I'm trying," she pleaded, but it wasn't enough, just not enough. The water was closer and closer, racing up to meet us . . .

"A little more!" Lyriana yelled, and her hand shot out to grab Syan's.

And then . . . something happened.

It was like all the air drew in around them, pulling in like a breath, and then burst out in a thunderous rushing exhale.

The whole world throbbed and crackled, a rush of energy that sizzled through my skin like the deepest shiver. Syan let out a gasp, and then she was glowing. The streaks in her hair blazed brilliant, sapphire meteors cutting through black. Her tattoos surged with a light so bright, it was blinding. Her zaryas leapt up into position, and then zipped out, spinning in a beautiful spiral that left streaks of color glowing in their wake.

"You're . . . you're . . ." Lyriana stammered, still staring at her hand clasped in Syan's.

"I know!" Syan replied, and even though her back was turned to me, I could almost feel her grin. The platform caught itself, leveling out, and then it surged up, up up up, lifting boldly away from the river. Zell pulled Ellarion back up, and I let out a triumphant whoop of my own. I had no idea what was happening, but it was *amazing*.

The platform cleared the rest of the river confidently, and the two mages gently dropped us down onto the sandy bank. Ellarion rolled off, clutching the sand between his fingers, howling with relief. Zell clasped my shoulder, and my father, *my father*, let out a little laugh of delight.

Lyriana and Syan stood together at the base of the platform, staring at each other. Lyriana had let go of Syan's hand, and the magic had faded out of her; her hair was a flat black now, her tattoos dull. But there was nothing dull about the way they were looking at each other.

"You drew from me," Lyriana said, beaming. "Our magic, it combined, grew together. Like nothing . . . nothing I've ever felt . . ."

Syan pressed a hand to her chest, gasping. "Your power was within me. I could feel all of you there. I could see you. . . ."

"I know . . . like we were one . . ."

"I've never felt anything like that," Syan said, staring down at her hands. "Have you ever done that before?"

"No. I'm not sure *anyone* has." Lyriana finally let herself go, slumping down into the sand on her knees, breathing hard. Her whole body was slick with sweat, her shirt clinging to her chest. Whatever that had been, it had taken a lot of out her; her face looked sickly, colorless, and it was clear she could barely stand up. Syan clasped her shoulder, then pulled away, as if she'd done something inappropriate.

"I know we still have a ways to go," Ellarion said. "But can we all just take one moment to appreciate how totally awesome that was?"

"Moment taken!" I grinned back, and ran over to give Lyriana a hug. "You guys! That was incredible!"

"It was something else," Zell said, coming over to join us, and then Ellarion was there, hugging his cousin close. Syan stared, a little uncertain, and then I reached out a hand to pull her in as well, and all of us were there, huddled together in the sand, hugging and laughing and cheering. My father sat alone on his knees nearby, watching us, and I swear for one moment, I think I saw him smile.

I knew the journey would be rough. I knew there was more darkness and pain ahead. I knew it would get a lot worse before it got better, if it ever did.

But we had this moment, this one moment of triumph. And I soaked it all up.

ELEVEN

LOSING OUR HORSES MEANT WE HAD TO MARCH ON FOOT through the Southlands. I'd thought that maybe we could just use Lyriana to power up Syan and have her do that Cutting thing to move us along, but that hope died when we saw just how badly it had drained Lyriana, how it took her nearly two days before she was able to walk for more than an hour without needing to rest. So no magical fast travel. Marching it was.

That meant long, slow hours, walking until our feet bled, the sun beating down way too hot for the middle of fall. It meant camping wherever we happened to be, curling up in the dirt, shivering under blankets when those chill plains winds streaked by. It meant blisters and aches and constantly, *constantly*, pouring dirt out of my boots.

I. Hated. Marching.

For a while, the landscape this side of the Adelphus didn't look that different from the ones we'd just been in. But with every mile we went farther south, the land turned drier, harsher, more barren. Those little shrubs and trees I'd gotten so used to became rarer and rarer, even as the dirt under-foot turned more to brittle sand. Those lovely sheep (and their tasty tasty meat) stopped showing up, and by the second night there, Syan was trying to convince us all that fried lizard didn't taste that bad, which was a hell of a leap when I didn't even like *looking* at lizards. Our skins ran dry pretty quick, so we had to stop every few hours for Lyriana to use her magic to pull weird-tasting water from scattered cactuses. The Southlands was mostly a desert, with its cities clustered along the fertile lands by the Adelphus and its offshoots. We needed to avoid all that, at least until we got to Tau Lorren. Which meant the never-ending slog of the long-ass desert hike.

The grind wore us all down. Ellarion's jokes trailed off, and my father looked even grumpier than usual. Even Zell's stoic facade began to crack, with little outbursts of annoyance or frustrated grumbles. Lyriana seemed the worst of all, her brow perpetually furrowed, her expression deeply troubled.

I came up to her one night, hunkered down by her side as she worked her magic on a stubby brown cactus dotted with twitching yellow flowers. "Hey," I said. "You okay?"

"Hmm?" Her hands moved in delicate circles around the cactus, its frame pulsing as if something was crawling around inside it. Super gross. "I'm just thinking."

"About . . . ?"

Her tongue poked out over her lower lip as she pulled her hands wide. Droplets of greenish water melted out through the cactus's skin, hovering in the air like fat pearls. "What happened back at the river." Her voice dropped to just above a whisper. "With Syan."

"Yeah, that was something else," I said. "I'm guessing no one's ever combined magic like that before?"

"It wasn't just our magic that combined," Lyriana said, choosing every word with care. "It was all of us. I could feel her thoughts, her emotions, her memories. I could remember playing with wooden dolls by sandy banks, could remember how her mother smelled when she pulled her in close, could remember her brother's laugh." She gently waved her hand, guiding the water drops into an open skin. "It's like, in that moment, we were one person."

"That sounds . . . invasive," I offered.

"It wasn't bad." She glanced over to the far side of the camp, where Syan was sitting next to Ellarion, talking to him as he stared at the inert zaryas. "Syan is a good person. There's a real kindness in her, a decency. She genuinely wants to help everyone, no matter the cost."

"Sounds like someone I know." I grinned. "Maybe you two were already kind of the same person to begin with."

Lyriana looked away, back at the skin, where the last droplets were plopping in. I thought she'd smile, but she frowned instead. "There was something else, though. Something in her thoughts I can't shake, an image that I kept thinking about, like a bad dream."

"What image?" I asked, even though I kind of didn't want to know.

"I saw fire, Tillandra. Towering waves of fire, bigger than the Godsblade, scorching across the world, destroying everything in their path. A storm that swallows the world." Her voice dropped so low it was almost inaudible. "Zastroya."

"That's what Syan talked about, right? What she said would happen if we didn't stop Miles?"

Lyriana nodded. "I'd thought it was a metaphor, or some Red Waster religious thing. But what if it isn't? What if she's talking about something that'll *really* happen?"

I swallowed. "Then . . . it's all the more reason to stop Miles."

Lyriana nodded, screwing the cap on the skin, her worry hardening into determination. "Damn right."

We marched on. And the morning of our third day in the Southlands, we stumbled onto a battlefield.

From the distance, it didn't look that different, because, well, the desert kind of all looked the same. We could make out shapes as we approached, upright blackened silhouettes framed against the bold red disc of the setting sun, but I figured they were just cactuses or something. It was only when we got closer that I realized the sand below my feet had turned black, that the rocks all around us were scorched and shattered. That the silhouettes were *people*.

Not living people, of course. Statues. Soldiers turned to stone mid-strike, their anger and fear permanently frozen on their cracked faces. There were about a dozen of them still standing, and a dozen more scattered around in broken chunks. And that's just the ones who were turned to stone. So many more bodies lay all around us, young men and women, stabbed and burned and crushed. They were Southlanders, their heads shaved bald, wearing shingled silver armor and leather sandals, many still clutching their spears. There were other bodies too, royal soldiers wearing Kent colors, a few robed men who I think had been bloodmages. But the Southlanders outnumbered them ten to one.

The sprawl of the field was too wide to walk around, so we walked through it instead, taking care not to disturb any of the dead. I'd seen my share of carnage, of course, but this still managed to unsettle me, bury deep in my gut and twist. The massacre at the Godsblade had been terrible, but it had also been kind of unreal, a whole room turned to ash in a blink. But this, this was so much, so vivid, so real. Raw gaping wounds, caked in dried blood. Hands clutching unspooled intestines. Heads cleaved in half. So many dead, just left to rot in the baking sun.

"What happened here?" Syan asked, more curious than affected.

"A battalion of Southlander soldiers must have run into a royal company," my father said. "I didn't know Miles's army had gotten this far south. The war is going even worse than I thought."

We passed another one of the statues, a hearty man holding a spiked mace. Deep fissures cracked his face, but I could still make out his young handsome features. "The Southlanders," Zell said. "They don't have magic."

Lyriana shook her head. "No. They never have."

"And yet they charge into battle against those who can do this." Zell reached out, pressing a hand to the statue's face. "True bravery."

"The spirit of men fighting to be free," my father said.

Ellarion, at the front of our group, let out an irritated snort. "Are you admiring them? Seriously? They died fighting *your* soldiers."

"I never sent soldiers into the Southlands, only to hold the border. This is Miles's work," my father insisted. "I've always viewed the Southlands as cousins to the West, free men struggling against the Volaris' chains. I never wanted this war."

"No King ever wants a war," Zell scoffed. "Yet history

is built on the bodies of the people who died in them."

My father turned to Zell, looking at him, like he was really seeing him for the first time. "What's that supposed to mean?"

"It means you don't get to wash your hands of blood because your great conquest didn't turn out how you wanted it to. You don't get to pass all the failure off on Miles," Zell replied.

"And what would you know of guilt and failure, son of Grezza Gaul?" my father replied.

Zell stiffened, and I found myself holding my breath. "I know less than you," Zell said, pushing down the anger. "But I know that my guilt is mine and mine alone. I know that actions I took, choices I made, have resulted in unspeakable harm. And I know that's on me. On me to fix. On me to atone for. On me to carry as a weight until my dying day." He gestured out at the battlefield, at the corpses, at all the blood. "And this place? That village back there? The thousands killed across the length of the kingdom? That's on you."

My father shook his head. "No. I don't accept that. Everything I did, every choice I made, was to free my people, to end the tyranny of Lightspire. I never wanted *this*."

I swear to the Old Kings, Zell actually rolled his eyes. "In all the time you spent with my father, did he ever tell you the parable of the archer?"

"I can't say he did." My father shrugged, stepping over the body of a woman impaled on a spear. "We weren't exactly friends. Just allies of convenience."

"It's one of the oldest tales in the Hall of Gods," Zell said. "Once, in the old days, when the Twelve walked the earth, a young archer wanted to prove that he was the best. So he laid an apple at the base of the steps of Zhal Khorso, and fired an arrow from the very highest spire. And his arrow flew, the truest shot, and it would have struck the apple right through. But at the last moment, a young mother saw the apple and went to pick it up, to take home for her son. And his arrow caught her right in the side, and killed her."

"Grim story," Ellarion said, and Zell ignored him.

"The Grayfather descended from the Hall of the Gods, furious. 'Who has killed this innocent young woman?' he demanded. 'It was I,' the archer admitted, throwing himself on his knees, 'but it wasn't my fault! I merely meant to strike the apple! I never intended to kill her!' But the Grayfather was unmoved. 'And does your intent feed her children? Does your intent mend the heart of her grief-stricken husband? Does your intent bring her back from the veil?' And the archer cried, for of course it did not, and the Grayfather made his decree so that all could hear. 'You nocked the arrow. You let it fly. You face justice for the target you struck, not the target you aimed for.'"

He stopped, letting his words hang over us. "Well?" Lyriana demanded after a moment. "What happened to the archer?"

Zell stared at her like she was asking about the most obvious thing in the world. "They hanged him."

I expected my father to have some cutting retort, some cold line to justify himself. But he didn't say anything at all, just walked on, his head down. Had Zell actually gotten the upper hand? Had someone managed to win an argument with my father?

Soon enough, mercifully soon, we made it off the battlefield. The bodies grew scarcer and scarcer, the scorch marks faded, the only debris a few toppled husks of supply wagons. When we were finally clear of the last one, back on normal ground (if you considered sand normal ground), Lyriana turned around, facing the battlefield with closed eyes. Syan stared at her, confused, and I shot her a look not to pry. I'd seen Lyriana like this before. I knew what was coming next.

"Blessed Titans above," she intoned, her voice calm and reverent. "I ask you to sanctify this battlefield. Guide the souls of the dead to your arms above. Ease the pain of the living they've left behind." She breathed deep, her Rings giving off the same golden glow as her eyes. "Titans . . . grant us all your mercy."

I glanced away. I felt bad admitting it, but I always felt uncomfortable when Lyriana got religious. I knew it was a huge part of her personality, but I never felt more removed from her than when she was praying. I just fundamentally couldn't fathom it. How could she still believe? Especially after everything we'd seen?

Like pretty much everyone in Lightspire, Lyriana had been brought up in the Church of the Titans. Even out in the West, I'd known the story. The Titans were these all-powerful beings who came down from the sky thousands of years ago, back when mankind was still huddled in caves, eating meat raw and wearing furs. The Titans gifted mankind with fire and agriculture, taught us how to build cities and forge metal and all that other stuff. Then, after a century or so, they left, Ascending back into the heavens or wherever they came from. According to the Church, they left their magic Rings behind for the Volaris to find, because of all the people in the world, they trusted that family the most to carry out their Heavenly Mandate: to shepherd and guide mankind, to unite the Kingdom in their holy ways, and to make our species so great that we could join the Titans in their heavenly paradise.

Which . . . okay. I could see how, if all you knew was what the priests taught, you could believe that. But Lyriana knew more than that. She *knew* that the whole Heavenly Mandate thing was a load of horse shit, that the only reason her family had magic was because they lived in a tower with the giant all-powerful magic source that was the Heartstone. She *knew* that the Church was a propaganda tool of the old monarchy, preaching whatever it took to keep her family in power. And she'd been there right by my side when we'd stumbled into that crypt deep below the city, when we'd seen the bodies of Titans all around us: porcelain-skinned giants with rictus smiles, flesh rotting and taut like jerky, deader than dead and very much not Ascended.

And yet here Lyriana still was, eyes closed reverently, hands raised at her sides, a true believer. Tiny lights sparkled out of her fingers, glistening golden orbs that hovered over the fringes of the battlefield like stars. A Lightspire funeral tradition, the ascendance of the souls.

A hand clasped mine, warm and firm. I looked over to see Zell, standing next to me, gazing at Lyriana with . . . respect? He squeezed my hand, and I squeezed his back, and okay, that made being cynical a lot harder. Behind us, Ellarion bowed his head, lips moving as no words came out. Syan didn't pray, I don't think, but she folded her hands together like she did when she was using her zaryas, and let out a sound, a soft singsong exhale, like she was just barely whispering a melody.

My father alone didn't show any emotion, didn't change.

He watched us all, his expression hard, his eyes narrowed in judgment, and then he turned away.

"Grant us strength and fortune as well, blessed Titans," Lyriana said, and the glowing orbs of light flared brighter, twinkling suns dancing as they rose up over our heads. "Grant us the determination to complete our journey, and grant us favor when we stand before the leaders of Benn Devalos. Grant us the powers we need to defeat the forces of the Inquisitor, and the glory to take back your Kingdom." She hesitated for a moment, voice breaking. "And grant me the wisdom I need to mend this broken world."

Something stung at my eyes and I pressed myself into Zell, burying my face in his shoulder. The orbs of light rose higher, higher, growing brighter and brighter, a false sky of stars burning above the blasted landscape and its scattered dead. It was beautiful, even for a cynic like me.

Maybe Lyriana wasn't as hard to understand as I'd thought. Maybe we were more alike than I gave us credit for.

We all had our load-bearing convictions, after all.

TWELVE

SOMEWHERE ALONG THE NEXT FEW DAYS, I STARTED TO GET used to the desert trek. The flat stretches gave way to these beautiful sloping dunes that sparkled gold under the sun and blue under the moon. I got over the sour tang of the cactus water, and I tried one of Syan's fried lizards and was honestly uncomfortable with how good it tasted. That awful aching in my feet didn't go away per se, but it became so overwhelming that my brain just tuned it out, like the sound of rain pouring against your window during a storm.

And there was something else too, something that grew on me more and more, a calm in the solitude. It had been over a week since we'd seen another living soul, a week where the world didn't seem to exist outside the six of us. Out here in the silence, you could almost forget there was a war going on, that Miles sat on the throne of Noveris, that villages were being put to the torch. Out here, you could stare up at the endless sky or marvel at the sloping dunes, and lose your connection to the madness everywhere else. In the emptiness, I actually started to feel peace.

I think the others did, too. My father went whole days without speaking, lost in his own thoughts. Lyriana smiled more, especially when she was talking to Syan. And while Ellarion kept up his practicing, the desperation was gone, replaced with something else, something approaching hope.

I watched him one night as the sun set, standing at the camp's edge with Syan behind him. Her zaryas lay flat on a mat a few feet in front of him, and he stood in that rigid pose, his removed hands resting at his feet, his wrists crossed across his chest, breathing slow, long, and deep.

"Feel the fire circling the zaryas," Syan said, gently pressing a hand to Ellarion's back. "Feel the fire within you." Her voice was low, calm, soothing, the way someone talks when lulling a baby to sleep.

"I feel it," Ellarion whispered. A single sweat drop streaked down his cheek. "I feel the fire. I can see them. So clear. Blue and red and crimson. I *see* them circling the zaryas. I see . . . so clearly . . ."

"Then reach out to them with your heart," Syan whispered. "Bend those flames to your passion. Bend those flames to your soul. Bend them to the zaryas, and make them your own!"

Ellarion sucked in his breath, and I kind of did, too. I couldn't actually see the bands or flames or whatever, but his gaze was so intense, his eyes so bright, that I almost felt like I would, any second now. The air seemed to tighten, drawing around us, and there was that crackle, that hum of magic. I stared at the zaryas, waiting, watching, hoping so badly they would move.

There was a scraping noise, like something metallic pushing against earth, and I gasped, because was it really happening? But then I realized the zaryas were still lying still. No, there was something else moving on the ground. Ellarion's bronze hands twitched at his feet, the index fingers drawing lines in the sand.

He sighed, deflated, and the sense of magic vanished as quickly as it had come. "Damn it," he said.

"You're still trying to use your hands," Syan said, head cocked to the side at the prosthetics.

"I'm not *trying* to," Ellarion insisted. "It's just... instinctive. It's what my body wants to do. It's what I spent decades learning to do. It's how I—" He cut himself off, shaking his head. "Doesn't matter. I'm getting closer. This time, I almost did it. I swear I felt it. I almost made it work, I really did." He turned to Syan, and he was so achingly vulnerable it made my heart ache. "Please. I'm telling you. I'm close. I can feel it. Don't give up on me."

"I promised I would try to teach you," Syan said. "I won't give up now."

Ellarion nodded, then, with one more heavy breath, scooped up his hands. "My turn at watch. I'll be on that dune." It wasn't actually his turn, I don't think, but I got that he needed some space. I was about to head off to get a little space of my own when I heard Lyriana clear her throat from somewhere nearby.

I turned around to see her sitting on a rock behind us. I hadn't realized she was watching too, but Lyriana had a way of sneaking up like that. "Thank you, Syan," she said. "Thank you for everything."

Syan let out a weary exhale of her own, and walked

over to sit by Lyriana's side. "I just wish I could do more for him."

"You're doing so much."

Syan shook her head. "It's not working. He tries so hard and wants it so badly, but there's just nothing. No connection to the zaryas." She folded her hands together, cracking her knuckles with her palms. "Your magic and mine, they're just too different. It's like teaching a fish to fly."

"Maybe it's just enough that he's trying," I said. "Enough that he has hope."

Lyriana shifted in her seat, sliding over to face Syan. "Is it acceptable for you to teach him your ways? Will your people be mad when they learn?"

Syan stared at her, confused, like this had never occurred to her. "There's no rules against it. I mean, there's no rules about it at all. I don't think any Person of the Storm has tried it before." She thought about it for a moment, then sighed. "My mother will probably object. Once she knows."

"Your mother?"

"Syan Sellara of Benn Devalos, Torchbearer, Greatest of the Elders." Syan's gaze was distant, troubled. "She is a . . . stern woman. Passionate. Strong-headed."

"Greatest of the elders . . ." Lyriana repeated. "Is she in charge of your people?"

"A council of elders presides over my benn. My city," Syan clarified. "But yes. My mother sits at the center of the council. Her voice resolves all disagreements."

"So she's a Queen." Lyriana struggled, and failed, to keep herself from smiling. "And you're a Princess!"

"No, I . . . That's not a term we use . . ."

"Do you struggle with the expectations your mother's put

on you? Do you have trouble sleeping when you think about all the decisions you'll have to make? Do you hate how everyone looks at you like you're some kind of glowing magical creature? Do you wish, all the time, that you could just be a normal girl, even for a day?"

Syan stared at Lyriana, orange eyes wide. "Yes. Yes, to all of that."

"Mmhmm." Lyriana grinned. "You're totally a Princess. Same as me."

"If you insist," Syan said, but she glanced away with a little smile, and was she actually . . . shy? What was *happening* here?

"I'm serious, Syan," Lyriana insisted. "I know we're really different, but ever since we met, I've just felt like . . . like I don't know. Like there's something connecting us. Like you understand me. This makes *so* much sense."

"I've felt the same way," Syan said quietly, and I could see her eyes light on Lyriana's tattoo. "I think we were fated to meet. To bring our people together."

"It's what your people dreamed of."

I expected that to make Syan smile, but for some reason, she looked away with an odd, guilty look. "Lyriana, there's so much I haven't told you," she said. "My people can be . . . I mean . . . I can't promise they'll understand. And if they don't . . ."

"They will," Lyriana said. "Because you do. And if you and I can come together like this, to join our flames like we did at the river, then our people can, too." She stared at Syan, her eyes big and earnest, sparkling gold. "I believe in us. I believe in *you*."

Syan turned back to Lyriana and now her eyes were glistening too, and was that a tear running down her cheek? There was something happening here, something I was missing, but something very real and powerful all the same. "Lyriana," Syan said and as she reached out to touch her arm, the streaks in her hair burned a sudden vibrant blue, so bright it lit up the night around us, brighter than the brightest torch, and the energy humming around us was so strong and electric I could feel it in my teeth and my bones and my thundering heart.

Syan jerked back, surprised, and all that magic blinked out instantly. "I'm sorry," she said. "I didn't mean to . . . I shouldn't have drawn from you like that."

"It's fine," Lyriana said, even though she looked a little flushed. She stood up, adjusting her shirt, averting her gaze. "I should go. To bed. You know. For rest."

She left, and Syan did too, and I just sat there alone, trying to figure out what in the frozen hell had just happened. Whatever it was, I was grateful to be out here alone.

So of course, as the sun set, we ran into a bunch of people.

We huddled down on the top of a cresting dune, gazing down through our spyglasses at a caravan. To the naked eye, the other travelers were just tiny specs on the horizon, a huddle of little black dots in a wide stretch between two hills, but through the spyglass I could make out more details: big brightly painted wagons, sleek brown horses with beautiful black manes, the bustle of at least a dozen people setting up for the night. Two men hoisted up heavy tarp tents. A couple women built a deep fire pit, while a few others laid out big strips of meat. I'm pretty sure there was even a child, a little boy running circles around the perimeter.

My stomach growled, and my back sent a highly suggestive ache. Sleeping in a real camp would be *nice*.

"Well, they're not soldiers." Zell squinted through his spyglass by my side. "Only one of them looks armed, the bald guy hanging around the back. Probably a hired guard."

"Refugees, maybe?" Lyriana speculated.

Ellarion shook his head. "Awfully well-provisioned for that. I'm thinking merchants or vagabonds."

"Does it matter who they are?" I asked. "Isn't the real question what we're going to do?"

"Their campsite is a problem," Zell said. "If we want to march far enough out so they won't see us, it'll cost us half a day, easy."

"You said they had horses, right?" my father asked. He was the only one of us without a spyglass, seated cross-legged on the dune's slope. "We could really use some of those."

Lyriana shot him a glare that could freeze a volcano. "Titans restrain me, if you're suggesting we rob these people . . ."

"I will take no part in this," Syan added, her voice a dagger's edge. "The law of my people forbids banditry. Try to harm them, and I *will* stop you."

My father looked from one girl to the other, then shrugged. "Merely making an observation."

"So then we avoid them," Zell said. "We'll move at night, when they're less likely to see us. Take a long path around the valley."

Zell kept talking, but I barely heard him, because I was staring at something though my spyglass, trying to make sense of it. It was at the edge of the strangers' camp, near one of the men, a beefy Heartlander with an open shirt and billowing pants. He had something in his hand, something that was sparkling really bright, a hot white glint almost blinding to look at . . .

The lens of a spyglass.

"Ahoy!" he shouted, his voice echoing over the dunes. "Fellow travelers! We bear you no harm! Come, share our bread and wine, and grant us the gift of company!"

Ellarion jerked up, slamming his spyglass shut, as if that would do any good now. "Shit. So much for avoiding them."

"Should we flee?" Lyriana asked, already in motion.

Syan shook her head. "No fleeing a horse in the desert."

"Um, guys?" I cut in. "I realize this might sound kind of out there . . . but that guy said they have bread *and* wine." Everyone turned to stare at me. "I mean, they seem friendly, right? And if we can't outrun them anyway, what other choice do we have?"

"You want to take him up on his offer?" Ellarion said "No. Too dangerous. What if they recognize us?"

"I don't think they will," Lyriana said, scanning our group. "We don't exactly look like ourselves."

She had a point. The journey had taken its toll on us, and I'm pretty sure we just looked like a random band of drifters. Zell and Ellarion both sported long hair and messy beards. My father was working a mad-hermit look. Even Lyriana's radiance was dulled, her skin cracked from the dry winds, her short hair tangled. Our clothes were tattered, our bodies bruised. Maybe it was just wishful thinking, but I couldn't imagine anyone looking at us and seeing a band of fugitive nobles.

"Did I mention we have wine?" the burly guy shouted.

"We'll make something up about who we are," I said. "If things go well, we can eat some good food and have a drink, maybe buy some of those horses off them. And if it doesn't, Lyriana can do some awesome magic thing, and we can escape. It's worth a shot, right?"

Lyriana nodded, as did Zell, and Syan gave a little shrug. Ellarion stretched and groaned, the way he always did when he was agreeing to a bad idea. "Fine. But let me do all the talking. It's the one thing I'm still pretty good at." Then he turned, shouting down to the figures on the horizon. "We accept your offer, travelers! We shall join you shortly!"

We got ready as quickly as we could. We took most of our weapons and wrapped them up in a sheet, hiding them in Zell's big pack. Lyriana tucked her Rings into her pockets. Syan pulled her hood up over her head, hiding her face in its shadow, as if that mattered.

My father cleared his throat. "Not to be demanding, but I think these might raise some questions." He held out his hands, showing us the heavy iron manacles on his wrists, the chain dangling between them.

We all looked among ourselves uneasily, then Lyriana let out a long, irritated sigh. "You try anything, Kent . . . *anything* . . . and I'll kill you on the spot."

My father nodded. "Understood."

Lyriana reached out a hand, whispering under her breath, as the air around her hand pulsed with a hidden heat, like the surface of a road on a hot day. The manacles glowed bright, then crumbled into brittle chunks and fell to the desert floor. I winced at the sight of my father's wrists: raw and bloody, the flesh ground away, two bands of oozing wounds. He held them out to Lyriana questioningly, and she just turned her back on him.

Ice. Cold.

With all that settled, we headed down into the clearing between the dunes. The big guy, who I'm guessing was the leader of the caravan, was already walking our way. He was a Heartlander, his skin almost as dark as a Volaris', with his hair hanging down his back in long beaded ropes and his bare chest covered in curly black hairs. The two women flanking him were Southlanders, slim women in tight robes with their bald heads glistening in the light of the sun. And the man behind them, the hired guard, was an Easterner, a Sparran I think, his face painted white with golden serpents around his eyes and a scimitar at his hips. "Greetings, companions!" the Heartlander shouted, voice booming over the desert sprawl. "Well met!"

Ellarion led our company toward him, and clasped the man's hand in greeting. "Well met, indeed!" Ellarion said, and was he actually doing a voice? Like kind of a gruff sailor voice, I guess, a rumbling baritone? Was this how he thought all commoners sounded?

Why did we let him do the talking again?

"My companions and I have fallen on rough times," Ellarion went on, and yup, he was definitely doing a voice. "How lucky we are to encounter your caravan!"

"Lucky you are indeed!" The big man grinned, several of his teeth shining gold. "I am Varyn Magsend, and you have the pleasure of meeting the Jolly Company, the greatest vagabond troupe on the continent!"

Vagabonds, then. Traveling entertainers who roamed from inn to inn, performing songs and dances and plays for anyone willing to toss them gold. As far as people to run into in the middle of the desert, we could've done a lot worse.

"I am the leader of this merry group," Varyn went on. "These two beautiful visions are the Lyo Sisters, the greatest acrobats you'll ever meet. The muscled gentleman behind me is our protection, Pattos Sel Tyn Dee, and though he'll never admit it, he has a truly magnificent singing voice." The guard rolled his eyes. "In the camp, you'll find all manner of wondrous entertainers. We have actors, jugglers, singers, dancers . . . and cooks." He must have seen our eyes light up, because he let out a booming laugh. "I take it that holds some appeal."

"It's been a while since we've eaten well," I admitted.

"If I may ask, what brings you out our way? Not many people travel this part of the Southlands."

I winced, half expecting Ellarion to say something like *Oh, you know how we poors are, can't read a map to save our lives.* But when he spoke, it was actually pretty convincing. "My name is Jerrald Taye, and this is my sister Mara." He waved at Lyriana, who blinked, then curtsied. "We were leading a merchant train to deliver our goods to Tau Lorren. We'd hoped to cut through these lands here to avoid any trouble, but alas, found ourselves caught in the middle of battle." He let out an only slightly melodramatic sigh. "Our little band is all that remains."

Varyn spit angrily into the sand. "This war ruins everything."

"What kind of merchant train has Zitochi and Westerners?" Pattos, the armed guard, grumbled, resting one hairy hand on a scimitar's hilt. "I don't trust this."

"We specialize in goods from all over the Kingdom," Ellarion quickly cut in. "Celyse sells the greatest redwood stock of the whole West." I guess that was me, so I nodded. "Zayn is a nightglass merchant from the Zitochi tundra. And this Red Waster . . ."

"My name is Cella Cae," Syan said calmly, without even the slightest hint she was lying. "I sell candles."

Well . . . okay.

"What about him?" Pattos jerked his head at my father. "What's his deal?"

"Celyse's poor uncle Gregory," Ellarion said, shaking his head with deep distress. "He barely survived the battle. Lost both his sons. Hasn't spoken a word since. We suspect he's been rendered mute. Isn't that right, *Gregory*?"

My father nodded.

Against all odds, Varyn seemed to buy it. "Sounds like you've all been through a lot. All the more reason to welcome you to our camp for the night."

"I'm afraid we don't have much to pay you with," Lyriana said, and, like, why bring that up?

Varyn just shrugged. "The only payment we need is your company." He reached out, clasping a hand around her shoulder, and I wonder what he'd say if he knew he was touching the Queen of Noveris. "Come! Come! Dinner is almost ready!"

It might have just been the hunger or the exhaustion or the sheer relief at eating something that wasn't dried and/or lizard. But the dinner we had there was the single best meal of my life.

They laid out a row of soft cushions for us by a roaring fire, and we all huddled together, the six of us, as the company's cooks brought out an incredible assortment of Southlands cuisine. There were roasted goat skewers, topped with just the right amount of spice and dipped in a tangy mint sauce. There was a creamy milk soup with chunks of potato, and bowls of seasoned rice. There were plates of fruits I'd never seen before, yellow pears covered in spikes and furry green apples with a surprisingly tart kick. And there was the dessert, Sinners'

Secrets, the flaky sugar-coated cubes full of cherry jam and rosewater liquor, my literal favorite thing in the world, ever. Oh, the Sinners' Secrets.

A reasonable person would've paced herself, knowing that after weeks of lean eating, she should go easy. I was not a reasonable person, so I gorged myself on every single delicious thing and then lay there, slumped against Zell, rubbing my incredibly full stomach. Next to me, Lyriana nibbled delicately on a long green fruit, while Syan slurped down her third bowl of soup. My father sat behind us, legs crossed, eating his rice in silence. For better or worse, he was playing along with Ellarion's ruse.

The vagabonds hustled all around us, practicing their arts and enjoying the cool night air. The acrobat sisters did handstands and contortions, climbing up one another in a form that seemed almost like a dance. A big bearded Southlander worked on his juggling; he could toss four daggers, easy, but as soon as he added a fifth, they came crashing down, making me wince every time. Three young people who I'm guessing were actors sat in a huddle, poring over pages of a script. And Varyn managed it all, flitting from group to group, before eventually wandering our way.

"I see my honored guests have eaten well!" He beamed, taking a seat at our fire. "You really must have been on the road a long time."

"We cannot thank you enough for your generosity," Lyriana said. "May the Titans bless you and your company."

Varyn waved her off. "Vagabonds rely on the kindness of strangers. It's only fair that we offer the same."

"If I may ask, what are you doing out around these parts?" Ellarion said, still chewing a hunk of goat.

Varyn glanced around, then leaned in. "In truth? We're hoping to find someone to get us across the Adelphus, so that we can tour around the Heartlands."

Ellarion blinked. "That seems awfully dangerous, with the war and all."

"Times of war are when vagabonds are most needed," Varyn replied with a shrug. "We bring light in the darkness, a night of happiness in a season of pain. What we do isn't just a pleasure. It's an obligation." He looked back at his company with a smile. "Heartlander, Southlander, Westerner, Zitochi. Everyone needs joy in their life."

"I'll drink to that," Zell said.

"Is that your way of sending me a hint?" Varyn shot him a sly grin, then reached into a pack at his side. He drew out a glass bottle full of a pale green liquid, and popped the cork. "It's your lucky day, my Zitochi friend."

He tossed Zell the bottle, and Zell sniffed it suspiciously. "What is it?"

"The Green Dream," Varyn said. "There's a tree that grows in scattered groves throughout the Southlands, nourished by underground streams, a tree that flowers with succulent green berries. Properly fermented, they make the finest liquor in the entire continent."

"It smells strange. Sour," Zell said, still wary, and shot me an uncertain glance. I mean, on the one hand, we were on a journey to save the kingdom, trying to keep up a complicated lie while surrounded by at least a dozen strangers. On the other hand, I *really* wanted a drink. I looked to Ellarion for guidance, and I could practically see the gears in his head whirring as he tried to decide the best course of action.

Then Syan reached over, took the bottle from Zell's

hands, and took a long swig. She slumped back in her seat, a grin slowly spreading across her face, and handed it over to Ellarion. "Trust me. You'll want to drink this."

So we drank, one by one, passing the bottle back and forth. I don't know if I'd call it the *best* drink I'd ever had (some of those Lightspire wines were hard to top), but it tasted pretty damn good, like lemonade with a kick. I'm guessing it was stronger than it tasted, because after my second drink I felt a warm blossoming glow in my stomach, tingling all the way to my fingertips, and a resounding conviction that what I really needed was more.

The night got a lot hazier after that.

I can vaguely remember songs and jokes and music, and the actors of the company performing a rough version of their latest play. I remember the warmth of the drink and the dancing shapes in the fire. I remember glancing back at my father, who was still watching the whole thing in silence, and wanting to talk to him but also wanting to never talk to him again, my thoughts a tangled mess.

Also I think I maybe puked on a cactus?

My next, clearest memory came from later in the night, when the sky was totally dark and the canopy of stars sparkled overhead. I was resting by the fire, sobering up against Zell's chest, with Lyriana and Syan on either side of me. There was music playing, a pair of strumming guitars and a jangling flute, and in the main sprawl of the camp, encircled by the wagons, people were dancing. Most of the company was up on their feet, twirling and clapping and laughing. Varyn was there, feet springing here and there in a wild jig, and the little boy and the acrobat sisters and the actors and . . .

Ellarion? Yup, there he was, no doubt, a big drunken grin

on his face as he twirled a buxom young Southlander girl in a circle. I sat up, watching him, and it took my tipsy brain a second to realize what was so weird about him. It's not that he looked different. It's that he looked like he'd used to, like the old Ellarion, the one who'd flirted with every girl in Lightspire, the one who'd strutted through the city like he owned every inch of it.

"He looks so happy," Lyriana said, obviously on the same wavelength. She was wobbling a little, the way she always did when she was drunk, and it was adorable. "I haven't seen him smile like that in months. . . ."

"I haven't seen him *flirt* like that in months," I replied.

"Those are probably related," Zell said from behind me. His cheeks were flushed red, and his mouth bent in a tiny smile. "Good for him."

There was a boisterous shout from the circle, and now Ellarion was dancing with a different girl, an older woman with graying hair, and everyone was clapping and laughing. Behind me, Zell shifted, and I leaned back into him, feeling the softness of his lips as he leaned over to kiss my forehead. "Do you have anyone special waiting for you back home?" I asked Syan. "A boyfriend or a lover or, I don't know, how do you guys do marriage?"

"No. No one special," Syan said, gazing out at the circle where the first girl Ellarion had danced with was smiling at us. "But my people treat marriage differently than you stillanders. All marriages are arranged by the Kindler, a wise woman who matches children up to best combine families for the good of the benn. When a person turns twenty, the Kindler presents them with three options, and they choose the one they like best. It is all very structured."

"Oh," I said. I knew intellectually it'd probably be rude to question her further, but, counterpoint, I was drunk. "But what if you don't love any of the three of them? Aren't you just, like, unhappy for the rest of your life?"

"Love like that has nothing to do with marriage," Syan explained. "Marriage only determines your home and your line of succession. If you love your spouse, then that is very fortunate. But if you do not, then you find that passion with others, as you see fit." She paused, considering her words, like she was worried about offending *us*. "The People of the Storm do not believe in owning a body the way stillanders do. Every Person is a free soul, and should not be bound, not by law, not by force. Marriage determines the home. But the spirit and the body will always be free."

I was struggling to follow. "So like . . . everyone just has lovers?"

"If that's how you choose to understand it," Syan said. "Everyone is different. Some have one companion they spend their time with, like you stillanders. Others, like my mother, prefer . . . what's your word? Flungs?"

"Flings."

"Flings," Syan repeated, then rose to her feet, adjusting her robe as she paced toward the camp's center. "I like this melody. I think I'll go dance now."

"And I think I need some sleep." Lyriana yawned big. "Before I embarrass myself any further."

Behind me, Zell rose, and extended me a hand. "I think I'll go for a walk. Would you care to join me?"

I glanced back to where my father lay on his side, asleep, then took Zell's hand in mine. I felt the warmth of his skin and the cold chill of his nightglass. "I'd love that."

We walked for fifteen minutes, maybe, just far enough to round the edge of a dune, and then collapsed into each other, hungry, desperate, tumbling into the sand. I ripped his shirt off, running my hands along his scarred chest, and he kissed his way all along me, my neck, my collarbone, my arms, my thighs. We hadn't made love like this in ages, frantic, playful, laughing as we nibbled each other, breathing deep as our bodies burned against the desert's cool sands.

Afterward, we lay together, naked, staring up at the wide expanse of stars overhead. The din of the camp was finally dying down, the boisterous music down to a single mellow singer, the voices all quiet. Zell kissed me, again and again, and I held him so close it hurt.

"This is what I want," I whispered, tracing my fingertips through the soft hairs on his stomach. "Just this. Forever. I could be happy with that."

Zell craned his head to me, and all I wanted was for him to say the same thing, that he could be happy with this, too. "I love you so much" was all he said.

"Not too late to run away, you know. We could just stay out here, the two of us, under the stars."

"You know I couldn't do that."

I sighed. "I know. But at least we have tonight."

He pulled me close. "At least we have tonight."

THIRTEEN

I WOKE UP THE NEXT MORNING WITH MY HEAD POUNDING so badly it felt like my brain was trying to force its way out of my eyes. The sun above was viciously bright, and I scrambled up, covering my face, moaning. I'm not going to say it was the worst hangover anyone has ever had. But I'm not *not* going to say that.

I'd passed out lying next to Zell, who was still sound asleep on the desert sand. That had seemed like a great idea the night before but now I felt super-exposed. I pulled my clothes on (and threw Zell's vaguely on top of him, covering up what I could), then staggered my way back toward the camp. I needed water, a pillow, and a dark tent to collapse in. Not necessarily in that order.

The camp was mostly still when I arrived. Smoke waved over ash pits, filling the air with that crisp morning-after-a-fire smell. Relics of the night before were scattered everywhere: empty bottles, picked-over skewers, Ellarion snoring on a rock. Not far from him were the mats laid out for us, and I could see my father asleep on one, curled onto his side. There was something weird about seeing him like this, something exposed and vulnerable. In that morning light, he looked *human*, just a regular person.

One of the tents on the far side of the camp wobbled as the flap opened. Syan crawled out, her robe loosely pulled around her body, her hair messy and uncombed. She pulled herself up to her feet, and through the open flap behind her I could see someone else sleeping in the tent: the Southlander girl from the night before, the one who'd smiled at us, naked and content.

Well.

Okay then.

Syan closed the flap behind her, then made her way through the camp, shielding her eyes from the sun with her hand. She dug around in her pack until she found a water-skin, then slumped down in the sand and chugged. I flopped down at her side.

"So . . ." I said, glancing at the tent she'd come from.

"So," she replied and handed me the skin.

The morning dragged on, hot, bright, and languid. Slowly the camp woke up, as vagabonds gathered to clean and pack for their journey. They brought us a breakfast of bread and honey, which was pretty much all I could handle. Zell came over, still shirtless. Ellarion spent half an hour trying to find his left boot. Lyriana futzed about, helping the vagabonds (even when they politely insisted she not). The Southlander girl emerged from her tent and waved flirtatiously at Syan, who bashfully glanced away.

A little before noon, we were ready to part ways. The vagabonds had packed up their camp amazingly (it defied all reason how they fit all that stuff into a pair of wagons), and our little band was up and dressed. My hangover had receded to merely painful, so I made my way toward the edge of their wagon train, where Lyriana and Ellarion were saying their good-byes to Varyn Magsend.

"I cannot possibly thank you enough," Lyriana said. "Your hospitality . . . it meant everything."

"Nah! It is I who should be thanking you!" Varyn boomed. "There is no greater blessing than the company of new friends. Which is why I'd like to offer you this gift." He paused, drawing out the moment, because I don't think he was capable of doing anything without dramatic flair. "Three fine horses, to hasten your journey!"

"What?" Ellarion said, but there was Pattos, the hired guard, leading a trio of beautiful brown beasts our way, their eyes soft, their noses snuffling. My aching feet cried out in relief at the sight of them. I've never wanted a horse more.

"Oh, no, we couldn't possibly take these!" Lyriana said, and I almost slugged her.

"I'm not giving you a choice," Varyn replied, his voice firm despite his smile. "The desert is vast and cruel, and I could not possibly let you and your companions wander it on foot. If something were to happen, the Titans would curse me forever."

I could see Lyriana calculating the rules of etiquette, and saw the exact moment she gave up. "Thank you so much, Varyn. I will always, *always*, remember this."

"And I will always remember you." Varyn took Lyriana's hand in his, raised it to his lips, and ever so slightly bowed his head. "Your Majesty."

We all froze staring at each other. Was this good? Bad?

How long had he known? How had he known? How could he have not known? My eyes flitted from Ellarion to Lyriana, but they looked as stunned as I felt. "I . . . I don't know what you mean . . ." Lyriana stammered, uselessly.

"The errant word of a loyal subject, nothing more." Varyn turned away. "May your journey be peaceful and prosperous. And may the sun once more rise to a true Volaris on the throne."

Then he was gone, puttering away to bark orders at his companions and load up his wagons.

"Well," I said at last. "Pretty glad we didn't rob them, right?"

So we set off on horseback, me with Zell, Lyriana with Syan, and Ellarion, hilariously, with my father, riding those majestic Southlands horses across the desert. With the freedom of riding came a little more time in each day, time to settle into a routine. In the mornings, we kept busy around camp, gathering prickleberries or drawing water. Sometimes Zell and I would spar, mostly out of habit; other days, we'd break off to hunt, and I'm proud to say I managed to catch a grand total of seven lizards and one weird hairless thing Lyriana called a sand-hare.

In the nights, we'd make camp and huddle around a fire, eating whatever meager meal we'd scraped together, and then we'd tell stories. I can't remember how we'd gotten started doing that, but it became habit quickly enough, a way to kill time in those lonely dunes. Lyriana recited histories of the Volaris, from the great Mage-Queen Morella, who traveled the entirety of the Heartlands healing the sick, to the tyrant Ortego, the King so awful he was murdered by his own sons just to keep the people from rioting. Ellarion told hilarious (and almost certainly exaggerated) stories from his youth, like the time he broke into the High Priest's house and tried on his robes, or how he had to flee naked from a professor's house after spending the night with his daughter. Zell went through the parables of the Zitochi, some of which felt staggeringly profound and others I couldn't figure out for the life of me. Syan told us a bunch of Red Waster stories, which were always about animals: the jackal who swallowed the sun, the beetle who yearned to be a man, the snake who burrowed to the center of the world. When it was my turn to talk, I just reenacted my favorite childhood novels as best as I could from memory: Muriel the wanderer, the twins who loved a mountain, and yes, the Princess of Jakar and her flying carpet.

Even my father told a story, just once, late at night in the stillness when we'd all finished. He told us a story from the days of the Old Kings, about a young Western fisherman who was captured by K'olali pirates and forced to be their slave. For years, he worked with them, plundering up and down the shore, and earned their respect for his skill with the sword. He became the captain's favorite slave, given status above most of the other pirates, a cabin of his own, and all the plunder and drink he could ever want. But one day, the pirates sailed back up the coast, to the Westerner's own village, and demanded he help them raid it. He agreed, all up until the last minute, and then he plunged his sword through the captain's heart and took the wheel, crashing the ship against the rocks and killing them all.

Everyone else was listening, gazes rapt, but I just felt cold. "That's not how you told it to me," I said.

My father craned his head my way. "What?"

"When I was a girl. That's not how you told me the story,"

I repeated. I hadn't thought of that story in years, had let it slip deep into the cracks of memory, but him telling it had brought it back up with a surge. I must have been five or six, no older, right around the time he was marrying Lady Yrenwood and getting ready to knock her up with his *real* heirs. We'd taken one of our rides into those foggy redwood forests of my home, down to a blacksand beach. There, by the mostly buried ruins of an ancient Western castle, we'd sat and looked out at the waters as he'd talked. "You told me the fisherman took control of the ship, that he threw the captain overboard and beat all the pirates in a swordfight. That he landed on the shore and his people welcomed him home and he lived happily ever after. The end."

For once, my father looked puzzled. "I told you that?"

"You did."

"Well, that's not the real ending." He looked away, green eyes darting to the fire. "The ship crashing on the rocks . . . that's how it really ended."

"It's so sad," Lyriana said, and then suddenly caught herself, like for just a moment she'd forgotten who my father was. "I mean . . . of *course* you'd tell a story like that," she said, and for the first time, it didn't seem like she really meant it.

After a few days of riding south, we began to turn our horses east, toward the Adelphus River and its fertile shores. With each mile we crossed, the soothing monotony of the desert began to end, and more and more signs of life began to appear around us. Palm trees began to pop up like signposts on the horizon. Spiky little bushes framed tiny ponds, and little foxes with tiny horns nipped playfully at our horses' hooves. Irrigation canals cut through the desert like massive serpents, huge stone tunnels funneling water from the Adelphus. We passed well-trod roads, spotted quiet little villages, and steered clear of processions of travelers, their camels laden heavy with goods.

And then there were the ziggurats. I actually gaped when I saw the first one, a massive building made of carved yellow stone, half-submerged in a dune. It was like the ancient-ruins version of one of those stacked cakes you saw at fancy Lightspire parties, layer atop layer, each smaller than the last, before culminating in a spiral tower at the top. A lot of it had crumbled and the top of the tower was gone, but even from a distance, it was impressive as hell.

"The last remnants of the Old Southlands Empire," Lyriana said, noticing my slack-jawed awe. "Before Lightspire conquered these lands, there were hundreds of ziggurats, maybe thousands. Now there's just ruins."

"Just like the West," my father muttered. "A great Kingdom, and all that's left is crumbled stone."

Ellarion rolled his eyes. "The Southlands Empire was dust before the first pilgrims crossed the Frostkiss Mountains to the West. Your comparison is facile."

"Not to those willing to listen," he said, and his eyes found mine. I looked away, back to that majestic ruined ziggurat, its frame grasping out of the sand like a skeletal hand. And I had to admit I kind of agreed with him.

We rode on. And five weeks after leaving the Unbroken camp, five long aching weeks, we arrived at Tau Lorren.

The city loomed on the horizon from miles away. From a distance, it actually reminded me of Lightspire: I could see big stone walls and domed roofs, hundreds of smoke-stacks and a bustling crowd outside. But the closer we came, the more I could see how different it was. Lightspire had a homogeneity, a certain consistency in its architecture across all the neighborhoods. But Tau Lorren was a chaotic jumble. Some buildings were brick, others stone, and some were this weird glowing green rock. Wide elegant towers stood next to sprawls of thatch-roofed huts. Crumbling ancient walls gave way to newly painted stretches that led to rickety wooden extensions. People bustled about everywhere: on the walls and roofs, lined up around in camps stretching all around the city's walls. Behind the city the Adelphus River roared, teeming with the multicolored sails of hundreds of ships.

And where Lightspire had the Godsblade, jutting out of the heart of the city like a sword driven into the earth, Tau Lorren had the Greatest Ziggurat, an enormous stacked palace that loomed over the rest of the city. It was the capital of the Province, the home of the young Dyn. The absolute last place we wanted to end up.

Getting into the city was actually pretty easy. We pulled our hoods up as we approached and blended into the busy stream of traffic, lost in the crowd of pilgrims and merchants and travelers. There were guards at the gates, of course, tall and armored Southland soldiers who searched wagons and interrogated anyone they thought was suspicious. But we didn't have to worry about them. As we approached the gate we'd chosen, one that was small and out of the way, we dismounted those beautiful horses and left them tied to a post for some lucky person to find. We approached the gate, held hands, and Lyriana cast that Glimmer over us, the one that made us invisible. I worried someone might notice six travelers just disappearing, but the whole line was so loud and chaotic that no one even looked our way.

Lyriana dropped the Glimmer once we were in the city itself, and we reappeared in the safe confines of an alley, behind a tavern that smelled of spiced liquor and sizzling meat. "What now?" Lyriana asked.

"To the southwest of the city is a neighborhood called Wanderer's Garden," Syan said. "That's where we'll find more of my people. They'll be able to give us the supplies we need to head into Izteros." She craned her head, orienting herself by the shape of the Greatest Ziggurat. "If we can get there without being caught, we should be fine."

"That's one big if," Ellarion added. "The Dyn will not take kindly to us being in his city. We need to keep our heads down, move quickly, and not draw any attention." He glanced at me. "No matter how good the meat smells."

"Are you sure this will work?" Lyriana asked Syan.

"No," the Red Waster replied, as if it were a ridiculous question. "I'm just sure that it's our only choice."

On that ominous note, we pulled our hoods back up and took off. Syan led the way, guiding us through the maze that was Tau Lorren. If Lightspire was an ornate garden of a city, meticulously plotted circles within circles within circles, then Tau Lorren was a wild overgrown sprawl. Lightspire had alleys connecting the busy streets, but as far as I could tell, Tau Lorren was *all* alleys, narrow passageways between noisy buildings that jutted at nonsense angles, branched chaotically together, and, at least half the time, led to bricked-over dead ends.

I'd been worried we'd stand out, but that turned out to be a nonissue; the population was mostly Southlanders, sure, but there were plenty of people from other Provinces— Heartlands refugees and Eastern Barony merchants, folks who'd settled here long ago or who'd come fleeing the war.

And the whole place was so loud and chaotic, no one really paid us any mind. It had been ages since I'd blended into a crowd, since I hadn't been "the traitor's daughter" or "the Unbroken fighter" but just another random face.

It was nice being back in a city, nice to be so surrounded by people. The place was packed. Huge crowds bustled everywhere. Merchants hawked wares like fresh fish and glistening fruit. Vagabonds performed on elevated stages. Children splashed around in long stone fountains and leaped daringly from rooftop to rooftop. Little silver cats with useless vestigial wings prowled the dusty floor, their eyes glinting at us from the shadows of the alleys. Southlander youths sat in a schoolhouse, their heads still unshaved, slumped bored at their desks. A fight spilled out from an overflowing tavern, broken up by a pair of soldiers who came running. Under the statue of a Titan, its features decidedly Southlandish, sat a gathering of priests, sitting cross-legged with their eyes shut and hands folded together.

I'm not sure what I'd expected from this place. With all the talk of the war, I think I'd expected something more awful and oppressive, burning buildings and marching soldiers everywhere. But no. For all the conflict to the north, Tau Lorren was still a city at peace, a city where people ate and played and worshipped, a city where life went on as it always had. I thought of that battlefield we'd passed, of the ash fluttering in the air of Torrus. And I prayed to the Old Kings that we'd stop this war before it came here.

"Just a little farther," Syan said. We were deep into the city, close enough to the Greatest Ziggurat that I could make out more details. It was at least seven layers tall, the bottom as wide as a whole castle and the top the size of a house. Its stone was ancient, unbleached, but packed so tight it looked like it'd still be standing a thousand years from now. And there were figures all along it, motionless, standing out in rows along the edges of the levels. I'd thought they were trees or maybe statues, but now I could see that they were soldiers, rigid, spears in one hand and shields in the other. There must have been at least a hundred of them. Did they just stand there like that all day? Was that their job? How many soldiers did this Province have?

We rounded a corner onto a cramped market street. Little shops lined the sides. At the far end, past a wide, round fountain, was a four story building, the biggest in the area. Though the rounded windows I could see kitchens and bedrooms, families making meals and children playing. A housing building then, for many families.

"So, Syan. When we get to this Wanderer's District," Ellarion began, "do you think we could get so—"

But he never got to finish the sentence, because that's when the earthquake hit.

I heard it before I felt it, a booming crash like thunder from below. Then the ground lurched so hard it hurled me off my feet, sending me slamming on my side into the stone. People screamed all around us, as stands collapsed and windows shattered, as trees toppled and stone cracked. This was brutal, the worst earthquake I'd ever felt by far. The ground jerked under me like a bolting horse, tossing me back and forth, skinning my knees and bruising my arm. Dust and sand billowed up all around us, stinging my eyes and clogging my throat. It was less than a minute but it felt like forever.

Then it stopped. I gasped, pulling myself onto all fours,

my heart beating like it was going to burst out of my chest. The roaring had ended, but the other sounds continued, the screaming and the sobbing and the yelling, the howls of a city wounded. Putting a hand over my eyes, I squinted through the cloud of dust, searching for my companions. Zell helped Lyriana up, and my father huddled with Ellarion, a bloody cut in his left arm. Only Syan still stood, her legs locked, her face gritted with determination.

This was bad. This was really bad. But at least we'd all made it.

"Oh no," Lyriana said, her eyes wide with horror. I followed her gaze and I saw it in the clearing dust, that tall building at the market's edge, or what was left of it. The top two stories had collapsed forward, toppling into the street, leaving only a massive pile of rubble and stone, broken up by the remains of what had just been people's homes: chunks of broken furniture, colorful fragments of torn rugs, here and there a stone splattered with red.

Then I heard it. We all did. Voices coming from within that pile of rubble. Howling and moaning and crying.

By the Old Kings. By the Titans. There were survivors in there.

"Help them!" someone screamed. A few people ran forward, burly laborers, scrambling to dig frantically in that pile. For a second I couldn't figure out why they were just doing it with their hands, uselessly tugging on huge hunks of stone, and then the realization hit me like a leaden weight. They didn't have mages out here. This was all they could do.

Lyriana obviously had the same thought. "We have to help them!" she said, rolling up her sleeves.

"No," my father growled, and even reached out to grab

Lyriana's arm. "You do that, you'll draw every guard in the city onto us. We can't get involved!"

"I am not letting them die!" Lyriana jerked her arm away, and there was a surge of energy around her, a crackling rush of air like an electric breeze. Heads swiveled our way and a few people gasped, but it was too late because we'd already crossed the point of no return. Lyriana strode forward, eyes blazing, and wrenched both hands into the air. The top layer of rubble lifted with them, massive stone slabs hovering like leaves on a breeze.

Zell didn't waste a second. He sprang forward, pushed through the crowd, and then he was on the stack, digging through it, hurling aside a broken table to reveal a slumped woman beneath. Ellarion ran after him and Syan did too, and then we were all in it, rifling through debris toward the agonized voices. The Southlander laborers gaped at us but only for a moment; right then, the only thing that mattered was saving as many lives as we could.

I wasn't thinking then, just acting. I grabbed a pillar of stone and pulled on it, even as my palms shrieked in pain. Next to me, Zell was hoisting an injured woman onto his shoulder, and Syan was on her knees, combing through a pile of crushed rock toward a sobbing voice underneath. Lyriana saw me struggling and flicked her wrist my way, lifting the stone up out of my hands and revealing even more debris below. And my father . . .

I'd lost sight of him. I squinted up, but between the billowing dust and the frantic crowd, I didn't know where to begin looking. He was gone. Shit. Shit shit shit! We'd lost him. All that care, all that precaution, and in one moment, we'd gone and lost our most valuable hostage.

And of course he took off now, when we were distracted *saving people*, like the total asshole he always was. He must have just been waiting this whole time, watching for the perfect moment, and now he was gone, gone like—

"Tilla!" Ellarion's scream jerked me out of my thoughts. I spun around to see him standing over a wide wooden beam on a heap of rubble, glaring down furiously at his left hand. It was twitching weirdly, the metal fingers contracting and clenching like he was playing an invisible guitar. "It's not working!" he yelled at me, eyes scorching out of his skull. "I think I got something caught in the gears! I need your help! Now!"

I followed his gaze down at his feet, below the wooden beam, and underneath it I saw a tiny arm, a kid's arm, jutting out against the stone. Before I could think, before I could breathe, I was over by his side, both arms hooked around the beam, straining, pulling, lifting as hard as I could. My muscles throbbed and my back flared and I could feel the splintered wood tearing into my palms, but all that just made me pull harder. The beam budged a little, just a little, and I could see underneath it, could see the tiny child (still moving, still moving!) trapped below.

Then someone was alongside me, hunched down, holding the beam with two arms and lifting with a low guttural grunt. Messy long hair. A tall lanky build. And furious sparkling green eyes.

My father.

I didn't ask or question or even think. I just gritted my teeth and strained and together the two of us jerked that heavy beam up and shoved it aside, sending it clattering down the side of the debris pile like a log rolling down a hillside.

I staggered back, hands bleeding, muscles burning, and my father knelt down and grabbed the child. She was a little girl, maybe five years old, in a loose tan dress blackened with dirt, her eyes lidded, her skin bruised and cut. My father scooped her up in his arms and pulled her out of the rubble, slumping back down. She was breathing, thank the Old Kings, and she coughed, and he slumped back, cradling her close to his chest.

She reached up with a tiny hand, placing it on his cheek.

And even in the chaos of the moment, as the city howled and the streets burned and the air hung heavy with smoke and ash and the crackle of magic, I felt this sudden stillness, this second of calm. I looked at my father holding this little girl, saw his eyes widen with tenderness and surprise, saw him press her against his chest.

"Shhh," he whispered, his voice softer than I'd heard it in a decade. "It's okay. It's okay. You're okay."

There were tears in his eyes.

Tears.

"None of you move!" an accented voice barked, perfectly shattering that second of calm. "Hands in the air! Now!"

I'd been so focused on lifting that beam, I'd lost sight of the world outside this crumbled building. The crowd had dissipated. The dust had cleared. And surrounding us from all sides were Southlander soldiers, their long flat spear-blades sparkling as they leveled them our way. I threw my hands up instinctively, as did Ellarion and Syan. Only my father remained still, but he had an injured child in his hands, and I'm pretty sure the soldiers knew better than to mess with that.

"You too, *mage*," one of the soldiers growled, swiveling his spear to jab the point at Lyriana. He was a big guy, stocky, his bald head covered in jagged tattoos. The commander, I'm guessing.

Lyriana's eyes flicked toward him, still glowing bright. She could crush him with a flick of her wrist, could bring the earth smashing down around every one of his soldiers, could get us all out of here before anyone even blinked.

But she didn't, because she wouldn't, because spears or not, these were just Southlands soldiers doing their job. The glow faded from her eyes, and she folded her hands together behind her head.

"We surrender."

FOURTEEN

THE SOLDIERS BOUND OUR HANDS IN FRONT OF US (SO MUCH for Lyriana's magic) and marched us through the city, past gawking crowds and distracted rescue workers, to the steps at the bottom of the Greatest Ziggurat. And then they marched us up them. It had looked like a lot of steps from a distance, but let me tell you, it was a *lot* of steps walking up. Especially because they took us all the way to the top.

The Greatest Ziggurat was basically a palace, with most of the levels made up of things like dining halls and nobles' quarters and big fancy baths. The very top level was the throne room, the Dyn's Chamber. From the outside, it wasn't particularly impressive: a big block of ancient yellow stone maybe two stories tall, its walls smooth and undecorated. But as they shoved us in, through a rounded, carved arch, I realized the simplicity was probably the point.

We Westerners liked to decorate our Halls with tapestries and fancy chandeliers, and the rich folks in Lightspire couldn't build a bathroom without throwing in a fancy golden filigree and some shimmersteel. But the chamber of the Dyn was plain, aggressively plain, so plain it actively made you admire its emptiness. The towering walls, the ceiling, the floor were all bare stone. So the only thing you could look at, the only thing you *had* to look at, was the Dyn of the Southlands, Rulys Cal himself.

Cal sat on a throne made of yellowish-orange sandstone, so impeccably polished it looked smooth as glass, with his feet resting in a small inlaid water basin at his feet. He was younger than I was expecting, in his early twenties maybe, with smooth bronze skin and sharp, lean features. He was dressed simply: a white, almost-translucent robe that gave way to a wrapped skirt, leather sandals, and at least four golden rings on each hand. Most notable of all was his hair. Every other man in the Southlands shaved his head bald, but Cal had beautiful long black hair, a serpentine ponytail that stretched down to his waist, clasped tight every fistful or so with a jade bracelet.

His soldiers shoved us forward at spearpoint, driving us all the way up to the throne. Cal didn't even look up (which, ultimate power move). He just rifled through a little serving bowl beside his table, piled high with fruit. "Ellarion Volaris. Queen Lyriana Volaris. And unless I'm mistaken, the bearded gentleman is none other than the former King Elric Kent himself. Which I'll admit is quite the surprise because all three of you are supposed to be dead." He plucked a juicy-looking pear out of the bowl and wiped it against his robe. "They say it's a great misfortune to see a ghost. I can't imagine what it means to see three at once."

Ellarion took point. "Great Dyn," he said. "I suspect there

has been a misunderstanding. We are but a group of humble travelers en route to—"

"Oh, stop it," Cal said, his voice a blade, and now his eyes finally flicked up to us: narrow, intense, the irises brown flecked with blue. "Bad enough you lost your hands, but you've apparently lost your sense, too. I know who you are, you simpleton. Lie to me again, and I'll start executing you one by one."

Ellarion looked like he was going to say something, then thought better of it and backed down. That left Lyriana to talk. "Great Dyn, I apologize for my cousin's attempt at deceit. He was merely trying to protect me." She bowed her head, something I'd never seen her do before. I guess the situation really was that desperate. "Your words are true. We are who you say we are."

"Well, of course." Cal reached down into his robe and drew out a little paring knife. Its handle was jade, its blade not even two inches long, but there was something menacing about it all the same. "Now perhaps you'd like to tell me what you're doing skulking about my Kingdom?"

"We came to seek an alliance with you, Great Dyn," Ellarion tried again. "Together, we can stand against our common enemy, the Inquisitor Hampstedt."

"And you sought to do that by sneaking into my city?" Cal sliced off a strip of the pear's skin. "Another lie which makes you officially more trouble than you're worth." He jabbed his knife in the air at Ellarion. "Kill him."

The soldiers drew back their spears and I lunged forward, bolting up to my feet, the words bursting out of my mouth. "No! Wait! I'll tell you the truth! We're just passing through to get to the Red Wastes!"

Cal raised his hand, and the guards stopped, the points just a few inches from the base of Ellarion's spine. "And why, pray tell, would you possibly be going there?"

Ellarion shot me a glare and Syan dropped her head, but we were past the point of trying anything clever. "They have mages. Really powerful ones, like Syan here. We're hoping we can convince them to join our cause."

Cal stopped, considering, his eyes boring a hole clear through me. "Well, that must be the truth, because I can't imagine anyone would come up with that ridiculous a lie." He cut the pear again, slicing off a long strip of skin. "So the brutal little Inquisitor sits alone on the throne, and the great fallen royals come to beg the help of the Red Waster mages. Things truly have gotten desperate up north."

"You know of our mages?" Syan asked.

"It appears everyone on this continent thinks me a fool." Cal rolled his eyes. "Your people have a whole neighborhood in my city. Of course I've heard rumors of your mages, capable of great and terrible things. And every spy I sent south to look into it never came back, which all but confirms it as true."

"Then you understand why we're here!" Lyriana exclaimed. "You can help us."

Cal didn't seem to be in a helping mood. "I understand that you seek to reclaim your throne without even considering the army actually fighting the usurper who sits in it. And I find myself wondering why that is."

"Your *army* needs every bit of help they can get," Ellarion growled. "Or do you not know what's happening out on your border? Miles's soldiers have pushed into your Province and are making their way here right now."

"It's my Kingdom, not my Province," Cal sharply

corrected. "And I know exactly where Miles's army is. They get exactly as far as I let them. Given that they're only fighting a third of my forces, I consider it impressive how we've held them thus far."

"Only a third of your forces . . ." Ellarion repeated with dawning understanding. "Then the rest are . . ."

"Marching on Lightspire." Cal smiled. "They crossed the Western Branch of the Adelphus three weeks ago. While Miles squanders his men slogging through desert and hunting your little rebellion, the real threat flies toward him like a spear. By the end of the month, they'll be setting Lightspire to siege." He flicked his wrist, sending the last strip of pear skin onto the floor. "Didn't see that coming, did you? No, you never could."

Lyriana stood there, struggling for words, and Ellarion looked toward the floor. A part of me was thrilled, because uh, a full-blown army attacking Miles was unquestionably a good thing. But that left the six of us here with even less to offer.

None of us seemed to know what to say, so my father rose up. "Great Dyn, if I may . . ."

Cal had been doing a great job seeming cool and indifferent, but my father's voice cracked that facade. His jaw clenched and his nostrils flared, just a tiny bit. I could see it now, the hate and fury, burning with him. "I ought to slit your throat here and now, Kent," he said. "But I'm feeling generous. Speak."

"Your army might catch Miles by surprise, but they'll never take the city," he said bluntly. "When you declared war, Miles and I spent weeks preparing the city for every eventuality. Including a full-scale siege by *all* of your forces, much less two-thirds." I could see Cal wanting to contradict him, but my father just kept going. "The walls have been reinforced with shimmersteel. Every gate secured. A hundred blood-mages sit at the riverfront, ready to set it ablaze in a second's notice. The Skywhale circles above, ready to unleash hell. And even if you somehow managed to breach the city, you'd find yourself riding straight into a slaughter. For every bloodmage Miles has out, three sit waiting within." My father stared Cal down. "With all due respect? You've sent your men to their deaths."

"But imagine if you had an army of mages backing you," Lyriana cut in before Cal could reply (or, you know, stab). "Dozens and dozens of them, mages that can move your army miles in the blink of an eye, mages that make Miles's most powerful soldiers look like children at their first lesson. We could get you that."

Cal's eyes flitted to Syan. "Is that true?"

She glanced away with . . . what was that? Uncertainty? "It is."

"So you propose an alliance after all, just in the most roundabout way." Cal set his pear down by the fruit bowl. "And suppose I agreed? Suppose we fought together, your mages and my soldiers, and we took the city back and mounted that whelp's head on the wall. What then? Your people would cheer for the return of their Queen. You'd take back the throne. And I would . . . what? Head back down here with what remains of my army to serve as High Lord? Grovel as I bend the knee?" He shook his head. "No. *No.* Hampstedt and Kent may have killed my kin, but it was your family, Queen Lyriana, that enslaved my people. It was your family that slaughtered their way through these lands and destroyed the great empire of my ancestors. It was your family that got us in this fucking mess to begin with!" He lunged up out of his throne, knocking over the fruit bowl, and there was the emotion, the passion, that fury bursting out. He stalked toward Lyriana, so close she jerked back, and jabbed that paring knife through the air to emphasize his words. "I will never bow again. I will be a King, or I will die trying. Nothing less."

Lyriana had nothing to say to that, so Cal turned away. "Take Queen Lyriana to the dungeons. Kill the others."

I looked to Lyriana and Ellarion, like, *Please get us out of this mess,* but they gave me nothing, just fear. This was really happening. I braced myself, waiting for the guard to grab me, because if nothing else I was going down fighting.

And then my father spoke. "Great Dyn!" he yelled, even as the guard jerked him back. "There is another way!"

The guards looked at Cal, who raised a weary hand to stop them. "Speak."

"I understand how you feel. Believe me, no one knows it more than I do," my father said. "I was the first to raise arms against the Volaris. I risked everything so that my people could live free. I vowed to never bow again. I took my crown by force, and I lost it the same way. But . . ." His gaze flitted toward Lyriana knowingly. "There are other ways to become a King."

A long moment of silence lingered over us, as the words set in (and also as I tried to figure out what he meant). Lyriana, though, she got it. I saw a gamut of emotions run across her face: shock, dismissal, then, a weary sigh of resignation. "Great Dyn," she said, eyes closed. "Kent speaks the truth. If you honor this alliance . . . if you help me take back my throne . . . I shall reward you with a place by my side." She swallowed. "As my husband."

"No—" Ellarion gasped, but the rest of the room was silent. I don't know why, but hearing her say that was somehow even more shocking than, you know, being sentenced to death. Even Zell looked stunned.

"Your husband," Cal repeated, staring at Lyriana with his head cocked to the side.

"You'd be King."

"A puppet King," he said, but he was clearly considering it. "Everyone knows the real power would sit with you."

"But you'd still be King," Lyriana insisted, and was she really pushing for this? For marrying *this* guy? "You'd be there, guiding me, helping me, speaking for your people. And one day, your child would sit on the shimmersteel throne."

Cal was silent for a long time. I could see the struggle playing out in his head. And I felt it. I desperately wanted him to say yes for my sake, and I just as badly wanted him to say no, for Lyriana's. "And in exchange?" he said at last. "What would you ask of me?"

"Only that you let us go," Lyriana replied. "If we die in the Wastes, then nothing changes for you. And if we succeed, then you get everything you ever wanted."

Cal took a bold step toward Lyriana. "And how do I know you aren't lying? That you won't betray me the second you have power?"

Lyriana's eyes narrowed. "I swear by the Titans above, by the Ascension, by the souls of my murdered father and mother. I give you my word."

Cal looked at her for a long time, an unfathomable series

of emotions flitting across his face. Finally, he nodded. "All right. I may live to regret this, but all right. I accept your bargain. I will let you go, and fight alongside these mages of yours. And when we win, I'll rule Noveris with you." He reached down to Lyriana's bound hands, and with one flick of his knife, cut through the ropes. Then he raised her hand to his lips and kissed it, tenderly. "My Queen."

"My King," Lyriana replied, her gaze distant, her voice flat.

Cal stepped back from her, nodding at his guards. "New plan. Put them up in the guest chambers. Make sure they have everything they need for their journey."

"That's it?" Ellarion asked. "We're good?"

"Almost," Cal said, and I *really* didn't like the way he said that. "There's still the matter of Kent here. The debt I owe him." He paced over to my father, who stood, grim and resolute, unblinking. "I said I would let you all go, after all. I didn't say what I'd do before then."

"What are you talking about?" Lyriana demanded.

Cal shot her a smile as gentle as it was cruel, as he laid one hand on my father's shoulder. "Consider this me claiming my dowry."

Then he leaned forward and drove his paring knife into my father's side, just below his ribs. My father let out a choked grunt, and I fought back a scream. "That's for my father," Cal said, then he jerked out his knife and stabbed again. "For my mother." Another stab. "For my brother."

He took a step back. My father was still standing, teeth clenched, sweat streaking down his forehead. The side of his shirt turned a deep red, and I could see blood running down his side. The wounds weren't deep, and they weren't mortal, but they must have hurt like hell. He stood all the same, breathing hard, refusing to back down.

"And you know what? This is for everyone else," Cal said, and then he drove the knife into my father's right eye.

Now my father screamed, a horrible pained wail, and dropped down to his knees. Lyriana clutched a hand over her mouth, and the guards closed in tight around us, spears leveled, practically daring us to try something. Cal held my father there, grinning, and then he jerked the knife out, sending rivulets of blood and globs of eye streaking across the floor. My father collapsed, clutching his face, and crimson seeped out through his fingers. "*Now* we're good," Cal said, wiping his blade on his shirt. "Take them away."

FIFTEEN

THEY PUT US UP IN SOME ROOMS ON ONE OF THE UPPER
levels of the Greatest Ziggurat. They were nice enough: spacious and well-furnished, with bowls of fruit and bottles of
chilled wine. That morning, I would've given anything to flop
down in a place like that, but I found myself a little distracted
by my father, sprawled out on one of the beds, bleeding out of
the gaping hole that had been his right eye.

The guards just dropped us there and left, not even bothering to get a medic, so it fell to Lyriana. And even though
she hated my father as much as Cal did, even though she
would've been totally justified in letting him bleed, she pulled
up a chair to his bedside and worked her Healing Arts, pressing her hands to his wounds, cupping a palm around his eye,
whispering under her breath as her Rings glowed green and
the air filled with the smell of fresh dew and budding flowers.
I sat there, watching as the ragged cuts clotted and healed,
as the skin refolded itself into white scars, as the horrible
crater in his head mended itself into a sunken fleshy patch.

There was only so much she could do, of course. Healing Arts hastened the body's natural healing processes, but they couldn't do anything your body wouldn't do on its own. So that eye was like Ellarion's hands. Gone for good.

It must have been at least an hour (and a bottle of wine), before she finished. Finally, she stepped away, leaving him lying there, his remaining eye shut, breath slow and deep. I kind of thought he was knocked out, but when Lyriana got out of her chair, he spoke, just once, in a voice barely above a whisper. "Thank you."

"You saved all of us with that marriage idea," Lyriana replied, refusing to look at him. "Consider us even."

She stepped out of our room onto the balcony. Zell, Syan, and Ellarion had all headed down into the Izterosi neighborhood to get us the supplies we'd need for the journey, which meant my options were joining her or staying in the room with my father and his heavy breathing and the bubbling patch of mottled flesh slowly forming over his eye.

I hit that balcony like no one's business.

Lyriana stood by the railing, gazing out, and I walked over to join her. Tau Lorren was beautiful from above, a sprawling maze of little houses and shops and taverns, lit up by thousands of lanterns, alive with bustle and noise. It looked like most of the fires had been put out, like the worst of the earthquake's damage had been cleared away. The sky overhead was a lush turquoise, and the moon a perfect silver crescent, reflecting like a current of magic on the surface of the Adelphus.

I smiled a little, because damn it was pretty, but Lyriana just gazed out with a distant, troubled look. Given her day, I didn't blame her. "So," I said, trying to think of the least awkward way to broach the topic. "You're engaged now."

Lyriana turned to me with a weary shrug, like, was that really the best I could do? "I suppose so. Not that I feel any different."

"Are you really going to go through with it? Marry him, I mean?"

"I made a vow, Tilla. I keep my promises." Lyriana nodded. "When we win this war . . . *if* we win this war . . . I shall take Rulys Cal as my husband."

"And . . . you're okay with that?"

"I understand how marriage works," Lyriana said with just a tiny hint of annoyance. "And I've known since I was a little girl that my marriage would be one of political convenience. I'd always assumed it would be to bring some powerful family into the Volaris fold or resolve some growing tension among Lightspire nobility. If my marriage secures the alliance to save the Kingdom . . . well, that's better than I could have ever expected."

"Well, okay, yeah," I said. "But you must have some personal feelings about it, right? We're talking about the man you're going to spend the rest of your life with. The man you're gonna . . . you know . . ." Why was I suddenly feeling bashful? *"You know."*

"Yes. I know." Lyriana rolled her eyes. "I've known what love feels like, Tilla. I've known heartbreak. And for that matter, I've known a fair bit of random pleasure as well. I don't need any of that in my life." She turned back to the city sprawled out below. "What I need is a Kingdom at peace. What I *need* is the will, the strength, and the wisdom to be a good ruler. If Rulys Cal can help me find that . . . I'll be happy to call him husband."

"Huh. Right." I paused, then couldn't help myself. "On the bright side, you guys are going to make some cute-ass babies."

Lyriana turned to me gravely, then cracked a smile. "I suppose he is . . . somewhat attractive. When he's not gouging people's eyes out, anyway."

"If we ruled out every guy who's gouged out an eye, who'd we be left with, right?"

I was mostly joking, but Lyriana looked at me thoughtfully. "What about you and Zell?" she asked. "When this is all over, are you two planning to get married?"

"Are we . . . I . . . well . . . I mean," I stammered, because I didn't actually know the answer. It's not that I hadn't thought about it. Being real, I'd imagined every single detail of our wedding (and more than a few of our wedding nights). It's just that those thoughts felt like whimsical daydreams, filed in my brain alongside childhood fantasies like "riding a dragon" and "being a Princess." I couldn't bring myself to think of them as things that could really happen. "I don't know," I said at last. "I mean, I want to. I love with him all my heart, and I can't ever imagine being with someone else. But it just doesn't feel like that day will ever come."

"The war will end," Lyriana insisted.

I shook my head. "This one will. But what about the next one? And the one after that?" I don't know why I was telling her all this, but it was spilling out now and there was no stopping it. "I just don't know that he'll ever let go, that he'll ever stop fighting. He's got this pain inside him, Lyriana, at his core, this feeling like he's just so guilty and awful, like he has to personally carry the weight of the world's problems on his shoulders. And I don't know if he's going to let go of that."

I dabbed at my eyes with the inside of my wrist. "I don't know if he even can."

Lyriana leaned over and hugged me, and I buried my face into her shoulder. "He'll grow. He'll change. We all will."

"I hope so," a voice said from behind us, and I turned to see Ellarion, leaning against the door frame. "Sorry. Hope I'm not interrupting private . . . girl . . . time."

"You are, but it's fine." Lyriana stepped away from me. "I thought you were going with the others to secure provisions."

"I was," he said. "But then I saw a tavern on the way, and they were serving strong honeyed ale, so I told Zell and Syan to go on ahead. And I went in and ordered myself the biggest glass they had." Lyriana shot me a look equal parts disappointed and concerned, a look Ellarion caught immediately. "I didn't drink it, if that's what you're thinking. I just sat there staring at it for a long time, and then I paid and left. What would the point even be? An hour of relief, a restless sleep, and then I'd feel just as bad tomorrow."

"Um, Ellarion?" I asked. "Is something wrong?"

"Is something wrong?" he repeated with a scoff, strolling out to rest along the balcony's edge. "You mean, besides the fact that we've lost the Kingdom, the rebellion's defeated, and the situation is so dire my dear cousin has to sell her hand in marriage to *Rulys Cal*? No. Nothing's wrong."

Lyriana rolled her eyes, zero patience for the dramatics. "I can make my own choices, thank you. And that's not what this is really about, is it?" She paced over to his side. "If you want to talk, *talk*. Tell us what's wrong."

Ellarion turned to her, then sighed. "I'm tired. And bitter. And angry. So angry all the time."

"About your hands?" I offered.

"No, actually. I got over being angry about that long ago," he said. "I'm angry about everything else. Did you see how Cal looked at me? How he talked to me? I'm the *Archmagus*, for the Titans' sake, and he treated me like I was nobody. He was ready to kill me to make a point. *Elric Kent* was a more valuable hostage." Ellarion's nostrils flared, and his eyes smoldered. "He looked at me like I was nothing."

"Ellarion . . ."

"It's not just him, either. It's everyone. Galen. The vagabonds." Ellarion paused, like he was debating, and then decided to go there. "Even you."

"No, I don't . . . I . . ." I tried.

"You do, though," Ellarion pressed. "I can see it in your faces. The pity. The sadness. The way you all look away when I'm training with Syan, like it's so pathetic. Like I'm just poor broken Ellarion, and you all feel so bad for me all the time."

"I—I mean . . ." I had an instinctive rootless impulse to defend myself, but I'd also learned that any time I felt that, it meant I was probably in the wrong. "I'm sorry. I'm sorry that I made you feel that way."

Ellarion took a deep breath and turned to Lyriana, his red eyes glowingly dimly through the night. "Let me ask you something. When you were a child, and you imagined being Queen, what did you think about? What went through your head?"

"If I'm being honest? Mostly worries," Lyriana replied. "I worried if I would be a good Queen. I worried if I would know how to make difficult decisions, if I was smart enough, if I was compassionate enough. I worried every day that I wouldn't be good enough."

"Of course you did," Ellarion said. "And do you know what I thought about, when I imagined being Archmagus?

I thought about the monuments they'd build in my honor. I thought about the songs they'd sing. I pictured the crowds gathered, chanting my name, and I imagined the history books, and how they'd call me *Ellarion the Great* and *Ellarion the Magnificent* and talk about how I was the most astounding Archmagus of all time."

"That's not *all* you thought about."

"No, it is," he insisted. "It really is. That's all I cared about. Being great. Being celebrated. Being amazing. All the things an Archmagus is supposed to care about, like bringing light to the masses and helping the smallfolk and all that, well, that was just a means to an end. A step on the road to glory." He slumped down into a chair with a weary exhale. "I don't want it anymore. I don't need monuments or songs or parades. I just need people to look at me like I'm a person. I need people to stop underestimating me. I need people to understand that I'm still *me.*"

"I understand," Lyriana said, and she walked over and gave him a hug. "You're my cousin. And you're smart and resourceful and clever and kind. You're the most important person in my world. And you're so, so far from nothing."

"You're also super good-looking," I added. "I mean, don't forget about that."

Ellarion shook his head, curly locks swaying. "Thanks."

"Feel better?" Lyriana asked.

"A little," he replied. He smiled, and Lyriana smiled, and I guess I did too, but it was hard to look away from the sadness in his eyes and the worry in hers. A cold chill blew over us, swaying the curtain over the balcony's door.

I fought back a shudder.

The next morning, as the sun rose over the city's sparkling

pools and bustling bazaars, we made our way to the southern gate. Syan hadn't been joking about provisions. There were heavy packs of food and big leather skins filled with water, new shining blades and thin ochre robes, the kind that were supposed to help us deal with the heat. And then there were our rides.

"What in the frozen hell are those?" I yelled the second I stepped through the gate.

I don't know what I'd been expecting to take out into the Wastes. Horses, maybe? Camels? But apparently I was totally off the mark because waiting for me out there, laden with our goods, were four massive, disgusting, hideous lizards. And I mean *massive*. These things were easily the size of a carriage, with six leathery limbs giving way to uncomfortably human hands. Huge tails thick as tree trunks lashed behind them, flicking up dust and sand. Their skin was a dull green, covered in bumpy scales the size of my fist, that didn't so much sparkle in the sun as absorb it. And their faces were the weirdest of all: long snouts that gave way to wide, fanged mouths, and bony skulls lined with four eyes, two big and red, two beady and black.

"Terzans," Syan said, gently petting one's head. A long purple tongue flicked out to lick her hand, and I had to fight back a gag. "Wonderful creatures. They were born in the Storm just like us. You won't find a better companion to brave the sands."

I looked to my friends for backup. "Seriously?"

"Syan says they'll get us through the desert," Zell said, and Lyriana just shrugged. "I think they're kind of cute."

"Well, *I* think they're big monster lizards with freaky-weird people hands." I knew this was a petty thing to be protesting, but also, I *really* didn't want to ride one. "We can't just take horses?"

"A horse will spook at the first sign of a storm," a man's voice said from beside me. I spun to see a young Izterosi guy, leaning against an exceptionally big terzan thing. He had shaggy black hair lit up with streaks of silver, wide brown eyes, and a gap-toothed smile that was instantly endearing. "Trust me. Out in Izteros, a terzan is the only way to go."

I blinked at him. "Um . . ."

He extended a hand, and clasped my wrist when I reached for it. "I am Trell Tain of Benn Selaro. I've been hired to be your Torchbearer."

"I thought Syan was our . . . that."

"My flame will relight once I reach the sands, but it won't be enough. Making it out all the way to Benn Devalos is too risky with just one Torchbearer," Syan said matter-of-factly, and it was starting to dawn on me how little I actually knew about what came next in our journey. "The Dyn has paid Trell to escort us."

"He offers a fortune," Trell said, beaming, and I had to wonder if he had any idea what he was getting into. "The elders at Benn Selaro will be so amazed when they hear." He shot Syan a wide grin. "Perhaps our benns can finally resolve their differences? Perhaps our adventure will forge a bond!"

"Mmm," Syan said, looking away. There was a weird vibe here, something going on between them, but I had no idea what it was. At this point, I was only like 95 percent certain that a benn was a kind of city.

"Come on," Ellarion said, climbing onto his disgusting lizard monster like it was no big deal. "If we're not back with Syan's mages before the Southlanders attack Lightspire they'll all get wiped out. We need to ride as fast as we can." He glanced at me. "That means you, Tilla."

I hated every second of this, hated climbing onto that thing's back, hated how slick its skin felt and the way its beady black eyes flitted around. Even the fact that I was riding on one with Zell and could wrap my arms around his waist wasn't helping. "This is my personal hell. You know that right? Personal. Hell."

"I'm sure you'll somehow get through it," he replied, and I could see the corners of his mouth twitching as he tried to hide that smile.

Syan gave a command, a sharp cry that ended in a whistle, and the beasts took off, plodding down the road with their hands slapping the ground, jostling us from side to side with each stride. Trell and Syan led, followed by Ellarion and Lyriana, then me and Zell, and last of all my father, riding alone, a black eyepatch mercifully covering the awfulness that was his right socket. We trudged forward in that line, past merchants and travelers and rows of soldiers, out through the arched southern gate and to the sprawling desert beyond.

As we left the city, I glanced back, and that's when I saw him. A lone figure standing atop the gate, watching us go. Dyn Rulys Cal. His hair hung long and neat down his back, and he'd traded out his sheer robe for a suit of blinding golden armor and a curved sword sheathed at his side. His face was stern, distant, but as we looked up at him, he balled his right hand into a fist and pressed it against his heart.

On the terzan in front of me, Lyriana let out a long, sad exhale. Then she raised her own fist and did the same.

Cal smiled.

SIXTEEN

I'll give the Red Wastes this. The name is *extremely* literal.

We're talking massive, sloping dunes, the vibrant crimson of a blooming rose, endless sprawls of sand in the smoldering red of a sunset's heart. I'd never seen anything like it, never imagined anything like it, an ocean of color brighter than any painting I'd ever seen, that sparkled like a million diamonds in the sunlight and glowed a gentle orange even in the dead of night.

It wasn't just the color (though a lot of it was the color). It was also the scale. Once we were out in the Wastes, four days after leaving Tau Lorren, it was like everything else in the world had vanished. There was just sand, beautiful and vibrant crimson sand, stretching out in all directions as far as the eye could see. There were no rocks, no plants, no wandering animals or birds circling overhead, just this great red sea with its mountainous waves and placid surface. Every now and again we'd pass a slab of crystal, reflective as a mirror, jutting out like a spike or lying flat like a buried relic. Other than that, it was just red sand forever. It was stunning, astounding, impossibly peaceful and serene.

I had no idea how anyone could possibly live out here.

The sun bore down hot overhead, but the terzans didn't seem to mind. They just marched forward, padding effortlessly over the dunes, leaving a trail of handprints in their wake. At night, we fed them hunks of dried meat from our packs, and they cuddled up in a big slumbering pile of snorting nostrils and floppy hands. Mine was apparently named Gribshanks, and I'll have it noted that at no point in the journey did I ever come to like him.

Navigating was its whole own challenge, because there were exactly zero landmarks to guide us. Trell and Syan led the way, gathering side by side every few hours to do some weird magic that involved their zaryas zipping around overhead, leaving grids of glowing lines in the sky. Lyriana and Ellarion spent twenty minutes one day debating how it worked, and when they finally asked the Red Wasters, they'd shrugged and said "It just does."

Three days into our journey, the Waste Sickness began to hit. I'd been feeling weird all day, a low rumbling nausea building up in my gut, a dull throb stabbing in the sides of my head. I'd figured it was just me, but as we settled into camp, I could see that the others were feeling it too; Zell rubbed at his temples, and my father wobbled unsteadily on his feet.

"Do you feel that?" Lyriana asked Ellarion, squinting all around like the sun was in her eyes. "In the air. It's like . . . like . . ."

"Magic," Ellarion answered, his brow slick with sweat, his teeth gritted. "All around us. But it's raw, unfocused, like . . ."

"Like that Titan crypt," Lyriana finished. She looked

down at her hand, and a tiny burst of flame enveloped it, flared purple, and vanished. "I didn't do that. I mean, I didn't mean to do that."

"It happens to all stillanders who venture into our lands," Trell said casually. "The People of the Storm don't feel it. We were born to the sands. Their power runs through our veins. But for your kind . . . it can be hard to endure."

"Some warning would have been nice," I said, and now I was definitely seeing little red spots in the center of my vision. "Is this just how it's going to be?"

Syan snorted. "Here. This will help." She turned to rummage around in a heavy pack, and I realized her hair had changed again. After the crossing at Torrus, the colored strands had faded to a dull gray, but they were starting to shine again, a soft blue.

"You're absorbing the magic," Lyriana said, obviously noticing the same thing. "That's why you're not sick. You're breathing it in and out like, like air."

Syan shrugged. "If that's how you'd like to think of it." She found what she was looking for in the pack and turned around, holding a few dried-looking brown leaves in her open palm. "From the sashtu plant, which thrives out in the sands. Chew these. They'll help."

Lyriana looked at them skeptically, and then another burst of fire shot out of her, this one popping off by her head like a firework. "Fine," she said, chewing the leaf with a grimace.

They tasted bitter and had an awful texture, like chewing on a crumbling twig. But within ten minutes, the nausea had passed, and within half an hour, the headache was gone, too.

The nights out in the Red Wastes were cold, a chilling cold that you felt in your bones and made your breath hang heavy in the air. Lyriana tried to warm us by making orbs of Light, but her magic was just too messed up out here; they popped and crackled, bursting apart in showers of sparks, and one even turned into weird gooey worms that wriggled off into the sand. So we relied on Syan and Trell. Every night, as the sun set, they sat together at the center of our camp, eyes closed, hands folded, working their magic. Trell had his own zaryas, and I'm guessing his were the cheap ones to Syan's luxury goods: chipped wooden balls lined with dulled metal, the paint on them faded and a distinct wobble in their twirl.

But hey, they worked, and that's what mattered. Their zaryas flitting in elegant spirals overhead, Syan and Trell made fires burst out of the sand, pillars of spiraling orange and gold that radiated blessed heat in all directions and burned of their own free will. Even fifteen feet away, the air was so cold you could feel your hair freeze, but the pillars kept us warm through the chill of night, giant candles blazing in the dark.

It took me four nights to make the connection. "Ohhhh," I said, staring up at the majestic tower of flame. "*That's* why you're called Torchbearers."

"You figured it out, huh?" Trell chuckled. "It's not a perfect translation, but it's close." His accent was softer than Syan's, his tongue more confident. I'm guessing he'd been living in Tau Lorren for quite a while.

"It's amazing," Ellarion said. He sprawled out on a blanket, chewing on his leaf, resting on his wrists. He'd had to take his hands off that morning; all the magic in the air had been causing them to go haywire, clenching and jabbing and clicking uncontrollably. "This whole desert is beyond inhospitable. The best explorers and mages in Lightspire wouldn't have made it two days. And yet the Red Wasters have been out here all along, surviving effortlessly, with a solution to every problem. It's like they've perfectly acclimated to the environment."

"We didn't 'acclimate' to this environment," Trell said, enunciating every syllable in the word. "We were gifted the power to control it."

"What do you mean?"

Trell came over and hunkered down cross-legged opposite us. When he spoke again, his voice had a new quality, slow, rhythmic and just a little grandiose, like he was reciting a story he'd heard hundreds of times. "Long, long ago, this land was not a desert but a forest, sprawling and lush, with towering trees and flowing rivers. The Sunfather had made it such, and while he admired its beauty, as the years passed, he felt lonely that he had no one to share it with. So one morning, he reached down from the sky, and he forged a man and a woman out of dirt. These were the first Izterosi, the first people of these lands. And they thanked the Sunfather for the gift of life, and settled all across this land."

Trell had been talking to just Ellarion and me, but the way he spoke managed to pique everyone's interest. Lyriana came over to join us, waterskin in hand, and Zell set down the blade he was sharpening. Even my father swiveled around, just a little. The only person who didn't seem to respond was Syan, who sat on the other side of the flame, arms crossed, gazing out into the night.

"But the Nightmother, she was jealous," Trell continued. "She was a demon, a monster, as cruel as the Sunfather was kind. She descended from the stars with her thousand siblings, cloaked in the swirling chaos of the Storm, and they enslaved the Izterosi. They forced us to build their city, a terrible monument of stone and glass. They put us to the lash, murdered any who dared oppose her. It was an era of darkness, of suffering, of pain."

"Trell," Syan cut in sharply, her back still turned. There was something weird going on with her, a discomfort, a tension. "You don't have to tell them this."

"Why not?" Trell shrugged. "We're taking them to your benn, aren't we? Are you really worried about keeping secrets?" He looked at us, and especially at Lyriana, who I'm pretty sure he had a thing for. "Would you like to hear more?"

"Yes, definitely," she replied.

"Right, then," he went on, and even though Syan's back was turned, I could somehow feel her rolling her eyes. "The Sunfather heard his children's cries, and he could not bear to see their suffering. So he reached deep into himself and drew forth his flame, and he brought that flame down on the Nightmother and her siblings. A rain of fire from the skies that destroyed their city, that toppled their towers, that set the demons aflame and burned them to ash. The Nightmother fled to Kaichkul, the Black Prison, and the Sunfather sealed her in there, where she rages to this day, plotting her revenge."

"Wouldn't your people have died in the fire, too?" Ellarion asked, which, kind of rude.

"Oh yes," Trell said. "The fire destroyed the forests, leaving only the scorched red sand. And many, many Izterosi died, martyrs so their children would live. And live they did." Trell reached up and placed a palm against his chest. "For all the Izterosi that survived were kissed by the flame of the sun. And we carried that flame deep in our hearts. With the fire of the Sunfather burning within us, we built our benns and learned to thrive in the heart of the Storm. With that flame, we made this land ours." He paused for dramatic effect. "And that is how we came to be. The People of the Storm, the Izterosi, the children of the Sunfather, the protectors of the flame."

A thoughtful silence hung over us, and I gave what I hoped was an appreciative nod.

"That's a nice story," Ellarion said at last.

Trell scowled. "It's not a 'story.' It's our history."

"Sorry, I . . . I didn't mean to . . ."

"You stillanders think you know *everything*," Trell said, and it was pretty clearly that Ellarion had struck a nerve. "You're so sure that your stories of 'the Titans' are true, when you have nothing to go off but the words of some gray-haired old priests. Pah." He spit to the side. "What I told you is the real truth. I can feel the Sunfather's fire burning within me, see his face in the sky above. I've seen the Black Prison with my own eyes and—"

"Hang on," Ellarion interrupted. "This Black Prison is a real place? You've physically been there?"

Trell nodded. "At the furthest southern border of Izteros, there is a place called the Ghostlands. The sand there is black and brittle, the air tainted and vile. Spirits roam it at night, howling in pain and fury. And lying at the heart of that place is an ancient prison of the darkest stone, a monument that keeps the Nightmother trapped within. It is forbidden to set foot in the Ghostlands, the greatest of all crimes. But I've stood at the edge. I've seen those evil sands! I've *been there!*"

"Hey, it's okay," I said, and I shot Ellarion a glare that he hopefully understood meant *Not another word.* "I believe you." And I mean, I actually did. After everything we'd been through and seen, after every shocking revelation, why would I doubt this?

Trell could tell, I think, because he nodded appreciatively.

"Thank you. I apologize for my outburst. It's just . . . a difficult memory." He leaned back on his hands, his youthful features looking sunken and haunted in the light of the towering flame. "Some elders teach that the prison is weakening, that our flame can only guard it for so long. One day, they say, the walls will shatter, and the Nightmother will be free, and she will unleash Zastroya."

"Zastroya," Lyriana repeated. "The Storm That Will Consume the World. Syan was telling us about this. How your people have been dreaming of it."

Trell blinked. "What is this now? I don't kn—"

"Enough," Syan said, so sharply that we all turned to stare at her. When she turned around, her brow was furrowed deep, and her eyes were furious narrow slits. I pulled back, surprised. I hadn't seen her like this before, this visibly angry and upset, not even when she was talking about her brother. Something had really gotten under her skin.

"Syan, I apologize," Trell tried. "I was just telling them . . ."

She ignored him, pacing over to the supply pile. "I can feel a storm coming. Tomorrow will be a difficult day." She pulled out our sleeping mats and tossed them down onto the sand. "We should all be sleeping, not sitting around blabbing our tongues."

Her tone was so harsh I didn't even bother telling her that that wasn't an expression. She took her mat and stalked off toward the outskirts of the camp. Trell wandered over to check on the pillars, and Ellarion shook his head. "What in the frozen hell just happened?" I asked.

"I don't know," Lyriana replied, her eyes on Syan. "But it worries me."

It pretty much felt like we had to go to sleep after that,

so I slid my mat alongside Zell's and curled up in his arms. "What'd you think of all that?" I whispered, my lips just inches away from his ear.

"I think the world is bigger and stranger and wilder than any of us have ever imagined," he replied, dark eyes staring up at the stars. "And the more I travel it, the more certain I become of how little I know. I believe in the Twelve. Lyriana believes in the Titans. Trell believes in this Sunfather and Nightmother. But what's true?"

"Well . . . something's gotta be true, right?" I replied, and honestly, I'd been hoping more to gossip about Syan's reaction than to get all heady and philosophical. "I mean, someone's right and everyone else is wrong?"

"Maybe. Or maybe we're all right and wrong," Zell replied. "Maybe all of these ideas are our attempts sense to make sense of something greater, something bigger than we could really comprehend." He breathed deeply, and my head rose and fell with his chest. "It's like we're all part of this giant tapestry, but we can only see our individual threads. You're a red thread, so you think the whole tapestry is red, and I'm blue so I think everything's blue. We've all taken our tiny little stretch of knowledge and imagined the whole world flows from it. But really, none of us have any clue what the whole is. None of us can see the tapestry itself."

We lay there for a minute quietly, letting his words sink in. "Is there anything we *can* be certain of?" I finally asked.

I expected another heavy thought, but Zell just craned his head down to me and smiled. "I'm certain you're here. And I'm certain I love you." He kissed my forehead, his lips soft, and I squeezed him close. "Maybe we can't ask for more than that."

I drifted off there in his arms, and woke up a little while

later, sweating and panting from a nightmare. Daytime was still a ways off, the sky dark and beautiful overhead. Everyone else was still asleep around me, the camp still and quiet save the snuffling of the terzan pile. I knew I should probably go back to sleep, but I had that middle-of-the-night restlessness, so I extracted myself from Zell's arms and stood up, stretching my legs and fumbling for a drink of water.

That's when I saw him. My father, sitting by the fire's edge, his back turned to me and his head craned up toward the top of the pillar. A part of me knew that the right thing to do would be to just go back to sleep, but the part of me that was wired was a lot louder. So as quietly as I could, I walked over and sat down by his side.

He glanced my way, a little surprised, and by the Old Kings did he look like hell. His remaining eye was bloodshot and exhausted, his beard frayed, his hair tangled and messy. He looked so old, so much worse than he should have at forty years. This was the legacy of a life of scheming and ambition, a life of brutal decisions. You could win the world, but you'd still look like shit.

"Tillandra," he said, and his voice sounded different, huskier, heavier. I could smell wine on his breath, and I noticed the skin, half-empty, at his side. Was this why he'd stayed up when we'd all passed out?

"You've been drinking," I said.

"It dulls the pain." He shrugged. "Lyriana's magic might have saved me, but . . . it all still hurts."

"Oh," I said, and wasn't sure really where to go from that.

"It's funny," my father said, leaning back with a little wobble. There were a lot of things I had a hard time imagining my father doing (like smiling, or saying "I love you"), but being drunk was probably at the top of the list. He was always so stiff and collected, every word measured, I figured his body was immune to alcohol, like it just burned up the second it hit his lips. But here he was, definitely at least a little tipsy. "My uncle Tobias Kent had an eyepatch. Did I ever tell you that?"

"No . . . ?"

"Well, he did. As a boy, I always thought it made him look so impressive and ominous, so commanding. I dreamed of having one when I was grown up." He laughed, a short brittle sound. "I can tell you now. It's not worth it."

"You do look more ominous and commanding?" I offered.

He laughed again and offered me the wineskin, and I took a deep swig. This was too weird a conversation to have sober. "Can't sleep? I never slept well, either. Too many thoughts colliding in my head." He paused for a moment, turning to face the flame. "You know what I can't stop thinking about?"

"What?"

"That girl," he said. "The one from Tau Lorren. The little one we rescued from the rubble."

"Uh . . ." I said, because what was there to think about? The last we'd seen of her, a group of Southlanders had rushed over to take her out of his arms. "I'm sure she's okay. . . ."

"It's just been so long since I've held a child. I'd forgotten what it's like. How small they feel. How vulnerable. How important." His voice was distant, his eye transfixed by the fire. "I don't believe in regrets. But of everything I sacrificed for the people of the West, there's none I regret more than the time I could've spent being a father." He shook his head. "I was never there for you. For any of you."

Any of *us*. It actually took me a moment to realize he was including his other three daughters, his legitimate children, my younger half sisters, Celyse, Kat, and Tara Kent. Holy shit. I'd spent a good decade wallowing in anger toward them, consumed by my bastard jealousy that they got to be legitimate, and now I actually had to stop and think to remember their names. It had been that long. "Are they back in Lightspire? My half sisters, I mean."

My father shook his head. "I didn't want them coming to Lightspire until I was sure it was safe. So I had them stay back at Castle Waverly with their mother. It's only a matter of time, though."

"A matter of time?"

"Celyse is the true heir to my throne, by law. Miles only rules as Regent because she's not of age." His expression hardened. "And we both know him well enough to know he'll never let that happen."

"Shit," I whispered, my mind spinning with images of Miles's soldiers storming the halls of Castle Waverly, hacking down their door as the girls screamed. I'd hated them when I was younger because their existence was a massive, glaring reminder of my bastardom. But they were still just three little kids, the oldest, what, twelve years old? "We won't let them die," I said. "I promise."

"It's not just about that," my father said. "It's about all of it. The choices I've made that brought us here. The choices I've made that have put my children in harm's way. The choices I've made my whole life." He leaned back on his hands, chin to the sky, and he'd never looked more human. "I sacrificed everything. I gave up the life we could have had. I gave up being a father. I killed so many people. I brought so much pain. And all of it, all of it I did for my people. For the greater good." He breathed in deep. "But what if there is *no* greater good? If that's just something we tell ourselves to justify doing what we want? If every solution just makes new problems? If intent and consequences don't matter, and the only thing you can be judged on is the choice you made in the moment? If I was so lost staring off into the distance, I lost sight of what was always in front of me?"

"I don't understand. Are you saying you feel guilty or something?"

"I've accomplished everything I ever dreamed of. I destroyed the Volaris. I freed the West. I was King. *King*. And none of it made me feel even a fraction of what I felt holding that little girl in Tau Lorren." He turned to me, and his eye sparkled. "What I felt when I held you."

I turned away, because I was not even remotely ready to deal with this. I just couldn't. Not here. Maybe not ever. There was just too much emotion in me, too many years of yearning and hating and longing and loving, too many conflicting images of the same person. How could I feel so many things at the same time? Looking at my father was like looking at a reflection in a shattered mirror, the same image in a dozen jagged shards: the father who'd doted on me when I was a child, the distant Lord whose approval obsessed me, the ice-cold strategist who'd gotten my brother killed, the ruthless tyrant who'd bombed a ballroom full of innocents, and now this, this earnest troubled man, this sad drunk hounded by regrets.

How dare he be a person *now*?

"I can't do this," I said, standing up and trying to hide the quiver in my voice. I couldn't let him see this, couldn't let him see how he made me feel. He didn't deserve that. "This was a mistake. I just . . . I can't."

"I'm sorry," he said, still facing the flame. "I shouldn't have said anything."

I knew I should have just kept walking and ended this conversation and left him there. But I couldn't hold it in. "Actually, you should have," I said. "You just should have said it years ago. When you still had a chance."

"Tillandra, wait," he said, and *then* I walked off, leaving him by the fire, all alone in the still night and the deafening thunder of his thoughts. He didn't say anything else, but he didn't need to, because I'd seen it in his face right before I'd turned away, a look of genuine honest hurt.

I'd spent a year dreaming of getting revenge on my father, of toppling his Kingdom and bringing him to justice, of holding him accountable for every last crime. But I'd never imagined I'd be capable of hurting him like this, of cutting him inside.

Of making him feel the way I'd felt for so long.

SEVENTEEN

THE STORM CAUGHT US THE NEXT DAY.

We saw it just after we rose, a speck of dark clouds hovering on the horizon, getting a little bit bigger every minute. From here, it didn't look like much. It was still just clouds, right? A storm is a storm?

Syan and Trell didn't seem to think so. The closer it came, the more concerned they got, and by the time they halted our train and huddled up, pointing and talking in hushed tones, I was starting to get worried. The storm was bigger now, a sprawl of darkness that filled the sky ahead, and I could already tell these were not ordinary clouds. The colors were all wrong, too vibrant and inconsistent: here was a patch of vivid purple, here a dark red, here a swirling miasma of onyx black and moss green. Bursts of lightning lit it up from within, hot flares of blinding gold and orange. And there was the sound, not the low rumbling of thunder but a relentless, growing chittering, like a swarm of locusts. The magic tainting the air here, that storm was full of it; my stomach twisted at the sight, and Lyriana wobbled on her feet like a drunk.

"Damn, that's bad," Trell said, squinting. "At least a four-fister."

"And we've just got the two of us," Syan replied, her expression grim.

"We could try to ride around it, see if it's thinner at the edges. . . ."

Syan shook her head. "Too risky. We have to hold fast here and hope for the best." Her tone was confident, authoritative, and Trell didn't argue. He looked at least five years older than Syan, but it was clear she was in charge here.

"Uh, sorry, not trying to interrupt," Ellarion said, raising one hand, "but are we in danger?"

"Yes."

"Is there anything I can do to help? Maybe we could lend you our power, like when we were crossing the river?"

Trell looked confused, understandably, and Syan shook her head. "No. Protecting us from the storm will take total precision, which we can't do with unknown power. Just . . . stay out of our way."

So we did. I huddled together with the others as Syan and Trell worked, moving with the speed and finesse of experts. First they set up a perimeter, using their magic to summon pillars of flame all around, ten total, forming a circle fifty feet in diameter. Syan's zaryas weaved from pillar to pillar, dragging strands of flame behind them like needles pulling thread, winding around the pillars to form a net of flame all around us. Trell paced the center of the circle, his zaryas spiraling in the sand to form sharp crystalline slabs that jutted out like fingers from invisible hands. He fished a bunch of thick ropes out of his pack and used some of them to tie up the terzans, then tossed the remainders to us. "You'll want to secure yourselves to the slabs. Just in case."

"Just in case *what*?" I demanded. I was scared, but a weird kind of scared where I didn't actually know what I was scared of, which also made me angry. My stomach was fluttering, and my knees were shaking. It was hot in the circle of pillars, unbearably hot.

Trell ignored me, which was probably for the best. Zell picked up a rope and looped it around his hand. I looked to him for reassurance, and just found a little smile. "What?" I asked.

"Always figured I'd die at the end of a blade." He shrugged. "Going out in a storm might be an improvement."

"Is that a joke?"

He reached down and squeezed my hand, even as he looped the rope around it. "We'll make it through this, Tilla. We've made it through so much else."

Syan had finished whatever she was doing with the borders and turned back to us, her zaryas zipping to their usual hovering spot over her shoulders. Her fire-net was as good as it was going to get, I guess, with at least five or six flickering strands connecting each pillar. The storm was close now, and moving fast; the sky was dark overhead, the sun almost blotted out, and that chittering sound had turned into a deafening clatter, like the sky was full of thousands of chattering teeth. Next to Syan, the terzans were freaking out, snuffling and snorting, slamming into each other and biting the air with those big drooling mouths. I really hoped their ropes would hold.

"Listen here," Syan shouted, her voice barely audible over

the storm. Her face was slick with sweat, her breath hard and sharp, and her hands, always so steady, trembled at her sides. "We're about to enter a very serious storm. Trell and I have created a barrier that protects this circle, and will hold it strong until the storm has passed. Your hope for survival—your *only* hope—is to stay in the circle. Do you understand?"

"Sure, yeah," I said, my eyes on those clouds. They were so much worse up close, shifting and writhing like waves in a crashing sea, those bursts of light within accompanied by thundering blasts that sounded an awful lot like screams. "Why would I leave the circle?"

"This is no ordinary storm," Trell said, and like, no shit. "You may see things. Hear things. Feel things. In the heart of a storm, you cannot trust your senses. You can only trust the rope."

"Please," Lyriana pleaded. "There must be something we c—"

But before she could finish her sentence, the first bolt struck. It scorched out of the sky maybe fifteen feet outside of the circle, a jagged spear of crackling light, and hit the sand with an explosion of sparks. I screamed and fell back, Zell just barely catching me, as Ellarion gasped and my father shielded his face.

"Now!" Syan screamed, and she and Trell sprang to position, folding their hands together as they turned to face the surging storm. Their zaryas zipped up above us, the four orbs spinning together over our circle, and a shimmering dome of fire stretched out above us, branching out from all the pillars to form a canopy over our heads. It reminded me of the Shields mages made, but where those were purple bubbles that moved like veils in the wind, this was more like a skin of flame, a sheer shell of burning light. It was bright, so bright, and I raised a hand to cover my eyes.

And all at once, we were in the storm. The hungry clouds enveloped the sky, blotting out the sun and swallowing us in a darkness like the dead of the night. Winds swirled around us, thick gusts that blew sand into my face and made me squint my eyes. Rain poured down, and while the dome of fire kept it from hitting us, I could see it outside the circle, the droplets hitting the sand with bursts of steam and ash. And the sounds, by the Old Kings, the sounds: the howl of the wind, the crash of thunder, and voices calling to us from all sides, screaming and sobbing, gibbering in unknown tongues and shrieking my name over and over again.

"Hold strong!" Syan shouted to Trell, and it looked like it was taking all of their effort to keep their zaryas up and working above us. The dome of fire buckled and trembled, shock waves cascading through its veil like ripples in a lake. The pillars of flame around us swayed and shook, bending in the increasingly violent gusts of wind.

My heart was in my throat, my lungs burning. I clutched my rope tightly with one hand and grabbed Zell's shoulder with the other, digging in my nails as I held on to him. He wrapped an arm around my waist, holding me tight, and I could feel his heart thundering. My father lay before us, teeth gritted, eye squinted, and Ellarion stood in front of him, stunned, arms at his side.

"Look!" Lyriana shouted, drawing my attention away. She was pointing outside the circle, at the spot where that first lightning bolt had struck, and once I looked I immediately regretted it. The sparks that had shot off the blast hadn't fallen. They hovered in the air like fireflies, flickering and crackling, wafting about like a dandelion tuft in the breeze. But it was the ground below them, where the bolt had struck, that was the real problem. There was a blackened spot there, a scorch mark, and the sand in it was . . . moving. That darkness snaked out like tendrils, spreading, and tufts of it were growing, reaching up into the air with twitching branches and sinewy sprouts, wobbling and grasping and covered in bristly little hairs. It was like looking at *wrongness* itself, something that fundamentally shouldn't be, a feeling that twisted my stomach with profound revulsion, and of course because that wasn't enough, one of the tendrils swiveled to me and I could see now in the fist-sized clump of sand an eye, a thick red eye, staring at me through a yellow pupil that dripped like the yolk of a runny egg.

"Titans protect us," Lyriana whispered, "Titans protect us, Titans protect us," but it wasn't the Titans that were protecting us, it was Syan and Trell and their dome of fire, a dome that was looking weaker and weaker every second.

Then another lightning bolt hit, this one closer, just a few feet from the circle, and a huge jag of stone shot up out of the earth where it had hit, a slab of red crystal covered in bulbous barnacle-y growths that opened and closed like sloppy mouths. That was the last straw for the terzans, I guess. They jerked away, horrified, letting out panicked braying wails.

One of them, the gray one Syan and Trell had been riding, pulled hard enough to break free. Its rope tore with a loud snap and even as Trell screamed "No!" it took off lumbering in the other direction. With a low, keening warble it smashed into the net of fire, its tough hide darkening with scorch lines in the flames, and then it was out, alone in the storm. For one second it seemed fine, like it would actually make it. And then . . . it changed. It stumbled forward and screamed, and its scream warped, from a husky bray to a wet sloppy gasp, like it was vomiting and choking all at the same time. Its body shifted and twisted, the back legs ballooning with a rubbery stretch, its front limbs atrophying into skeletal husks. Chunks of crystal stabbed out through its back, and its eyes burst open as flowering vines shot out of the sockets. The whole thing vibrated and trembled and then it exploded in a massive burst of chunky blood and crumbling bone.

Zell had been wrong. I'd take a sword over that any day.

The dead terzan was the least of our problems, though. The bigger issue was the protective net. There was a hole where the terzan had smashed through, the strands of flame between the pillars broken, and that meant the storm was getting in. A blast of wind shot through, swirling sand into our faces, our eyes, and with it came a cold, a chilling cold even though we were surrounded by flame. My skin burned and my stomach roiled and my mouth flooded with the taste of rotting food and spoiled milk. I fell forward, gagging, which meant I'd lost Zell, the only thing keeping me from totally freaking out. And as I looked up at the hole, I saw something else, something moving in the dark of the storm, something *alive*. It was a man, sort of, like if you buried a man up to his waist in the sand, and it was dragging itself toward us with its hands. It was the most terrifying thing I'd ever seen.

"Seal the gap!" Syan screamed at Trell. "Now! Before it gets in!"

"I can't!" he sobbed back, and now I could see tears in his eyes. "If I let go here, the whole roof will collapse!"

With a roar of her own, Syan pivoted toward the gap, one of her zaryas whistling down to try to rebind it. It zipped frantically between the pillars, pulling together new strands, but they were thin and weak, buckling with the wind, extinguishing before they could bind. Up top, without Syan's help, the dome of flame was giving in; a spot tore open, a hole the size of my fist, but it was enough for rain to pour down into our circle, scorching-hot rain that hit the sand with bursts of sulfurous green steam. There was too much all around us, too much happening, too fast. Lyriana was crying and my father was screaming and Trell let out a desperate sob even as Syan cursed and the hole at the top was tearing open wider and wider, more rain flooding in, and that thing was still out there, that crawling man-thing, getting closer and closer, and I could see now it didn't have a face, just a wide shrieking hole lined with teeth, and no, please no, not this, anything but this, anything but this!

And then . . . there were two new zaryas.

They shot past me, streaking like hummingbirds, glowing with a radiant white light, and zipped around one of the pillars, and when they emerged they were pulling a thick strand of flame, one they wove deftly around the next pillar over. That crawling thing recoiled, stymied by this new barrier, and I just sort of stared dumbstruck as these new zaryas flitted back and forth, patching the holes and dragging new strands, and then they stopped for one second, hovering still, twitching from side to side like they were looking for a task. I got my first good look at them and suddenly it all made sense.

These zaryas weren't orbs.

They were hands.

Mechanical prosthetic hands, made of the finest bronze

in the Kingdom. Floating in the air, the fingers dancing, tugging strands of flame like they were ribbons in a fair.

I spun around and there was Ellarion, standing upright, his jaw clenched and his eyes hardened with determination. His arms were outstretched, moving, guiding his prosthetic hands through the air, and in that moment, he looked more like an Archmagus than ever.

Syan stared too, mouth agape, but only for a moment. Then she spun back to business, pulling her own zaryas up to help Trell patch the dome overhead. "Seal the wall!" she barked at Ellarion, like it wasn't an absolutely enormous deal that he was helping at all. "I'll hold the roof!"

"I'm on it," Ellarion responded, his flying hands getting back to work, but I could see it on his face, underneath the determination and focus, a twitch in his lips he couldn't hide: a smile. His hands, his zaryas, flew through the air gracefully, bending flame and winding strands of light, securing against the howl and the fury.

Working together, the three of them managed to keep our little circle safe until the storm had passed. The whole thing lasted maybe a total of fifteen minutes, though of course it felt like an eternity. Winds howled, lightning bolts shot down, and I saw more shapes moving through the billowing sand: slithering serpents and lumbering giants and something huge and awful that flew overhead at one point, a ten-winged beast with a tentacled maw.

But then it ended, just as quickly as it had come. The clouds passed, and sunlight appeared again, soft rays more wonderful than anything I'd ever felt. The howling of the wind left, and the chittering sound, and that awful feeling in my stomach. The horrors inside it, if they were even real, left with it. When the storm had gone, there was no sign of anything strange around us, save a few chunks of charred terzan and a single slab of still orange glass.

When it was all settled and done, when the last rush of wind had vanished, Syan collapsed down into the sand, panting, and her zaryas plopped with her. Trell did the same, collapsing to his back, gasping like he'd just surfaced from the depths of the ocean. The dome flickered and vanished, and half the pillars went out, blown out like candles. Only Ellarion still stood, the muscles in his neck taut, wrists pressed together. And only when he saw the others relax did he do the same. He toppled onto his knees, breathing deep. His hands flitted toward him, puttering out halfway, hitting the sand fast and leaving long skids.

Lyriana was the first to move. She sprinted toward her cousin and wrapped him up in a hug so intense it nearly knocked him over. "Ellarion! You did it!" she said. "You did . . . did incredible magic!"

"I . . . I guess I did, yeah," he said, staring down, and he sounded more surprised than anyone. "All this time, I was so focused on not using my hands . . . but they were the key after all." He shut his eyes, but that didn't stop the tears streaming down his cheeks. "They're my zaryas."

Syan walked over, shaking her head, and her expression was somewhere between stunned, proud, and embarrassed. "That was the real problem," she whispered. "You couldn't connect to my zaryas. You needed your own."

"And you saved us all." Zell walked over to clench Ellarion's shoulder, easing him to his feet. "You're a hero."

Ellarion made a sound, a sob so joyful it broke my heart, and then I was hugging him, and Lyriana pulled Syan in, and my father stood and clapped, and we were all together, crying and holding each other and laughing, letting it all spill out. We'd made it, made it through the blazing hell that had been the storm, and come out the other side.

If we could get through that, we could do anything.

EIGHTEEN

WE DIDN'T ENCOUNTER ANY OTHER STORMS ON OUR JOURNEY, which, thank the Titans and the Old Kings and everyone else. It was just three quiet days of steady trekking over crimson sands and sleeping under gentle skies. And after that, we finally came to Benn Devalos.

I couldn't see it at first, not until we'd hiked to the top of a long, sloped dune. Then we reached the summit, and I looked down and actually gasped out loud.

It had been ages since I'd seen anything but desert, since my eyes had seen a natural color besides bright red. But sprawled out there between the dunes was a hidden valley of vibrant green and sparkling blue, an oasis paradise. At the center was a lake, wide and bean-shaped, its surface slick and reflective as a mirror to the sky above. Plants flourished around it: tall palms and leafy papyrus and patches of jutting reeds. But I barely noticed any of that because I couldn't stop staring at the cluster of buildings all around the lake, at the full-blown city.

I don't know what I'd been expecting from Syan's benn. A camp, maybe, like the Unbroken had? A tent-village, like you saw in the history books? But this was so much more than that. There were at least a hundred buildings below us, elegantly laid out around the lake like rows of plants in a garden. I couldn't tell what they were made out of, a slick tan material somewhere between sandstone and crystal, but it shone like gold in the bright sunlight. They had domed roofs with skylights made of translucent green stone, and they ranged in size from small family homes to a massive three-story building on the lake's edge. Gazing down from the dune's crest, I could see the people of the benn going about their day: artisans bartering goods in the market, cooks turning skewers lined with vegetables and fruit, children running and laughing while fishermen labored on boats dotting the lake.

I clearly wasn't the only one impressed. "By the Titans," Lyriana whispered. "It's amazing."

"All this time, you had this out here," Ellarion said, his voice just a little accusatory. "A city like this. A paradise. And we thought it was just a barren wasteland. . . ."

"How is this possible?" Zell asked. "Does the whole city withstand the storms?"

"There are soft places in the deserts where the storms don't go," Trell explained. "No one knows why. But those places are where we built up the benns."

"How many are there?" my father asked. "How many benns?"

"Twelve total," Trell boasted, and Syan shot him a glare like, *Why are you telling him that?* "Mine is about a week's ride to the east. When the elders learn how much gold I've made . . ."

"Twelve cities. Hundreds of people. Dozens of mages." My father let out a low laugh. "Miles has no idea what's coming."

"It's more than that," Lyriana said. "The implications of this are overwhelming. This changes everything."

"How so?" I asked.

"The reign of the Volaris is justified by the Heavenly Mandate: the Titans gifted us their magic so that we could guide mankind toward greatness, to be the shepherds that unite all the people of Noveris in prosperity and peace," Lyriana said. "That's how we justified everything. That we were creating the greatest world possible. That for all our flaws and failings, we were still the best option."

Ellarion nodded, clearly on the same train of thought. "We brought order to chaos. We were the clenched fist keeping the world from falling apart. Every war, every law, every jail, and every death, all of it was worth it because there was no better way."

Lyriana's eyes were fixed on the village. "But if this civilization exists . . . if they're living out here in peace and prosperity, in the most inhospitable climate in the world . . . then maybe it's all wrong. Maybe it's all a lie, and always has been."

I shot Zell a skeptical look, and he nodded, knowingly. It was nice that they were getting it. But had it really taken them this long?

Lyriana must have picked up on the awkwardness, because she cleared her throat and adjusted her collar. "We can talk more about this later. Right now, we need to get into that city and talk to the elders. This is the moment it all comes together. The moment the war turns. Right, Syan?"

But Syan glanced away, unable to meet her gaze. I didn't

get it; she'd completed her mission, gotten us all the way down here, survived storms and earthquakes and raging rivers, but here, on the border of her own city, she looked more hesitant than ever.

"Is everything okay?" I asked.

"I just want to say one thing," Syan said, staring out. "Whatever happens next . . . whatever they say down in the benn . . . I am so grateful to all of you. I've never really had friends. Not like you all. And I . . ." She swallowed hard, her voice just a little choked up. "Thank you. For coming this far. For trusting me. It's meant more than you'll ever understand."

"Syan?" Lyriana asked, reaching out to touch her shoulder.

But Syan just jerked it away. "Come on," she said, with an icy resolve. "It's time."

Well, *that* was ominous.

We marched in silence down the dune, toward the sprawl of the benn. The closer we got, the more impressive it looked. The buildings were all impossibly smooth, their surfaces so slick I couldn't make out a single brick or stone, their glistening tan frames decorated with intricate carvings and drawings. Shimmering crystal water cascaded out of fountains, as crystalline rooftops sparkled green and gold. Flowers were everywhere (in the middle of the desert!), wide planters brimming with flora the likes of which I'd never seen before: tall blue stems with prickly yellow bulbs, winding ivy with huge red berries, and what I can only describe as "sunflowers but at the same time roses"? And everywhere, *everywhere*, were zaryas, whistling through the air, hovering over people's shoulders, a skyscape of fluttering little orbs like a flock of hummingbirds.

The scale of it all was hitting me, the scale that had so

stunned Lyriana and Ellarion at the top of the dune. Lightspire was a city fueled by magic, sure. But this was a city built entirely out of it, a city shaped from magic itself.

There was something else off too, something I couldn't put my finger on until we were almost at the city's edge. "There are no walls," I said. "No guards either. No gates. It's just open."

"Why would they need them?" Zell replied in front of me, holding the terzan's reins tight. "The storm is the greatest wall any city's ever had."

So we just sort of strolled in, tethering our terzans to a hitching post outside the benn and following Syan in on foot. But just because we didn't get held up doesn't mean we didn't make a splash. By the time we set foot on the polished cobblestone that made up Benn Devalos's streets, it felt like everyone in the city was watching us. Some of the braver ones, heavyset men with pointed beards and stern-looking women with beads in their hair, actually hung out on the streets to stare. Most of the others just watched from the safety of their windows: gray-haired elders shaking their heads, young men and women whispering, kids pointing and gaping. I was starting to recognize common Izterosi qualities: olive skin, orange eyes, sharp features, and black hair glowing with multicolored strands. And there was something else they had in common, too. None of them looked happy to see us.

Which I guess made sense. I mean, none of them had ever seen someone who wasn't Izterosi before, much less a crew of two Volaris, two Westerners, and a Zitochi, much *less* a crew that looked as ragged, messy, and battle-scarred as we were. They'd probably reconsider that no-guards policy after we left.

No one said anything, though. Not until we crossed into a round little plaza outside of that wide hall, surrounded by plants that looked like bright red palm trees with watermelon-size berries. Waiting for us at the end of the plaza was a severe-looking group of older Izterosi, arms folded across their chests, faces etched with deep scowls. Their zaryas buzzed over them in a swarm, with a low hum that felt kind of menacing.

A woman stepped forward from that crowd, and I knew right away this was Syan's mother. Her face was almost identical, just twenty years older, with a crinkle of crow's feet by her eyes and deep furrows in her brow. And there was something about the way she held herself, a proudness to her manner, like there was absolutely nothing you could say that would remotely faze her.

But if this was Syan's mother, why didn't she look happier to see her daughter? Why did she look so pissed?

"Syan Syee," she said, her voice hard and furious. Four zaryas, *four*, fluttered over her, two above each shoulder, jerking back and forth with a crackling energy. "What in the name of the Sunfather is the meaning of this?"

I looked to Zell and Ellarion for support, but they looked just as confused as I felt. There was something we were missing here, something Syan hadn't told us, something big and awful. I looked back around, at the benn sprawled out behind me, at the faces staring from the windows, and a horrible truth twisted in my gut. Those people hadn't been staring at *us* with hate in their eyes. They'd been staring at *Syan*.

"Syan? What's going on?" Trell demanded, suddenly alarmed. "Was this not approved?"

But Syan just ignored him. "Mother," she said, and there was a quiver to her voice, a weakness that made my blood run cold. "Please. I can explain everything if you'll only listen. These are great leaders from the Stillands. They're—"

"Not where everyone can hear you!" her mother cut in, and the hum of the swarm of zaryas behind her rose to a drone. "Inside the hall. Now."

"Um . . ." I said, hoping someone else would jump in and help, maybe offer some insight, but the wagon was rolling and there was no turning it back. The elders ushered us into the hall, that big three-story building, with Syan sheepishly following. I turned to Lyriana, my expression hopefully communicating *What do we do here?* But Lyriana just shook her head and followed. There was nothing we could do, not until we knew more, maybe not even then. We'd come all this way. We had to see it through, one way or another.

The hall was simple, simple as a room built of slick magic stone could be. Fires flickered within perfect glass orbs, mounted in recesses all along the ceiling. A semicircle of elevated chairs lined the room's back wall, and we stood on the cold floor in front of them as the elders took their seats. Their zaryas settled down, slotting into small round grooves in their chairs, where they spun idly in lazy circles. There were seven other elders, husky men with bushy eyebrows and slim women with thick metal necklaces, but none of them spoke. It was clear Syan's mother ran the show.

"Now then," she said, once we were all in and the doors shut tight behind us. "Tell me, daughter. Who are these stillanders you've brought into our benn?"

"These are the great leaders and rebels of the Kingdom of Noveris," Syan said. "The former King, Elric Kent. The true Queen, Lyriana Volaris. Archmagus Ellarion, the greatest of their mages. They come here seeking our aid."

"Our aid," Syan's mother repeated, her face curdled like

the words were rotting in her mouth. "What could they possibly need our aid for?"

"Your Majesty," Lyriana cut in, putting on her best voice of regal deference. "If I may be permitted to speak, I—"

"My title is Elder Syee," the woman replied, her voice hard as a hatchet. "And the only thing you're permitted to do, *girl*, is stay silent and know your place."

Lyriana stepped back, stunned. I was, too. I don't think anyone had ever dared to speak to Lyriana like that.

"Mother, they come seeking our aid in their war." Syan was stumbling over her words and looking way, way too pale. I'd seen Syan stare down Jacobi and battle a storm of monsters, but I'd never seen her look even one-tenth this scared. "A terrible usurper sits on the throne, building an army of abominations. We can help these rebels turn the tide, restore peace, and put a stop to the horrors ravaging their land."

"And why would we possibly do that?" the Elder Syee replied. "For millennia, our people have stayed out of the affairs of stillanders. Why would we change that now? What would we have to gain? What could possibly justify such a monstrous breach of our laws?"

"Respected Elder, if I may." Trell stepped forward, head bowed low. "On behalf of Benn Selaro, I apologize profusely for any part I played in this. I had no idea that these stillanders were unwelcome. I was merely a guide, and I mean the people of your benn no ill will."

"You may merely be a guide, boy, but you are no fool," Syan's mother replied. "You know the laws of our people. You know stillanders are forbidden from setting foot in our sands. And I'm sure you knew that you ought to consult with your own benn's elders before taking on a job like this." Her gaze narrowed. "You knew this was wrong, and you let your greed blind you. I have no sympathy for that."

Trell stepped back, hand clutched over his mouth, eyes watering. My breath caught in my throat. Just how screwed were we?

With Trell cowed, the Elder Syee turned back to her daughter, and I swear the air in the room dropped ten degrees. "Syan Syee. Daughter of mine. Enough talk. Where is your brother?"

"He . . . he . . ." Syan tried and then she broke, collapsing to her knees, tears streaking down her cheeks. "I'm sorry, Mother. I'm so sorry. He's dead. I couldn't protect him. I couldn't save him. I'm so, so sorry."

Syan's mother's zaryas spun furiously in their slots. The other elders leaned back in their seats, like they were bracing for an explosion. For one moment, her face had an emotion besides indignation and grit, a look of real anguish. Then she pulled it in, hid it behind a snarl, and there was only the cold anger again. "You stupid girl," she said, voice barely a whisper. "You stupid, selfish, miserable girl." And even though I knew I should be scared, and I was scared, I also felt pissed, because what mother dared talk to her kid that way? What mother looked at her own child with that much venom and hate?

"I'm sorry, Mother," Syan begged. "I'm sorry!"

"So this is what it's come to, you ungrateful cur," the Elder Syee growled. "You dragged your brother onto your fool's crusade. You got my boy, my sweet wonderful boy, killed. And now you come to us, violating our people's ancient laws, dragging stillanders into our benn to . . . what? Get revenge? Is that truly how low you've sunk?"

"It's not about revenge!" Lyriana cut in, and I guess she'd decided not to know her place after all. "It's about saving the world. It's about Zastroya!"

The whole room went silent. The zaryas stopped spinning. The elders looked from one to another, perplexed, and the Elder Syee composed herself, folding her hands neatly together in front of her face. "And what would *you* know of Zastroya?"

"It's the end of everything. The Storm That Will Consume the World. And it's somehow connected to Miles and his bloodmages." Lyriana stepped forward, which, bold choice. "I know you've seen it too, that you've all been dreaming about it. I know the dreams started around the time Kent took over. I know—"

But the Elder Syee cut her off with a laugh. "Is that what she told you?"

Lyriana looked at her, then at us, then finally at Syan. "Yes?"

"I'm sorry," Syan whispered, unable to even look up. "I'm so sorry."

"Then it seems we are all victims of my daughter and her passions. That no matter how we scold and guide and punish her, she just drags more and more people into her madness." The Elder Syee shook her head. "Tell them, daughter. Tell them the truth."

My heart was pounding, my hands shaking, and I desperately needed to get out of this room. How had this all gone so wrong, so quickly? What had we missed all this time?

I wanted Syan to answer, to tell her mom to piss off, to assure us that everything was okay. But Syan just sat there, face hidden, breath ragged, unable to speak. So her mother sighed wearily and spoke for her. "Of course. You can lie to Kings and Queens, but the one thing you can't do is tell the truth." She turned to Lyriana, looking at her less with fury and more a profound pity. "We have *not* all been dreaming of Zastroya. I've never dreamed of it in my life. The only person . . . the *only* person . . . who dreamed of it was her. My daughter. The lunatic."

"What?" I asked.

"It's a tragic illness, the madness." The Elder Syee shook her head. "Syan's father had it, and his grandmother before him. First come the dreams, terrible visions of death and chaos, tormenting them every night. Then the hallucinations, vivid nightmares all around them even when they're awake. Soon enough, they don't know what's real anymore. They kill themselves. Or others."

It hit me all at once like a punch in the gut, like the air had been sucked out of the room. Syan had been lying to us. This whole time, she'd been lying. This wasn't some special mission for her people, it was just her own personal obsession. And her people couldn't care less. Syan had led us out here, into the desert, away from our Kingdom and our cause, on a wild dream at best and a total lie at worst.

That answered *that* question. We were *completely* screwed.

"I'm *not* mad, mother," Syan insisted, with the labored desperation of someone who's had to say this all too many times. "The dreams were real! Zastroya is coming!"

"We tried to help her, to comfort her, to convince her that her delusions weren't real," Syan's mother went on. There was love in her voice, buried somewhere deep, but it was smothered under layers of anger and disappointment. "I'd braced myself for the worst. But never in a thousand years did I think she would be foolish enough to venture into the Ghostlands!"

A murmur ran through the room, and Trell burst up to his feet, jerking away from Syan as if he'd just learned she was carrying the plague. "I didn't know!" he yelled, sounding equal parts furious and terrified. "I swear it! I swear! I would never have helped this blasphemer!"

"I needed to know the truth," Syan said. "The dreams kept calling to me, telling me to go out there, to the prison."

"To the Nightmother!" Trell howled, and I was honestly a little worried he was going to get violent. "To the demon, the destroyer! You went to *her*!"

The Elder Syee ignored Trell, going on as if he wasn't even there. "When my daughter returned, wild-eyed, raving, talking of what she'd seen in the Ghostlands, my heart broke in half. She was beyond helping, beyond redemption. There were some in this room that felt the compassionate choice would be to end her. But that is not our way. So I banished her instead." The Elder Syee's eyes flared bright. "I never thought she'd return. I never thought she'd find more ways to break our laws. And I *never* thought she'd drag my sweet innocent boy into her madness."

"The Nightmother sends warnings of the end," Syan said. "She showed me the lands of Noveris, and the abominations, and the usurper King. She showed me the symbol!" She turned back to us, her eyes wild, and I had the horrible realization that this was her trump card, the moment she thought it would all turn. "Look at Lyriana's tattoo, mother! It's the symbol I drew. The symbol I always drew. You recognize it, right?"

A hushed silence hung over the room. The Elder Syee

squinted at Lyriana's tattoo, and I could see a flicker of recognition. "Yes, I suppose that does resemble it."

"Well, there you go!" Syan said. "I was telling the truth. This is all destiny. This is the Nightmother's will. Our people were meant to join flames, to fight together!"

But the Elder Syee's face was still cold as ever. Maybe colder. "So you got this girl to tattoo your symbol onto her arm. And you thought that would convince me?"

"What?" Syan said, and I could see the exact moment it crushed her. "No. I didn't . . . I didn't convince her of anything. She had the tattoo when I met her. . . ."

"It's true. It's the ancient symbol of the Titans. I got it months ago," Lyriana said. "There is truth in your daughter's words. The visions—her visions—they led her to me."

"If you really believe that, you're as delusional as she is," the Elder Syee said.

"Look. There has clearly been a mistake made here," Lyriana said in her most perfectly mannered diplomatic voice. "But I believe we can still work something out. Forget the past. Let us talk as the leaders of two people. . . ."

"No. There will be no talk," the Elder Syee said. "Your presence here is a violation. My daughter's presence is a blasphemy. There is only one outcome here. I spared you once, daughter. And I have lived to consider it my greatest regret." She closed her eyes. "You all must face the sand's justice. For my son's sake, if nothing else."

"You betray his memory," Syan whispered.

The Elder Syee sat forward. "What was that?"

"You heard me," Syan replied, and now there was something new in her voice, an edge, a fury, a gathering storm. "Kalin came with me because he believed me. He had not seen the dreams, but he trusted in my words, in my passion. When all of you turned your backs and cast me out, he stood with me. And when he died, he died fighting to save others. To save *stillanders*." She rose to her feet, standing tall to stare her mother down. "You may remember him as the sweet boy you held in your arms. But I remember him as the proud man who fought for his beliefs, no matter the cost. If he were here today, he'd be standing by my side. And he'd hate who you've become."

The Elder Syee pulled in her breath through her teeth, and I've never seen anyone look more enraged. The air hung heavy, tense. The other elders stared at her nervously. For one long endless minute, no one spoke.

"I wish you'd died," she said at last, "and he'd lived."

The Elder Syee's zaryas rose up, bursting out of their grooves in her chair. They spun wildly in the air in front of us, spooling around each other like fishing rods drawing in their catch. There was a loud sucking noise, like the world sharply drawing in through a straw, and then I was on my knees, gasping, hacking for breath that wouldn't come. My lungs burned in my chest, and the sides of my head felt like they were being crushed by an invisible vise. I'd expected a blast or a strike, a fireball or a wave of ice. But this was worse, so much worse.

She was pulling the air out from the room around us, drawing it out of our lungs. She was suffocating us where we stood.

The others went down all around me: my father clawing at his throat, Lyriana helplessly flailing, Zell dragging himself forward by his knuckleblades, teeth clenched in a furious grimace. But the Elder's zaryas just kept whirling, all four of them, faster and faster, and that horrible burning feeling got worse and worse. My vision blurred, flared red. My body felt like it was on fire from the inside. I hit the ground face-first, gagging, gasping, and the last thing I saw was Syan lying next to me, her face bloodless, her eyes wide with a broken resignation.

I'm sorry, she mouthed to me.

Then the darkness took us.

nineteen

"Tilla."

Hands shook me. A voice, familiar, called my name. I felt only pain, and swam through a murky darkness.

"Tilla!"

With way more effort than it should have taken, I opened my eyes. I was lying on the ground, I think, on something soft and sloping. There was a wide blue sky above, and a figure leaning over me, his face blurry but familiar. I let out a groan and blinked, and he swam into focus. Zell.

Zell.

Memory rushed back to me like water pouring from a breaking dam. I wanted to shoot up, to scramble to my feet, to look around and figure out where in the frozen hell we were and why I was still alive. But I was in way, way too much pain to do that. My lungs still felt like they'd been hollowed out with a carving knife, and my throat was dry and scratchy. The sides of my head throbbed. Every inch of my body hurt.

So instead I just sort of lay there and moaned. "Why . . . How . . . *What?*"

"We're alive," Zell said, and I felt the warmth of his hand clenching mine. "She didn't kill us."

"Not right away," another voice, Ellarion's, said from somewhere nearby. That was enough to get me up at least a little, rolling over onto my stomach and pushing myself onto my hands and knees. I was on sand, coarse sand as black as nightglass. This wasn't like the blacksand beaches back home, though, where it sparkled all pretty in the light. This sand was a deeper black, darker, like it was pulling in all the light around it. That sand stretched out around me as far as I could see, an endless stretch of charred desert that somehow strained my eyes to look at. Behind me, maybe fifty feet away, the sand gave way to what looked like a cliff face, dropping down into a crater; besides that, there was nothing, not even dunes, just a forever sprawl of sandy night. And that's just what I could see. Worse was the feeling in the air, a sweaty, sticky tangible magical energy, curdling my stomach and making my eyes water. If it was bad in the desert on our way in, it was so much worse here.

The rest of my group was laid out around me, also going through the motions of getting up. My father was on his feet, staggering; Lyriana was helping Syan up; Ellarion was pacing around, gazing out at the horizon. "Where are we?" I asked. "And . . . why?"

"The Ghostlands," Syan answered, her voice distant. Her eyes were cast down with shame, unable to look at any of us. "It is against the laws of the Izterosi for the elders to take a life. They could not kill us. But they could bring us here, send us over the border with a Cut, and turn away. The justice of the sands."

Lyriana looked down, crestfallen. "We've been left here to die."

I glanced down, realizing for the first time that all my stuff was gone. My sword and scabbard, even my water flask. They'd left us with just the clothes on our backs.

"You!" a voice screamed, and I realized I'd forgotten the last party member. Trell. He stood upright, his hair wild, an expression of crazed fury on his face. "This is all your fault!" He rushed toward Syan, and though they'd taken his zaryas and anything else he could use as a weapon, he looked ready to strangle her with his bare hands. "Blasphemer! *Blasphemer!*"

"Stop," Zell said, putting himself in Trell's path. "There's no need for that."

"You don't understand." Trell tried to push past Zell, but that wasn't happening; Zell stepped around to block him, pressing a hand to his chest. "She lied to us. She betrayed us. She doomed us all!"

"I have to admit, he's right," Ellarion said. He turned toward Syan, and when he spoke his voice had equal parts hurt and anger. "All this time. Our whole journey. It was based on a lie. You brought us out here, to the very reaches of the world, on a promise you could never deliver. How could you?"

"It's not like that," Syan replied, her voice ragged. "I thought my mother would listen. I thought when she saw who you were, when she saw Lyriana's tattoo, she'd believe me. I thought this was fated. I thought it was meant to be." She swallowed hard. "I thought she'd want to avenge her son."

"She *is* avenging him," Trell said, glowering. "Don't you see? His death is *your* fault. You're mad. And you've dragged us all down with you!"

"I'm not mad!" Syan cried. "I swear. The dreams are

real. Zastroya is coming. Yes, the visions come from the Nightmother. But she chose me to bear her warning, like my father before me. She sent me the dreams because she needs me to save the world! She spoke to me!" That last part was new. "In all the dreams, all of them, the same message, the same words. *Find me. Help me. Save the world.*"

"Listen to yourself!" Trell yelled. "The *Nightmother* spoke to you and *you* listened? Madness! Utter madness!"

"I believe her," Lyriana said.

Now we all stopped, staring at her, the only sound the whistle of the wind over the sand. "What?" Ellarion asked at last.

"You heard me." Lyriana rose to her feet, staring all of us down. "I don't care what her mother said. I believe Syan. I think she's telling the truth."

"But . . . but even she admits she lied," Ellarion countered. "I mean, about the dreams, she was the only one having them."

"That doesn't mean they're not true." Lyriana stood firm, and Syan stared up at her, cheeks streaked with tears. "When Syan held my hand, when our flames joined, I saw those same visions. I saw the fire. I heard the Nightmother's voice. And I know, I know what I saw, what Syan saw, is real. I think Zastroya is coming, and it has do with Miles. I think she brought us here for a reason."

"You think it's real," Ellarion repeated. "Zastroya. The Storm That Will Consume the World."

"Yes," Lyriana replied, and this was a Lyriana I hadn't seen in ages, maybe not since the war had started: assured, confident, and certain, unflinching in her beliefs. "Look. A year ago, you and I would have sworn up and down that no

Westerner could ever do magic. We were wrong. A month ago, we would have said that there are no cities in the Red Wastes, and certainly no mages. We were wrong. If there's one thing that's clear to me, it's that what we've been taught is true is likely not, that what seems impossible might well be happening." Lyriana turned to me. "Tilla, remember what it was like when you were telling us about the bloodmage who attacked you, and none of us listened? When the whole city thought you were mad?"

I nodded. "Yeah. It was the worst."

"Well, I don't want to do that to anyone ever again." Lyriana pressed a hand to her chest. "The only thing I can rely on is what I feel. And my heart tells me Syan speaks the truth."

Syan stared up at her, and it was as if nothing else existed but the two of them. "Thank you," she whispered, like no one had ever said this before. "Thank you."

Zell cleared his throat. "We can figure out the truth later. Right now, we need to focus on getting out of here."

Ellarion nodded, and I could see the exact moment he switched into strategist mode. "Right. You said they made a Cut to get us out here. Can you make a Cut to get us back?"

Syan shook her head. "They took my zaryas. I could make new ones, but I'd need materials. Stone, metal, something to smooth them."

"And time," Zell said. I followed his gaze and now I saw it, a rapidly growing dot in the sky to our west. A gathering storm. "We need to move fast."

"Could we just run?" I asked. "Like to the nearest benn?"

"That's miles and miles away," Trell replied. "And even if we got there, they wouldn't l—"

"All of you," my father cut in. It was the first time he'd spoken since we'd woken up. "You need to see this." He stood at the edge of the downward-sloping crater. "Now."

We made our way over to him, to the cliff's edge. Then we stopped and stared.

It was a while before anyone spoke again.

The crater was massive, maybe the size of a whole Lightspire block. Its surfaces were perfectly smooth and slick, like someone had reached into the sand with a giant bowl and lifted it straight up. And in the very middle of it was a tall, rounded structure that I couldn't take my eyes off of. Jutting out of the sand was the top of a tower, a long massive spire maybe five stories tall. The roof was a rounded dome, smooth and polished; the body was spiraled with thick curves, like a serpent wrapped around a staff. It was coated in ash and soot, but even underneath that, the original shimmersteel shined through, glistening like the scales of a fish in the sun's light.

"The prison!" Trell gasped. "The Nightmother's prison!"

"That's no prison," Ellarion said, his voice a million miles away. "That's the Godsblade."

I felt like my head was going to explode. Because it was undeniable. That's what it was: the Godsblade, the giant Titan building at the heart of Lightspire, the ruin around which the city was built, the tower that housed the throne and the court and the Heartstone. It was here, or the very top of it was anyway, jutting up out of the sand like a sword stabbed into the dirt. The Nightmother's prison, the center of the Ghostlands, was the Godsblade.

"How?" I demanded. "How is this possible?"

"The story Trell told us," Zell said, his eyes locked on the structure. "The Nightmother and her siblings, coming from the sky to enslave the people. Could they have been . . . Titans?"

"They built the Godsblade in the Heartlands," Lyriana speculated. "Perhaps they built another out here? One that fell to ruin when they Ascended?"

"A second Godsblade. That could mean a second Heartstone!" Ellarion said, actually jumping with the realization. "This explains everything. The Izterosi mages, the storms, the magic everywhere out here. It's all connected. All of it!"

Lyriana turned to Syan, who looked mostly perplexed by our reactions. "You've been down there? Did you go inside?"

"No. I couldn't find a way in," Syan said. "I just touched the surface, and that's when the visions came strongest, most deafening and overwhelming." She reached up to the sides of her head, rubbing her temples. "Can you not hear it? The voice, so loud and clear . . . *Find me. Help me. Save the world.*"

I definitely did not hear a voice, but I was now firmly with Lyriana in the "nothing is impossible, just roll with it" camp. "We should go in there, right? See what's inside?"

Zell nodded, looking out at the horizon, where that little blip of darkness was now five times its size. "Even if we can't find any magic, it'll be shelter from the storm."

"Go in there?" Trell scoffed. "Do you understand what you're saying? That's the Nightmother's prison! The house of darkness and chaos and terror! We can't *go in.*"

Lyriana stepped over and put one hand on his shoulder. "Trell of Benn Sevalos. I'm sorry that we dragged you into this mess. I'm sorry that you've suffered for our journey. I'll do everything I can to make it right." She squeezed. "But we need to go in there. You can come with us or you can stay out here, but I doubt you'll be safer all alone when the storm hits."

I could see the exact moment he broke down, when his fear outpaced his conviction. "Madness," he said, "utter madness," but when we started moving, he walked with us.

Making it down the slope wasn't too bad; I slipped only two, maybe three times, and Zell was always there to help me. The sand had this weird way of crunching underfoot, almost like ice, and we left a long trail of our footprints down the side. Worse, way worse, was the feeling in my head. Everything around me was blurry, my nose was stuffed, and there was this endless throb, like thumbs being ground into my temples. I could see stars and taste blood, and it felt like every cell in my body was screaming *This is bad! Turn back!*

But there was nowhere else to go, so on we went. Seeing this second Godsblade from above had been weird enough, but being up close felt truly like we'd crossed into a fever dream. Here were the slick symmetrical octagons, the grooved sides, the telltale glow of shimmersteel. This was definitely the Godsblade. Except, you know, just the very top of it, jutting out of the black sand of a cursed desert.

"I think I found a door," Lyriana said, approaching a flat circle carved in the building's side, with a slick slate of shimmersteel grooved into the wall next to it. By my estimation, only the very top story of the building was visible here, the rounded dome that, in the Lightspire Godsblade, housed the massive chamber with the Heartstone. Was that what was waiting for us inside? Was the rest of this Godsblade down there, below the sand? What *else* was down there?

"I found the door as well," Syan said, "but I couldn't figure out how to open it." She pressed one hand to the building's side. "The voice is so loud. Unbearable. It wants us to open it. To come in."

I was going to suggest that maybe listening to the voice in Syan's head wasn't the best idea, but before I could, Lyriana reached out a hand toward that grooved slate. She ran her fingers over its surface, and it glowed to life, displaying a perfect blue trace of the symbol she'd drawn. Syan clasped a hand over her mouth, and Trell looked ready to pass out.

With a rusty hum, that round circle in the wall glowed a vibrant blue and then vanished, revealing a passageway into the side of the building.

"It worked." Lyriana stared at her own hand in disbelief. "The *open* symbol, the one the priests taught us as an ancient rune of the Titans . . . it actually worked."

"It's all connected," Ellarion repeated. "Titans here . . . Titans there . . ."

We stepped through the opening, because what else were we going to do? The room inside was small, just barely big enough for all of us to fit in, with a different carved circle in the opposite wall, its own slate grooved into the wall next to it. Once we were all in, Lyriana touched this second slate, drawing the rune again.

I expected the second door to open, but instead the first one reappeared behind us, sealing us in. A soft red light shone down on us from the ceiling above, though I couldn't make out any lamp. The room got warmer, a lot warmer, the floor beneath us glowing orange as drafts of heat wafted up. The walls around us hummed, louder and louder.

Then . . . I don't quite know how to describe it. There was a rush of wind into the room, fluttering my clothes, and a surge of magic in the air, that awful sickly crackle. The smell of ash filled my nose. And there was this feeling, this awful feeling, as if something was reaching into me, snaking invisible tendrils into my body, probing and grasping. I gritted my teeth and dug my nails into Zell's hand, while the others around me all stiffened and gasped. The hum grew louder, the room grew hotter, the lights burned bright, and all I could think was what an incredibly stupid way to die.

It stopped, as sharply as it had started. The lights above dimmed, the heat vanished, and that horrible feeling went away. The door in front of us, the one leading deeper in, glowed and vanished, revealing a long shaft leading into darkness.

"What was that?" I asked. "Does anyone have any idea what just happened?"

Lyriana looked to Ellarion, and he shrugged. "We've long left behind anything close to understanding," he said. "All we can do is keep going."

That wasn't technically true, because we could also, you know, break down crying or bang on the walls or just stand there screaming in terror. It didn't seem like anyone else was open to that.

Lyriana stepped over the door's lip and flicked her hand to make an orb of Light appear. It was clear the air here was still full of raw magic; her first orb flickered out, her second stretched like a balloon before bursting, but her third worked right, floating alongside us to illuminate our way. As soon as she did, she let out a little shriek. Because this was a wide chamber all right, a wide and round room about the size of the grand hall back in Castle Waverly. The walls were lined with rows and rows of heavy stone chairs, stacked up above one another like shelves in a cupboard, all the way up to the ceiling.

And in every chair was a Titan.

I'd seen them before like this, in the catacombs below Lightspire. These looked a lot like those had: hulking human forms at least nine feet tall, their bodies slick and hairless and nude. Their skin was white as snow, their heads bald as eggs, and every one of them somehow had the same face, with a bony nose and lips curled ever so slightly in a subtle smile. Their eyes were shut, their heads reclined a little, with some kind of strange shimmersteel tube hooked into the bases of their skulls.

"What is this?" Trell whimpered. "What are *they*?"

"Titans," Ellarion whispered. "It's another Titan crypt."

My heart leaped into my throat. The last time we'd been in a Titan crypt, the wild magic in the air had nearly driven all of us mad, had sent me into a horrific nightmare vision of my brother's corpse. I was *not* doing that again. "We should go. Now."

"No, wait." Lyriana raised a hand, as if testing the breeze. "It's different in here. The air isn't as corrupted. I think we're safe."

"Are we really going to take that chance?"

"If they have a Heartstone, it'll be in here." Ellarion gestured toward the end of the room. "We need to at least look."

So we went on, through this sprawling hall, past one creepy dead Titan after another. The hall gave way to a rounded wall that I'm guessing was the inside of the dome. Just like in the top floor of the Godsblade in Lightspire, there was a second shimmersteel dome sitting in front of it, where the Heartstone would be. But this dome was cracked, a big chunk of the front missing. I could see something inside, a husk of trembling rock, black and colorless, like a stone dug out of a long-dead fire. If this was the second Heartstone, then all the magic had long since drained out.

There was something else at the end of the room, too. In front of the smaller dome there was a single throne, this one twice as big as the others. Long shimmersteel cords stretched out from the chair, snaking like vines into walls all along the room. A Titan sat in it just like the others, but this one seemed more important somehow; bigger, more imposing, its seven-fingered hands hooked into slots built into the chair.

"I might not know about the Titans, but I'm guessing that was their leader," my father said.

"The Nightmother," Trell whispered. "It's her. It's *her.*"

"What happened out here?" Lyriana asked. "Why did they all die?"

"The Heartstone's broken," Ellarion said, equal parts horrified and awed that it could even happen. "I can't imagine that went well."

"I don't understand," Syan said. I thought she was responding to Ellarion, but she was looking at something else, a long black wall at the far end of the room, past the Heartstone. It was broken up into panels, each at least a single story tall, their surfaces smooth and dark as nightglass. "The voice . . . it's coming from in there."

She reached out a hand, and even as Lyriana yelled "Wait, no!" she touched the wall's surface. The panel lit up around her hand, a halo of blue encircling it the way the floors would light up underfoot in the Godsblade, and then it spread out until the panel was glowing, then the one next to it, then the one after that. Syan jerked back but the panels kept glowing, and it took me a second to realize it wasn't the surface itself but a glowing layer of light in front of it, like a floating magical skin, a series of translucent panes hovering in the air.

"It's a gallery," Ellarion said, transfixed, and sure enough, images were appearing on those panes. Each held a single picture, if you could call it that, a glowing series of lines that pulsed with light, flickering in and out of existence. In some moments, they were crystal clear, as detailed as the lavish oil portraits of themselves that nobles liked to hang around their mansions. In others, they were more like hieroglyphics.

I didn't get it, but Lyriana did. "It's a history," she said. "The history of the Titans. Look." She stared up at the first panel, which showed a ray of light descending from a starry sky with a giant nude figure within. "'The Titans came from the heavens above,'" she said reverently, and even a skeptic like me knew that was the first line of scripture. "'From the stars beyond the sky.'"

"Look at the next one," Ellarion said. This one showed a map of the continent, not that different from the one we'd plotted our route on, except it was floating and made of light and so detailed you could make out trees swaying in forests and clouds drifting over mountaintops. Two dots on it glowed red: one in a sprawl of grassy plains I knew were the Heartlands, and the other down here, in the Red Wastes. "Two Titan cities. Lightspire, and another. Here. Where we are now." He shook his head. "All this time we thought we were chosen . . . and there was a whole second Titan city just to the south." He let out a noise that was maybe a laugh, if a laugh could be deeply sad. "There was nothing special about us at all."

"You should probably keep looking," Zell said. His eyes were on the third panel, and when I saw this one, I actually gasped. It showed people, humans, undeniably our ancestors, dressed in clothes that were little more than rags. And it showed what the Titans had done to them. It showed the humans dragging huge stones across the plains, laboring away with hoes and shovels in fields of grain, mining deep in dark, damp mines. I saw faces slick with sweat, backs straining from yokes, bleeding hands and weeping eyes. And everywhere our ancestors labored, the Titans stood behind them, watching, judging, not with malice or cruelty but with that awful smiling calm.

"No," Lyriana gasped, and I felt sick. I'd heard the slaves theory before, back when I'd been going through my questioning phase. But it was one thing to hear the theory, and another to see it so vividly.

"It's as I said!" Trell cried. "The Nightmother and her siblings! They enslaved us! For centuries and centuries!" He jabbed a finger at the image accusingly. "You see? You see it now?"

The next pane showed the fruits of their labor: a Godsblade, erected in the earth, and a city springing up around it like ivy: first buildings of wood and stone, then structures of metal and glass, and finally dozens and dozens of towers of shimmersteel. The Godsblade itself grew taller and taller as levels were built below it, turning it into the majestic spire it became, surrounded by a city of wonder. An image of a Titan appeared before it, as tall as the building itself, a moving statue made of glowing light that loomed over all the city's denizens. No wonder we thought they were gods.

But it was the next panel that really caught my eye. It showed a series of images, flickering, flashing, almost too fast to follow. I saw what looked like a battlefield from above, as armies of Titans surged toward each other. I saw fire raining from the sky onto a tower, the tower I'm pretty sure we were in, colossal meteors of searing orange that flattened the city around it, that burned the jungles to cinders, that left only charred sand. And then I saw the streets of an undemolished city, Lightspire, but things weren't looking great there, either. The Titans collapsed to their knees, clutched at their throats, tore at their faces. Thick white blood streamed down their cheeks as their eyes melted in their skulls.

"A war," Zell mused. "Between the two cities. Fire and plague, the magic of destruction."

"They killed each other," Lyriana said, and I could hear the exact moment her faith broke. "There was no Ascendance. No great vision for mankind. No purpose. No *point*. Just more war and death, forever."

"Nothing ever changes," my father whispered.

"There's another panel," Syan said, and she was right. This was off to the side, a little disconnected from the others, and if the last panel of war had been hard to follow, this one was incomprehensible. I saw raging fires and trembling earth, pulsing storm clouds and surging rivers. I saw a flickering rune that looked just like Lyriana's, and I saw an endless procession of screaming faces. It was chaos, total chaos, like looking into the last few seconds of a nightmare.

"My dream," Syan whispered. "This is my dream. This right here. All of it. How?"

"Maybe it's a—" Ellarion began, but he never got to finish his sentence, because right then the Titan in the throne sat up and opened its eyes.

TWENTY

THE NIGHTMOTHER'S EYES WERE BLUE, AN IMPOSSIBLE ICY blue like the depths of the hottest flame, full of color with no iris or pupils. She craned her head up toward us with an odd stiffness, and I could hear the crunch of her bones, like someone cracking their knuckles, if their knuckles were their whole body. The pipe, cable, whatever, that had been hooked into the base of her skull fell limp to the ground, and she drew her massive pale hands out from the grooves on the throne.

I screamed and staggered back, stopped from sprinting only by Zell grabbing my shoulder. Trell collapsed onto the ground, and Lyriana raised her hands, defensively. But the Nightmother barely seemed to notice. She rose up to her feet slowly, one cable detaching at a time, and rolled her head across her shoulders with a stretch. Standing up, she was so much scarier than sitting down, her massive frame towering over us, her enormous alabaster body shining bright in the light from the panels. There was this air about her, an aura of utter power and indifference. She took a step forward, and as her bare foot hit the shimmersteel floor the lights in the room turned on, casting the whole chamber in a faint bluish glow.

At last, the Nightmother saw us. She froze in place, her head tilting very slightly as she took in the sight of our party huddled together. Her expression didn't change; I'm not sure it *could* change. But there was something in her manner that I read as confusion.

Then she spoke. *Spoke* isn't really the right word, though. Her lips didn't move, and there was no sound. She just stared at us, her eyes blazing blue, and a voice sounded in our heads, reverberating around the inside of our skulls, a rumbling deep voice that boomed within us.

Who are you? she asked. ***What is the meaning of this?***

"Die, demon!" Trell screamed. He moved fast, too fast for any of us to stop him. With a shriek, he whipped a small knife out of a hidden sheath in his boot and rushed forward.

The Nightmother didn't move. Her hands lay still at her sides. But her eyes flicked to him, just the slightest bit.

Trell froze mid-stride. He jerked up off his feet, into the air, a terrified look on his face, hanging like a marionette. And then . . . he crumpled. It was like he was being squeezed by a giant invisible fist, crushed like a wad of paper in someone's hands. With a sickening crunch and a spray of blood in all directions, his whole body caved in on itself until it was a fleshy lump about the size of a watermelon. Then the Nightmother flicked her hand, bored, and what was left of Trell went flying, tossed to the side like a piece of garbage, leaving a long wet streak across the chamber's floor.

Syan screamed and Ellarion jerked back. Zell threw up a fist, the gesture for *freeze*. "No. One. Move," he said, his voice low and firm. "Don't try anything."

The Nightmother swiveled back to regard him, and then she noticed Lyriana. Well, more specifically, she noticed the orb of Light hovering next to her. Finally, she seemed interested. *How are you doing that?* she demanded. *Explain yourself.*

"The . . . the Light?" Lyriana asked, still staring at the horrifying remains of Trell. "It's magic. An Art."

Magic, the Titan repeated, like she was tasting the word. *No. That should be impossible. You can't use the Deep Magic. You're just apes.*

"Apes?" I asked, because I had to.

The Nightmother ignored me, focused entirely on Lyriana. *Prove it. Make another. Now.*

"Uh, okay." Lyriana raised a trembling hand, turning it over in a simple circle. A second orb appeared, this one duller than the first, but burning nonetheless.

The Nightmother stared at it for some time, and then she laughed, and that was the worst of all, a rumbling thundering laugh mocking me from within my own mind. *Oh, remarkable. Utterly remarkable. Apes using the Deep Magic. Whenever you think you have everything figured out, the universe still finds a way to surprise you.*

She turned away and raised her hand, her seven fingers bending into an incredibly complex form; I noticed, for the first time, that each had an extra knuckle. Behind her, the blackened ember that was this place's Heartstone gave off the faintest light, its exterior quaking like the surface of a lake when there's a distant tremor.

Then images appeared. They were like mirrors, I guess, or windows, squares of light, hanging in the air all around us, bright blue and just a little translucent. Some showed pictures of the desert outside, while others were covered in arcane runes and symbols, flickering as they streamed down like droplets of rain on a pane of glass. I had no idea what was going on, but I could tell this was magic on a whole other level, a mastery worlds beyond what any human could do. The Nightmother waved her hands, beckoning one pane closer, and examined it. *Seven hundred and seventy-eight years. Far too soon to be woken. Yet I am awake nonetheless.*

Awake? Was that the difference between this and the chamber we'd found in Lightspire? That had been a crypt, a place to preserve the dead, and this was a chamber for the living? Were all the other Titans around us just . . . asleep?

I didn't like that at *all*.

The Nightmother waved her hand, ushering the square in front of her away. *Why are you here?*

"You called me here," Syan said. She had dropped to her knees, her head bowed in deference, which I think the Nightmother found amusing. "You sent me the dreams. You warned of Zastroya. You asked me to come find you."

I did no such thing, the Nightmother said, then turned curiously to examine more of the glowing panels behind her. *Ah. Yes. I enchanted those to send my story out for any of my kind who survived the war. But your minds should never have been able to receive their message.* She paused, thoughtful. *Unless your minds changed. Unless the residual energy altered your capacity for magic.* She moved her hands again, and they spun on her wrists in a way that made no sense, full 360-degree rotations. I felt a warmth pass over me, and Syan let out a little gasp. *There it is,* the Nightmother said. *Will wonders never cease? There were none left who could do magic . . . so the magic created those who could use it.* She clapped her hands, and the screens vanished, leaving her burning blue eyes boring right into us. *How many are there like you?*

We all looked at each other uneasily, like maybe this wasn't something we should answer. "Mages?" Lyriana said at last. "I mean, hundreds. Thousands if you count the blood-mages and the Torchbearers."

No. Too many. Far too many. The panels behind the Nightmother dimmed, and I swear she was getting taller. *Have the earthquakes started again?*

"There have been earthquakes, yes," Ellarion said. "Getting worse and worse. But what does that have to do with—"

Then it has already begun, she cut in, and it really sounded like was she getting angry. *History repeats itself. First the earthquakes. Then the firestorms. The seas rise, the skies burst. And for all we sacrificed, for all we gave, this world will be lost to darkness.*

"Zastroya!" Syan exclaimed, sounding almost relieved. "The Storm That Will Consume the World. It is real. You *were* trying to warn me. Nightmother, I heard your call!"

Night . . . mother? she repeated, at once incredulous and condescending. *Oh, you pathetic apes. You took the distress signals I sent out and your mushy brains turned them into what? Myth? Legend?* She took a step toward us now. I was scared, that kind of deep bone-level scared where you can't even scream or run, you just sit there, frozen, desperately wanting it to be over. *Foolish creatures. Your minds can't begin to comprehend what's happening. You end the world without even understanding what you're doing!*

The air around us pulsed with gathering energy, and the Titan's hands clenched tight, shimmering with surging heat. Lyriana stepped forward, head held high, but I could see her knees trembling, her hands shaking, the fear behind her bold gaze. "Great Titan," she said. "I am Lyriana Ellaria Volaris, true Queen of Noveris. I do not claim to understand what's happening here. It's obvious that much of our understanding has been . . . misinformed." Her eyes flitted to the panel showing the enslaved workers, but her expression didn't waver. "But I can tell you that we came here because we want to prevent whatever catastrophe it is that you're describing. We want to save this world from ourselves." She took another step forward, and that was maybe the bravest thing I'd ever seen anyone do. "We come as your allies."

My allies, the Nightmother repeated, glancing down at her. Her expression hadn't changed even once since she'd stood up, still that placid smiling mask, but I was starting to read her body language. She looked curious. *Perhaps you do offer something of value. Perhaps this problem and its solution are one.* I could smell something in the air, a dusty chemical scent like the floor of an apothecary. *You pledge to me your service, little Queen? You vow to carry out my will?*

"Could we maybe find out what your will is first?" I blurted out.

The Nightmother jerked her head up to stare through me, and oh boy did I wish I'd kept my mouth shut. *You ask for understanding? Yes. You will perform better with knowledge.* She gestured back toward the panels with an open hand, her seven fingers unfurling like an anemone. *You saw the Wall of History?*

"We saw that you came from the stars," my father said, and even though his voice was calm and affectless, I tensed up. "We saw that you enslaved our ancestors."

Yes, the Nightmother said, with absolutely zero indication she saw anything wrong with that. *Through their labor, we built two great cities: Kaichkul, here, and Veshtanar to the north. Through their labor, we built the Great Towers. And through their labor, we forged our greatest achievement: the Heartstones.* She glanced over her shoulder at the massive black slab, glowing with only the faintest light, and was that a hint of real sadness?

The Heartstones granted us magic, the means to bend the rules of physics and usher in an era of true wonder. Through them, we transcended our original bodies, and adopted these perfect forms. We outgrew hunger and pain and want. We created paradise.

"And yet?" my father asked.

And yet, our actions carried a terrible price. We saw, too late, what happens to a world when its very reality becomes unraveled. The Nightmother glanced down. *It started with earthquakes. Then storms, surging from the seas, swallowing the coast. Then the mountains began to slide, and the forests began to rot, and we realized, truly, the damage we'd done.*

"You caused Zastroya," Syan said, a hand over her mouth.

We began it, the Nightmother said. *A world can only sustain being bent for so long before it breaks. It was clear the two great cities could not keep using magic. One of them would have to stop. And yet those fools in Veshtanar would not listen.*

"You went to war," Zell said. "Neither of you would give up your magic. So you slaughtered each other over it."

I had thought they would see sense when they saw the superior numbers of my army. But those cowards sank even lower than I could imagine. The ground below her feet trembled, little motes of dust rising to dance at her ankles, and a few tiny sparks of flame flicked around her hands. *Their mages unleashed the rain of fire on my city, on my civilians, defenseless, unarmed. They destroyed it. They killed thousands. This room, this scattered few, huddled here in the safety of the tower, are all that remain.*

"And you retaliated," my father said.

Oh yes, the Nightmother replied with an uncomfortable amount of relish. *I had a weapon of my own. A plague that fed on magical energy, that ate away flesh it had touched.* My eyes darted toward that mural with all the dead Titans, their skin sliding off their bones like a layer of curdled milk. *And I unleashed it on the world.*

"You killed all of them. All the Titans who lived in Lightspire."

In the world, the Nightmother clarified. *I annihilated my own kind. With one simple act, I murdered nearly a hundred thousand of my kin. I saved the planet, saved my kind and yours. I made the only right choice. I served the greater good. I—* She stopped, collecting herself. *The other survivors and I sealed ourselves in here. We put ourselves into a deep sleep, intending to emerge in a thousand years, when the plague would fade away, and the land would be safe to settle again.*

And yet here I find myself, awakened too early, and for all my efforts, the continent is threatened yet again, she said, and it was unnerving how calm she sounded about it. *You miserable apes have accessed the Heartstones, and you abuse them, pushing them to collapse, straining them until they break and unleash world-rending chaos.*

"The bloodmages," my father said. "In just one year, Miles created hundreds of new ones. That must be what's causing the earthquakes."

"Then Syan's visions were right," I added. "The blood-mages . . . Miles . . . they're tearing the world apart."

"Zastroya," Syan said. And in a way, it was only fitting, the final awful turn of the knife to cap off all the horrors that had come before. Miles ruined everything he touched, destroyed everything he came near. *Of course* he'd somehow find a way to put the whole world at risk.

The enormity of it sank in, stunning us into silence. All of us except Lyriana. "So we really were nothing to you," she said.

You were useful, the Nightmother replied. *As you are useful now. Together, we may yet stop this.*

"How?" Syan demanded. "How do we stop Zastroya?"

Your little mages are widespread, but they are still weak, delicate. Nothing compared to my kind. The Nightmother's hands darted through the air, faster than my eyes could follow, and the glowing panes whirled around her, flickering and pulsing, strange runes and numbers scrolling down their surfaces. *I can grant you my power. The power to truly use the Heartstones, the power to target and cull.* She extended her hand, and something hovered above her palm, a pale yellow crystal turning slowly in the air. *As I wiped out the threat among my people . . . so you can do the same to yours.*

"That's . . . the plague?"

A variant on it, the Nightmother said, with a definite hint of annoyance. *Modified to target your delicate human physiognomy. Take it to the Heartstone in Veshtanar, little Queen, and channel its power. The rest is up to you.*

"I don't understand," Lyriana pressed. "This crystal will kill the bloodmages?"

No. That won't be enough. It'll kill every single magic

user. The Nightmother's hands waved again, pulling a glowing pane up in front of her with images of Lyriana, Syan, and Ellarion. *Don't worry. I crafted it so that you three would be immune. Consider it a gift.*

"A gift? You're talking about killing thousands of people!"

They will die anyway. Within ten years at most, the Heartstone will burst. And everything will burn. Your people. Mine. Everything. She jabbed the crystal forward, this time more aggressively. *You kill a few to save your whole race. That is the cost of survival.*

Lyriana rose to her feet, eyes burning, hands balled into fists. "I refuse it," she said. "I refuse you. I refuse all of this!"

The Nightmother stepped forward, and the light around her seemed to bend, creating a massive shadow behind her that reached up to the ceiling. It was like she grew ten feet taller, like the world was shrinking behind her, like everything was trembling with the thunder of a gathering storm. I jerked back, we all did, except Lyriana, who stood proud and strong. *You do not speak like that to me, little ape,* she said, and now her voice was deafening, a roar in my skull so loud it hurt. *I gave you an offer. Now I give you a command. Do as I say, or I will . . .*

Then she stopped, her shadow shrinking, that rumble and roar vanishing. She just looked at us, perplexed. *The craft outside. More of your allies?*

"What?" I said. "What craft?"

The Nightmother stared at us like the answer was evident. *It landed a few minutes ago.* She flicked her hands through the air and one of those panes stretched out huge in front of us, like those massive tapestries that draped the walls in Castle Waverly's Great Hall. But this pane was moving, showing us an image like we were looking out through a window. There was the building we were in, the second Godsblade, jutting out of the desert sand. And next to it was something else, something big and gray, something it took my eyes a moment to recognize.

The Skywhale.

"Is this real?" Zell demanded. "Is this happening now?"

Of course, the Nightmother said, and now I could see lots of figures moving in the image, armored men rushing forward to the Godsblade's side, to the wall of the rounded dome we were standing in. There were at least two dozen of them, maybe more. And behind them, at the ramp leading down from the metal ship's maw, a man in a long black coat, with a shimmersteel circlet resting on his curly blond hair.

Miles.

I looked around wildly, from wall to wall, my body torn between the desperate need to start running and the understanding there was nowhere to run to. My legs felt weak, and my breath caught in my throat. Next to me, Zell clenched his hands into fists, and Lyriana's fingers bent into a combat form.

This was happening. This was actually happening. Miles had actually followed us all the way across the continent, had somehow landed his ship just outside the walls.

Miles was *here*.

What is the meaning of this? the Nightmother demanded. On her pane, the men came up to the side of this Godsblade, right up to the wall of the dome at the top. The room we were in right now. I turned to the wall with horror, the wall they were just on the other side of, and then I staggered back. Now I knew where to go: as far from that wall as humanly possible.

"Those are our enemies!" Lyriana exclaimed. "The ones who are using all the magic! The ones we need to stop!"

Why have they come here? she asked, and like, good question, lady. The soldiers were doing something, pressing something against the wall, I think, and then they ran back the way they'd come, sprinting away and ducking low in the sands.

"What is that?" Zell demanded, pointing at the pane. The Nightmother pinched her fingers, and the image expanded on the side of the building's wall, where the men had been pressing their hands. They'd left something there, stuck to the surface. A disc in a leather case, like a compass. With a burning, dancing, flickering light behind the glass.

A mage-killer.

Oh no.

"Run!" I screamed, and the wall blew open with the roar of thunder.

TWENTY-ONE

THE BLAST HURLED ME OFF MY FEET AND SENT ME FLYING, slamming me hard into the wall at the chamber's end. My vision flickered yellow and red, and pain shot through my spine. Dust billowed into the room, a thick cloud that stung my eyes and burned my lungs. I pulled myself up onto one hand, trying to take stock of what was happening.

There was a hole where the wall had been, a massive hole maybe five men wide, looking out into the sprawling black sand beyond. Chunks of shimmersteel debris lay on the ground around it, sparkling and twitching, pulsing with magic, like snakes writhing in the sun. Flakes of ash fell like snowflakes, and embers smoldered all over the ground. I squinted through that haze and I saw them, waves of soldiers drawing their blades. And beyond them, I saw that same shape, that figure in the black coat, that shadow that filled me with equal parts fury and fear.

Then I heard his voice, loud, clear, unmistakable.

"Kill them!"

With a roar, the soldiers charged forward, sprinting in through the hole, their swords shining in the wan light. I jerked back, scrambling for anything I could use as a weapon, but before I could react, the Nightmother let out a horrifying noise, a bellow that scraped like a shard of glass on the inside of my skull, a howl that ripped at my bones from within. She flailed out her hands, all fourteen fingers twisting like they were grabbing invisible clouds out of the air.

Something was happening to her. Something awful. She dropped to her knees with a thud that rattled the floor, and let out a choked gasp all the more terrifying because her face was still smiling. With one clawed hand, she pulled at her throat, even as her veins throbbed within her skin, as her eyeballs quivered and melted away.

The magic plague she'd released. The one that had killed almost all of her kind. She'd been safe before because we'd passed through that locked room, the one that had burned away the traces on us, but with the wall gone, she was exposed. . . .

She fell forward on one hand, and the skin on it cracked with deep bleeding rivulets, rotting on the bone. *NO!* she howled, deafening in my head.

That was all the wave of soldiers needed. "Get them!" Miles shouted, and they rushed forward, through the breach.

Zell was the first to strike. He lunged forward, bouncing off a wall with a leap, and caught the first soldier right in the side of the neck with his knuckle blades. The soldier collapsed with a gurgle, spraying crimson everywhere, and then Zell was up and moving, catching the next soldier under the ribs and dropping the one behind him with a bladed punch to the face, stabbing four clean holes into the center of his forehead.

Then the others were getting up all around me, bellowing as they rushed forward: Lyriana surrounded by pulses of blue light, Ellarion with his hands floating over his shoulders, Syan and my father with nothing but their fists and howls of fury. We were really doing this. We were fighting it out.

One way or another, it ended here.

I leaped to my feet and ran forward. One of the Western soldiers charged right at me, a small man with a pointed beard and a short sword in each hand. He swung the right one down in a chop and I weaved effortlessly around it, streaking behind him and delivering a spinning elbow to the side of his head. He stumbled away and turned back to me, wobbling on his feet, dropping one of his swords with a clatter. He reached for it, but he was too slow, too disoriented. I rolled, plucked it off the ground, and brought it up in a sweeping slash that slit him open from belly to chin.

Thirty-one.

Then the others were moving, too. Lyriana sprang forward, hands outstretched, and shot out a blast of rumbling force that sent soldiers flying. A soldier came up behind her, blade drawn, but before he could strike Syan tackled him to the ground. She didn't have her zaryas but that didn't stop her from smashing his head once, twice, three times against the metal floor. Ellarion's hands streaked through the air, carrying a ribbon of flame between them that cut through the charging line like a hot wire, decapitating at least four of them in one go. And Zell was a blur of nightglass fury, bounding from one enemy to the next, effortlessly dodging their attacks, leaving only slumped bodies and streaks of blood on the walls.

"Tilla!" my father's voice yelled from behind me. I spun

and there he was, on his knees, with a meaty Westerner holding him in a headlock, huge sweaty bicep clenched tight around his throat. With one hand, my father clawed at the man's arm, and with the other he reached out toward me, grasping, begging . . .

This time, I didn't hesitate. I tossed him my sword effortlessly, an underhand lob. He caught it and jabbed it back over his shoulder, driving it up to the hilt into the soldier's chest. The man let out an aggrieved noise, blood bubbling out of his lips, and then he let go of my father and crumpled back and lay still.

My father sprang back up to his feet, gave me an appreciative nod, and tossed the sword back to me. I shot him a smile, a wild-eyed combat smile, and let myself, for one second, taste the rush of victory. The soldiers around us were all dead or dying. Had we won? Had we actually *won*?

Then I turned back to the hole in the wall, to the Skywhale beyond, to Miles at the top of the ramp. I saw the confident grin plastered on his face. And I saw the force massing behind him, charging our way.

Bloodmages. At least two dozen of them. Their bodies crackling with energy, their bloodshot eyes throbbing with magic, their hands clouded in fire and ice and shadow. The soldiers we'd fought were just the disposable infantry. This was Miles's real power. And there was no way we could take them.

"Get back!" Lyriana screamed, throwing up her hands to cast a rippling purple membrane across the hole in the wall. And not a moment too soon, because the first few bloodmages were already attacking, slamming Lyriana's shield with jagged husks of rock and swirling blasts of light. She strained, gritting her teeth, but her Shield buckled and rippled, already fraying at the ends. There was no way it would hold. And when it fell, we'd be trapped with nowhere to run. I looked to Zell, to Ellarion, to my father. All their expressions said the same thing.

We were dead.

Help me, the Nightmother's voice cried, at once behind me but also still in my head. I turned back and there she was, lying on her stomach by the foot of her throne. She looked *awful*. Her skin had melted into a liquidy gray goo, hanging off her bones like wet paper on a stick. Her eyes had leaked out of her skull, streaking down her cheeks. Her whole body was shaking, like there were a million tiny insects burrowing in her skin, just trying to tear free.

And it wasn't just her. All the Titans, the dozens and dozens sitting in rows around us, were doing the same thing, writhing and flailing and gasping as their bodies dissolved around them. My stomach twisted as the enormity hit me. Miles hadn't just killed the Nightmother. He'd killed all the Titans, for good.

Take it, the Nightmother said, and reached out her hand, well, what was left of her hand, which was mostly a bony claw with a few ragged strips of skin dangling off it. That thing was still hovering above it, that slowly-spinning yellow crystal.

I don't know why I did it. Maybe because I didn't want to close off the option, no matter how unthinkable. Maybe because as terrifying as she was, there was something still pitiable about her, dying all alone on a cold floor. Maybe it was just the desperation of the situation. Whatever the reason, I ran forward, kneeled down on the shimmersteel floor and grabbed that crystal out of the Nightmother's hand.

I figured it would be, I don't know, solid. Instead, it

crumbled instantly in my palm, vanishing into my skin. I let out a gasp, and then . . .

I don't really know how to explain this next part. All I can say is that in that moment, everything changed. *I* changed.

The second that crystal absorbed into me, it was like I became . . . someone else. Became the Nightmother. It was only a second, a single moment, but that moment stretched out across eternity. A current surged through me, like I was being struck by lightning from within, like every cell in my body was vibrating and pulsing. My hands tingled with fire, my stomach lurched. The world flashed and throbbed a rainbow of impossible colors, the floor bleeding magenta, the walls writhing pink, every surface shimmering like a fish's scales in the sun. I tried to look at my hands, but they were simultaneously my hands but also a baby's hands but also an old woman's hands and also just bones and also a floating web of veins pulsing with blood. The way the Heartstone changed and shifted, somehow many different shapes at the same time? That's how the world had become.

And then there were memories. They weren't mine, but they were in my head now. I remembered staring at the cold vastness of the stars. I remembered the piteous mewling of the hairless apes as they beheld my visage. I remembered standing here, on this very spot, holding a yellow crystal, feeling the weight of the knowledge that I was going to kill thousands.

It was too much. Too many thoughts, too many memories, too many sensations. My head throbbed, my eyes burned, and I felt like my brain was going to explode. Panting, gasping, I jerked away toward the rest of the room. That just made it worse.

It was still the same hall I'd been in. But it was so much more. Ribbons of energy danced all around us, green and purple and white. Blue panes, the kind the Nightmother had been using, hung all around me, thousands and thousands of them, all flickering and pulsing with information. I could see my friends up ahead, frozen in place, blades drawn, as Lyriana's Shield cracked and shattered, but I could also somehow still see them everywhere else in the room at once, ghostly afterimages of where they'd been, trails of movement that showed them running and fighting and killing. I could see the Heartstone, could see all the magic within it, so much raw power still trapped within that smooth glass frame.

And I could see the bloodmages marching down toward us, twenty-seven of them in total. I could see the pulsing energy around them, could see their sick, polluted blood sizzling through their veins, could see the gathering storm that was their attack.

But I could also see how fragile they were, the weakness of their little hearts. The frailty of their brittle bones. Tiny little sacks of flesh, barely held together by tendon and sinew, so small and weak.

The Heartstone pulsed, and I could see lines, like arteries, leading from its frame to the bloodmages. Each was connected to it by this invisible strand, a conduit for magic. And all it would take was the simplest push.

Lyriana's Shield burst apart, the membrane ripping open like a cloth stretched too thin. She screamed. Zell gritted his teeth. My father closed his eyes.

Without thinking, without even really understanding what I was doing, I stretched out one hand and drew from the Heartstone. Just the tiniest bit. Just a drop. I pulled just the teensiest bit of that energy out of it and then with my other hand I hurled it out, sent it out to the bloodmages pulsing along those tendrils.

They burst apart. Every single one of them. One moment, they were there. And the next they were gone, violently exploding into clouds of misty blood and bone.

For one long endless moment, everything was still. No one moved. No one even screamed. We all just stood there, rooted in place, my friends on one side of the hole, Miles on the other, and a stretch of sand stained red with the remains of the bloodmages in between.

"Wh what?" Lyriana stammered. She hadn't seen me do it. None of them had. They had no idea I'd taken the crystal. No idea that I'd just singlehandedly killed all of Miles's best men.

Thirty-one plus twenty-seven is fifty-eight.

My number was fifty-eight.

Miles was the first to react, the first to break that lingering stunned impasse. "No!" he screamed, and turned to run back into the ship. But before he could, my father wound up and threw his sword.

It whistled through the air, spun over once, and then plunged right into the top of Miles's left shoulder. He screamed and toppled back onto the ramp, and then we were on him, all of us, sprinting out through the hole and across those black sands and up the ship's ramp. Miles staggered to his feet, trying to run, but Zell slammed down on top of him with a knee to his chest and some knuckleblades to his throat. I reached the base of the ramp just in time to see Miles throw up his hands, gasping. "Surrender!" he screamed. "I surrender!"

Then it was silent and still. All of his men were dead or

bleeding out. All of the Titans had dissolved. And all of us were there, at the base of the Skywhale, standing together, panting, staring down at Miles Hampstedt. The Inquisitor. The Regent of Noveris. The man who had brought so much harm. The boy who had cost me so much. And he just lay there, hands up, eyes winced shut, begging for mercy.

We'd won.

Holy shit.

Holy. Shit.

We'd actually won.

I looked to the others, from face to face, as all of us took in the enormity of what had just happened. They still didn't understand it, didn't know that I'd been the one who'd killed all those bloodmages, but in their defense, I didn't actually understand it, either. Standing by the Heartstone, surging with its power, I'd felt like a god, seeing the joints of the world exposed, capable of anything. But now, even twenty feet away, all of that had faded. I didn't see beating hearts or ribbons of energy or . . . any of it. I felt like myself again. Mostly.

Ellarion slumped down, his hands hovering over his shoulders. Lyriana glared with a look at once triumphant and furious. Zell was all business, keeping Miles pinned, but there was a hint of something else, the tiniest curl of a smile. My father just shook his head. And Syan . . .

Her face was weary, streaked with blood, gaze a thousand miles away, but she still moved with an incredible speed. She bounded past me, over Zell, and lunged toward Miles with a dagger drawn.

"No!" my father yelled, catching her wrist, jerking her back. "We need him alive!"

"His men killed my brother! They killed the Nightmother!

He did all of this!" Syan yelled. Miles jerked away, trying to scramble up the ramp, but Zell kept him pinned. "He has to pay!"

"I know," Lyriana said. She extended one hand to gently touch Syan's cheek, and Syan first bristled, then softened, at the touch. "He will. But first I have to take my Kingdom back."

"I can get you home," Miles pleaded, and in that second, whatever new dignity he'd accrued, whatever commanding aura, was gone. This was the Miles I'd always known, scared and desperate, saying anything to save himself. "I can make the army stand down and the bloodmages surrender. But you need me alive to do that. You understand that, don't you?" Then he had the audacity to look at me, right at me. "Tell them, Tilla!"

The others looked to me. I shrugged. And I stepped forward and punched him in the face.

TWENTY-TWO

IT'S STILL A LITTLE HARD FOR ME TO WRAP MY MIND AROUND how fast the next part happened.

One moment, we were back in the fallen Godsblade, staring at the pane in terror as Miles's soldiers charged our way. And the next, he was our prisoner, and we were soaring through the sky in his hijacked ship.

Okay, maybe it wasn't exactly one moment. Even after capturing Miles, we still had to clear the Skywhale and make sure there weren't any of his men hidden away. It was mostly empty. There was a young soldier who lunged out from a closet (and caught a blade in the throat for his trouble), an old steward who practically fainted when we found him, and a stodgy Western navigator up in the captain's quarters who took one look at us, with the bound Miles in tow, and began yammering about how he knew how to get us home.

And there were the Hands of Servo, the mages imprisoned within the wings who performed the magical Arts that kept the ship afloat. Miles had plucked them out of the prison camps and kept them locked up in the Skywhale for the past three months, threatening to kill their families if they dared defy him. These poor mages looked beyond broken: gaunt and thin in frayed rags, with haunted eyes and trembling hands. Lyriana freed them from their cages in the Skywhale's wings, blasting open the doors with bursts of force, and they collapsed to their knees in front of her, clutching at her legs, kissing her hands as tears streaked down their cheeks. "The True Queen," they sobbed. "The True Queen has returned!"

It was a lot.

With the Hands freed and Miles shoved into a cell, the Skywhale was ours. The Hands were more than happy to help us, of course, in part to repay Lyriana but also because what was the alternative, stay here in the desert and die in a storm? So they took their places back in the wings and the rest of us gathered together in the bridge, sitting in black leather chairs. My father took the helm, which was a series of elaborate dials and tubes. True to his word way back when, he did know how to fly it, barking orders into the tubes: "Hand one, lift off. Hand two, lift off. Hand three . . ."

The Skywhale rumbled beneath us, wobbling from side to side. I clutched my armrest. Next to me, Zell smiled, looking awfully calm for a guy about to fly in a giant metal ship. I guess after everything we'd been through in the past few weeks, what else could you do, right?

"All Hands, full blast!" my father shouted, and then with a rolling roar from outside and the jangling rattle of vibrating metal, the Skywhale took off. I felt my stomach drop as we lifted off, the way it always did in an aravin, and through the window outside I saw the ground vanish, the horizon recede, replaced only by the clear blue of sky.

We were up high soon, like, really high, the fallen Godsblade looking as tiny as a child's toy, the sprawl of desert a sandpit. My stomach still felt uneasy, but I couldn't help but smile as well. We were flying, actually for-real flying. The Skywhale . . . and the sky itself . . . was ours.

I wish Galen could've seen us. I hoped he was okay.

"This is amazing," Lyriana said, and I realized she was by my side. "Beyond amazing." The others came to join her: Zell and Ellarion and Syan, and we all stood together, gazing out at the world below.

"Never in my wildest dreams would I have ever imagined this." Ellarion's eyes glistened with tears of real joy.

Zell's face was harder to read: awed, reverent, a little uneasy. "We sail the heavens as Gods," he said, voice barely audible.

Behind us, the navigator was plotting a course on a long map draped across a table, while the steward prepared us chalices of wine. Both of them had pretty much immediately flipped to our side, which said volumes about their loyalty to Miles. And speaking of the devil . . .

With our course firmly plotted back toward Lightspire, Zell went down into the ship's lower level and came back with Miles. His hands were bound together with an iron chain, his hair tousled, his cloak sweat-soaked and clinging tight to his frame. A huge purple bruise blossomed on his cheek where I'd slugged him, just below the long scar he'd gotten fighting out West. He'd grown a beard since we'd last talked, thick and blond, and it almost covered up his round cheeks and soft features. I'd kind of hoped he'd still be frantic and begging, like he'd been out on the ramp, but something in his expression had changed. That desperate look was gone, replaced by a pinched steeliness, an air of angry determination.

I liked that a lot less.

Zell shoved him down in a chair as the rest of us formed a tight circle. "Here's how this is going to go," Ellarion said, rising to his feet. "We're going to ask you some questions. You're going to give us answers. If you don't, we're all going to work out our issues with you. And I think I speak for the group when I say we've all got a *lot* of pent-up issues."

Miles rolled his eyes. "You can drop the tough-guy act. I'll tell you whatever you want. Not like it matters at this point."

Ellarion looked like he kind of wanted to keep the act going a little longer, but Lyriana cut in. "How did you find us out here?"

"We caught a group of your Unbroken friends fleeing into the Heartlands. One of them, Kelvin Del Te Rayne, gave you up. Took quite a bit of persuasion, too. Poor guy. Not much left of him." I wanted to punch Miles again, so bad. "He said you lot had taken off for the Red Wastes, to recruit some army of Waster mages. I would've written it off as a ridiculous lie—but I'd seen what that girl could do." His eyes flitted to Syan.

"And you dropped everything to come down here after us?" I demanded.

"Well, I had to. I mean, if there was even a chance of more of . . . her . . ." Miles shrugged. "I left Jacobi in charge of the city. He can handle it for a few days."

A few days? I guess that's how long it took to cross the distance in the Skywhale. The thought was staggering.

"You left Jacobi in charge?" my father repeated with disgust, and Miles flinched at his voice. "With two-thirds of the Southlands army approaching, you're not even there to defend the city yourself?"

"He doesn't know about the Southlanders," Zell said.

"Oh, I know, *Zitochi*," Miles said, dripping venom. "And I know their little crusade is doomed. The City Walls have been reinforced and fortified. There's five hundred new bloodmages just waiting to defend them. The Southlanders ride to their death."

Five hundred new bloodmages. I glanced at Lyriana uneasily, the visions of the Nightmother flashing in my head. Miles had no idea what he was doing. No idea the danger he was putting us all in.

"Yeah, well, it doesn't matter now, does it?" Ellarion said, staying on topic. "You're our prisoner. And if you want to live to see the end of the week, you'll order all your bloodmages to stand down."

"I can negotiate a surrender, yes." He shifted uneasily in his seat. "You'll have to get me to the capital safely, of course. Arrange a meeting with Jacobi somewhere neutral. I can take it from there."

"I'm sure you can," Lyriana replied, her tone making it clear he'd do no such thing. She stared at him closely, head cocked to the side, taking him in. "It's so strange."

He eyed her warily. "What is?"

"I've thought about this moment for so long. Since that tower in the Nest, really, when you betrayed us. When Jax died." Lyriana's voice choked up on that one, just a tiny bit. "I've dreamed of seeing you like this, bound and defeated, utterly at my mercy. I've played this out so many times in my head: how you'd grovel and beg, how you'd apologize, how you'd finally pay for everyone you've taken from me."

"Your parents were casualties of war," Miles said, harder than I would've thought he was capable of. "And I never meant for Jax to get hurt. *Never.*"

"Keep his name out of your mouth, you son of a bitch," I growled, and then I was lunging forward, only Zell's grip keeping me from punching him all over again.

Luckily, Lyriana had me covered, slaying instead with words. "It doesn't even matter," she said. "This isn't satisfying. And now I get that it never could be, could it? Because you'd never get it. You'd never understand what you took from us. You'd never understand how everything that's happened is your fault. You'd never understand how awful you truly are. You're incapable of it, of seeing anything beyond yourself and your fears and your desires. You're just too small and broken."

Miles's nostrils flared as he twitched in his chair, wrists straining against the bonds. "I freed the Kingdom from *your* family's tyranny," he hissed. "I invented bloodmages! I built this ship! I've transformed the world! My name will live on forever! What's small about that, huh? What's small about that?"

"Everything," Lyriana said. "But if there's one thing that brings me comfort, it's this. You've gotten everything you could have ever wanted. You've managed to kill and con and ruin your way into becoming the most powerful man in the Kingdom. But when I look into your eyes, all I see is loneliness and pain. You're on top of the world and you still see yourself as the victim. You might just be the most miserable person I've ever met." She turned away, back to the window. "So that's why it doesn't matter if I bring you to justice or not. You've already built your own personal hell."

"You don't know me!" Miles yelled, all composure gone.

"You don't know me at all! I'm happy! I'm plenty ha—" and he never got to finish that sentence because Zell shoved a gag in his mouth. He bit at it, thrashing, spitting wordlessly, and even though he was our prisoner, I jerked away. He had such anger in him, always frothing below the surface. How had he become like this? Had he *always* had this inside?

"I think we're done here," Zell said. "Should I take him back to the cells?"

We nodded, pretty much as one. Zell dragged Miles down, even as he continued to kick and howl, and when Zell came back, he downed his whole chalice in one gulp.

"So," I said. "Miles wants to arrange a surrender."

"It's a trap," my father replied, not looking away from the helm. "I don't know how, but I'm sure of that. Wherever he arranges the meet, he'll have an ambush waiting."

"I know," Lyriana said. "That's why we're not going to Lightspire. We'll find the Southland army and join up with them."

We all turned to stare at her. "What?"

"I swore an alliance with Rulys Cal. His men represent the best chance we have at taking the city. With them, the Skywhale, and Miles as prisoner, we should be able to pull it off, no matter how many bloodmages he has."

I nodded. Made sense. Though a part of me was still hoping, for Lyriana's sake, that we could win this thing without the Southlander's help, that she wouldn't be forced to marry some guy she barely even knew. That seemed like the least of her concerns.

"Miles isn't your only prisoner," my father said quietly. I blinked at him, and then I remembered. Right. *Him*. "I'm the King of Noveris, remember? The bloodmages might be

Miles's creatures, but the rest of the army should still be loyal to me. Put me in the right place and I'll negotiate the surrender."

"You're the *usurper*, not the King," Ellarion growled, "and why should we trust you any more than him?" There was a weird hollowness to the statement, though, like he was just saying it out of formality. After all, we clearly already did trust him, at least a little. He was the one standing on the deck, unbound in any way, a sword at his side. He was the one piloting the ship that was keeping us all alive. Somewhere along the way, he'd stopped feeling like a temporary ally, and more like a real one. But that time was rapidly coming to an end.

Lyriana was obviously having the same thoughts. "Lord Kent, if we do take back the city, if I do reclaim my Kingdom, what will you do?"

"The same thing I always said I'd do," my father replied, still refusing to turn around. "I'm not enough of a fool that I don't know when I've been beaten. You'll take Miles's place on the throne, and I've seen enough to know that you'll be a thousand times the ruler he is. Probably a thousand times the ruler your father was as well." His voice was flat, but I swear I heard just the tiniest moment of hesitation. "All I ever wanted was to see Miles pay for his betrayal. After that . . . I'm ready to face the Queen's justice."

"You acknowledge me as Queen," Lyriana said softly.

He turned around, looking at her, and in his eye I saw no hate, no anger, just acceptance. "I do."

A long silence hung over all of us. Zell squeezed my shoulder, and I poured myself another chalice, because there was one more ugly turn this conversation had to take. "There's something else we should talk about," I said. "The Night-mother's words. Her visions. The whole thing about the end of the world."

"If we believe her—and I do—then our problems are just beginning," Ellarion said. "Even if we take the city back, those bloodmages will still be out there, working their Arts. Using the energy of the Lightspire Heartstone. Bringing about the end of the world."

The weight of it hit us all at once, so heavy it felt like it would drag the Skywhale out of the air. We'd been so focused on defeating Miles and taking back the Kingdom, but all this time there was something happening that was so much bigger, so much more awful, something we'd been a part of even as we'd tried to do the right thing. It put our whole mission into its terrible context. What did it matter who sat on the throne if it was all going to burn anyway?

Ellarion let out a long exhale and then a bitter laugh. "It's always something else, isn't it?" he said. "We're about to win this war and *still* lose everything."

"No," Lyriana said. "There must be something we can do. A way to control the bloodmages."

"Not just them, remember?" Zell said. "It's all mages. All magic. You included." His voice was flat, without judgment, but Lyriana still looked stung. "Its mere existence brings the world to ruin."

"Then we control all mages," Lyriana tried. "There has to be a way . . ."

"They're spread out all over the land," my father said. "Dozens in every major city. You'd never be able to imprison them all."

"That's not what I was suggesting!" Lyriana glared at him.

"Laws to prohibit the use of magic, messengers to educate the population on the risks . . ."

But as she said the words, it was clear even she wasn't buying it. The temptation would always be there, and so long as people had the power, they'd use it.

I hadn't figured out how I was going to tell everyone about the whole "oh by the way I may have absorbed the Nightmother's dark power" thing, and I kind of didn't want to; it scared me, honestly, knowing that it was inside me, knowing what I was capable of. But *not* telling them felt like it would be way worse, and if there was anything I learned backed in Lightspire, it's that keeping secrets like that just comes back to bite you in the end.

So I took a deep breath. "There is . . . another way," I said, and everyone turned to look at me. I held out my hand and opened it wide, and the Nightmother's yellow crystal appeared there, hovering just above my palm.

The reaction was instantaneous. Everyone jerked back like I'd burst into flames, Ellarion's hands rising up above him, Lyriana almost falling out of her chair. "What . . . How . . . ?" she stammered.

"During the fight, the Nightmother was dying. I took the crystal and . . . I don't know." How could I begin formulating the words for what had happened when I could barely understand it myself? "It's like she's in me now. Her thoughts, her memories, her powers. She's inside of my head, inside of me, but she's also *not*, because it's like there's this wall, and—"

"The bloodmages," Zell said quietly. "The way they all just burst apart. That was you."

I nodded, and I know it was ridiculous to feel guilty, but I still somehow did. "Yeah. I pulled energy from the

Heartstone, and I sent it right back at them. I just . . . somehow knew how." I swallowed deep, because the next part was even worse. "And I think . . . I think if you got me to the Heartstone in Lightspire, I could do what she told us to. I could unleash her power to stop all the mages."

"You mean kill them?" Lyriana said, and that seemed to shock her even more than the light crystal floating in my hand. "The bloodmages who pose a threat?"

"I don't think it's that specific," I said, and I don't know how I knew that, but I definitely did. "At that scale, it'll just be indiscriminate. Without actually seeing them, I'll have no way of knowing who's a bloodmage and who isn't. I'll just send out the pulse and every mage out there will die."

"You're talking about innocent people," Lyriana gasped.

"Those people will die anyway," Syan said, her voice soft, her gaze down. "Zastroya doesn't care if you're innocent or guilty. It swallows all."

"You can't be suggesting—"

"She's right," Ellarion said. "I hate to think about it. But if it's the only way to stop the end of the world . . . if we have to kill a thousand to save a million . . ."

"Thousands," Zell cut in. "Plural. Thousands."

I stared at the crystal in my hand and felt sick to my stomach. It was so beautiful, so bright and delicate, it was impossible to think that it'd be capable of something so terrible. And even if we all agreed to it, I'd still be the one doing it, the one making the ultimate call. I'd be the one with the blood on my hands. It's not like I'd just be able to target the bad. Men, women, children, innocent and guilty alike, all dying that horrible death because of me. How would I live with myself afterward? Would I fall asleep every night thinking about them? Or would I harden, convince myself it was for the greater good, refuse to look back on what I'd done?

"It doesn't matter now," my father said, jerking me, us, out of that. "The first thing we have to do is take back the throne. Everything else we can decide after that."

Ellarion nodded, and Lyriana did too, and I breathed a deep sigh of relief. Maybe it was a cop-out. But I'd take not having to weigh the decision for every second I could. I closed my palm, and the crystal vanished as if it had never been there, as if the power to kill the population of a city wasn't residing inside me.

I'd started tracking my kills as a way to keep the war in perspective, to remind myself of the cost of what I'd done. It kept me grounded. It kept me whole.

What would I do when the number was too high to count?

TWENTY-THREE

ONCE THE NOVELTY OF FLYING THROUGH THE SKY WORE off, the Skywhale turned out to be pretty damn boring.

The navigator estimated it would take us a day and a half to get back, and while that had seemed impossibly short at the outset, after our fifth hour or so in the air it felt excruciatingly long. I paced restlessly around the ship. I polished off the last of the wine. I watched through the portholes as the Hands worked, alternating shifts in the wings, and tried not to think about the fact that the will of six men was all that was keeping us in the air.

Night fell around the time we were leaving the Red Wastes, crossing over into the Southlands. The others seemed to have found ways to occupy themselves: My father was still on the bridge, manning the controls, even though the ship seemed to mostly be flying itself. Ellarion was busy with the navigator, grilling him on the details of the ship, trying to figure out just how much power its cannons packed. And Zell was napping down in the soldiers' bunks, because he had the supernatural ability to fall asleep if he needed rest no matter how anxious he was.

So I wandered instead to the viewing deck. This was simultaneously the best and scariest part of the ship, a rounded balcony jutting off the captain's quarters where you could sit and look down at the world below. The view was incredible, way better than looking out the windows: you could stare directly down at the landscape, feel the rush of wind in your face, marvel at how high we were. You could also fall over the waist-high railing and plummet to your horrific death, but no one but me seemed to care about that.

I'd thought it'd be empty, but as I approached the metal door I could see through the porthole there was already someone there. Syan. She was right up against the railing, staring down at the inconceivably high drop, her back turned to me. I started to turn to head back inside, but there was something off about her, something in the way she was slumped against the railing, that made me hesitant to abandon her. She'd been through a lot in the past few days, more than any of us; I might've become the vessel for the power of an ancient terrible being, but that was still probably easier than the confrontation she'd had with her mother.

So I slid open that door and stepped outside, onto the slick metal surface of the deck. Syan didn't even look up.

"Hey," I said, walking over to her. It was a perfect night out. Above, the sky was clear, the stars sparkling like diamonds, the moon a perfect white disc. I wasn't going to go all the way to the balcony's edge because, uh, no, but I went out enough that I could look over and see the world below. The desert of the Southlands sprawled before us, but in the moonlight it looked more like a dark sea, the dunes glistening like frozen waves.

"Tilla." Syan turned back to me. "I'm sorry. Do you want the balcony?"

"Naw. It's fine. I just wanted to talk. You okay?" I asked, though honestly, the answer was pretty clear in how awful she looked. Her hair was messy, hanging in tangles around her shoulder, and her orange eyes were puffy and weary.

"Not really," she said. "Take care not to step on the zaryas." She nodded her head down, toward the floor by her bare feet, and yep, sure enough, there they were, two smooth stone orbs lined with bands of slick sharp metal. "I found them in the jail cells, locked away in a chest with other weapons. They were my brother's."

"Oh," I said. "Good. I mean, not *good*, but, good that you found them, and, uh . . ."

"It doesn't matter," Syan said, mercifully cutting me off. "I came out here to attune to them, and then . . ." She trailed off, clutching the railing tight and gazing off to the south, to the sprawl we were flying away from. On the horizon I could just barely see the edge of the Red Wastes, a thin line of darkest crimson.

"And then?"

She breathed deep. In the darkness, the streaks in her hair were brighter than ever, burning like cold flames that gave off a gentle halo of glowing blue. "I am never going home again," she said, her voice barely above a whisper. "No matter what happens, this is it. This is the last time I'll ever see it."

"You don't know that . . ." I tried.

"I do," she replied. "I will never see my family again. I will never walk the streets of Benn Devalos or bathe in the Crystal Spring or watch the sun rise over the red sands." A single tear streaked down her cheek like a raindrop. "Even if we take the throne back. Even if we prevent Zastroya. I will never be permitted to return."

"I'm sorry, Syan." I wanted to hug her, but wasn't sure if that would be okay. "I had to flee my home too, you know."

She turned back to me. "What was it like? Your home?"

"Beautiful. Nothing like this, of course. It was a forest, a real forest, not like that piddly crap you see in the Heartlands. There were redwood trees that reached all the way up into the sky, and foggy hills littered with the ruins of ancient stone castles, and blacksand beaches that looked out onto the Endless Ocean. And if you came out at night and looked to the sky in the West, you'd see these bands dancing there, green and blue, like ribbons in the stars. The Coastal Lights." Was I crying too? Yeah. Apparently, I was. "There's nothing in the whole world like it."

"You miss it."

I rubbed at my eyes with the back of my hand. "Every day. But life goes on. I promise you, it goes on."

"I hope so," she replied, even though it was clear she didn't believe it. There was so much pain in her eyes, so many layers of hurt and loss and shame. "I am sorry I lied to you, Tilla. To all of you. I never thought it would go like this. I never thought I would be so wrong."

"It's fine," I said. Objectively, I probably should have been angrier, but after everything we'd been through, it was impossible to hold a grudge. "You did what you thought you had to. And it worked out, right? We captured Miles and got the Skywhale and . . ." I thought of the other thing we'd gotten, the power burning in me, that horrible looming decision. I decided to move on. "If we'd stayed back in the Heartland, we probably would've just gotten captured. This is the best outcome, you know?"

"It is not just about the outcome. It's about what I believed! It's about . . . about . . ." Syan said sharply. "I believed my dreams came from the Nightmother because she needed me to prevent Zastroya. I believed I'd been chosen. I believed I was special." Her zaryas twitched on the floor by her feet. "But it was all a lie. The Nightmother did not care about us. There is no Sunfather looking over my people. Those creatures, those 'Titans,' they made this world into what it is now, and they looked at us like lowly beasts." The Skywhale dipped, sending a gust of wind billowing through her hair. "It's a lie. All of it. Everything I ever believed is a lie!"

"You're not the only one," a voice said from behind us. Lyriana. She stepped out onto the balcony and walked past me, over to Syan by the railing. "Trust me. I know exactly how you feel."

"You do?" Syan asked.

"Of course," Lyriana replied, like how could anyone think otherwise? "I grew up in the faith of the Titans, Syan. I dedicated my life to their service. I prayed to them in times of need. I sacrificed so much to try to live in their image. And even after everything that happened, after the fall of my Kingdom and the deaths of my family and the horrible things we saw in the crypt, I still believed. With every fiber of my being, I *believed*." She gazed out at the landscape below. "My whole life was built on a lie."

Syan turned to look at her, taking it all in. She seemed to soften, just a little. "How are you able to deal with it?"

"I have no idea," Lyriana replied. "Honestly, it takes every-thing I have not to just collapse screaming. There's so much going on inside me. I feel shame and confusion and anger, so much anger."

"And pain," Syan added.

"And pain," Lyriana repeated. "A pain deeper than I thought was possible. I've felt loss and heartbreak, but this . . . this is beyond that. It's a pain in my soul."

"What do we do now?" Syan asked. "How do we get past this? How do we know what to do?"

Lyriana was silent for a while, staring out at the night. There was something different in her expression, something I'd never seen before. Even in a tattered tunic, her hair dirty, her body bruised, she looked indomitable, majestic. Somehow in that moment, on the balcony of the Skywhale, her golden eyes blazing in the night, she looked more like a Queen than ever. "We have to do it ourselves," she said at last. "We can't rely on the past. We can't turn to our parents. We can't follow a path laid out for us by those that came before. It's up to us to find the way forward. We're the trailblazers now."

Syan leaned toward her, hesitant, almost trembling. "We'll be alone."

And Lyriana turned to her and smiled. "No. We'll have each other," she said, and then she leaned forward and kissed Syan.

For one moment, Syan was surprised, her eyes wide, and then she leaned into it, kissing Lyriana back, slow, tender, the kind of kiss that made you desperately want someone to kiss *you* that way. The air around them pulsed and crackled, literal sparks of magic whirling all around. I let out a little gasp as the current shot through me, as Syan's hair pulsed the most vivid beautiful sapphire blue, as the light around them dimmed and the whole world burned like it was on fire. They were together for a second, and then pulled apart, staring into each other's eyes.

"You . . . I . . . I don't . . ." Syan stammered.

"The last time I really liked someone, I didn't kiss them until it was too late," Lyriana said. "I'm not making that mistake twice."

Syan stared at her and then smiled and leaned in, kissing her a second time, long and deep. I had a lot of follow-up questions for Lyriana, like, for starters, *what*? But I knew they'd wait, because this was one hell of a moment and I wasn't going to stop that. The two kissed for one wonderful perfect endless moment, and then finally pulled apart.

"Now I know we have to survive," Syan said at last.

"Why's that?" Lyriana asked.

"Because I can't die without doing that again." Syan grinned and wrapped her arms around Lyriana, pulling her close. I could barely believe what was happening, but I was also grinning ear-to-ear, the grin you have from seeing something realized that you didn't even know you wanted. They were so cute it made me want to cry.

As badly as I wanted to stay and get all the details, this was very much their moment now, so I stepped back into the stillness of the Skywhale and made my way back down to the soldiers' quarters. Zell was there, on his side on one of the bunks, his eyes shut, his breath slow and gentle. I was really tempted to wake him and tell him all about, uh, *that,* but he looked so peaceful when he slept, so serene. Looking at him, you could believe he was just the gentle boy who held me in his arms, the boy who kissed my neck and whispered in my ear, not a hardened warrior whose kill count was probably in the triple digits. What would he do if the crystal was his? Would he hesitate?

It wasn't worth thinking about. I lay down on the bed beside him and wrapped one of his arms around me, pressing my whole body against his and sinking into his warmth. He stirred just the tiniest bit, and even in his sleep he held me close and buried his face into my hair.

"I love you," I whispered, and kissed the soft skin of his arm. I didn't know what the future held. I didn't know how we'd go from here, or what decisions I'd make, or who I'd have to become. I didn't know how many more moments I'd have like this.

So I savored this one for as long as I could.

TWENTY-FOUR

I MUST HAVE NODDED OFF, BECAUSE MY NEXT MEMORY WAS being gently shaken awake by Zell. "Hey. Tilla. We're almost there."

With a groan, I forced my eyes open. The bunk wasn't much, just a hard slab with a thin mattress, but it sure beat a bedroll on the sand; I could've happily slept there for another, I don't know, ten hours. Still, I blinked and pulled myself off the bed with a bare minimum of grumbling, following Zell up to the captain's quarters.

It was midafternoon, I think, sunlight streaming in through the Skywhale's windows and the blue sky visible outside. The others were there: Ellarion and my father gazing down at the land below, and Syan and Lyriana standing side by side, not *quite* holding hands but almost, their fingertips just centimeters apart. Lyriana glanced over her shoulder at me with a sheepish smile, and I have never ever wanted to gossip more.

"We're about two hours away from Lightspire," the

navigator announced stiffly. "The encampment of the Southlander army should be nearby."

"No kidding," Ellarion said. I made my way to a window and looked down, and now I could finally see what they were all staring at. We were in the Heartlands, all right, sprawling plains and golden wheat fields as far as the eye could see. The Adelphus River surged below us, a massive blue serpent winding its way through the continent. And I could make out villages too, as tiny as children's toys, little houses and castles that looked like I could reach out and pick them up.

But we weren't looking at the fields or the river or the villages. No, all our eyes were on the long stretch of darkness cutting its way across the landscape like a scar, a stretch of trampled land and smoldering ash, littered with little black husks that I'm pretty sure were the remains of houses. It was like the battlefield we'd passed through but longer, an unbroken line, like someone had run over the continent with a gigantic plow.

The Southlands army had marched through here. And they'd left nothing standing in their wake.

"There, look! Lightspire!" Lyriana said, craning her head at one of the windows. I did the same and now I could almost see it too, on the horizon: a wide blurry shape that I think was the city's walls, a glowing emerald tower that had to be the Godsblade. And all around it were tendrils of smoke stretching into the sky, hundreds of them, like an infestation. The city was burning. The siege had already begun.

"Now, this is the tricky part," Ellarion said, his brow furrowed deep. "We'll want to land near the rear of the Southlands army, with enough distance that we can safely touch down and exit the ship. They'll definitely assume we're hostile, so the most important thing is making sure they know we're on their side. . . ."

I stepped back, because I was still too groggy to dive into the details of planning anything. I hadn't planned to sleep so long, so my brain still expected hours more time on the Skywhale to eat and relax and get ready. Things were moving too fast. I wanted more time up here, more time at peace with my friends, more time before the next battle or confrontation or awful decision.

"You ready?" Zell said.

"Yeah," I lied. Relaxing and resting I could get later. But there was one last thing I had to do now.

I slipped away while the others strategized, pocketing an iron key off the table, and made my way to the back of the ship and down that spiral staircase into its underbelly. I was back down in the jail, that cold room with the three heavy doors, lit up only by the yellow light of a Luminae. I swallowed deep, tried to calm the unease in my stomach, and approached Miles's door.

I knew this was probably a bad idea, okay? I knew nothing good would come of it. But I had to try. Once we landed, we'd hand Miles over, and I probably wouldn't see him again until he was swinging from a gallows or being mounted on a pike. I wouldn't shed any tears for him. But for my own peace of mind, for my own sense of closure, I had to talk to him one last time. I had to tell him how I felt, to make him really know what he'd done. I had to have that.

So I pulled open the door and there he was, slumped on the floor, wrists bound together with a thick iron chain. He craned his head up at me, and he looked even worse than before. His skin was so pale it was almost translucent, his eyes sunk deep into his skull, his lips cracked and swollen. His hair hung greasily along his face, and his hands were trembling, just a little. Still when he saw me, he couldn't help but smile. "Tilla," he said. "You came to see me."

"Yeah," I replied. "We'll probably never talk again, so . . . yeah."

"I take it I won't be the one negotiating a surrender. Smart. I wouldn't have let me do it, either." He leaned back, nodding, oddly resigned to his fate. "So what's the plan? Hand me over to the Southlanders?"

"I'm not going to tell you our plan," I growled, even though he'd pretty much already guessed it. "That's not why I came here."

"No. You came to say good-bye," Miles said. And the weird thing is, he was kind of right? I mean, for everything that had happened, for everything that he'd done, for how much I hated him . . . he was still the boy I'd grown up with, one of my first friends, someone who knew me on a level that almost no one else did. I had to say good-bye to that part.

But I wasn't going to give him the satisfaction of admitting it. "I came to tell you how I really felt," I replied. "Do you have any idea how much you hurt me, Miles? How much you took from me? Do you even understand what your betrayal did?" I shook my head. "I've been stabbed and cut and beaten. But nothing hurt me worse than what you did." I gestured around me at the jail cell, at the table covered in bloodied torture tools. "Do you see this, Miles? Do you see what you've built, what you've become? Do you have *any* shame?"

Miles breathed in sharply, nostrils flaring. I could see him struggling to temper his words. "Look. I'm not going to claim I always made the right decision. Obviously, I'm not happy with how things turned out. And believe it or not, I was crushed when I heard about Jax. Really. I know he and I didn't always get along, but he was my friend too, Tilla." I hated hearing him saying it, hated Jax's name on his lips, but I had to admit he sounded sincere. "But you have to understand. When it comes to the Kingdom, the bloodmages, the war, all of it, I only did what I had to in order to survive. I never had a choice. Not really."

"Bullshit!" I almost-yelled. "You always had a choice. And you chose to kill so many people. . . ."

"Like you haven't killed?" Miles replied. "Come on. I know you've got blood on your hands."

Fifty-eight, I thought, but didn't say. "That's different. That was in battle."

"But what put you in the battle? Was it your own choice? Or was it the path of life that had been set for you, forces beyond your control shoving you into that moment when all you could do was kill or be killed?" Miles argued. "Your father was the one who forced me to be his right hand. Your father was the one who forced me to lead men onto the front lines. Your father was the one who made me what I am!" He was getting louder now, his voice starting to crack. "While you were living it up in the fancy city, drinking and dancing and screwing around with the Zitochi, I was hiding in a trench, digging an arrowhead out of my thigh and holding a man as his guts spilled out of his stomach! If you want to blame anyone for this, blame your father. But no. He's up there, a free man, and I'm the one rotting in a cell."

Miles had technically put my father in that very same cell, but this wasn't the time to get into it. "My father did a lot of awful shit, and he's going to pay for it," I replied. "But at least he has the decency to own up to it and take responsibility. At least he doesn't always try to blame someone else for his choices!"

"Choices," Miles repeated, closing his eyes. "What a weird word. Like I'd ever have chosen this for myself. Like I'd ever have chosen this mantle, this world, this fate." He leaned back against the wall of his cell, chained wrists hitting the ground with a clank. "I never wanted to be a King, you know. Not even as a little kid. Ruling and making decisions and ordering armies and all of it . . . just the thought made me want to throw up." There was a wistful quality to his tone, more earnest than I'd heard him since before the betrayal. Was his impending death breaking him down? "All I ever wanted was a big library to lose myself in, and good friends, and a nice safe home to come back to. All I ever wanted was . . . was . . ." He trailed off, lost in the thought.

"It's still not too late," I said, and I don't know why I was reasoning with him, why I somehow felt bad. Coming down here had been a mistake. "You can use the time you have left to try to make things right. You can fix all the damage you've done."

"No. It is too late. The minute your father demanded I create mages for him, my fate was sealed." Miles looked up at me, right at me, his gray eyes meeting mine. "You know what I think about all the time, Tilla? Our journey through the West. When we were running from our parents, all together, just a scrappy band of bastards. You, me, Zell, Lyriana, Jax, all of us. Camping together under the stars and telling jokes by the riverside and relying on one another to survive. It's hard to believe, right? We were in mortal danger, chased by horrible mercenaries, abandoned by our own families." He smiled weakly. "But I think that's the happiest I've ever been."

"You could have had that, Miles. That life. Those friendships. You could have kept all of it."

"Yeah. If you hadn't chosen Zell."

There it was. The dodge. The blaming. The refusal, at every turn, to just own up to his choices. This was who Miles was, who he'd always be. Lyriana was right; there was no point talking to him.

I got up, reaching for the door, ready to slam it in his face. "Well. This went about as well as it could. Time to get ready to land."

Something changed instantly in Miles's manner. He stiffened, and that earnest emotion vanished from his eyes, replaced by a cold cunning. "So we're landing, then? Sooner than I thought. I always suspected the Hands were holding out on me." He cleared his throat and stretched out his bound wrists, fingers flexing. "Right, then. Let's get this over with."

"What?" I asked, pushing back, even as the knot of unease in my stomach turned into plunging dread. We'd missed something. Something big. Something bad. I reached for the handle of the door to slam it . . .

But before I could, the air curdled with the sickly pulse of bloodmagic. My skin tingled like someone was scraping it with a dull blade, and I fought back a gag as my mouth flooded with the taste of smoke and ash, as my ears filled with the sound of scraping metal. Miles's eyes flickered, and that dull gray glowed brighter and brighter, hot and metallic, like sunshine on the edge of a blade.

"No," I whispered, but it was too late. Miles leaned back, and I could see it now, underneath him, a hidden compartment built into the floor of the cell . . .

And a spent syringe lying within.

Miles had just made himself a bloodmage.

He flared out his pointer fingers, and the chain between his wrists snapped apart, whistling toward me through the air like a hurled dagger. I tried to duck, but it was too late; it caught me in the neck, hitting hard, and wrapped around my throat like a clenching fist. My vision flared red. Pain shot through me. I gasped and wheezed, begging for air.

In front of me, Miles rose to his feet, a bemused look on his face. He twirled one hand in a lazy half circle, and the chain relaxed just the tiniest bit, enough for me to breathe. I collapsed down to my knees, rasping, panting. "You took the serum."

"I had to," he said with a growl. "I'd hoped to avoid it. But the second you locked me in this cell, you left me no choice." He waved his hands in the air, and the door's hinges burst off. "It's funny. I still haven't figured out why the serum activates such different abilities in people. I suspect it's tied into innate psychology somehow. I'd kind of hoped for fire or lightning but . . . well, controlling metal is kind of me, right?"

On my hands and knees, the chain still tight around my throat, I fumbled toward him. On the one hand, I could barely breathe. On the other, I wanted to claw his eyes out. I gritted my teeth and strained to channel the Nightmother's power, to pop Miles like the tumor he was . . . but there was nothing. I needed a Heartstone for it to work.

"Try anything, and I *will* choke you out," Miles said. "I don't want to. But I will. You understand?"

"Yes," I wheezed, begging him to turn his back, to give me a chance.

"Good. Then let's go."

He ushered me up the spiral staircase, holding me out in front of him like a shield. "What's your plan?" I managed to get out. "We still control the ship."

"You do. Which is why I'm taking it back," Miles replied, shoving me through the door into the upper hallway.

Lyriana was there, idly walking from one room to the other. "Tilla!" she yelled in shock at the sight of me, and jerked her hands up, preparing an Art . . .

"Do it and she dies!" Miles barked. "I mean it! I'll crush her throat!"

"Do it, Lyriana!" I tried to say, but the chain squeezed tight so all I got out was a gurgle. It didn't matter. At the sight of the chain, Lyriana dropped her hands. "Don't hurt her!" she yelled, and even though she was saving my life, I wanted to smack her. You couldn't give in to Miles. Not ever.

"Into the captain's quarters!" Miles bellowed, and Lyriana backed through the rounded doorway into the cozy padded study. The others were all in there, and they fumbled up out of their seats as Miles stepped into the doorway with me at his side. Zell whipped out a blade, and Ellarion raised his arms, his hands whistling into formation at his back.

"What is this?" Syan demanded. "How is he free?"

"Blood . . . mage . . ." I got out. My eyes met Zell's, and I could see the murderous rage inside him, the whirring of his mind as he ran through every possible way to clear the room and save me. He was like a cat, poised, tense, ready to pounce. But the opening just wasn't there. Not with a chain crushing my neck.

"So you took the serum after all," my father growled. He alone hadn't gotten up, glaring at Miles from his chair. "You're even more shortsighted than I thought."

"Oh, really?" Miles's voice cracked. "Sure seems to have worked out pretty well for me." Ellarion's hands twitched, and Miles shot him a glare. "Try anything, and she dies. I'm serious."

"He won't do it," my father said to the others. "He's in love with her." That was a weird thing to bring up right now, even if it was true. "We can take him. We have to. Now!"

The three mages didn't move, but Zell did. I guess he trusted my father or he knew Miles or both. With a low hiss, he spun and threw his sword . . .

Which Miles stopped effortlessly in midair with a single raised hand. "Idiot," he said, and flicked it back, the blade clipping the side of Zell's arm. He let out a grunt and toppled down, clutching it even as the blood seeped out.

"No!" I screamed, pushing forward. This asshole. This miserable piece of shit. I would tear his face apart with my nails. I would bite open his throat. I would crush his skull with my bare hands. I would—

Do nothing at the moment, because the chain held me tighter than ever. I could see the others backing away uneasily, glancing at each other, trying to come up with something. Lyriana streaked over to Zell's side, pressing a single glowing hand to his wound.

"What's your plan, then?" Ellarion demanded. "You think you can take all of us?"

"Oh, Archmagus. I already have." Miles grinned. He had this voice he put on in these situations, this sneering cocky manner that he must have thought sounded cool. "I'm actually pretty proud of this one. You see, the captain's quarters is a retrofit. It wasn't part of the original Skywhale, which was conceived as a military ship. I had it installed when it became clear I'd be spending a lot of time on it." He smiled, and there was none of that sweet boy there, no earnestness, just a sneering cruelty. "Do you see where this is going?"

"No," Syan gasped. "No!"

"Yes." From back in the doorway, Miles jerked up both hands, fingers clawed, and massive rifts cut through the metal of the walls, the metal holding the room in place. Lyriana let out a scream and the whole room tilted down at a rough angle, causing all of my friends to tumble backward. The hiss of the wind shot over us, and I could see the sky through the cracks, the clouds below. My heart leaped into my throat.

He was cutting off the room. The whole room. He was going to rip it off and let it fall away. And he was going to keep me.

"Do something!" my father screamed.

But it was too late. Miles brought his hands together over his head, and the rifts connected, a clean cut that severed the captain's quarters from the body of the Skywhale, leaving the doorway we were standing in a portal out the side of the ship. Lyriana threw up her hands. Syan sprang to her feet. Zell, still fallen, reached out. The room shuddered, hanging by just a few strands of metal, tilting down lower and lower.

Miles grinned.

And I did the one thing he didn't expect. With all the force I had, with every ounce of strength in my body, I jerked forward, pulled myself out of his magic's grasp, out and through the doorway. My foot touched the floor of the room just as it ripped off.

"No!" Miles screamed, but there was nothing else he could do.

Like a nest blown off a tree in a storm, the captain's quarters tore away from the Skywhale and plummeted down to the world.

With me in it.

TWENTY-FIVE

As a kid, I'd always been fearless when it came to heights. I would scale the parapets of Castle Waverly, run along the ramparts, and sit up in the watchtowers with my feet dangling over the edge. My stepmother, Lady Yrenwood, would tut-tut and shake her head, telling her precious daughters not to be like me, that one day I'd fall to my death.

I guess she was right.

One moment, I'd been standing in the doorway of the Skywhale with Miles. Now I was in the detached captain's quarters, screaming and clutching a wall as we hurtled toward the ground from hundreds of miles up. The whole room had tilted at a 90 degree angle, so the far wall was now the floor and we'd all gone smashing down into it. At the top was the ragged hole where the room had connected to the ship, and through it I could see the sky above, bright and blue and beautiful, and the gray husk of the Skywhale, sailing harmlessly away. The wind howled around us, so loud it was deafening, and I felt a huge force holding me down, pinning me to the wall (floor?) like I had a hand on my chest. All the furniture had fallen down around us, so I could barely see anyone, just a tumble of chairs and tables, loose papers whistling wildly by us. I strained around, trying to find Zell, to make sure he was okay, to hold his hand in the end.

How long did we have? Twenty seconds? Ten?

"Lyri! Syan!" Ellarion's voice screamed from somewhere beside me. "Air currents! Lift! Now!"

"I'm trying!" Lyriana yelled, and I could see her now, standing upright, her hands soaked in Zell's blood. Syan was next to her, fumbling for her new zaryas even as the ground lurched away beneath us. Lyriana jerked a hand up hard, and there was a sudden surge from below us, a jostling that sent us bouncing up. Our fall slowed, a little, into more of a float. She gritted her teeth, sweat streaking down her face, her whole body taut and trembling. Her eyes burned a furious gold, the pupils sinking away as she dove deeper and deeper into Heartmagic. "It's heavy . . . so much . . ." she gasped.

"You've got this!" I yelled, and there was another jolt as a second current swooped in to support us. This one caught us even more, but it also shoved the back of the falling room upright, tilting us sharply forward. The hole at the top swung down as the room re-leveled to be back at the side, and then it was shaking and tilting down. I could see the ground below, the stretch of amber field. We must have covered at least half the distance and were now just three hundred feet up or so. Still enough to dash us into little pieces when we hit the ground.

Then the room tilted even more, and now the hole was below us, and we were all sliding toward it. Tables and chairs hurtled down into the void. I screamed and shot out a hand, grabbing onto a post in the wall. Ellarion wrapped his arms around one next to me, Syan clinging to him, and now I could see Zell too, his arm still bleeding, hanging on to a crack in the wall with one hand. And Lyriana . . .

She was still standing upright, working her Lift! She slipped and fell forward with a shriek, plunging toward the abyss. "No!" I yelled, but I was too far, all of us were too far. She hurtled down toward the edge, even as her Lift wore off and we plunged down faster . . .

A hand shot out and grabbed her wrist, catching her just before she went over. My father. He clutched her close, holding a railing with his free hand, teeth gritted, letting out a roar of exertion. He'd caught her, stopping her right before she went over, and threw her back, toward the far end of the room, toward Ellarion and Syan. Her eyes met Ellarion's, even as we fell, and he yelled "Shields!"

In that moment, that one critical moment, the three mages acted as one. Lyriana shot out one hand to grab Syan and another to grab Ellarion. Syan's zaryas shot up into the air; Ellarion's hands rose up above him. "Shields!" Lyriana roared, her eyes full gold, her voice thunder.

And they appeared all around us, a spiraling band of rippling purple membranes surrounding the falling room. I'd seen a Shield before, of course, but the three mages threw up one after another, Shield after Shield, enveloping the room, nesting it in, wrapping it up like bandages, sealing it tight.

Then we hit the ground. The Shields took the impact, or almost all of it, absorbing it, keeping us safe like a glass egg nestled within hundreds of pillows. I felt their energy as they took the shock, felt them buckle and strain and break. The Shields took the blow, but we still hit the ground hard.

The room shuddered and shook. We all lifted up, flying

from the floor to hit the ceiling and back to the floor. The walls shuddered and bent. What little furniture was left came crashing down. A cloud of dust billowed up around us. That surge of energy, that power, that whatever, vanished instantly, replaced only by incredible aching pain, flaring through what felt like every inch of my body.

And yet . . . I was alive.

I pulled myself up, coughing through the dust. We were on the ground now, all right, and through the hole in the side I could see the stretch of field where we'd landed, making a pretty decent little crater. The room itself was all banged up; the walls were cracked and shattered, twisting into jagged chunks, and a big sliver of the ceiling was hanging on by a thread. All the furniture was shattered, hunks of splintered wood.

And yet . . . we were alive!

I turned to look for the others. There was Lyriana on all fours, coughing as the glow left her eyes, and Syan, bleeding from a cut in her forehead, helping Ellarion to his feet. Zell made his way to me, clutching his arm, his hair tousled, his face caked in dirt, but a smile on his face nonetheless.

"You did it!" I beamed at the mages. "You saved us!"

"I . . . I just . . . I . . ." Lyriana tried, but couldn't find the words. That was fine. She'd done more than enough.

"Uh . . . guys . . ." Ellarion said, staring toward the back of the room with a grimace. "Look."

I followed his gaze and . . .

My stomach leapt into my throat. No. Oh no.

My father lay against the farthest wall, slumped down in a heap. He was lying very still, barely moving, and that's probably because a jagged spiral of twisted metal was bursting out through his chest like a massive bloodied spear. He'd been thrown onto it when we landed, and it had skewered him clean through.

No. No no no.

Not now.

Not like this.

I ran over to his side, bounding over the debris, and fell to my knees beside him. "Father. Can you hear me? Father!"

He craned his head up to me weakly, his one eye bleary. Blood trickled down his lips, soaking his beard. "Tillandra," he said, each syllable a labor. "You're alive. Thank the Old Kings." He tried to look around, but it was clear he was having trouble focusing. "The others? The Queen?"

"We all made it, Father." I hadn't touched him in who knows how long, probably not since I was a little girl, but I grabbed his hand, squeezing it tight. "We're safe."

His lips twisted into the tiniest hint of a smile. "Good." Then he coughed, a horrible rasping cough, and his chest shuddered and I saw just how much blood he'd already lost, how slick the floor was. "Damn. Shame to go like this. I'd hoped to see it through to the end."

"You're not going to die here," I said, and the reality of it was crushing, suffocating, closing in around me. I looked to Lyriana for help, but she just shook her head. Healing Arts could only repair what the body would do on its own. And no body could recover from this.

"Listen, Tilla," he said, each breath a bloody wheeze. "I need to tell you this. Before it's too late. I've made a lot of mistakes in my life." He squeezed my hand tight. "But you are not one of them."

"Father . . ." I tried, and my eyes were burning and my hand was trembling and my breath was trapped in my throat.

Was this really happening? I'd thought about my father's death so many times in so many ways, but I couldn't believe it was actually here. "You can't die. Not now. I still don't know what to do. I still need your help."

"You'll figure it out," he said, looking at me, really looking at me. "You're a marvel. You're smart and resourceful and the bravest fighter I've ever met. And you've surrounded yourself with incredible friends. Whatever challenge you'll face, you'll overcome." His grip was getting weaker, fading away. "Win this war, Tilla. Fix what I've broken. And then . . . live for yourself."

"What do you mean?"

"Go somewhere far away. Make a home. Put war and death behind you." The others were gathered around me, silent, but it was hard to see them through the tears. "Keep Zell close. He's a good man. You two can build a life together . . . find the happiness I never did." He was fighting now, fighting to stay lucid, to stay alive. "Be kind. Be brave. Be better than me."

I squeezed tight, so tight, trying to will my life into him for just another moment. "I will. I promise."

He swallowed tight, and seemed to pull himself together, just a little. He craned his head to the side, trying to look past me. "Is the Queen there?"

"She is."

"Then listen close." He pulled his hand out of mine, and reached up to touch my cheek. "By the laws of the Old Kings and the laws of the Kingdom of Noveris, under the eyes of its True Queen, I hereby declare Tilla Kent to be my true-born daughter, and the rightful heir to House Kent." His gaze met mine. A single tear streaked down his cheek. "You are bastard no more, my love."

This was it. This was really it. The words I'd spent the first sixteen years of my life dreaming about. And they were coming like this, so long after I'd given up on hearing them, after their meaning had changed in every way. "I love you," I told him. "But I don't forgive you."

"I know," he whispered with a proud smile.

Then he died.

I sniffled and clutched his limp hand to my lips and tried and failed to blink away the tears. Zell reached down and squeezed my shoulder and I pressed my cheek against him. My father was gone. He was really gone. There was so much more I wanted to say to him. So much more I needed to know. So much more we could have done if we'd only had more time, if we'd only talked more, if we'd only, if we'd only—

"Someone's here," Syan said, pulling me out of that thought. I spun around to look, and yeah, she was right. There were people emerging from the fields to surround our fallen room. A lot of them too. Kind of a mob. Most were Heartlanders, with a few Southlanders and Easterners in the mix. A few were dressed like soldiers, but most just looked like smallfolk. They held makeshift weapons, pitchforks and clubs and rusty blades, and stared at us like they wanted to attack but weren't quite sure if they should.

I turned to the others for guidance, and they all looked as confused as I was. It suddenly dawned on me that I didn't know where we'd landed or who they were or what in the frozen hell we were doing next.

Then the crowd parted and a man stepped forward, a man with a crisp tunic and a familiar face, a man staring at us with his jaw wide in disbelief.

"No fucking way," Galen said.

TWENTY-SIX

WE STOOD THERE FOR A MOMENT, NOBODY MOVING, AND then Lyriana was the first, bounding out from the rubble of the shattered quarters to grab him in a hug so hard it nearly knocked him off his feet. We all emerged one by one, looking like utter hell: our hair tousled, our faces stained with ash and blood, our clothes barely rags at this point. I was surprised to see Galen, of course; when we'd last left him, he was taking the remains of the Unbroken and heading east to recover and rebuild. But he looked vastly more surprised to see us, which makes sense because we'd literally fallen out of the sky in front of him. He held Lyriana tight and waved weakly at us and it took nearly ten minutes before he was back to his usual self again, marching us forward while filling us in.

Galen, it turned out, had been almost as busy as we had. After the fall of our camp, he'd fled with the remaining Unbroken to the East. He'd had some luck at first, regrouping with some small rebel groups and rebuilding his numbers, until an attack on a grain caravan had turned out to be an ambush. They'd lost another dozen men, including poor Kelvin, and Galen had been forced to flee once more. The survivors were pursued into the south, and just when things had looked hopeless, they'd managed to run into the oncoming vanguard of the Southlands army, fresh off crossing the Adelphus. Galen convinced the army's leader that he was an asset, and brokered an alliance between the Unbroken and the Southlanders. I didn't ask if that meant Galen had to marry him, badly as I wanted to.

"So who are all these people?" Lyriana asked. We were walking through Galen's camp, though even calling it a camp was a stretch. It was more a long messy train, a procession of at least two hundred smallfolk, sleeping in shoddy tents or just out in the night air. We'd left the captain's quarters behind, walked away from the cold, still body lying inside. My chest was heavy, my heart refusing to admit it had really happened. My father was dead. My father. Was dead.

I couldn't think about that, couldn't handle dealing with the whirlwind of warring emotions just waiting to come tearing out. So I pushed it all down and just tried to focus on looking at the people around me. Here three old men sat, cooking scrawny-looking game over a crude fire pit. Here a pair of women practiced their sword work using blades so rusted they looked ready to break.

"They're rebels," Galen said, beaming. "Well, aspiring rebels mostly. Smallfolk who've put their lives on hold to join our ranks and fight the tyranny of the Inquisitor with everything they have. Every day, their numbers grow as more and more arrive."

"I don't understand," I said. "Why now? Why like this?"

Galen jerked his head to the north, past the sprawl of

commoners. There, laid out across the wheat fields, was the bulk of the Southlands army. I could see huge pitched tents and rows upon rows of wagons, could hear the clatter of blades and the clanging of hammers and the rumble of men's voices, blurring together like a distant river. I'd never seen an army on the march, but the sheer size blew me away: there had to be at least two thousand soldiers there, maybe more, marched right up to the very heart of the Kingdom itself.

Lightspire. The city sat in the distance, and from here I could make out the details more clearly. Tall stone walls surrounded it, and they still stood, despite the army camped outside. Normally, I would've been able to see the roofs of some of the tallest buildings from here, like the domed temple spires, but right now, the city was hidden behind thick clouds of smoke billowing up from behind the walls, like the whole place was burning in there. Tiny shapes, dozens of them, paced the ramparts. Bloodmages. Every now and again, one of them would make a sharp movement, and there'd be a flash of light, a bolt of lightning or a blast of flame screeching down, keeping any potential intruders at bay.

I remembered riding up here, what, a year and a half ago? How majestic and beautiful the city had looked. How worried I had been about what the King would think of me. How certain I was that I'd never see my father again, and how certain I was that I'd never want to.

If I had known . . . if I could've just talked to him more . . . if only I'd protected him, if I hadn't gone down to Miles, if I—

Zell must have seen the look on my face, because he reached out and held me close. "The smallfolk are joining you because of the Southlander army?" he asked.

Galen nodded. "Oh yeah. The people of this Kingdom are

sick and tired of this bloody regime. They want their Queen back, and they're ready to fight for her. They just needed to know it was possible." A young man with a bow pressed his fist to his heart as we passed, and Galen returned the salute. "I've never been the biggest fan of the Southlands. But say what you will, they really came through here. Seeing them march through the Province, driving Miles's army back, in open defiance . . . it was exactly the push the people needed." There was a sense of pride to his voice, an optimism I don't think I'd ever heard before. "Four minor Lords have thrown in their lot with us. Dozens more are pulling back. Reports are coming that the city itself is in rebellion, that insurgents take to the streets. And every village we pass, our ranks here swell and grow."

"So you're what? A recruiter?" Ellarion asked.

"It's what I've always been good at, right?" Galen replied. We'd gone farther up his camp now, and I think we were entering the "skilled rebel" section; armored defectors practicing their forms alongside surviving mages from the old regime, like a pair of Hands sculpting a floating ball of earth or a sole Knight of Lazan, off in the distance, twirling a blade of shimmering flame. "I ride behind the army and give my speeches in the villages we pass. It's amazing, in a way. We're stronger than ever, and we're finally in a position to make Miles suffer." He looked around the camp. "If we keep this up, by the time winter breaks, we'll have a formidable army all on our own."

"By the time winter breaks?" I asked. "I don't understand. That's months from now. Why would we still be here in winter? Aren't we taking the city back?"

"That hasn't gone as well as we'd hoped," Galen said, his

expression dark. "Miles pulled all of his forces back to defend it. We've tried to breach it but between the walls and the bloodmages, it's just resulted in a lot of dead Southlanders." His troubled look made me think he'd seen a lot of that up close. "That's why we've gone into siege mode. Sooner or later, their food will run out. Sooner or later, the city will burn from within. Sooner or later, winter will come. In three months, it'll be ours."

"I don't think we have till winter," Lyriana began, but she was cut off by the loudest, most boisterous shout I'd ever heard. I turned and there he was bounding toward us, Marlo Todarian, his apron dirty and his hair wild around his head, with the quietly smiling Garrus closed behind. I was so damn happy to see them.

"Tilla!" Marlo grabbed me up in a hug, lifting me off my feet, while Garrus gave the others a curt salute. "You're alive!"

"It's. Good. To. See. You. Too," I squeezed out from the depths of his arms. He smelled like oatmeal and potatoes.

"Titans be blessed," Garrus said with a little nod. That was a weird phrase to hear these days, but I let it go. "I'll make sure there's a bowl of stew waiting for you."

"Don't suppose it comes with a glass of ale."

"I've got my own special little supply," Marlo said with a wink, then turned to Galen. "We were actually coming here to ask about the prisoners. There's some dissent regarding how much we should be feeding them."

"Prisoners?" I asked, and Galen jerked his head to the side. There, a row of miserable-looking men sat on the ground, mostly Westerners, their wrists shackled together to their ankles. Their faces were pallid and sweaty, veins throbbing under their skin. One leaned over and vomited, a noxious black bile.

"Bloodmages," Zell said.

"About that," Galen said, glancing away with a hint of guilt. "The Southlanders insist on keeping them. They've been draining their blood, trying to use it to make their own serum. About time, I say."

"They're making their own bloodmages," I said. I felt sick to my stomach. "No . . . no, they can't do that."

Galen blinked. "Why not?"

We all looked at each other uneasily, and then Lyriana spoke. "There's something you should know."

It took a while for us to catch Galen up to speed. We told him everything, well, almost everything: our journey across the Adelphus, the night with the vagabonds, the earthquake in the Southlands, the deal we'd made with Rulys Cal. He took that in stride, more or less, but the more we got into what happened to us in the Red Wastes, the more perplexed he got; by the time we were talking about meeting an actual Titan, he was staring at us like we'd all collectively lost our minds. He grinned when we told him about capturing the Skywhale, and scowled when we told him how Miles took it back. But when we told him the last part, about the Heartstones and the magic and the end of the world, his face darkened, curling into a cold fury worse than I'd ever seen on him.

"You're telling me," he said at last, each word a labor, "that every single new bloodmage brings the world closer to ruin? That even if we take back the throne, we still have to deal with every bloodmage out there or we'll all die?"

"Not just bloodmages," Syan corrected. "All the mages, period. Except for me, Ellarion, and Lyriana, that is."

"That's a price we'll just have to pay," he said, which was really easy for him since it wasn't his choice to make. "We have to do the thing. Get Tilla to the Heartstone and have her use the crystal. Kill them all and save the Kingdom."

"Kill *thousands* of people?" Lyriana demanded. "No. There has to be another way."

"There isn't. The Titan said so herself," Galen said, with way too much authority given that he hadn't even been there. "We have to do it."

Lyriana's gaze narrowed. "You almost sound eager."

"To kill the bloodmages who've taken so much from us? Yeah. I'm eager," Galen growled. "And I'm eager to prevent the end of the world."

"Maybe it *should* end," Zell said. "If we do this, what makes us worth saving?"

"Are you serious right now? Are you actually—"

"Stop it!" I yelled, and they all went quiet. "Stop talking, all of you. I'm the one with the crystal in me. So this is my decision. My choice. And I . . . I . . ." It all felt too much. The power surging inside me. The weight of the choice in front of me. The city lying ahead, the army all around, and the room lying behind me, the crushed captain's quarters, and the still form within . . .

I turned my back on all of them. "Right now, I have a father to mourn."

TWENTY-SEVEN

WE WESTERNERS DON'T USUALLY BURN OUR DEAD; WE BURY them in graveyards, or in the case of nobility, inter them in crypts below our castles with majestic statues that watch over them with cold, regal eyes. But we weren't in the West, and I wasn't about to bury my father here, in the Province he'd so hated, the Province he'd broken himself trying to conquer, the Province that had, in the end, taken his life.

So I went out to the farthest edge of the camp and built a pyre there, dragging logs away from the woodpile and stacking them up. My arms ached and my fingers bled but I couldn't stop, no matter how tired I felt. After a moment, Zell came to join me. He didn't say anything. He didn't have to. Together, we stacked log upon log upon log, built up an interlaced mound, laid down the kindling. A few of the peasants watched us, confused, but none approached; they could tell something heavy was going on.

By the time we finished building it, night had started to fall, the sky a soft purple, the sun slipping behind the horizon.

Despite it all, I still couldn't bear the thought of carrying my father, so Zell did it, emerging from the crushed quarters with my father's body limp in his arms. He looked so small like this, a bundle of flesh and bone wrapped in bloody cloth, his eye shut, his hair hanging low. How could someone so powerful, so important, so utterly monumental, become just *this*?

Zell laid my father down on the pyre, and turned to me. I took a torch from a nearby fire pit and lit the kindling. Then the flames spread, climbing up the wood like hungry vines, swallowing my father in a shroud of orange and yellow and red.

Zell's hand found mine, and we stood there, still, like the statues that watch over the dead in the crypts of the West. Tears streaked down my cheeks, but they were quiet tears, the kind that came not with heaving sobs but a broken heart. "I feel like I should say something," I whispered. "But I don't know what to say."

Zell turned to me. The firelight danced in his soft dark eyes. "May I?"

"Of course."

He stepped toward the pyre, and raised out one hand. When he spoke, it was in Zitochi. *"Khezhta koral zal toro. Khezhta van rella zar. Khezhta per tel mar dezhta kharr."*

"Was that a prayer?" I asked as he stepped back.

"A poem," he replied. *"May the winters stop freezing and the fires stop burning. May the beasts sheathe their claws and the warriors hang up their blades. Then, at last, may the tortured man find peace."*

I leaned into him and he put his arm around my shoulders and held me there as the pyre burned and burned, as the smoke grew and night fell. I don't know how long we stood there like that. An hour, maybe two. But soon the sky was dark and the camp was still, save the distant murmur of a whispered conversation and the rustling of the wheat fields. In the distance, the light of the Godsblade cut through the night, a pillar of illumination driven into the earth. One way or another, my journey would end there.

"What're you thinking about?" Zell asked.

We were sitting at this point, side by side in the dirt, staring at the flickering embers of the pyre. "Just what happens next," I replied.

"What do you mean?"

"I don't know what to do, Zell. There's so much pressure on me. Galen wants me to use the crystal. Hell, everyone wants me to use the crystal. And I want to defeat Miles and save the world but . . . but I'd be killing thousands of people. And everyone else could go on with themselves, talking about how it was the right choice and they would've died anyway and all that. But I'm the one who'll have to live with it. I'm the one who'll have to go to bed every night picturing their faces. I'm the one who'll carry the weight." I swallowed deep. "And I don't know if I can do that."

Zell was quiet for a long time, taking it all in. When he finally spoke his voice was low, haunted. "It's not right," he said. "It shouldn't be you."

"What do you mean?"

"You don't deserve to have this pressure on you," he said. "You didn't do anything to deserve it. *I'm* the one who aided the Ragged Disciples. *I'm* the one who helped your father take over. I'm the one responsible for all this." He shook his head. "If anyone should have to carry that weight, it's me. I deserve it."

I turned to look at him. He'd shaved in the Skywhale, so his face was smooth, and in the dancing orange light of the pyre, he looked young, younger than usual. In that moment, he wasn't the hardened world-weary killer he so often looked like. He was just a boy of eighteen, my boy, looking sad and lost and scared. "You deserve it?" I repeated. And in that moment, it was like . . . like I somehow truly and fully understood him. I'd been with Zell for a year and a half. I'd fought alongside him, slept in his arms, stared into his eyes as our bodies became one. But somehow it was right there, in that field, with the moon bright overhead and the pyre glowing faintly, that I really truly knew him. "Holy shit. This is how you cope."

"How I cope?" he repeated.

"With the uncertainty of the world. With all the chaos and fear and the pain. You put it all on your own shoulders. You think everything bad that happens in the world is a punishment for mistakes you made. You feel like you have to solve it all, like it's all your fault and responsibility, like everything awful is about you and the only solution is for you to fight and suffer . . . because that's actually easier than the alternative." The words were just coming out, spilling forth, and I knew they might seem hurtful, but that's not how I meant them. These were just truths, truths I was seeing for the first time, the most important truths there were. "What you said about my father, how he had to just keep swimming forward, how he can't stop for a moment or he'll die . . . you're exactly the same way, aren't you? You have to believe this is all your fault and you're the only one who can fix it. You have to keep fighting and bleeding and suffering. Because if you stopped then you'd have to face the real truth."

Zell stared at me in silence. I could see the emotion in his face: the hurt, the anger, the defensiveness. His nostrils flared and his brow furrowed, and I could see the moment where he was about to turn away and storm off, to push back against what I was saying by throwing up a wall between us. I could see him struggle.

And then I saw him shove that away. I saw him swallow his pride. I saw him breathe deep and push through the defensive instinct and force himself to take it in, to hear my words, to really listen to me. I'd never loved him more.

"And what is the real truth?" he quietly asked.

"That life's not fair or just or meaningful," I replied. "It's just random. Bad things happen for no reason. Good people have to carry burdens for no reason. And you'll never ever *ever* be able to solve everything or take it all on yourself. You can keep on going, always fighting till you bleed, always searching for the next battle, just stewing in your guilt and pain. Or . . ."

"Or?"

"Or you can let go," I said, and I somehow knew I was talking to myself even as I was talking to him. "You can let someone else take over. You can let someone else carry the weight." I closed my eyes, feeling the night's cool breeze, the pyre's distant warmth. "This isn't about you, Zell. It's about me. It's my choice."

"And what do you choose?"

"The only thing I can," I whispered. "It's not fair or just or right. I don't deserve this, and I haven't earned it. But it's fallen on me, so I need to stop running and whining and hoping someone else will have the answers. I need to stop thinking about my feelings, and start thinking about everyone else. It doesn't matter how I'll feel when it's done. It doesn't matter the burden I'll carry. I need to think of the greater good."

"The greater good," Zell repeated.

"Back in Tau Lorren, I had this talk with Ellarion about how he always wanted to be this big hero. How he dreamed of being honored with statues and songs and fawning crowds. But that's not what being a hero is, is it? Being a hero doesn't mean getting rewards or praise. Being a hero means suffering so other people don't have to. Being a hero means pain."

"Heroes don't get happy endings," Zell said.

I turned to look at him. "Another Zitochi saying?"

"No." He smiled, just the tiniest bit. "Just one of my own."

I took a deep breath, and at once felt the relief of having finally made a decision and the crushing burden of what that meant. "I'm going to have to do it, aren't I?"

Zell nodded. His brown eyes never looked kinder, gentler, more appreciative. "I love you so much," he said. "Whatever you choose, I'll be right by your side."

"I love you too," I replied. "And you'd better be."

Then I pulled myself to my feet. I had a fire burning in me, a sense of momentum, and I had to keep it going before inertia and doubt could set in. I walked back into the main camp, away from the pyre, toward a little campfire in the middle. My friends were seated around it, Ellarion and Lyriana and Galen and Syan, and they all looked up at me as I approached.

"Well?" Galen asked.

I opened my palm and the crystal appeared, hovering, rotating, clear for everyone to see. "I'll do it," I said. "Get me to the Heartstone, and I'll use the crystal. I don't want to, but I don't have a choice."

Lyriana let out a heavy breath, and Syan glanced away. Galen nodded, pleased. "Then we just need to find a way to get you to the Heartstone." He turned toward the city on the horizon, its ominous looming walls, its grasping pillars of smoke. "That's . . . the hard part."

"Luckily for all of you," Ellarion said, "*I* have a plan." He rose to his feet and stretched out his arms, his knuckles cracking with a metallic scrape. "We build our own Skywhale. One that's small and fast, a slick attack craft for a small team. Galen, you and the Southlanders wage an assault on the other side of the city, drawing their guard. We fly up, over the wall, and then Syan uses her Cutting Art to warp us into the Godsblade itself." He glanced at her. "You *can* do that, right?"

"It would be difficult to land a Cut that precise," Syan said with some consideration. "But if you could get me close enough . . . yes. I think I could do it."

Ellarion grinned and folded his arms across his chest. "Well? Admit it. It's a good plan."

"No," Galen replied wearily. "It's a terrible, doomed, suicidal plan that puts our most valuable assets at risk on a completely unproven strategy. But at this point, I've learned better than to doubt you lot. If I tried to stop you, you'd probably do it anyway."

I nodded. "Fair. Totally fair."

"Just one last question," Galen asked. "Say it works and you manage to get your team into the Godsblade. What then? Miles will be holed up in there with dozens of his best men, his best bloodmages, and Archmagus Jacobi. They're all going to stand between you and the Heartstone. What's your plan for them?"

"Same plan we've always had," Zell said, walking up to our group through the dark of night. "We fight."

"You'll die," Galen replied.

I turned toward him, and then my eyes flitted beyond, to the edge of the camp, where the captured bloodmage prisoners still sat slumped in the dirt. An idea formed in my mind. A terrible idea, something awful and dark and monstrous, the kind of idea you felt awful for even thinking. The kind of idea a good person would never voice. The kind of idea you could never take back.

But we were past that threshold, weren't we? What mattered now wasn't being good. It wasn't being heroes. It was doing whatever it took to defeat Miles and save the world. And I knew this was the one thing he'd never see coming.

I took a deep swallow. "Actually," I said, "I think I have an idea."

TWENTY-EIGHT

IT TOOK TWO DAYS TO GET US READY FOR THE MISSION. Two days of Ellarion working with some blacksmiths to fashion a vessel. Two days of Lyriana and Syan practicing their magic together out in the fields, giggling as they found new ways to synchronize their Arts. Two days of sparring with Zell and drinking with Marlo and staring at the specter of the city in the distance, at the looming tower that held the inevitable. Two days of savoring every moment before the world changed forever. Two days of trying to ignore the screams coming from the tent on the outskirts of camp, the one where Galen took the most irredeemable of the bloodmage prisoners. Two days of feeling like two days wasn't enough.

You know what I definitely did find time for? Catching up with Lyriana. I ambushed her the first night in her tent, while Syan was busy, pulling the flap shut behind me and plopping down on the bed beside her with an expectant grin.

"Can I help you?" she asked, but even she couldn't hide her smile.

"Uh, yeah?" I replied. "You and Syan! Tell me everything! How long has this been a thing?"

"I've had feelings for her for some time," Lyriana admitted. "I just wasn't sure how to act on them."

"I'd say you did a pretty good job." I grinned at her. "It's just . . . I thought you liked guys."

"I do. But I also like girls," Lyriana said. "I've always felt some . . . attraction. But I never thought to act on it. For one, the Queen of Noveris has always married a man, as per the custom, so it felt . . . I don't know. Inappropriate or something. There would've been gossip and rumors and all that." She leaned back on her hands, grinning so wide it made my heart swell. "I don't care anymore, though. To hell with what anyone thinks. I really like Syan. She understands me in a way no one ever has. She makes me so happy. The way I feel when I'm with her . . ." She let out an adorable sigh. "I don't know. It's just something else."

"You two look just unbearably cute together," I said. "The last few days have been awful, but seeing you this happy makes it worth it."

Lyriana smiled, but I could see some worry behind it. "I know it probably won't last," she admitted. "I mean, we'll probably die during the mission. And if we don't, then there's still my engagement to Rulys Cal. I know this will probably have to end."

"If there's one thing we've learned in the past two years, I think there's nothing we know with any real certainty," I said, feeling weirdly profound. "If you like her, if she makes you happy, then fight for her. Make it happen."

Lyriana cocked an eyebrow. "You sound like Zell."

"Zell's usually right."

Lyriana looked down, but I could see a faint glow in her golden eyes. "Let's hope so."

Then those two days were up, and it was go time. We gathered together in a clearing southeast of the city as the sun slipped behind the horizon, framed by fields of swaying wheat, the beautiful sunset swallowed by the chaos and smoke of the city. In the end, after a lot of debate, we'd decided to send six of us on the mission: me, Zell, Ellarion, Lyriana, Syan, and Aeron, a former Hand of Servo and the most qualified mage we could find to man the ship.

At Lyriana's insistence, we told him what the plan would entail: that if I got the crystal to the Heartstone, he would die. To my surprise, he accepted it.

"I was always ready to die for you, my Queen," he'd said. "And at least this way, I'll take all those bloodmages with me."

We'd been given the pick of Galen's stores, and were strapped as hell and ready for war. I wore tight leather armor, thick bracers around my forearms, a chain-mail undershirt and tall new boots. A brand-new short sword (also named Muriel, because I've never been creative) sat sheathed at my hip, and I have to say, after weeks of traveling in chafing clothes and fighting with cracked swords, it felt pretty damn good. A pair of curved nightglass blades crossed Zell's back in an X; Ellarion's hands hovered over his shoulders, ready to strike; and Lyriana had a look that I could only describe as badass battle Queen, wearing a black leather tunic with long gloves and tall boots and a little dagger at her hip.

I just wish our ship looked remotely as impressive. It was either the Skydolphin or the Skyshark, depending on who was talking about it, but lying out in the clearing, it looked more like a Skyminnow. It was a narrow metal half cylinder maybe the length of a longboat, with two wooden benches on each side and barely room for six people. Two flat cloth wings jutted out of each side, wings that could rotate a full 360 degrees through poles that jutted into the ship.

Looking at it, I felt a knot of fear tighten in my stomach. For the last two days, this had seemed abstract, a good plan on paper that some other people would do. But now, gearing up to get in the ship, the reality was setting in. I'd made a lot of reckless decisions the past two years, but this probably took the cake. We were running—no, *flying*—headfirst into the single most dangerous place in the entire kingdom. We'd made it this far through courage and cunning and a whole lot of luck, but that had to run out someday.

And I had a really bad feeling today was that day. "We're really doing this, huh?"

"The battle's under way." Zell nodded toward the city's western side. A massive cloud of dust blocked off most of my vision, but I could see jagged bursts of fire popping through the hazy lightning in a storm, could hear the clang of metal and the crackle of magic and the shouts of commanders. The Southlanders were attacking, and true to Ellarion's plan, it looked like most of the bloodmages were focused on protecting the city from them. The flank was clear. "We're not going to get a chance like this again," Zell said.

"Then let's do it," Ellarion replied. His hands fluttered down to his wrists, clicking on, and he took a seat toward the ship's rear.

Lyriana and Syan sat at the front, Ellarion and Aeron in the middle, me and Zell at the back. I was the last one to go, but for some reason, my feet weren't moving. It wasn't just the fear, though yeah, there was plenty of fear. But it was also knowing that as soon as I sat down in that ship, I'd cross the point of no return. I was going into the Godsblade. And I was either dying there or killing thousands of innocent people. The Tilla I was, the Tilla I liked being, the life I'd built, the friends, the love . . . none of it would ever be the same.

"Wait," I said, and every head turned to me. "I just . . . I just want to say thank you. To all of you. For the support and the friendship and just everything." Lyriana gave me a soft smile, and Ellarion tipped his head. "The world is a raging trash fire. But you all are amazing. And no matter what happens next or what the future holds, I'll never forget what we've had. I love you all."

They all nodded (even Aeron, which, thanks) and let the moment hang. I stepped over the ship's side and took my seat on the bench next to Zell. Heavy purple clouds blotted out the sky overhead, and in the distance, I could hear a thunderous blast as something exploded, something big. The ground trembled, and screams, so many screams, cut through the air. "Let's do this," Ellarion said.

Aeron nodded his head and, with a sharp breath, began. He flexed his palms out, twisting them around. The air around us hummed with magical energy, sending a weird, warm tingle down the length of my body. The ship beneath us began to vibrate and I felt that rush once again, and now we lifted off the ground, first just a few inches, and then, with a whoosh, up into the sky, the ground vanishing below us. As Aeron pushed the air up under the wings, we rose and rose, higher and higher, until the wheat field below us looked like a child's playhouse, until the top of the city walls looked level.

"All right," Ellarion said, and I could almost, almost, feel him pushing down the fear. "Forward! To the Godsblade!"

Aeron reached down, grabbing the pole that controlled the wings, and turned them 90 degrees, so they were perpendicular to the ground. "Hold on tight!" he yelled, and a second gust hit us, this one pushing us forward, toward the city. The wind rushed through my hair, even as the vessel under me trembled and wobbled. We were like an arrow fired out of a bow, plunging at the Godsblade, and nothing could stop us.

The city grew bigger, closer. As we streaked its way, I could make out all the little details that were obscure from afar: the bloodmages patrolling the walls, the lights flickering in the Godsblade, the sweeping fires raging within.

"Syan, go!" Ellarion screamed. We were coming up on the wall now, closer and closer, and I could see the bloodmages start to look our way, to notice the tiny craft barreling toward them. "Make the Cut!"

"I can't!" Syan yelled back. Her zaryas hovered in front of the ship, twitching, streaking in messy lines. "I need to get closer!"

The craft beneath us shook, tipping one way and the other. I hated this, *hated* this. My nails dug into Zell's palm. We'd flown across most of the meadow now, almost up to the wall, where the bloodmages were pointing and shouting. At the front of the ship, Syan's brow had the deepest furrows I'd ever seen, sweat streaking down her cheek, the blue streaks in her hair burning like Luminae.

A horn of alarm blared from the wall, and one of the bloodmages raised his hands overhead. A ball of flame appeared above him, a scorching red mass, and with a roar he flared his hands out and sent it hurtling toward us, a blazing meteor cutting through the night. "Fireball!" I screamed, because what else could I do?

"On it!" Lyriana replied and jerked her own hands up, fingers contorting into intricate shapes. A viscous purple membrane rippled out of her palms, like water hanging in the air, enveloping us in a protective bubble. A Shield. And not a moment too soon. The ball of flame slammed into it, shattering into dozens of blazing streaks that slid along the surface. Our ship lurched hard from the blast, and I let out a scream as I slammed into the side. Aeron moved fast, jerking his fists up, stabilizing us and keeping us going.

And that was just the beginning. The Shield kept us safe but it also drew a whole lot of attention our way, turning us into a luminescent purple bubble flying right into the city. More horns blared with increased urgency, and I could see the bloodmages on the wall scrambling to the front, charging up with magical energy. The Southlanders' distraction had gotten us this far, but we were rapidly becoming target number one.

"Syan! The Shield won't hold off all of them!" Lyriana yelled. Her voice bounced around the Shield's bubble with an intense echo that only made it seem more urgent. "You need to get us in, *now!*"

"I can't quite line it up from here!" Syan replied, and she was full-on panting at this point. Her zaryas flitted back and forth with a manic intensity, but never quite formed that X. "If I make the Cut without focusing on exactly the right spot, I'll kill us all!"

That much was definitely true. During the two days we'd spent prepping, I'd watched Ellarion try to learn to Cut, attempting to move an apple from one stump to another. It had only resulted in cleaving it down the middle and fusing half of it with a nearby rock. I was very much not interested in dying like that.

"Faster!" Ellarion turned to Aeron. "Get us in before they can fire the volley!"

"Trying!" Aeron yelled back, and our little bubbled ship shot forward. I hung on to the bench with both hands as it jostled, the metal vibrating beneath me like it was going to come apart any second. I felt like my heart was going to explode in my chest, like the world was growing fuzzy at the borders. Zell closed his eyes, chanting a prayer. Ellarion's hands clutched the sides of the ship so hard they actually started to dent it. We were almost at the wall now, about to sail right over the line of bloodmages. I could see at least three fireballs forming, could see a bloodmage surrounded by pulsing yellow electricity, could see two of them forming what looked like a giant lance of ice.

We weren't going to make it.

We were going to die.

"I've got it," Syan said through gritted teeth, and her zaryas were glowing now, radiant blue stars dancing in the air. "I've got the sight. Lyriana, drop the Shield."

"What?" Lyriana demanded.

"Now! I can't pull us through while it's up!" Syan screamed.

"But—"

Then Syan looked back at Lyriana and their eyes met and even here, in a rickety metal ship fifty stories in the air, tossed to and fro, under attack by dozens of bloodmages, there was a sudden wonderful calm. "Trust me," Syan said.

Lyriana nodded and closed her hands.

The Shield vanished.

The bloodmages flared out their palms, and the fireballs shot toward us, the lightning hissed through the air, the lance of ice flew like a spear.

Syan's zaryas shot across each other, forming a perfect glowing X of white light, an X that cut through the skin of the world, an X that wrenched us in like water to a whirlpool.

The world bent and twisted, pulled out like a fun-house mirror.

And then we were inside.

The ship wasn't flying anymore, but it was still moving, our momentum sliding us across a shimmersteel floor like the world's fastest sled. My breath was trapped in my chest, my hands clenching the bench, as my brain struggled to make sense of where we were. A wide chamber. Inlaid Luminae. Shimmersteel walls. Cathedral ceiling. Figures streaked by, soldiers, their faces hidden in helmets, their voices a chorus of shouts and screams.

"Hang on!" Zell yelled, and I looked up to see the chamber's wall coming fast. A single Western soldier, a brawny fighter with a face covered in tattoos, looked up to see us just as our ship's prow slammed into his chest. We lifted him off his feet, drove him backward, and then smashed hard into the wall, plunging the ship clean through him, impaling him to the front of the ship like a bloody reverse-masthead. We all flew forward, tumbling onto each other, hurtling toward the front. I landed right on Zell, right in front of that poor sod of a soldier. And finally, finally, we were still.

I pushed my head up, air rushing into my lungs. The good news was, Syan had successfully gotten us into the Godsblade. The bad news was that we were definitely not in the chamber of the Heartstone. No, this was two stories below it, in the massive hall where the King held court. I could see the shimmersteel throne at the end of the room, empty, grand, bright, and sparkling. And between it and us, I could see two dozen Western soldiers.

We stared at them. They stared at us. One endless second of confusion hung still in the air.

Then the closest Western soldier let out a roar and charged, his ax raised high overhead.

Even here, after what we'd just been through, my khel zhan training kicked in. I leaned over the ship's edge with one hand, drew Muriel with the other, and thrust her out, point first, right into the soldier's chest, running him through before he even had a chance to swing. He let out a choked gasp, glaring down at me, and then his ax fell from his hands and he fell back and lay still.

Fifty-nine.

The second the man's back hit the ground, the room exploded into chaos. The other soldiers rushed forward, coming in at us from all sides, but my companions were up and fighting. I felt a hand press down on my back as Zell bounded over me and caught the next soldier in the chest with his knee, dropping the two to the ground as he delivered a brutal knuckleblade punch to the side of his throat. Blood sprayed out, dark and red, and Zell was already bounding off him, drawing his swords from his back. The nightglass blades sparkled yellow and blue in the light of the Luminae, and cut dazzling streaks as Zell whirled into the crowd. Another group of soldiers were charging us from the other side, but our mages had it covered. Aeron threw out his palm, shooting a gust of wind that knocked the soldiers down, and then

Lyriana flared out her hands, lifting them up and slamming them together, tossing them around like dolls. But even as they dropped, there was another wave coming, and another, and another.

This wasn't how it was supposed to go. We should've been in the tight chamber of the Heartstone. We should've had the chance to do this clean. But we were here now and there was only one way out. Fight or die.

With a roar of my own, I hopped over the side of the ship and charged forward, across the room, into the fray. Halos of light glistened on the shimmersteel floor under my feet. Muriel swung light and easy in my hands, cutting through the air, clanging against armor, sinking into flesh. Bodies collided. Blades struck and sparked. The room pulsed thick with magic, with scorching tendrils of flame and howling gusts of wind. Syan's zaryas whistled like bladed hummingbirds, tearing open throats and punching holes through chests. Rivulets of crimson lashed through the air like paint off a brush, splattering the walls. I screamed and slashed, rolled and stabbed. I felt warm blood splash across my face and didn't even flinch. In that chaos, I was not a person. I was an instrument of death, a tool of war, forged by my father's betrayal, hardened by Zell's instruction, set to purpose against the men who'd stolen this Kingdom. I was the hammer and the nail, the scythe and the flame. I was a pounding heart, a clenched fist, a howl of righteous fury.

Sixty.

Sixty-one.

Sixty-two.

Sixty-three.

One soldier came at me, swinging a mace. I dodged to the

side and put Muriel through his cheek. *Sixty-four.* Another swung at me from behind, clipping my side with his dagger, and I grabbed his wrist and pulled him forward, onto my blade. *Sixty-five.* Poor Aeron went down, an ax in his back, and I avenged him by hurling Muriel like a knife, right into his killer's chest. *Sixty-six.*

I reached down to grab another sword, leaving myself open for half a second. Not a long time, but long enough for a tall thin soldier to charge me with a spear. He would've gotten me too, if Zell hadn't swooped in, leaping from the side to ram his sword into the man's ribs. Our eyes met. Zell's face was slick with blood, his hair wet, his knuckles dripping. But he was alive and I was alive and we smiled at each other, the half-crazed wide-eyed smiles you can only have on a battlefield.

Then he sprang up as two more soldiers rushed at us, fancy-vested royal guard. Bloodmages. They flared out their hands in unison and flickering yellow-blue bursts of lightning shot out, streaking toward us, and then blasting apart as they struck the shimmering purple membrane of a Shield that had materialized right in front of our faces. "I've got you!" Lyriana shouted, and then Ellarion's hands were in the air, whirling wildly, catching the ribbons of lightning and sending them right back into the bloodmages who'd cast them, tearing clean through them and leaving little more than fluttering scraps of cloth.

And with their deaths, the room was quiet again.

I slumped to my knees, panting. My eyes still scanned instinctively, searching for the next attacker, the next swinging ax, the next slashing blade. But none came. The soldiers were dead. All of them. Their bodies, so many of them, littered the floor like fallen leaves. There was so much blood, you couldn't even see the shimmersteel, except for subtle halos of light that glowed around the corpses. The burned ashy residue of magic hung stagnant in the air, and a half-dozen tiny fires smoldered.

My body abruptly become a body again, not a weapon, and with that came a whole lot of pain. My muscles burned, and my lungs throbbed. The cut in my side stung badly, as did a gash on the back of my calf that I didn't even remember getting. Looking around, I saw my friends were in the same shape: blood-soaked and bleeding, bruised and stumbling, but alive. Alive!

"We did it." Ellarion staggered forward. His hands fell limp to the ground, and he looked around the room with a stunned, disbelieving smile. "We actually d—"

But he didn't get to finish that sentence, because a jagged lance of gnarled stone burst out through his stomach.

I screamed and fell back, scrambling for a sword. Ellarion stood there, trembling, blood bubbling out through his quivering lips, and then keeled over. A figure moved behind him, emerging from the shadows, a tall gaunt man cloaked in darkness, with serpentine tendrils of smoke flaring behind him like wings made of dusk.

Archmagus Jacobi.

We all moved at once, leaping up, drawing blades, but it was too late. He'd waited the whole time for this moment, for the second when he'd have an advantage, and he moved with impossible speed and precision. His sunken black eyes darted around the room, taking us all in. His long elegant fingers whirled and contorted, as his wrists spun and his hands flared.

One of those tendrils shot at me, a striking viper, and tore through the side of my leg, and then it was like I'd been filled with ice. My leg went numb and stiff, and I crashed down to the ground. My whole body was frozen, locked, cold. I pushed as hard as I could, begged it to move, to crawl, to fight, but I just lay there, limp and useless. Lyriana flared out her palms, hurling a ball of flame his way, but Jacobi twisted a hand at it, blowing it up just an inch in front of her and sending her slamming into a wall. She bounced off it hard, hit the ground, and lay still. Syan's zaryas whistled toward him, but he raised another hand, and they hurtled off uselessly to the side, and then he lashed her with one of those tendrils too, driving it through her arm and sending her crumbling down.

That just left Zell. Zell, who was racing across the room like a blur, Zell with a blade in each hand and death in his eyes. He ran at Jacobi's back and leaped through the air, his nightglass swords drawn back to deliver a cutting blow. But Jacobi craned his head back to him, and cut a harsh line with a hand, and Zell froze midair, suspended like a marionette.

"Pathetic," Jacobi sneered, and clenched his fist. Zell's left arm jerked back and with a horrible brittle crack it shattered just between the wrist and the elbow, white bone bursting through the skin like a knife through leather. I screamed, my eyes blurry, and even though my whole body still felt frozen, I crawled forward, dragging myself by my nails. A sword. All I needed was a sword.

"Let him go," a voice choked out. It was Ellarion, slumped against a wall, his whole front soaked red. That gnarled stone lance had caught him just below the ribs, running him clean through. He looked bad, real bad. The color had drained from his face, and his eyes were glassy and distant. With every breath, he spat blood, and his wrists lay limp by his side.

Jacobi waved a hand dismissively, sending Zell hurtling into a pillar, and then spun around to face Ellarion. "Now this . . . this is curious," he said, his voice a cruel purr. With measured footsteps he paced toward Ellarion, stepping over the corpses of his soldiers. His tendrils drew back, hanging at attention, a mass of tense vipers. "At last I meet my predecessor. The great Archmagus Ellarion." I wanted so badly to fight, to stab, to bite his worthless throat, but my body wasn't letting me. "It's a shame, really, what happened to you. If you weren't so broken, you might actually have made a worthy adversary."

"I would've wiped the floor with you," Ellarion growled through bloody teeth. I don't know what he was doing. Distracting him? Drawing him away? Just talking shit?

"A bold claim." Jacobi cocked his narrow head to the side, and he smiled, a mean tight little smile that pissed me off like none other. But even as he talked and honed in on Ellarion, there was something happening behind him, something he didn't notice. Two small bronze shapes lifted off the floor, slowly, carefully, rising up with a silent precision.

Ellarion's hands.

"This is what I don't understand." Jacobi gestured in the air, conjuring another gnarled lance out of nothingness. "The others are all skilled fighters and mages, clearly. But you? You're nothing. A shadow of a mage. A sad, broken wreck. Why would they possibly bring you all along?"

Even with a lance through his stomach, bleeding out on a cold floor, Ellarion laughed. His floating hands were now up above Jacobi's shoulders, tensed, with the pointer and middle fingers extended.

The bloodmage still hadn't noticed. "See something amusing?"

"Yeah, actually," Ellarion replied, and his eyes blazed like the heart of the sun. "The very last asshole dumb enough to underestimate me."

Jacobi's eyes widened and he spun around, gasping as he realized the threat. Ellarion's hands jerked down in an X, crossing fast, Cutting through the skin of the world with glowing light.

For one moment, nothing seemed to happen. Jacobi just stood there, rigid, back to us, arms drawn out. Then he turned around, and I saw the mess that he'd become. The Cut hadn't taken him, not quite, but it had taken enough. It was like someone had reached down with a giant spoon and scooped a big hunk out of his front. His face was gone, leaving just an oozing wet cavity in the front of his head, and most of his chest was gone, too. His body wobbled and fell back onto the ground. I was about to wonder where the rest of him had gone, and then I heard a wet splat from the far side of the room. Fair enough.

That cold numbness vanished instantly, and my body returned to me. With a gasp I jerked myself up, onto my hands and knees, feeling the rush of sensation return. Everything was tingling, pins and needles, but it didn't matter because I could feel again. I could see the others moving, too: Syan rising to her feet, Lyriana on her knees, Zell slumped against a pillar, cradling his broken arm.

But Ellarion didn't rise or move. He just lay there, sprawled out, his eyes struggling to focus even as a look of satisfied pride lit up his face. "Cousin!" Lyriana yelled and ran over to his side. She pressed her hands to his wound, and her Rings glowed a vibrant green. "Hey. Hey! Stay with me!"

"I'm with you," he said, head lolling back. His hands fluttered gently to the ground, settling in repose by Jacobi's messy corpse. "But let's skip the whole 'I can heal you, no you can't' thing, okay?" He gestured weakly with a wrist at the lance running him through. "I'm not walking away from this."

A heavy knot tightened in my chest. I couldn't watch. I'd been slashed and stabbed and run through with magic, but this hurt so much worse. I couldn't lose anyone else. I couldn't.

"It didn't hit anything major," Lyriana insisted, barely able to get the words out. "I can heal this. I really can."

"Maybe. But not here. Not now." Ellarion shifted up, and I wish he hadn't because it made me see just how much blood he'd lost. "There's a door behind the throne that leads to the royal chambers. There's a flight of stairs at the end straight to the Heartstone. Miles'll be there. I'm sure of it." He closed his eyes. "You have to go. Finish the mission. End this war." A hand reached down and squeezed my shoulder. Zell. I looked up at him and saw the pain in his lowered gaze, the somber look on his face.

"We're not leaving you," Lyriana pressed, her eyes watering with golden tears. "We'll find a way . . ."

"I'll slow you down, and you know it," Ellarion said, and I could tell he was trying to sound resolute even though his voice was quivering. "Besides. It's only a matter of time before reinforcements come barging through the main door. I'll hold them off and buy you time."

I leaned forward, biting my lip, trying to focus on the

pain in my body because it was better than the pain in my heart. I pressed my palm to the wall behind him as hard as I could, and as I did the shimmersteel glowed underneath it, the glistening metal texture thawing away like frost to reveal a window. For the first time, I looked closely at the city beyond. And my breath caught in my throat. "Lyriana," I whispered. "Look."

From the distance outside the city walls, I'd seen the towers of smoke and assumed parts of the city were on fire. But looking out now, from within, I realized it wasn't parts. It was all of it. As far as the eye could see, the city was a blazing ruin. The beautiful mansions and ancient temples, the bustling markets and majestic gardens, were all gone. Looking out that window, I saw crumbled buildings and sprawling rubble, raging fires and scrambling little shapes I knew were people. Flickers of light went off all over, like crackling fireflies, and it would've been pretty if I hadn't known they were bursts of bloodmagic. The city, the whole city, home to so many innocent men, women, and children, was a war zone. How long had it been like this? A day? A week? A month?

I'd been dwelling obsessively on how many people the plague would kill. But how many would die just today if I didn't use it? How many had already died?

I saw the shock cross Lyriana's face as she looked out, and I knew whatever I was feeling, she had to be feeling a hundred times worse. Lightspire was just a city where I'd lain low for a few months, but it was her home. Every happy memory of her childhood, of her parents, of her life, had happened inside these walls. And Miles had destroyed it, like he'd destroyed so much else.

"Please," Ellarion said. "Don't make me beg."

Syan knelt down by Ellarion's side, her zaryas gently levitating over his wound. "I can stay with him," she said to us, a hitch in her throat. "I can't save him but . . . I can make sure he's warm and comfortable. Make sure he's not alone when . . ." She trailed off, cleared her throat, and looked down. "You three go. Use the crystal. Save the world."

"Okay." Lyriana turned away from the window, her chest heaving, and she did that thing where she stiffened up, that thing where she was steeling herself to do something she wasn't ready for. "Just . . . give me a second."

Zell nodded. He crouched down by Ellarion and grasped his shoulder, squeezing it tight. "It's been an honor to fight alongside you," he said. "And an honor to call you friend."

Lyriana wasn't moving, so I guess it was my turn, even though I hated this, I hated this so much. I leaned down and hugged him as gently as I could. "Look at you. A hero after all."

His eyes met mine, and for once, the glowing crimson didn't look angry or dangerous. It looked warm, inviting, kind. He smiled, a real smile, and a single glowing tear streaked down his cheek. "When they build the statue of me, make sure it captures how handsome I was."

I smiled, and realized I was crying, too. "It's a promise."

Then I stepped away and Lyriana came up, crouching by his side, pressing her head to his. "I love you so much, cousin," she whispered.

He reached up and held her, then craned his head up to gently kiss her forehead. "You're going to be the best damn Queen Noveris has ever seen," he said. "I know it." Then he coughed, a painful scraping cough that made the lance heave and sent blood to his lips. The light in his eyes was fading.

I could tell it was taking all his strength just to stay lucid. "Enough. Go. End this."

Syan squeezed his shoulder, and nodded to us. It was time.

So we left. Even though my heart felt like an anchor in my chest, even though it took every ounce of strength I had in me, we got up and turned away, leaving Ellarion and Syan, and heading across the sea of corpses toward the doors. Lyriana balled her hands into fists, magic flaring around her. Zell tore his shirt into a sling and stumbled forward, clenching and unclenching his good fist. I jerked Muriel out of that one soldier's chest and blinked away my tears, swallowed the pain, focused on the floor beneath my feet, the door in front of me, the fight ahead, the choice beyond. Anything but Ellarion, lying slumped against the wall, watching us go, that distant look in his eyes.

TWENTY-NINE

THE DOORS BEHIND THE THRONE GAVE WAY TO THE quarters where the royal family lived. We passed through a lovely private kitchen, a library covered with notes in Miles's writing, a bath with a heated shimmersteel tub. These rooms were as elegant and clean as they'd been back when I'd lived here, perfectly maintained. In these rooms, you could actually pretend the world was normal, that life was good. In these rooms, you could almost forget the Kingdom was burning.

The last room before the staircase up was the royal bedroom, a massive chamber with the biggest and fluffiest bed I've ever seen. The rest of the rooms had looked pretty much the way they had under the Volaris, but this room had been redecorated in the Western style: redwood panels on the floors and walls, candles affixed in iron holders, a heavy wooden desk. Paintings of Kents adorned the walls. I could recognize my grandfather, my grand-uncle, my stepmother and her three daughters. Closer to the bed was a mess that had to be Miles's. Just like him to move into the King's chamber at the first notice. Bottles of wine lay empty on the floor, along with crumpled clothes. A row of spent syringes lay alongside the bed, their glass tubes still stained with flecks of the blood-mage serum.

I'd assumed the room was empty, just like the others, but a small voice gasped as we approached. Hand on my blade, I peeked behind the bed, and inhaled sharply. Huddled there were three young Western women, about my age, maybe a little younger. They were in their smallclothes, the fancy silk kinds that noblewomen wore, with the garters and the lacy trims. They all had auburn hair, pale skin, green eyes, and freckles.

They all looked like me.

"Royal concubines," Lyriana said, looking over my shoulder. "A practice long forbidden."

"Apparently not anymore," I replied. My stomach turned, and I felt something I hadn't felt in a long time, a fury toward Miles that wasn't just political, wasn't just about avenging the people he'd taken. It was a fury that came from my very core, a fury that was all about me.

"Please don't hurt us," one of the girls begged. "We're just here for the money. I swear."

"Go," I said, my voice a dagger's edge. "Get out of here. Now."

They turned and ran. The world grew red at the edges, and my knees trembled, and it took Zell reaching out and grabbing my shoulder to snap me back. "Let's end this," he said. "Once and for all."

The King's bedroom had a private staircase up to the Heartstone, a small winding screw of delicate shimmer-steel that led to a heavy closed door. We made our way up together and stopped at the top. I leaned against the door, and through the other side, I could hear voices: soldiers, I thought, bloodmages maybe, and a commanding bark that I was almost certain was Miles.

I turned to glance back at the others. We looked like absolute hell. Zell's left arm hung in a sling. Lyriana bled from a long cut along her arm, and the gash in my side made every step flare with pain. We very much did not look ready to take on the world.

But what else could we do? We'd come this far. There was only one option left. My plan, the one I'd pitched to Galen back in the camp, the one that had cost me a good chunk of my soul. We all looked at each other for one long moment, breathing, preparing. "I'm ready," I whispered. Lyriana nodded. Zell did, too. I pulled the heaviest, deepest breath of my life into my lungs. And then I threw open the door.

The chamber of the Heartstone was a wide, round room with a domed ceiling. The stone itself, the Heartstone, the source of magic, was in the center, enclosed in a second smaller dome of incredibly thick shimmersteel. I couldn't see the stone itself now, because the dome was in its hardened nontranslucent state, but also because there were about a dozen men standing in the way. They were Westerners in loose robes, their skin pale and veiny, the veins in their eyes pulsing unnatural colors. Bloodmages. The best of the best. And standing in the middle of them was Miles.

The bloodmages raised their arms and opened their palms. Magic crackled in the air. I sucked in my breath and stepped forward, right onto the front line, my arms raised.

Everything came down to this moment. To this gamble. To my plan. And I didn't blink. Because if there was one thing

I was sure of, one thing I knew to my core, it's that Miles would hesitate before shooting me down.

"Wait!" Miles yelled.

The bloodmages froze. And I dropped low to one knee, which let Zell step up and hurl his sword. It was a perfect shot, and it streaked through the air like a missile, plunging right at Miles.

And froze, midair, an inch from his face. Miles's hand was up, fingers unfurled, palm wide. His eyes glowed gray, and the air hummed around him with the dull grinding of stone scraping on stone. The sword hovered there, useless, stopped. Miles looked past it, at me, with a look at once pitying and full of contempt. "Seriously, Tilla?" he said, waving a hand to spin the sword around, so its blade pointed right at Zell. "This was your big play? You do remember I can control metal, right?"

"Oh, I remember," I said, stepping back behind Lyriana. "I was actually counting on it."

Then Miles blinked, and his eyes flitted to the hilt of the sword, and I saw the exact moment he realized what was about to happen. Because there was something built into the hilt of the sword, a round metal ball attached to the end of the pommel. And inside that ball, behind a glass screen, there was something else: a gemstone crackling with trapped magical energy, flaring and flickering, a hurricane trapped in a bottle.

A mage-killer.

Many things happened at once.

Lyriana flared out her hands, and a purple Shield rippled out, filling the doorway's frame like a makeshift wall. Miles screamed and hurled himself to the side. A few of his mages sprang forward, trying to throw Shields of their own. The gemstone cracked, shattered, and burst.

The room rumbled and shook with the blast, an explosion of light and flame and energy that flooded the dome with a deafening roar. It hit Lyriana's Shield like a crashing wave, and she gritted her teeth and planted her feet, holding strong as it buckled and trembled. I couldn't see what was happening in the room beyond, because all I could see was swirling fire and crackling pulses of light.

Then it passed, the energy dissipating like a breeze. The room went still. I finally exhaled, my whole body trembling, and next to me, with a cautious pause, Lyriana dropped the Shield.

The chamber of the Heartstone, once so pristine and shiny, was now a charred ruin. Every surface was blackened, coated in ash. Strange crystalline growths sprouted from the shimmersteel, taking on the metal's glistening fish-scale look. The bodies of the bloodmages lay everywhere. Some, the closest to the blast, were in pieces, while others were still alive, barely, crawling and moaning across the floor, their skin scorched and cracked.

I'd hoped it wouldn't come to this. Killing so many just like that. Using the weapons of our enemy. But it was done. It was done.

None of us spoke. Zell took point, pacing over to the wounded bloodmages, and ending each with a single merciful thrust. Lyriana crossed to the dome and pressed her hand to the surface, causing the metal to turn transparent around her touch. The Heartstone was there, all right: a boulder that quivered like a liquid, that bent itself into impossible geometric shapes, that was somehow a half-dozen colors at once, that gave you a headache if you looked at it. I'd deal with that in a minute. Right now, I had a more pressing task.

Miles lay against the room's far wall. He'd managed to throw himself behind enough of the bloodmages that they'd taken the brunt of the blast, enough to keep him alive. But just barely. Whatever Shield had protected him had only blocked the left side of his face; the right was a blistered ruin, the skin blackened and raw, his eye a dripping socket. Little corkscrews of blue crystal twisted out through the skin of his forehead. His right arm had been taken clean off, and his chest rose and fell with ragged heaves, each sounding worse than the last.

I hunkered down next to him, and his one good eye flitted to me. When he spoke, his voice was a choked whisper. "Mage-killer," he said. "You made a mage-killer."

"I did," I replied quietly. There was only one way to make a mage-killer: by brutally torturing mages, breaking their minds and capturing their anguish within the Rings on their fingers. It had taken us six of the captive bloodmages before we got it right, six men dragged kicking and screaming into Galen's tent and carried out wrapped in sheets, six times Galen emerged with his hands stained red and a grim look on his face. It was unthinkable, unimaginable, the choice that separated us from our enemies, the line we never crossed. And I'd crossed it six times.

"I never thought . . ." Miles tried. Given that I'd just blown off half his face, you'd think he would've been angry, but he just looked sad, crushed, like he was so disappointed in me. "I never thought you'd do something like that."

"That's because you never really knew me, Miles," I said. "You just knew your idea of me." I had to say, for a moment I'd spent two years dreaming of, it felt weirdly sad. Lying there like that, totally broken, Miles didn't look like a cruel tyrant or a sinister bloodmage or the hateful little shit who sold me out back in the West. He just looked like the boy I'd once known, the boy I'd grown up with, the sweet boy who brought me mulberries, whose cheeks turned pink when he kissed my hand.

"It's over, isn't it?" he choked out.

I leaned forward and pressed Muriel's tip to his chest. "It is."

His eye met mine, and a single tear ran down his cheek. "All I ever wanted was you."

"I know," I replied, and pushed the sword in up to the hilt. *Sixty-seven.*

With the world's longest exhale, I stepped away. Miles lay there, cold and still, but he didn't matter anymore, because it was time for the next step, the final step, the moment when I'd change everything. The shimmersteel dome was now translucent, and inside, the Heartstone thrashed and writhed like a wounded beast, tendrils of grappling rock that slurped against the surface of the dome like hungry eels, flashing thousands of different colors at once.

"Do you know what you're doing?" Lyriana asked, and like, at this point, it'd be pretty bad if I didn't.

I closed my eyes and slipped into that other me, into the power that lurked behind my eyelids, the thoughts whispering beneath the running of my brain. The Nightmother. I let her take over, guiding my hands, pushing the power to the foreground. The world blurred, grayed at the edges, and I felt time slow to a crawl. Energy flared around me, colorful ribbons and dancing bands, tendrils of light and fury stretching out of the Heartstone, stretching into me. Shimmering green panes, just like the Nightmother's, hovered around me, covered in sliding runes and glowing symbols. I looked down at my palm and the crystal was there, yellow, spinning, so beautiful and pristine, almost like it didn't contain the deaths of thousands of people.

The room was silent and still, every eye on me, as I walked toward the Heartstone. This was the moment. The end of the line. All I had to do was press my palm on the shimmersteel frame, press the crystal through it, and let this bloodmage nightmare finally end. It was that simple.

But I couldn't bring myself to move.

The Heartstone sat there, waiting. The crystal spun in my hand. The tendrils of magic glowed around me. And outside, all around the tower, the city, the world, burned. I could end it. I could end it all now. I could *save the world*.

And still. I just stood there.

"Tilla?" Lyriana asked.

Zell just shook his head. "Let her think."

I wasn't thinking. Not really. I was just . . . feeling. Feeling the weight of the moment. Feeling the significance of what I was about to do flooding in around the edges of my vision, like I was drowning from the inside, like the world was a fist clutching me, squeezing tight. Their faces swam in my head, all the people I'd be killing, the men and women and children, anyone even remotely touched by magic.

I wanted to do it, to end this, but I couldn't will my body to move no matter how hard I told it to. I just . . . *couldn't*.

Do it! the voice inside me screamed. *You have to!*

And I could see her, the Nightmother, I could see how she'd done this, how she'd hunched over her own Godsblade, how she'd sentenced her own kind to death. I could see the hesitation and fear in her blank face, could sense her uncertainty, could feel her guilt and trepidation. She'd felt exactly like this, but she'd done it anyway, because she had to. Because she didn't have a choice. Because it was the only way.

Her choice had killed the Titans. It doomed her race to annihilation. It killed hundreds of thousands. And it led to the rise of mankind. It led to the triumphs of humanity, to the reign of the Volaris, to the Kingdom of the West, to my father, to me. Every moment of our history, every King and rebel, every child playing in the street and mage commanding the elements, all of it came from her choice.

Her choice that created my father. Her choice that brought me here. Standing in front of an identical Heartstone. Holding an identical crystal. Ready to do it all over again.

My knees trembled. My hand shook. I could feel the overwhelming weight of the cycles of history. Growth and death, conquest and rebellion, war and peace and war and peace and war. We just kept doing this, again and again, each generation bearing the burden of the one that came before, every child reliving her parents' mistakes, all of us doomed to repeat and relive and die praying our children will be better. And at the end of the day, it always came down to the same justification, the same pressure, the same sense of inevitability. We never wanted this. We just accepted it. For the good of our people. For the good of the world.

For the *greater good*.

And before I could think any more, before I could rationalize or talk myself into it, before I could let even one more voice speak inside my head, I spun around and flared out my hand and pushed all the energy inside me into that crystal and it exploded like a starburst, shattering all over the room, glittering and bright and useless, a skyscape of yellow stars that hung around us like flickering fireflies.

The power was gone. I'd destroyed it.

It was done.

If it had been silent before, then now it was a level below silence, a quiet that was overwhelming. Zell stared, stunned. Lyriana's jaw hung open.

"You didn't use it," Lyriana said at last.

"No. And now no one can," I said. My heart was thundering in my chest. I felt like I was going to faint. I'd done that. I'd really actually done *that*. I knew I should have felt guilt or shame or fear. I'd destroyed our only solution. I'd let the bloodmages run free. I'd doomed the world.

But all I felt was relief.

"Why?" Zell asked, without judgment. "You would have saved the world."

"Because a world that we have to kill thousands of innocent people to save isn't one worth saving," I replied, and even as the words came out, I felt their strength, felt *my* strength. "Because I'm not going to just be another cog in the wheels of history, churning along, repeating the same mistakes. Because sooner or later, someone has to take a risk to actually build a better future, and not just take the easy way out. Because I'm not going to become my father." I was shouting, I realized, but I didn't care. "We have to find another way. A better way. Or die trying."

"Zastroya will still come," Lyriana said quietly.

"Maybe," Zell said, and I could hear something new in his voice. Relief. "But maybe it won't. Maybe we'll find a better way, like Tilla said." He turned to me and smiled, and it felt like a weight as heavy as a boulder had been removed from my chest. "At least we can live with the choices we made. At least we can live with ourselves."

Lyriana nodded. "Damn right," she said. "But . . . what do we do now?"

"The one thing we should have done a long time ago," I replied, and even as I spoke an idea was forming in my head. "We tell everyone the truth." The crystal was gone, but I still had the rest of the Nightmother's knowledge in me, and that meant I could still see the glowing green panes, the ones that controlled this room. And I still somehow knew how they worked. My hands did the work automatically, drawing one in, tracing a rune, using the Titans' ingrained magical systems. A twist of my wrist brought up a single translucent button. I turned to Lyriana, my hand lingering over it. "So. Your Majesty. Ready to give your first real address as Queen?"

She blinked. "To who?"

"Everyone."

She stared at me for a moment, and then I saw comprehension hit. "Oh," she said. She ran her hands through her hair, smoothing it as much as she could, wiped some blood off her forehead, and took the deepest breath I've ever seen. "Okay," she said at last. "Do it."

I pressed the button. A green halo appeared under Lyriana's feet, and a beam of pale light enveloped her. The air sang with the low hum of deep magic, and I felt a buzzing in the back of my head, like a fingernail scraping against my brain. The room flooded with a blinding green light, but it wasn't coming from inside but outside. I spun to the far wall, which was now a window looking out on the city, and there was something in front of it, something massive and bright. I could only see a tiny bit of it from up here, but a hovering pane in front of me let me see the view from the outside.

Standing in front of the Godsblade, tall as the tower itself, was an image of Lyriana made of green light. She loomed over the city like an impossible statue, like a giantess, like a Titan. It had been almost a thousand years since anyone had seen a sight like this, a level of magic beyond anything any human had ever achieved. And everyone who saw it, everyone in the city or the fields beyond, dropped what they were doing and turned to gape. Westerners, Heartlanders, bloodmages, soldiers, men, women, children. In that moment, everyone was united in awe.

"Psst," I whispered. "I think you're on."

"People of Noveris!" Lyriana said, and even though I heard her voice in my ears from a few feet away, I *also* heard her voice the way everyone else did, booming and thundering in my mind, the way the Nightmother's voice had. And everyone could hear her like this. The people in the city below, sure, but also the merchants in the Baronies of the Eastern shore and the Zitochi in Zhal Khorso and Syan's mother all the way down in Benn Devalos. When Lyriana spoke, her words went out to every soul on the continent.

But still, somehow, she kept her cool. "I speak to you as your rightful Queen. The Usurper Kent is dead. The Inquisitor Hampstedt is dead. I have retaken the Godsblade. The war *is over*." Her voice was strong and authoritative, regal and commanding, the kind of voice you had to stop and listen to. It was a side of her I hadn't seen in ages, a composure I hadn't seen her display since the fall of Lightspire. I'd gotten so used to Lyriana the rebel, Lyriana the warrior, I'd forgotten how impressive Lyriana the Royal could be.

"We've all lost so much in this war. So many people have died. So many cities have burned. And we've all given up parts of ourselves, our souls, just to stay in the fight. Now, at long last, the time has come to put down our swords and take off our Rings. The time has come to build a peace." She swallowed deep, collecting herself. "I know there are many of you out there who will not want to accept this, especially coming from me. There are many of you who will blame my family for this war, for their conquests, for the way they ruled. I don't blame you for this. The Kings and Queens before me made mistakes. My family made mistakes. Their rule was not perfect, not just, not divinely mandated. I can't promise you I'll be any of those things. But I can promise you I'll try to be better."

I had no idea how her words were being taken out there, on the battlefields, in the streets. All I knew was that my heart was practically bursting with pride.

"The truth is, even if this war ends, the danger is far from over," Lyriana went on. "A far greater threat looms over the Kingdom. The use of magic has begun tearing our world apart. The earthquakes are just the beginning. If we don't unite as one people, if we don't end this conflict, if we don't all work together to find a solution, then it won't matter who sits on the throne. Heartlander or Westerner, Easterner or Southlander . . . we'll all burn."

She closed her eyes, and I don't think she'd ever looked more beautiful. "I am your Queen, but the truth is, I cannot order you to bow to me. You, the people, hold all the power. All I can do is tell you what I know. And I know we all face the most important choice in our history. We can unite as one and build a ship toward a better future. Or we can all drown together. If you'll trust me, if you'll give me a chance, I promise you I'll try to find a way forward. But in the end, the choice is yours."

Lyriana nodded to me, and I swiped my wrist again,

moving away the pane. The halo of light under Lyriana vanished, as did the giant projection of her outside. That scratching feeling vanished as well, so it's safe to say she was out of my head. "Well?" she asked. "How was I?"

"Magnificent," I replied.

"Hey," Zell said, his voice hushed and reverent. "Look."

He was pointing out the window, to the city below, and I walked over to look out, my stomach fluttering, because if this didn't work, if Lyriana's speech fell flat, then I'd kind of doomed the whole world. Lightspire sprawled out below us, and even though the fires still raged and the smokestacks still loomed, the city seemed different. Stiller. Quieter. There were no flashes of magic, no scurrying figures, no bursts of lightning or clanging blades.

All throughout the city, soldiers stared up at the Godsblade, whispering, muttering, praying. With tears in their eyes, they fell to their knees.

And laid down their swords.

THIRTY

LYRIANA'S CORONATION FELL ON THE FIRST DAY OF FALL, and naturally, I overslept.

A month had passed since the Battle of Lightspire. A month of reconstruction and rebuilding, of putting out the fires raging all over the Kingdom, both literal and figurative. It was a month of exhausting negotiations and fraught diplomacy, a month of endless letters and endless meetings, a month of long difficult conversations about what the future would hold. It took a month to bring order to the city and begin fixing all the damage that had been done, a month to clean up the Godsblade, a month to convince the holdout bloodmages and Western Lords to surrender, a month to put together a new government. Lyriana wasn't technically the Queen yet, just the Regent until her coronation, but it was a month that saw her scrambling to craft a vision of what her reign would be: policies that saw the nobility forced to share their wealth with the people, that created jobs for the poor and provided medicine to the sick, that prohibited the use of magic, that rebuilt the kingdom as a place that was, at least on paper, far more equal and just.

That was her, though. For me, it was a month of desperately needed rest. The city wasn't safe to wander for a Westerner, not yet, so I kept to the Godsblade, got myself a nice room in the upper floors. I slept in. I took long baths. I spent hours and hours in Zell's arms. To stay helpful, I baked bread in the kitchens to hand out to the smallfolk, and to relax I hung out with Lyriana and Syan whenever they were free. I celebrated my eighteenth birthday with fine Lightspire wine and a beautiful sunset and all my friends by my side. It wasn't all comforts and kisses; there were nights when I woke up screaming and days when my wounds itched and my eyes burned with sudden tears for everyone I'd lost. But still, little by little, life seemed to go on.

I thought of my father's dying words a lot. About what would happen if I ran away with Zell, if I went somewhere far, far away. Building a little cottage. Making a life. And putting all of this, all this responsibility and conflict and death, finally behind us.

But that was in the future. Right now, I had a coronation to get to.

I scrambled all morning to get ready, brushing out my hair, putting on jewelry for the first time in ages, slipping into the gown Lyriana had picked out for me. It was a Lightspire dress made of flowing blue silk, sleeveless, with golden ribbons tying up the back and little jeweled strands that crept up the side like ivy. It had been at least a year since I'd worn a dress, and I couldn't help staring at myself in the mirror, at the stranger I could barely recognize. My arms were buff, like, really buff, with biceps that put half the guys I'd known to shame. My shoulders looked broader, my stomach flatter, and even my hair looked unnatural flowing down, instead of tucked back in a ponytail. I never thought I'd look too tough for a ball gown, but here I was.

"You look beautiful," a voice said from behind me. I turned around and there was Zell, leaning against my door frame with a sly grin. He was wearing a tight black leather tunic with an icewolf fur trim around the collar, a trailing black cape, and matching gloves and boots. Small silver chains crossed his chest, and little tiny beads of embedded nightglass sparkled like a sea of dark stars. It was traditional Zitochi formalwear, an outfit he'd gotten as a gift from some Lord currying favor. It's funny. A year ago, the idea of Zell wearing Zitochi clothes to a formal event would've been unthinkable, because we'd wanted so badly to blend in. Now he wore them with pride.

"You look pretty damn good yourself," I said, crossing over to kiss him. And I meant it. He looked *amazing*. So amazing that I kind of wanted to just keep kissing him, to feel his arms around me, and maybe to slide my hands down and see what happened. Did we have time? I mean, maybe if we were quick . . .

He pulled away, smiling. "Later, my love," he said. "We have a coronation to get to."

Fine. *Fine*. I took his hand and followed.

The coronation was held in the throne room, naturally, a room I'd managed to avoid in the month I'd been here. They'd cleaned it up real nice: all the blood had been mopped up, all the bodies dragged away, the whole place as shiny and sparkling as it had ever been. The shimmersteel throne glistened at the end, and even after everything, it still looked majestic.

Zell and I were the last to come in, shuffling to our place at the front. The room was packed, with rows and rows of chairs that stretched all the way to the chamber's end. It looked like pretty much everyone of import had managed to make it out. In the front row were the special guests Lyriana had chosen to honor: Syan in a gorgeous white gown, Galen in a sharp black robe, even little Princess Aurelia, back home at last, looking utterly adorable. Behind us were the new Lords of the Heartlands, the fifth sons and castle regents and distant cousins who'd come into power after the fall of the nobility.

But I could see other Provinces represented too. One row was made up of the leaders of the Eastern Baronies, pale men and women with painted faces and bright red lips; I wondered if Markiska's parents were among them. Behind them were the Southlanders, with their white robes and bald heads. Rulys Cal was with them, watching us closely, like a cat poised to pounce. His engagement to Lyriana was one thing the Queen and I very much had *not* talked about; every time I tried to bring it up, Lyriana changed the subject, probably because of what it meant for her relationship with Syan. I didn't blame her. I knew we owed Cal a huge debt, that none of this would've been possible without the help of his army. But it didn't mean I liked looking at him.

And then at the very back were the Westerners, a handful of Lords who'd come out to represent the Province, the handful who'd survived: stern, hawk-faced Lord Tyre, the young Lady Millings, and heavy bearded Lord Collinwood, who I'd watched fall asleep in his beet soup a lifetime ago. They looked uneasiest of all, glancing around nervously, like they expected us to turn on them any second with blades drawn.

I didn't blame them. It's what they'd probably do if the tables were turned.

I swallowed deep, feeling the tinges of anxiety tickle at my stomach. The last time I'd been in a room with this many powerful people, they'd all died in a horrible fireball. Lyriana had assured me we'd be safe but . . . how could she be sure?

Zell's hand found mine and squeezed. I breathed deep, forced a smile. I'd made it this far. I'd make it further.

The music kicked in, a choir of young women singing in perfect harmony as a group of performers strummed violins and a blind old man played a majestic grand piano. In previous years, this would've been a ceremony infused with magic, the music augmented by the impossible geometries of the Mesmers, the room lit up by dazzling lights and ribbons of flying color. But magic was forbidden now except for emergencies, and so the whole thing had a humble, low-key vibe, the kind of thing you might see in a wealthy Western merchant's house. It was actually kind of nice.

The doors at the end swung open and Lyriana emerged. She looked so beautiful I actually gasped. She wore an ornate layered gown, a light cream that looked radiant against her black skin, with shining rivulets along the side and a flowing trail behind her. Her hair was braided in dozens of elegant strands, adorned with a crown of blue-and-yellow elderbloom. Long gloves went up her arms, and her golden eyes glowed bright and radiant.

Every head in the room turned to look at her and bowed in reverence. The music swelled. She walked forward, nodding regally at each delegation, her face a model of poise and grace. And for one second, one tiny wonderful second, our eyes met and I swear she cracked a smile.

Then she was up at the front of the room, at the foot of the throne. Normally, the High Priest would take over here, blessing the new monarch as the living herald of the Titans' will. For a lot of obvious reasons, Lyriana didn't feel comfortable with that, so instead, she had Archmagus Ellarion usher her in.

Yeah, that's right. Ellarion! After all those dramatic goodbyes, he'd made it out alive, thanks in no small part to Syan. We rushed back to them after Lyriana's speech and found him where we'd left him, unconscious, slumped against the throne room wall, surrounded now by the bodies of a dozen more Westerners Syan had killed to protect him. It had taken two weeks in the care of the Sisters of Kaia, but they'd saved his life. Sure, he'd lost twenty pounds and walked with a limp. But that spark was back in his eyes, the confidence back in his stride, and I'd seen him hit on at least four different girls in the last week alone. Ellarion was back in his element, and he'd never seemed better.

Today, though, he was all business, and managed to make it through the entire ceremony without cracking a single joke. He read Lyriana the vows of the throne, and she accepted all of them, pledging to be a faithful leader and serve the people and all that. It took nearly an hour, by the end of which I'd totally zoned out and was just staring blankly out the window. But then he ended and she rose to her feet and replaced her elderbloom crown with one made of shimmersteel and took her seat on the throne, and we all stood and clapped and cheered and damn if it didn't feel good. I knew there were still problems out there, a lifetime's worth: rebel bloodmages and uneasy alliances and the whole possible end of the world thing. But Lyriana was on the throne. At last. I had to celebrate that.

Then Lyriana spoke. "My assembled Lords and Ladies," she said. "I thank you all for making the journey to be here for this event. I know that you all have many responsibilities to your people, and that many of you may have apprehensions about what the future will hold. I know that we all have a difficult road ahead of us, that we have so much to rebuild and so many challenges to face. And yet seeing you all here, seeing us gathered together, not as enemies, but as friends once again, it fills me with tremendous hope." She smiled, a beaming, generous infectious smile. "For the first time in ages, I feel as though we might be able to make it to a brighter future.

"With that said, before we get to the festivities, I have one announcement to make," Lyriana went on. "My first Decree. And I believe it will be a fairly significant one. As the sitting Queen of Noveris, the sole monarch of the realm, I declare that th—"

"Your Majesty," Rulys Cal cut in, and every head swung to stare at him. His pact with Lyriana wasn't formally announced, but it was common knowledge, and the room shook with gasps and whispers. "I believe, before making any Decrees, we should confer? Perhaps make an announcement?"

I gritted my teeth, digging my nails into the skin of my palm. *Of course* Cal would try to make this moment about him. It was a power play, plain and simple, right now at the moment of Lyriana's coronation, and if she needed me to punch him in his stupid face, I totally would.

Lyriana didn't seem to need any punching. "Honored Dyn," she said, nodding her head like she'd seen this coming all along. "I understand why you'd want to speak with me. I know you've come here with great expectations."

"Expectations," Cal repeated, cautiously. "I don't consider

honoring a promise an expectation, but a vow. And you vowed we would be wed."

The murmur ran through the room again, even louder. So it was out in public now. Syan tensed up in her seat, and I sucked in my breath. But Lyriana looked totally unfazed. "I regret that I must disappoint you," Lyriana said. "There will be no marriage."

Cal's nostrils flared, and his face reddened. His countrymen all rose behind him, and everyone else scooted away, like this was really going to erupt into violence here and now. "You liar," he hissed. "How dare you? How *dare* you? After everything I did for you?" He turned away, fists clenched. "I should've known. Of course you'd betray me. Why would I trust a lying Volaris wh—"

"Honored Dyn," Lyriana cut in, the gracious smile never leaving her face, which felt like the ultimate power move. "Before you finish that sentence and say something you'll regret, I recommend you hear my Decree. After all, there's more than one way to become a King."

Cal blinked, frozen mid-word. "I'm listening," he said at last.

Lyriana cleared her throat. "As the sitting Queen of Noveris, the monarch of the realm, I declare that the borders of the Kingdom be immediately redrawn to end at the Evergreen Mountains to the east, the Adelphus fork to the south, and the Frostkiss Mountains to the west. I shall rule over only the original territory of Noveris, the Heartlands. All lands of conquest are returned to their people."

The room was dead silent. There wasn't even a rippling murmur now, because everyone was just too stunned for that.

Not just all the visitors either, who were gaping at the throne slack-jawed, but the rest of us as well. I stared at Lyriana, at her elegant smile, at the confidence and relief in her eyes. This was her moment of choice, her shattering the crystal, on a scale that was maybe even bigger than mine. With one sentence, she'd undone five hundred years of history. With one sentence, she'd changed everything.

I knew the rational thing would be to have some skepticism or doubt, or at least concern over what the future would hold. But screw that. I looked right at Lyriana and grinned, big and wide and proud. But her eyes weren't on me. They were on Syan sitting in the front row, Syan who stared up at her like she was looking at a goddess, totally and utterly in love.

Good for her. Good for them.

Rulys Cal was the first to break the silence. "Are you saying . . . ?" he asked, unable to complete the thought.

"I am. The Southlands are yours." Lyriana dipped her head in the subtlest hint of a bow. "*Your Majesty.*"

Cal stared at her for a while. His countrymen stared at him, and the rest of us stared at them. It felt like a whole lot was hanging on this moment. Then Cal nodded and forced a smile. "As you will, Your Majesty. And may the friendship between our Kingdoms be long and prosperous."

An Eastern Baron was the next to speak, a burly, exceptionally pale man with snowflakes painted by his eyes. "And our lands? The Baronies?"

"Free city-states once more, as they were in the days of old," Lyriana said, and I swear her smile seemed a little more genuine. "I imagine you'll have some very interesting conversations in your future." Her gaze flitted to the Westerners at the back. "And before you ask, the same goes for you, my Lords. The West is a free Kingdom once again."

The Western Lords didn't react, not immediately, but I saw them glance at each other uneasily. I got the feeling they'd be uneasy for the rest of their lives.

"Your Majesty," Galen said, and rose to his feet. He'd asked to serve Lyriana as her Inquisitor, and she'd accepted, on the condition the role was changed to Advisor; after everything we'd been through, everyone felt like maybe it was time to give Inquisitors a rest. "If I may have a word?" He spoke quietly, so quietly even sitting in the front row I could barely make out the words. "Your Decree is far easier said than done. There will be conflicts about borders and unhappy Lords and—"

"I know," Lyriana replied, her eyes not leaving the crowd, the smile not leaving her face. "And we have a lifetime to deal with the practicalities. But for tonight, let's enjoy the spirit of it, shall we?"

Galen nodded. "As you wish, Your Majesty."

The room was starting to hum again, a chattering wave that threatened to break into a roar. Lyriana rose from the throne and strode toward the crowd, one hand raised. "I know this is quite a lot to take in. I will take visitors all day tomorrow to hear concerns and address questions. But for now, let's put aside the politicking and enjoy one another's company. The war is over. The continent is at peace. And if I may compliment my Head Stewards, they've prepared a truly wondrous feast." She threw a wave toward the end of the room, by the doors to the Feasting Hall, where Marlo and Garrus stood in matching white suits, trying to look professional but unable to contain their smiles. "Let us adjourn."

It was a great closer, but it still felt like the room wasn't quite ready, still processing what had happened. So I did the only thing I could. I rose to my feet, turned back to the crowd and pressed my fist to my heart. "Long live the Queen!"

Then Zell was up, next to me. "Long live the Queen!" And Syan was up, and Ellarion too, and Galen, and then Cal was on his feet, and he shouted it too, and that was the symbol, the final blow that broke the dam. Everyone was up and cheering and crying, shouting and laughing, welcoming the future, consequences be damned. Even Lord Collinwood bellowed it, his voice thundering through the room. And in that wild noise, in that chaotic joy, Lyriana walked up to the front row and took Syan by the hands and looked into her eyes.

"Long live the Queen," Syan said.

"With you by my side, I will," Lyriana replied, and kissed her, and then I couldn't see anything because I was crying too hard.

The feast was, as promised, amazing. We dined on a buffet of foods from all over the Kingdom, well, the *Kingdoms* now: flaky meat pies from Lightspire, sizzling clams from the East, liquor-filled confections from the Southlands, and stuffed quail from the West. Ale and wine flowed, musicians played, and I let Zell twirl me on the dance floor while my whole body tingled with warmth. I saw Marlo hustling around to make sure everyone tried his favorite dishes, saw Princess Aurelia stuffing her mouth with cakes, saw Ellarion making out with an Eastern beauty, saw Lord Collinwood downing an entire flagon of beer in one gulp, and I even saw Rulys Cal smile, like, a genuine smile.

Lyriana fluttered around the room like a butterfly, chatting with all the Lords and Ladies, alleviating fears and making promises. I watched her like a hawk, and when she finally vanished through a side door for a breath of fresh air, I followed her out. She stood on a shimmersteel balcony, a rounded ledge fifty stories up that looked out over the city. The air was unusually warm for the fall, and the sky was bright and clear overhead, a thousand brilliant stars lighting up the night. Below us the city was . . . well, not rebuilt. But the fires were out and the columns of smoke were gone and it looked gentle, calm, at peace. Lyriana stood against the railing, gazing out in her cream gown, a vision.

"Hey, Your Majesty," I said.

She glanced back at me and smiled. "Please. I've got a lifetime of being called that. You of all people don't have to."

I walked over and joined her, leaning with my back against the railing. "How're you feeling?"

"Surprisingly good," Lyriana replied. "I have so much work ahead of me, I don't know how I'll ever rest, but . . . good. It's odd to say it, with the whole world still in catastrophic danger, but I think I actually have hope." She turned to me, and in that moment, her skin glowing in the moonlight, her golden eyes bright and pure, she didn't look like the regal Queen or the charismatic ruler I'd gotten used to. She just looked like my friend. "Am I out of my mind?"

"Well, you did just upend the power balance of the entire continent," I said. "You've got to be a little out of your mind to do that."

Lyriana snorted a laugh. "If you think that's bad, wait until I reveal my plan to hold a popular vote every five years to determine who should be the next monarch."

I stared at her. "Are you joking?"

"Zell explained how the Zitochi select their Chief of

Clans through a vote. It seems like a pretty good system." She shrugged. "Besides. What kind of a Queen would I be if my own people didn't want me to rule?"

I shook my head, because creating a way for her people to depose her was peak Lyriana. "How's Syan?"

"She's good, too," Lyriana said, glancing back into the feasting hall, where Syan was chatting with Ellarion on a bench. "She helped me craft some of the proposals. She misses her home a lot, but I think she's starting to settle in here, to find her place."

"You two seem happy."

"Oh, Tilla, you don't know the half of it," Lyriana said, and I could tell she was just dying to talk about it. "She's so smart and kind and insightful, and she just gets me, just understands me, like no one ever has. And she's funny too, when no one's watching, and oh, in the bedroom, she's just . . . I mean . . . wow." Lyriana glanced down, her cheeks suddenly flushed. "Too much information?"

"Maybe a little." I grinned. Together, we looked through the transparent doors into the feasting halls. The Barons were arguing about something, shouting at each other in that Eastern way that sounds like they're really mad but is actually just them mildly disagreeing, while Galen had a serious-looking chat with Cal. Lord Collinwood was passed out on a table, but the other two Western Lords stood behind him, whispering to each other while glancing around.

"When did you decide to do it?" I asked Lyriana. "Release all the conquered lands, I mean."

Lyriana shrugged. "I don't know. It's something I've imagined doing for a long time, I think, but never had the courage to really consider, not until you destroyed that crystal. After that, it just seemed like it was time to do the right thing, no matter the risk."

"Not to raise any doubt, but . . . won't it make regulating magic more difficult?"

"You know, I thought that, but I'm not convinced," Lyriana said. "The truth is, there's no way we're going to move past magic as a people without all coming together. Whether we're one Kingdom or four, we all have to agree to work toward a common goal. And if we have less war and conflict, less oppression and rebellion, maybe that'll be easier."

"Do you think we'll have peace? Between the new Kingdoms, I mean?"

"I hope so." Lyriana paused then, glancing out at the city below, like there was a thought she was struggling with. "Tilla . . . I do have one last favor to ask of you. And it's a big one."

"Sure. Anything."

"The Southlands will be fine; Cal's already been ruling as the Dyn for the past six months, and I trust him. And the Eastern Baronies will be too busy competing with each other to pose any threat. But the West is going to be a problem."

My heart sank, because of course my people were the ones who'd ruin everything. "Yeah. I know. A lot of those Western Lords were very loyal to my father."

"Yes. With your father gone, the West is poised for a huge power struggle over who will be its new King. We're looking at major unrest, a war between the Lords, one that could well spill over the border and restart the conflict we've just resolved." Lyriana pursed her lips. "Unless."

"Unless . . . ?"

"Unless the West rallied around a new leader, one who

unified the Lords and convinced them that peace was the way forward," Lyriana said, her gaze on the horizon. "Someone inspiring and impressive, someone with a bold vision for the future, someone who I could have a good relationship with. Someone the Lords could rally around." A chill breeze passed over us, and the shimmersteel walls of the Godsblade sparkled iridescent. "Someone who just so happens to hold the rightful claim to the seat of House Kent."

My stomach plunged, and my knees went weak. "No. You can't be . . . not . . . I mean . . . that's not . . ." Words had never felt more difficult, and I grasped the railing to keep from stumbling. "You're asking me to be . . ."

"To be a Queen," Lyriana said. "Trust me, it's not as bad as you'd think."

"That's easy for you to say!" I stammered. "I mean, you've trained for it your whole life. Me, I'm a bastard. A nobody. And now you're ordering me to go be a *Queen*?"

"I'm not ordering anything," Lyriana gently clarified. "What you do is your choice."

"They won't accept me," I tried. "I'm a traitor."

"You're a Kent. And as long as there has been a West, there has been a Kent on the redwood throne, ruling over it. Your name, your word, holds tremendous power. As, for that matter, does mine," Lyriana said. "Trust me. They'll accept you."

"Okay, but, even if they do, I'm not a Queen. I have no idea how to be one!" I shook my head. "I can't do it, Lyriana."

"Sure you can," she said, and she really actually meant it. "You're the bravest person I've ever met. You always do the right thing, even when the cost is unthinkable. You're smart and resourceful and a natural leader. And you'd make a better Queen than anyone else in the world."

My head was still spinning, my legs jelly. Sure, it was my choice, but it also very much wasn't my choice, in that there was no way I could ever actually say no. I *had* to do it. After everything we'd fought for, after everything we'd sacrificed, who would I be if I let it all go to hell again? If Lyriana was right, if this was the best way to ensure a continent at peace, of course I had to do it. For my father. For Markiska. For Jax.

"Shit," I whispered. That future, that cottage, that simple life with Zell, vanished into ash like the fleeting dream it had always been. Instead, I'd be going home. Back to the West, to Castle Waverly, and its towering redwoods and mist-shrouded beaches. I'd be going . . .

"I'd have to leave you," I said to Lyriana, and the sudden rush of emotion tightened in my chest like a fist around my heart. In all the chaos of the past two years, Lyriana had been a constant, my best friend, one of the only people I could always rely on. She'd always been there for me, whether it was riding through the West or cuddling after a Lightspire party or washing the blood off my hands in a rebel camp tent. The thought of leaving her behind made me feel like I was drowning. "I wouldn't see you anymore."

"We'd still see each other, silly," Lyriana said, but her voice was a little choked up in her throat. "Our Kingdoms would be close allies. We'd meet several times a year to make plans and negotiate. And I'll make sure the wine casks are always well-stocked."

I knew that was a joke, but I was still hung up on the two utterly unreal words that had come out of her mouth: *our Kingdoms.* And as I stood there on that balcony, the future looming in front of me like a gathering storm, I had the most vivid flashback to the moment when we'd met, at the Bastard

Table so long ago. I'd been a snotty bastard who only cared about impressing my father. She'd been a naive little Princess who'd never kissed anyone or hurt a fly. And now here we stood, two battle-scarred veterans, two hardened women, two future Queens. How had we gone from there to here? How much further did we have to go?

How was I ever going to do it without her?

I leaned forward and hugged her, really hugged her, pulling her into my arms and holding her close. "I love you so much, Lyriana," I said.

"I love you too, Tilla," she said, and kissed me softly on the cheek. Then she turned back to the party, taking my hand and leading me in. "Now come on. The night's still young and the future's still a ways off. Let's go have a drink."

"Or three," I said, then brushed my eyes with the back of one hand and followed her in.

EPILOGUE

I'D SEEN A LOT OF AMAZING THINGS IN MY EIGHTEEN YEARS. I'd watched a storm burst over the blazing red sands of the Red Wastes. I'd seen the Godsblade lit up like a pillar of light, sparkling a thousand colors against the darkness. I'd seen the Festival of Tears and the snows on the Frostkiss Mountains.

But still . . . nothing was prettier than a Western sunrise.

I stood alone in the sentry tower on Castle Waverly's eastern wall, leaning against the ancient stone of the parapet, gazing out at the sprawl of redwood forest below. The sun was rising up above the horizon behind me, painting the sky a beautiful rosy orange, with tinges of emerald from the fading Coastal Lights. Whenever I'd missed the West, it had always been images that came into my mind, but now that I was back, what I found myself noticing was all the other senses, all the little things I'd forgotten. The smell of the forest, smoky and earthy, like a campfire the morning after it had been put out. The sounds of the night, the whooshing of wind through the treetops and the distant hooting of owls. The crackle of frost underneath my boots as I walked, and the taste of the air, a hint of ocean salt.

I closed my eyes and took it in. When I'd left the West two years ago, fleeing across the border in Lyriana's caravan, I'd just assumed I'd never come back. I'd mourned its loss like I would the death of a family member, grieved and cried and come to accept it. You'd think being back would be thrilling, like someone you lost coming back to life, but instead it just felt like I was a ghost, haunting the memories of my former self. The halls I'd played in, the rooms I slept in, the tunnels where Jax and I had run and hid and laughed . . . they were all the same, of course, physically, but their emotional texture was all wrong, the memories of a life I'd long left behind. Being here felt like being in a dream I'd almost forgotten, floating in a haze.

A peal of childish laughter jerked me out of that thought. I turned to look back down into the courtyard, where three little blond girls were giggling as they chased each other around. My half sisters, my father's other daughters. Their mother, Lady Yrenwood, had begged me to let them stay, and of course I did, because I'm not some monster. I had to admit, they were growing on me, especially the middle one, Kat, who loved to mouth off at her mom and throw dirt clods at the boys who pissed her off. I smiled a little as I watched them sprint around, weaving circles around the ever-patient knights.

My knights.

It had been six months since my coronation, since I'd sworn the ancient vows down in the crypts of the Old Kings and taken on the redwood crown. Six months of traveling the Kingdom, six months of Lords bowing to me, six months of defusing territory disputes and glad-handing ambitious nobles and trying to get my brain to understand economics. Six months of weirdness like sleeping in the royal bedroom and being called "Your Majesty" and seeing young women copying my fashion choices. Six months of being the Young Queen.

My knights. My castle. My Kingdom.

Those words still sounded so weird. They always would.

A horn sounded from the castle gates, and I turned to see the flutter of white wings as dozens of birds swooped in from the forests, streaking in a wave through the slits in the castle's walls. Trained carrier doves, bringing messages from all over the continent, from the Alliance of the Four Kingdoms. They were slower than Whispers, and less reliable, but hey, they weren't made of magic, so it's what we had.

Would there be one from Lyriana? Hearing from her was the highlight of my month, in part because she was *really* good at writing letters. She always gave these great detailed updates about what was happening over in Lightspire: how she'd created a program of civil service for all the nobility, how Galen was importing shimmersteel to insulate the Heartstone and block its energy, how Ellarion was seriously dating an Eastern diplomat, how she and Syan had adopted the most adorable kitten.

I was supposed to visit her in two months, and I was counting down every day.

I missed her more badly than I could begin to express.

"Tilla?" a voice called from nearby. The door to the watchtower swung open, and I smiled as Zell leaned out. He still didn't have a formal title out here, but that's kind of because he was my everything: my bodyguard, my advisor, my best friend, my love. He looked good, damn good: his hair hung long around his shoulders, and a dark beard framed his face. And there was something else, something in his manner these days. He had a calm air to him, an ease that was so different from the tense, weary way he'd carried himself for the past two years. He looked relaxed. At peace. Happy.

"How'd you know I'd be here?" I asked.

"Because I know *you*," he said, and stepped forward to wrap an arm around my waist and pull me in close. I leaned back, pressing my face against the side of his neck, soaking into the firmness of his grip, into his touch, his smell. "What're you thinking about?"

"Nothing," I replied. "Everything. I don't know. What's on my agenda for today?"

Zell stifled a laugh. I'd gotten pretty damn good at talking to Lords and I was even starting to wrap my head around taxes, but I still couldn't manage a daily schedule for the life of me. "Breakfast with the head of the castle guard. Then a meeting with some merchants from the K'olali Isles to discuss trade policy. You promised the treasurer you'd take another economics session with him in the afternoon. And in the evening, a delegation of Lords from the southern swamps should arrive. I believe they're hoping you'll offer to pay to repair their castles, which were damaged in last month's earthquake."

"Ugggh," I groaned. "How're things with the Zitochi?"

"Better. They've accepted your legitimacy, and are open to a possible thaw of tensions." Zell had taken point on fixing Western–Zitochi relations, which were looking pretty bad after all the chaos and conflict. If it had just been me, I'm not sure they would've even been open to talks, but having Zell, a Zitochi, sitting by my side at the seat of the Kingdom . . . it opened a lot of doors. "The Conclave for Chief will be held in two months. If Clan Verax wins, I think we'll be fine. If it goes to Clan Tezza . . . well . . . it'll be more difficult. But I doubt it'll come to war. Not yet."

I sighed deeply. "It never ends, does it?"

His arm around my waist pulled me in closer, and his lips grazed the side of my neck. "No. But it gets better."

A warm morning wind blew over us. I turned around to face him and he leaned down and I leaned up and we kissed, long and deep and glowing. The problems of the future loomed. The specters of the past still stalked us. The wheels of history still spun.

But I had this moment. A sunrise. A breeze. A beautiful view. A letter from a friend. The laughter of children, the rustling of the trees. The arms of my boy, the warmth of his breath, the glint in his eye, the crease of his smile.

It never ends.

But it gets better.

I could live with that.

ACKNOWLEDGMENTS

Five years ago, I sat down and started writing a story about a group of royal bastards on the run from their diabolical parents. It's been a wild journey from there to now, writing the very last words of this trilogy, and it's one I could never have made without all of the amazing people who supported me along the way.

As always, thanks to the truly amazing team at Hyperion. Laura Schreiber is, objectively, a god-tier editor, whose insight and guidance helped shape this series every step of the way. Thanks as well to Cassie McGinty and Seale Ballenger for the phenomenal publicity, for great launch events and a truly memorable tour. And thanks to Mary Mudd, Levente Szabo, Sara Liebling, Guy Cunningham, Dan Kaufman, and the rest of Team Bastard. You all made this series possible, and I'm eternally grateful.

To my agent, Sara Crowe, for her endless support and encouragement. Onwards and upwards!

To the Casting Time Crew, for keeping me company

on all those late nights: Cat Valman, Owen and Adrienne Javellana, Jessica Yang, Chelsa Lauderdale, Sara Swartout, Coral Nardandrea, and Jeffrey Herdman.

To the writing peers whose invaluable wisdom and guidance helped me, you know, keep it together: Jilly Gagnon, Stephanie Garber, Tamara Ireland Stone, Kelly Loy Gilbert, Randy Ribay, Tara Sim, Traci Chee, Misa Sugiura, Parker Peevyhouse, and Dahlia Adler.

To the friends, who were always there with a laugh and a beer and a friendly word: Geoffrey Lundie, Sean McKenzie, Brendan Boland, Eric Dean, Max Doty, Kara Loo, Jennifer Young, and so many more.

Special thanks to Elisa Bandy for an exceptional beta read and some truly insightful feedback.

To my family for their endless support: Ann and Simon; Yakov, Yulya, Marina and Daniel. So much love.

To Sarah and Alex, the absolute best.

And finally, to all my wonderful readers. Thank you so much for taking this journey with me, for showing up to events, for sending love and reviews and support and Zutara gifs. It's all for you.

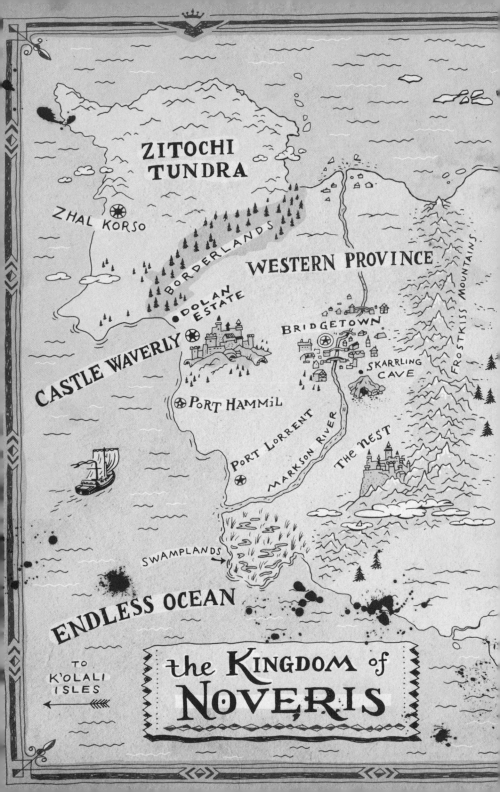